D0041021

THE

SILENCE

OF THE

GIRLS

THE
SILENCE
OF THE
GIRLS

· A NOVEL ·

PAT BARKER

DOUBLEDAY  NEW YORK

doubleday.com

DOUBLEDAY and the portrayal of an anchor with a dolphin are registered
trademarks of Penguin Random House LLC.

Jacket design by Emily Mahon
Jacket illustration: Engraving by Louis Charles Ruotte, drawn by François Gédéon
Reverdin, nineteenth century, after an antique sculpture at the Vatican Museums.
Bibliothèque Nationale. akg-images

LIBRARY OF CONGRESS CATALOGING-IN-PUBLICATION DATA
Names: Barker, Pat, 1943– author.
Title: The silence of the girls : a novel / Pat Barker.
Description: First edition. | New York : Doubleday, 2018.
Identifiers: LCCN 2018014387 (print) | LCCN 2018015358 (ebook) |
ISBN 9780385544214 (hardcover) | ISBN 9780385544221 (ebook)
Subjects: LCSH: Trojan War—Fiction. | Troy (Extinct city)—Fiction. |
BISAC: FICTION / Literary. | FICTION / Historical. | FICTION / War &
Military. | GSAFD: Historical fiction. | War stories.
Classification: LCC PR6052.A6488 (ebook) |
LCC PR6052.A6488 S55 2018 (print) | DDC 823/.914—dc23
LC record available at https://lccn.loc.gov/2018014387

MANUFACTURED IN THE UNITED STATES OF AMERICA

1 3 5 7 9 10 8 6 4 2

First United States Edition

For my children, John and Anna; and, as always,

in loving memory of David

"You know how European literature begins?" he'd ask, after taking the roll at the first class meeting. "With a quarrel. All of European literature springs from a fight." And then he picked up his copy of *The Iliad* and read to the class the opening lines. "'Divine Muse, sing of the ruinous wrath of Achilles . . . Begin where they first quarrelled, Agamemnon, the King of men, and great Achilles.' And what are they quarrelling about, these two violent, mighty souls? It's as basic as a barroom brawl. They are quarrelling over a woman. A girl, really. A girl stolen from her father. A girl abducted in a war."

—*The Human Stain,* Philip Roth

PART ONE

1

Great Achilles. Brilliant Achilles, shining Achilles, godlike Achilles . . . How the epithets pile up. We never called him any of those things; we called him "the butcher."

Swift-footed Achilles. Now there's an interesting one. More than anything else, more than brilliance, more than greatness, his speed defined him. There's a story that he once chased the god Apollo all over the plains of Troy. Cornered at last, Apollo is supposed to have said: "You can't kill me, I'm immortal." "Ah, yes," Achilles replied. "But we both know if you weren't immortal, you'd be dead."

Nobody was ever allowed the last word; not even a god.

I heard him before I saw him: his battle cry ringing round the walls of Lyrnessus.

We women—children too, of course—had been told to go to the citadel, taking a change of clothes and as much food and drink as we could carry. Like all respectable married women, I rarely left my house—though admittedly in my case the house was a palace—so to be walking down the street in broad daylight felt like a holiday. Almost. Under the laughter and cheering and shouted jokes, I think we were all afraid. I know I was. We all knew the men were being pushed back—the fighting that had once been on the beach and around the harbour was now directly under the gates. We could hear shouts, cries, the clash of swords on shields—and we knew what awaited us if the city fell. And yet the danger didn't *feel* real—not to me at any rate, and I doubt if the others were any closer to grasping it. How was it possible for these high walls that had protected us all our lives to fall?

Down all the narrow lanes of the city, small groups of women carrying babies or holding children by the hand were converging on the main square. Fierce sunlight, a scouring wind and the citadel's black shadow reaching out to take us in. Blinded for a moment, I stumbled, moving from bright light into the dark. The common women and slaves were herded together into the basement while members of royal and aristocratic families occupied the top floor. All the way up the twisting staircase we went, barely able to get a foothold on the narrow steps, round and round and round until at last we came out, abruptly, into a big, bare room. Arrows of light from the slit windows lay at intervals across the floor, leaving the corners of the room in shadow. Slowly, we looked around, selecting places to sit and spread our belongings and start trying to create some semblance of a home.

At first, it felt cool but then, as the sun rose higher, it became hot and stuffy. Airless. Within a few hours, the smells of sweaty bodies, of milk, baby-shit and menstrual blood, had become almost unbearable. Babies and toddlers grew fretful in the heat. Mothers laid the youngest children on sheets and fanned them while their older brothers and sisters ran around, overexcited, not really under-standing what was going on. A couple of boys—ten or eleven years old, too young to fight—occupied the top of the stairs and pre-tended to drive back the invaders. The women kept looking at each other, dry-mouthed, not talking much, as outside the shouts and cries grew louder and a great hammering on the gates began. Again, and again, that battle cry rang out, as inhuman as the howling of a wolf. For once, women with sons envied those with daughters, because girls would be allowed to live. Boys, if anywhere near fighting age, were routinely slaughtered. Even pregnant women were sometimes killed, speared through the belly on the off chance their child would be a boy. I noticed Ismene, who was four months pregnant with my husband's child, pressing her hands hard into her stomach, trying to convince herself the pregnancy didn't show.

In the past few days, I'd often seen her looking at me—Ismene, who'd once been so careful never to meet my eyes—and her expression had said, more clearly than any words: *It's your turn now. Let's see how you like it.* It hurt, that brash, unblinking stare. I came from a family where slaves were treated kindly and when my father gave me in marriage to Mynes, the king, I carried on the tradition in my own home. I'd been kind to Ismene—or I thought I had, but perhaps no kindness was possible between owner and slave, only varying degrees of brutality? I looked across the room at Ismene and thought: *Yes, you're right. My turn now.*

Nobody was talking of defeat, though we all expected it. Oh, except for one old woman, my husband's great-aunt, who insisted this falling back to the gate was a mere tactical ploy. Mynes was just playing them along, she said, leading them blindfolded into a trap. We were going to win, chase the marauding Greeks into the sea— and I think perhaps some of the younger women believed her. But then that war cry came again, and again, each time closer, and we all knew who it was, though nobody said his name.

The air was heavy with the foreknowledge of what we would have to face. Mothers put their arms round girls who were growing up fast but not yet ripe for marriage. Girls as young as nine and ten would not be spared. Ritsa leant across to me. "Well, at least *we're* not virgins." She was grinning as she said it, revealing gaps in her teeth caused by long years of childbearing—and no living child to show for it. I nodded and forced a smile, but said nothing.

I was worried about my mother-in-law, who'd chosen to stay behind in the palace rather than be carried to the citadel on a litter—worried, and exasperated with myself for being worried, for if our situations had been reversed she would certainly not have cared about me. She'd been ill for a year with a disease that swelled her belly and stripped the flesh from her bones. Finally, I decided I had to go to her, at least check she had enough water and food. Ritsa would have gone with me—she was already on her feet—but I shook my head. "I won't be gone a minute," I said.

Outside, I took a deep breath. Even at that moment, with the world about to explode and cascade down around my ears, I felt the relief of breathing untainted air. Dusty and hot—it scorched the back of my throat—but still smelling fresh after the foetid atmosphere of the upstairs room. The quickest route to the palace was straight across the main square, but I could see arrows scattered in the dust and even as I watched one soared over the walls and stuck, quivering, in a pile of dirt. *No, better not risk it.* I ran down a side street so narrow the houses towering over me let in scarcely any light. Reaching the palace walls, I entered through a side gate that must have been left unlocked when the servants fled. Horses whickered from the stables on my right. I crossed the courtyard and ran quickly along a passage that led into the main hall.

It seemed strange to me, the huge, lofty room with Mynes's throne at the far end. I'd first entered this room on my marriage day, carried from my father's house on a litter, after dark, surrounded by men holding blazing torches. Mynes, with his mother, Queen Maire, by his side, had been waiting to greet me. His father had died the year before, he had no brothers and it was vital for him to get an heir. So he was being married, far younger than men expect to marry, though no doubt he'd already worked his way round the palace women and thrown in a few stable lads for relish along the way. What a disappointment I must have been when, finally, I climbed down from the litter and stood, trembling, as the maids removed my mantle and veils: a skinny little thing, all hair and eyes and scarcely a curve in sight. Poor Mynes. His idea of female beauty was a woman so fat if you slapped her backside in the morning she'd still be jiggling when you got back home for dinner. But he did his best, every night for months, toiling between my less-than-voluptuous thighs as willingly as a carthorse in the shafts, but when no pregnancy resulted he quickly became bored and reverted to his first love: a woman who worked in the kitchens and who, with a slave's subtle mixture of fondness and aggression, had taken him into her bed when he was only twelve years old.

Even on that first day, I looked at Queen Maire and knew I had a fight on my hands. Only it was not just one fight, it was a whole bloody war. By the time I was eighteen I was the veteran of many long and bitter campaigns. Mynes seemed entirely unaware of the tension, but then in my experience men are curiously blind to aggression in women. *They're* the warriors, with their helmets and armour, their swords and spears, and they don't seem to see our battles—or they prefer not to. Perhaps if they realized we're not the gentle creatures they take us for their own peace of mind would be disturbed?

If I'd had a baby—a son—everything would have changed, but at the end of a year I was still wearing my girdle defiantly tight until at last Maire, made desperate by her longing for a grandchild, pointed at my slim waist and openly jeered. I don't know what would have happened if she hadn't become ill. She'd already selected a concubine from one of the ruling families; a girl who, although not lawfully married, would have become queen in all but name. But then, Maire's own belly began to grow. She was still just young enough for there to be ripples of scandal. *Whose is it?* everybody was asking. She never left the palace except to pray at her husband's tomb! But then she began to turn yellow and lose weight and kept to her own rooms most of the time. Without her to drive them, the negotiations over the sixteen-year-old concubine faltered and died. This was my opportunity, the first I'd had, and I seized it. Soon, all the palace officials who'd been loyal to her were answering to me. And the palace was no worse run than it had been when she was in power. More efficiently, if anything.

I stood in the centre of the hall, remembering these things and the palace that was normally so full of noise—voices, clattering pans, running feet—stretched out all around me as quiet as a tomb.

Oh, I could still hear the clash of battle from outside the city walls but, rather like the intermittent humming of a bee on a summer's evening, the sound seemed merely to intensify the silence.

I'd have liked to stay there in the hall or, even better, go out into the inner courtyard and sit under my favourite tree, but I knew Ritsa would be worrying about me and so I went slowly up the stairs and along the main corridor to my mother-in-law's room. The door creaked as I opened it. The room was in semi-darkness; Maire kept the blinds closed, whether because the light hurt her eyes or because she wished to hide her changed appearance from the world, I didn't know. She had been a very beautiful woman—and I'd noticed a few weeks before that the precious bronze mirror that had formed part of her dowry was nowhere to be seen.

A movement on the bed. A pale face turned towards me in the gloom.

"Who is it?"

"Briseis."

Immediately, the face turned away. That wasn't the name she'd been hoping for. She'd become rather fond of Ismene, who was supposed to be carrying Mynes's baby—and probably was, though given the lives slaves lead it's not always possible to know who a child's father is. But in these last few desperate weeks and months that child had become Maire's hope. Yes, Ismene was a slave, but slaves can be freed, and if the child were to be a boy . . .

I went further into the room. "Do you have everything you need?"

"Yes." Not thinking about it, just wanting me to go.

"Enough water?"

She glanced at her bedside table. I went round the bed and picked up the jug, which was almost full. I poured her a large cup then went to refill the jug from a bowl of water in the corner furthest from the door. Warm, stale water with a film of dust on the top. I plunged the jug deep and took it across to the bed. Four sharp slits of light lay across the red-and-purple rug beneath my feet, bright enough to hurt my eyes, though the bed was in near-darkness.

She was struggling to sit up. I held the cup to her lips and she drank greedily, her wasted throat jerking with every gulp. After a while, she raised her head and I thought she'd had enough, but she made a little mew of protest when I tried to take the cup away. When at last she'd finished, she wiped her mouth delicately on a corner of her veil. I could feel her resenting me because I'd witnessed her thirst, her helplessness.

I straightened the pillows behind her head. As she bent forward her spine was shockingly visible under the pallid skin. You lift spines like that out of cooked fish. I lowered her gently onto the pillows and she let out a sigh of contentment. I smoothed the sheets, every fold of linen releasing smells of old age, illness ... Urine too. I was angry. I'd hated this woman so fiercely for so long—and not without cause. I'd come into her house as a fourteen-year-old girl, a girl with no mother to guide her. She could've been kind to me and she wasn't; she could've helped me find my feet and she didn't. I had no reason to love her, but what made me angry at that moment was that in allowing herself to dwindle until she was nothing more than a heap of creased flesh and jutting bone, she'd left me with so very little to hate. Yes, I'd won, but it was a hollow victory—and not just because Achilles was hammering on the gate.

"There is something you could do for me." Her voice was high, clear and cold. "You see that chest?"

I could, though only just. An oblong of heavy, carved oak, squatting on its own shadow at the foot of the bed.

"I need you to get something."

Raising the heavy lid, I released a fusty smell of feathers and stale herbs. "What am I looking for?"

"There's a knife. No, not on the top—underneath ... Can you see it?"

I turned to look at her. She stared straight back at me, not blinking, not lowering her gaze.

The knife was tucked in between the third and fourth layer of bedclothes. I drew it from its sheath and the sharp blade winked wickedly up at me. This was far from being the small, ornamental knife I'd been expecting to find, the kind rich women use to cut their meat. It was the length of a man's ceremonial dagger and must surely have belonged to her husband. I carried it across to her and placed it in her hands. She looked down at it, fingering the encrusted jewels on the hilt. I wondered for a moment if she was going to ask me to kill her and how I would feel if she did, but no, she sighed and set the knife to one side.

Easing herself a little higher in the bed, she said, "Have you heard anything? Do you know what's happening?"

"No. I know they're close to the gates." I could pity her then, an old woman—because illness had made her old—dreading to be told her son was dead. "If I do hear anything, of course I'll let you know . . ."

She nodded, dismissing me. When I got to the door I paused with my hand on the latch and looked back, but she'd already turned away.

2

Ritsa was bathing a sick child when I got back. I had to step over several sleeping bodies to get to her.

She turned as my shadow fell across her. "How is she?"

"Not good. She won't last."

"Probably just as well."

I caught her looking at me curiously. The feud between my mother-in-law and me was well known. I said, rather defensively, perhaps, "She could've come with us. We could've carried her. She didn't want to."

The child whimpered and Ritsa brushed the hair back from his damp forehead. His mother was sitting only a few feet away, struggling with a fretful baby who wanted to suckle but was fighting the breast. She looked worn out. I wondered whether facing the future was harder if you were responsible for other lives. I had only my own burden to bear and, looking at that exhausted mother, I felt the freedom of that—and the loneliness. And then I thought that there were different ways of being connected to other people. Yes, I was childless—but I felt responsible for every woman and child in that room, not to mention the slaves crammed together in the basement.

As the heat intensified, most of the women settled down and tried to sleep. A few succeeded—for a time there was a rising chorus of snores and whistling breaths—but most just lay there staring listlessly at the ceiling. I closed my eyes and kept them closed while pulses throbbed in my temples and under my jaw. Then Achilles's war cry came again, so close this time some of the women sat up and gazed fearfully around them. We all knew we were approaching the end.

An hour later, hearing the crash and splinter of wood breaking, I ran up onto the roof, leant over the parapet and saw Greek fighters spilling through a breach in the gates. Directly below me, a knot of writhing arms and shoulders advanced and then retreated as our men struggled to push the invaders back. No use, they were pouring through the breach, slashing and stabbing as they came. Soon, that peaceful square where the farmers held their weekend market was trampled red with blood. Now and then, for no apparent reason, a gap would open in the struggling ranks and in one of those momentary clearings I saw Achilles raise his plumed head and look towards the palace steps where my husband stood with two of my brothers by his side. The next thing I saw was Achilles hacking his way towards them. As he reached the steps, the guards came running down to bar his way. I saw him thrust his sword upwards into the pit of a man's belly. Blood and urine spurted out, but the dying man, his face wiped clean of pain, cradled his spilling intestines as gently as a mother nurses her newborn child. I saw men's mouths open like scarlet flowers but I couldn't hear their screams. The noise of the battle kept coming and going, one minute deafening, the next muffled. I was gripping the parapet so hard my nails splintered on the rough stone. There were moments when I swear time stopped. My youngest brother—fourteen years old, barely able to lift my father's sword—I saw him die. I saw the flash of the upraised spear, I saw my brother lying on the ground wriggling like a stuck pig. And at that moment Achilles, as if he had all the time in the world, turned his head and glanced up at the tower. He was looking straight at me, or so it seemed—I think I actually took a step back—but the sun was in his eyes, he couldn't possibly have seen me. Then, with a kind of fastidious precision—I wish I could forget it, but I can't—he put his foot on my brother's neck and pulled the spear out. Blood spurted from the wound, my brother struggled for a full minute to go on breathing, and then lay still. I saw my father's sword drop from his loosening grip.

Achilles had already moved on, to the next man, and the next. He killed sixty men that day.

The fiercest fighting was on the palace steps where my husband, poor, silly Mynes, fought bravely to defend his city—he who, until that day, had been a weak, boorish, vacillating boy. He died with both hands gripping Achilles's spear, as if he thought it belonged to him and Achilles was trying to take it away. Mynes looked utterly astonished. My two older brothers died beside him. I don't know how my third-oldest brother died, but somehow or other, whether by the gates or on the palace steps, he met his end. For the first and only time in my life, I was glad my mother was dead.

Every man in the city died that day, fighting at the gates or on the palace steps. Those who were too old to fight were dragged out of their houses and butchered in the street. I saw Achilles, blood-red from his plumed helmet to his sandalled feet, throw his arm across the shoulders of another young man, laughing in triumph. His spear, trailing behind him, cut a line through the red earth.

It was over in a matter of hours. By the time the shadows lengthened across the square, the palace steps were piled high with corpses, though the Greeks were busy for an hour after that, chasing stragglers, searching houses and gardens where the wounded might have tried to hide. When there were no men left to kill, the looting began. Men like columns of red ants passed goods from hand to hand, heaping them up close to the gates ready to carry them down to the ships. When they ran out of space they dragged the corpses to one side of the marketplace, stacking them against the walls of the citadel. Dogs drooling ropes of slobber began sniffing around the dead, their lean, angular, black shadows knife-edged on the white stone. Crows came flying in, squabbling as they settled on roofs and walls, lining every door and window frame like black snow. Noisy, to begin with, then quiet. Waiting.

The looting was better organized now. Gangs of men were dragging heavy loads out of the buildings—carved furniture, bales of rich cloth, tapestries, armour, tripods, cooking cauldrons, barrels of wine and grain. Now and then, the men would sit down and rest, some on the ground, some on the chairs and beds they'd been carrying. They were all swigging wine straight from the jug, wiping their mouths on the backs of their bloodstained hands, getting steadily and determinedly drunk. And more and more often, as the sky started to fade, they gazed up at the slit windows of the citadel where they knew the women would be hiding. The captains went from group to group, urging the men onto their feet again, and gradually they succeeded. A few final swigs and they were back at work.

For hours, I watched them strip houses and temples of wealth that generations of my people had worked hard to create, and they were so good at it, so *practised.* It was exactly like seeing a swarm of locusts settle onto a harvest field; you know they're not going to leave even one ear of corn behind. I watched helplessly as the palace—my home—was stripped bare. By now many of the other women had joined me on the roof, but we were all too gripped by grief and fear to talk to each other. Gradually, the looting stopped—there was nothing left to take—and the drinking began in earnest. Several huge vats were wheeled into the square and jugs passed from man to man . . .

And then they turned their attention to us.

The slave women in the basement were dragged out first. Still watching from the roof, I saw a woman raped repeatedly by a gang of men who were sharing a wine jug, passing it good-naturedly from hand to hand while waiting their turn. Her two sons—twelve, thirteen years old perhaps—lay wounded and dying a few yards away from her, though those few yards might as well have been a mile: she had no hope of reaching them. She kept stretching out her hands and calling their names as first one and then the other died. I turned away; I couldn't bear to go on watching.

By now, all the women had come up to the roof and were huddled together, young girls in particular clinging to their mothers. We could hear laughter as the Greeks crowded up the stairs. Arianna, my cousin on my mother's side, grasped my arm, saying without words: *Come.* And then she climbed onto the parapet and, at the exact moment they burst onto the roof, threw herself down, her white robe fluttering round her as she fell—like a singed moth. It seemed to be a long time before she hit the ground, though it could only have been seconds. Her cry faded to a stricken silence, in which, slowly, stepping out in front of the other women, I turned to face the men. They stared at me, awkward now, uneasy, like puppies who aren't sure what to do with the rabbit they've caught in their jaws.

Then a white-haired man walked forward and introduced himself as Nestor, King of Pylos. He bowed courteously and I thought that, probably for the last time in my life, somebody was looking at me and seeing Briseis, the queen.

"Don't be frightened," he said. "Nobody's going to hurt you."

I just wanted to laugh. The boys who'd been pretending to defend the staircase had already been dragged away. Another boy, a year or two older, but backward for his age, clung to his mother's skirt until one of the fighters bent down and prized his pudgy fingers loose. We heard him screaming *"Mummy, Mummy!"* all the way down the stairs. Then silence.

Keeping my face carefully expressionless, I looked at Nestor and thought: *I will hate you till my last breath.*

———

After that, it's a blur. A few things stand out, still cut like daggers. We were led away, through the narrow side streets of our city, herded along by men with torches. Our jumbled shadows leapt up the white walls ahead of us and fell away behind. Once, we passed a walled garden and the scent of mimosa drifted towards us on the warm night air. Later, when so many other memories have vanished, I still get flashes of that smell, tugging at my heartstrings, reminding me of everything I lost. Then it was gone—and we were holding on to each other again, slipping and slithering along alleys cobbled with our brothers.

And so on to the beach, the sea dark and heaving, breaking curd-white against the black bows of their ships. We were pushed on board, urged up ladders by men wielding the butt ends of their spears and then made to stand crowded together on the decks—the holds being full of more perishable cargo. We took a last look at the city. Most of the houses and temples were ablaze. Flames had engulfed one wing of the palace. I only hoped my mother-in-law had somehow summoned up the strength to kill herself before the fire reached her.

With a great rattling of anchor chains the ships put out to sea. Once we'd left the shelter of the harbour, a treacherous wind filled the sails and carried us rapidly away from home. We crowded the sides, hungry for a last glimpse of Lyrnessus. Even in the short time we'd been on board, the fires had spread. I thought of the corpses piled high in the marketplace and hoped the flames would get to them before the dogs, but even as the thought formed I saw my brothers' dismembered limbs being dragged from street to street. For a time, the dogs would snap and snarl at the black birds circling overhead and the big, ungainly vultures waiting. At intervals, the birds would all rise up into the air and then settle slowly, drifting down like scraps of burnt cloth, charred remnants of the great tapestries that had lined the palace walls. Soon the dogs would have gorged till they were sick and then they'd slink out of the city, away from the advancing fires, and the birds would get their turn.

———————

A short voyage. We clung to each other for comfort on the tilting deck. Most of the women and nearly all the children were violently sick, as much from fear, I think, as from the motion of the waves. In no time at all, it seemed, the ship yawed and shuddered as she turned, against the tide, into the shelter of a huge bay.

Suddenly, men were shouting and throwing ropes—one rope snaked across the deck and hit my feet—or jumping down into the sea and wading, waist-deep, through foam-tipped waves onto the shore. Still we held on to each other, wet and shaking with cold now because a wave had broken over the bow as the ship veered round, all of us terrified of what was going to happen next. They drove the ship hard onto the shingle, and other men, scores of them, splashed into the sea to help haul her above the tideline. Then, one by one, we were lowered to the ground. I looked along the curve of the bay and saw hundreds of black, beaked, predatory ships, more than I'd ever seen in my life. More than I could ever have imagined. Once everybody was on dry land, we were driven up the beach and across a wide-open space towards a row of huts. I was walking beside a young girl, dark-haired and very pretty—or she would've been if her face hadn't been blubbery with tears. I grabbed her bare arm and pinched it. Startled, she turned to look at me, and I said: "Don't cry." She gaped at me so I pinched her again, harder. *"Don't cry."*

We were lined up outside the huts and inspected. Two men, who never spoke except to each other, walked along the line of women, pulling down a lip here, a lower eyelid there, prodding bellies, squeezing breasts, thrusting their hands between our legs. I realized we were being assessed for distribution. A few of us were singled out and pushed into a particular hut while the others were led away. Ritsa was gone. I tried to hold on to her but we were pulled apart. Once inside the hut, we were given bread and water and a bucket and then they went out, bolting the door behind them.

There was no window, but after a while, as our eyes became accustomed to the dark, there was just enough moonlight slanting in through cracks in the walls to let us see each other's faces. This was now a much smaller group of very young women and girls, all pretty, all healthy-looking, a few with babies at their breasts. I looked around for Ismene, but she wasn't there. Hot, close, airless space, wailing babies and, as the night wore on, a stink of shit from the bucket we were obliged to use. I don't think I slept at all.

In the morning, the same two men thrust piles of tunics through the door and told us roughly to get dressed. Our own clothes were dirty, wet and creased from the sea crossing. We did as we were told, numb fingers fumbling with fastenings that ought to have been easy. One girl, no more than twelve or thirteen years old, began to cry. What could we say to her? I rubbed her back and she pressed her hot, damp face into my side.

"It'll be all right," I said, knowing it wouldn't.

I was the first out. Remember, I hadn't been outside the house, unveiled and unchaperoned, since I was fourteen years old, so I kept my eyes cast down, looking at the ornate buckles on my sandals that glittered in the sunlight. Whoops of appreciation: *Hey, will you look at the knockers on that?* Mainly good-natured, though one or two shouted terrible things, what they would have liked to do to me and all the other Trojan whores.

Nestor was there. Nestor, the old one, seventy if he was a day. He came up and spoke to me—pompous, though not unkind. "Don't think about your previous life," he said. "That's all over now—you'll only make yourself miserable if you start brooding about it. *Forget!* This is your life now."

Forget. So there was my duty laid out in front of me, as simple and clear as a bowl of water: *Remember.*

I shut my eyes. Bright light shone orange on my closed lids stained here and there with drifting bands of purple. The men were shouting louder now: *Achilles! Achilles!* Then a roar went up and I knew he was there. Howls, laughter, jokes—jokes that sounded like threats, and were threats. I was a cow, tethered and waiting to be sacrificed—and, believe me, at that moment I'd have welcomed death. I put my hands over my ears and, gathering every last scrap of strength, made myself go back to Lyrnessus. I walked through the unbroken gates, saw again its unburnt palaces and temples, busy streets, women washing clothes at the well, farmers unloading fruit and vegetables onto the market stalls. I rebuilt the ruined city, repeopled its streets, brought my husband and my brothers back to life—and smiled, in passing, at the woman I'd seen being raped as she strolled across the main square with her two fine sons by her side . . . *I* did it. Standing at the centre of that baying mob, I pushed them back, out of the arena, down the beach and up onto the ships. I did it. *Me*, alone. I sent the murdering fleets home.

More shouting: "Achilles! Achilles!" Of all their names, the most hateful. Again, I saw him pause in the act of killing my brother and turn to look up at the citadel—straight at me, it seemed—leaving my brother lying there, pinned to the ground, before turning back to him and, in that poised, leisurely, *elegant* way of his, pulling the spear out of his neck.

No, I thought. And so I walked home from the market square down the cool, quiet streets, through the palace gates and into the darkness of the hall—the hall that I'd first entered on my marriage day. From there, I went at once to my favourite place. There was a tree in the inner courtyard, a tree with spreading branches that gave shade on even the hottest day. I used to sit there in the evenings, listening to music in the hall. The sound of lyres and flutes would drift out on the night air and all the cares of the day would fall away from me. I was there now, craning my neck to look up at the tree, seeing the moon caught like a glinting silver fish in the black net of its branches . . .

And then a hand, fingertips gritty with sand, seized hold of my chin and turned my head from side to side. I tried to open my eyes, but the sun hurt too much, and by the time I'd forced them open, he was already walking away.

At the centre of the arena he stopped and raised both hands above his head until the shouting died away.

"Cheers, lads," he said. "She'll do."

And everyone, every single man in that vast arena, laughed.

3

Immediately, two guards appeared and took me to Achilles's hut. "Hut" probably gives the wrong impression; it was a substantial building, with a veranda on two sides and steps leading up to the main door. I was taken through a large hall and into a poky little room at the back, hardly bigger than a cupboard and with no window onto the outside world. There, I was simply abandoned. Shaking with cold and shock, I sat down on a narrow bed. After a while, I noticed my hands were touching a woollen coverlet and I forced myself to examine it. The weaving was very fine, an intricate pattern of leaves and flowers, obviously Trojan workmanship—Greek textiles were nowhere near as good as ours—and I wondered from which city it had been looted.

Somewhere close at hand was a clattering of plates and dishes. A smell of roast beef crept into the room. My stomach heaved, I tasted bile and forced myself to swallow and take a succession of deep, steady breaths. My eyes were watering, my throat raw. Deep breaths. In, out, in, out. Deep, steady breaths . . .

I heard footsteps approaching and then the door latch began to lift. Dry-mouthed, I waited.

A tall man—not Achilles—came into the room carrying a tray with food and wine.

"Briseis?" he said.

I nodded. I didn't feel like anything that might have a name. "Patroclus."

He was pointing to his chest as he spoke, as if he thought I mightn't understand, and I could hardly blame him for that, since I was sitting there blank-eyed and dumb as an ox. But I recognized the name. The war had been going on a long time, we knew a lot about the enemy commanders. This was Achilles's closest companion, his second in command, but that made no sense at all, for why would such a powerful man be waiting on a slave?

"Drink," he said. "It'll make you feel better."

He poured a generous measure and held out the cup. I took it and made a show of raising it to my lips.

"Nobody's going to hurt you."

I stared at him, taking in every detail of his appearance—his height, his floppy hair, his broken nose—but I couldn't speak. After a while, he gave a lopsided grin, put the tray down on a small table beside the bed and left.

The food was a problem. I chewed a piece of meat for what felt like hours before spitting it out into the palm of my hand and concealing it under the rim of the plate. At first, I thought I wouldn't be able to manage the wine either, but I forced it down. I don't know whether it helped—perhaps it did. So much strong wine on an empty stomach made my nose and mouth feel numb; the rest of me was numb already.

From the hall came a rumble of men's voices, that grating roar that drowns out every other sound. The smell of roast beef was stronger now. *Our* beef. They'd driven the cattle away three days ago, before the city fell. An hour limped past. More shouting, more laughter, songs, the singing always ending with banging on the table and a burst of applause. Somewhere outside in the darkness, I thought I heard a child cry.

At last, I got up and went to the door. It wasn't locked. Well, of course it wasn't locked, why would they bother? They knew I had nowhere to go. I opened it inch by careful inch and the noise of songs and laughter became suddenly much louder. I was afraid to venture out, and yet I felt I had to *see*. Had to know what was going on. The poky room had begun to feel like a grave. So I tiptoed along the short passage that led to the hall and peered into the half-darkness.

A long, narrow hall with a low, beamed ceiling, smelling of pine and resin and lit by rows of smoking lamps that hung from brackets on the walls. Two trestle tables with benches on either side ran the whole length of the floor. Men, crammed shoulder to shoulder, jostled each other as they reached out to impale hunks of red meat on their daggers' points. I saw rows of shining faces with blood and juices running down the chins gleaming in the overlapping circles of light. Across the raftered ceiling, huge shadows met and grappled, dwarfing the men who cast them. Even from that distance I caught the stench of sweat, today's sweat, still fresh, but under that the stale sweat of other days and other nights, receding into the far distance, the darkness, all the way back to the first year of this interminable war. I'd been a little girl playing with my dolls when first the black ships came.

Achilles and Patroclus sat at a small table, looking down the centre of the room towards the outside door. They had their backs to me, but I could see how frequently they glanced at each other. Everybody was in high good humour, boasting about their exploits at Lyrnessus. More songs, including one about Helen, every verse more obscene than the last. It ended in a burst of laughter. In the pause that followed, Achilles pushed his plate away and got to his feet. To begin with, nobody noticed, then, gradually, the hubbub began to die down. He raised his hands and said something in that thick, northern dialect of his—normally, I had no problem understanding Greek, but I found his accent very difficult for the first few days—he was saying something about not wanting to break up the party, *but . . .*

He was laughing as he spoke, it was a sort of joke against himself. There was a chorus of jeers and catcalls and then somebody at the back shouted, "We all know why *you* want an early night!"

They began thumping the tables. Somebody started a song and they bellowed it out in time with the rhythm of their clenched fists.

Why was he born so beautiful?
Why was he born at all?
He's no fucking use to anyone!
He's no fucking use at all!
He may be a joy to his mother,
But he's a pain in the arsehole to me!

And so on. I crept back to the cupboard and closed the door, but then, as the singing went on, I opened it again, just a few inches, enough to be able to see into Achilles's room. A glimpse of rich tapestries hanging from the walls, a bronze mirror and, pushed well back against the wall, a bed.

A minute or so later, heavy footsteps clumped along the passage. Men's voices. I drew back, though I knew they couldn't see me. Patroclus went into the other room, followed almost immediately by Achilles, who threw his arm across his friend's shoulders, laughing in triumph and relief. Another successful raid, another city destroyed, men and boys killed, women and girls enslaved—all in all, a good day. And there was still the night to come.

They talked about having another drink—Patroclus had his hand on the jug handle ready to pour—but then Achilles nodded to the door where I was standing and flared his eyes.

Patroclus laughed. "Oh yes, she's there."

I stepped back and sat down on the narrow bed, pressing my hands together to stop them trembling. I tried to swallow, but my mouth was too dry. Seconds later, the door opened and Achilles's huge shadow blotted out the light. He didn't speak—perhaps he thought I wouldn't be able to understand him—just jerked his thumb at the other room. Shaking, I got up and followed him.

4

What can I say? He wasn't cruel. I waited for it—expected it, even—
but there was nothing like that, and at least it was soon over. He
fucked as quickly as he killed, and for me it was the same thing.
Something in me died that night.

I lay there, hating him, though of course he wasn't doing anything
he didn't have a perfect right to do. If his prize of honour had been
the armour of a great lord he wouldn't have rested till he'd tried it
out: lifted the shield, picked up the sword, assessed its length and
weight, slashed it a few times through the air. That's what he did to
me. *He tried me out.*

I told myself I wouldn't sleep. I was exhausted, but so tense, so
frightened of everything around me and most of all of him that
after he'd finished and rolled off me to sleep I just lay there, staring
into the darkness, as rigid as a board. Whenever I blinked, my lids
scraped painfully across dry eyes. And yet—somehow—I must've
slept, because when I looked again the lamp had burned low. Achilles was lying with his face only an inch away from mine, snoring
softly, his upper lip puckering on every breath. Desperate to escape
the furnace heat of his body, I flattened myself against the wall and
turned my head away so as not to have to look at him.

After a few minutes, I noticed a sound. Not a new sound—
I'd been aware of it even in my half-dreaming state. His breathing,

perhaps—but then I thought, *No, it's the sea.* Had to be—we were only a few hundred yards away from the shore. I listened and let it soothe me, that ceaseless ebb and flow, the crash of the breaking waves, the grating sigh of its retreat. It was like lying on the chest of somebody who loves you, somebody you know you can trust—though the sea loves nobody and can never be trusted. I was immediately aware of a new desire, to be part of it, to dissolve into it: the sea that feels nothing and can never be hurt.

And then, I suppose, I must have slept again because when I woke up he was gone.

Immediately, I was anxious. Should I have been up before him, getting his breakfast, perhaps? I had no idea how, on this desolate beach, food was prepared or even whether preparing it would be one of my jobs. But then I thought Achilles would have many slaves, all with different functions: weaving, cooking, preparing his bath, washing bedlinen and clothes . . . I'd be told soon enough what was expected of me. It was possible that very little would be required beyond what I'd already done. When I thought about my father's young concubine, the one he took after my mother's death, most of her duties had been discharged on her back.

The bed was cold. Sitting up, I saw he'd left one of the doors open. I was still trying to get my bearings. There were three doors: one leading into the small room—I'd already started thinking of it as the cupboard; another leading down a short passage to the hall; and a third that opened directly onto the veranda and from there onto the beach. Evidently he'd gone out that way, because the door was ajar and creaking on its hinges.

Pulling my mantle close round my shoulders, I went to stand on the threshold. A breeze blowing straight off the sea lifted my hair and cooled the bed-sweat on my skin. It was still dark, though a nail-paring of moon gave just enough light for me to see the huts, hundreds of them it seemed, stretching away into the distance. Between their dark, huddled shapes I caught tormenting glimpses of the sea. Turning my head to look inland, I noticed a faint glow in the sky, which puzzled me at first, until I realized it must be Troy. Troy, whose palaces and temples and even streets are lit all night. Here, the paths between the huts were narrow, blood-black. I felt I'd come to a dreadful place, the exact opposite of a great city, a place where darkness and savagery reigned.

From where I stood, on the threshold of Achilles's hut, the thunder of breaking waves sounded like a battle, the clash of swords on shields, but then to my exhausted mind everything sounded like a battle, just as there was no colour in the world but red. Cautiously, I ventured out onto the rough wood of the veranda and from there jumped down onto the sand. I stood for a moment, scrunching my toes in the gritty damp, relieved to be able to feel something, *anything*, after the numbness of the night. And then, barefoot and wearing only my mantle, I set off to find the sea.

Finding my way more by touch than sight, I stumbled upon a path that seemed to lead away from the huts, dribbling first along the edges of the dunes and then shelving steeply down onto the beach. For the last few yards the path became a tunnel, sand dunes topped with marram grass rising high on either side; I had to stop for a minute because the narrow space constricted my breath. At the back of my mind was the fear: suppose he comes back, suppose he wants me again and I'm not there? Moonlight shifted on blades of grass as they bent and swayed in the wind. I came out onto the beach beside a stream of brackish water that trickled between rocks and pebbles, widening as it reached the sea.

There was a new noise now, louder than the waves: a frenetic thrumming that sawed at your nerves. It took me a while to identify it as the sound of the ships' rigging slapping against the mastheads. The ships, most of them hauled clear of the tideline and supported on cradles, were a dark mass on my left. There were other ships anchored offshore—but these were little, fat-bellied cargo vessels as different from the lean warships as ducks from fish eagles. I knew the warships would be guarded against the possibility of a Trojan attack, so I backed into the dunes again and cut across a spur of scrubby heathland to the open sea.

Here, the dominant sound was that sword-on-shield clash of waves. I walked down to the sea, hoping to catch a glimpse of Lyrnessus where I guessed the fires that had destroyed the city would still be burning, but the closer I got to the water the thicker the mist became. It seemed to have come from nowhere—a dense fog, cold and clammy as a dead man's fingers, turning the black ships into spectral shapes that no longer seemed entirely real. It seemed odd that such a mist should form and linger on a night of high wind, but it freed me, making me invisible even to myself.

Out there, beyond the roiling waves, in the calm place where the sea forgets the land, were the souls of my dead brothers. They'd been denied funeral rites and so would be forbidden entry to Hades, condemned to haunt the living, not for a few days only but for all eternity. Again and again, behind my closed lids, I watched my youngest brother die. I grieved for all of them, but particularly for him. After our mother's death, he'd crept into my bed every night, seeking the comfort he was ashamed of needing by day. There, on that windswept beach, I heard him calling me—as lost, as houseless and beyond help as I was myself.

With no idea in my head except to reach him, I began wading into the sea—ankles, calves, knees, thighs, and then the sudden, cold shock as a bulging wave slapped into my groin. Standing there, splay-footed, the sand shifting under my feet, I put my hand down and washed *him* out of me. And then, clean, or as clean as I would ever be again, I stood, waist-deep, feeling the swell of waves lift me onto my toes, and set me down again, so I rose and fell with the sea. One huge wave picked me up and threatened to sweep me out of my depth and I thought: *Why not?* I could feel my brothers waiting for me.

But then I heard a voice. I thought for a moment it might be my youngest brother's voice. I listened, straining to hear above the roar of the waves, and it came again—definitely a man's voice, though I couldn't make out the words. And suddenly, I was afraid. I'd been frightened for days—I'd forgotten what it was like *not* to be frightened—but this was a different kind of fear. The skin at the back of my neck crawled as the hairs rose. I told myself the voice must be coming from the camp, somehow bouncing off the wall of mist so it seemed to be coming from the sea, but then I heard it again and this time I knew it was out there. Somebody, some*thing,* was churning up the water beyond the breaking waves. An animal—it had to be, couldn't be anything else, a dolphin or a killer whale. They sometimes come in very close to land, even beaching themselves to snatch a seal pup from the rocks. But then the drifting veils of mist momentarily parted and I saw human arms and shoulders, the gleam of moonlight on wet skin. More heaving, more splashing—and then, abruptly, silence, as he turned and lay face-down on the water, drifting backwards and forwards with the tide.

Men on this coast don't learn to swim. They're sailors—they know swimming serves only to prolong a death that might otherwise be quick and relatively merciful. But this man had been playing with the sea like a dolphin or a porpoise, as if it were his real home. And now he lay spread-eagled on the surface, staying in that position for such a long time I began to think he could breathe water. But then, suddenly, he raised his head and shoulders and floated upright, like a bottling seal. Seeing his face came as a shock, though it shouldn't have done, because I'd guessed already who it was.

I began to wade fast towards the shore, in a hurry now to get back to the hut and dry myself, because how on earth was I going to explain this? But in the shallows I was forced to slow down because I didn't want to splash and attract his attention. As I stepped onto dry land, I felt a quick, sharp stab of pain in my right foot. Something—a stone or a fragment of broken shell—was sticking into the sole of my foot and I had to bend down and pull it out. When I looked up again, I saw Achilles, not swimming now, but wading knee-deep onto the shore. I squatted down, held my breath, but he passed by without seeing me, both hands raised to wipe salt spray from his eyes. I let myself breathe again, thinking it was over, that he'd go back to the camp, but he just stood on the tideline, facing out to sea.

When he spoke I thought he was speaking to me and I opened my mouth, though I'd no idea what I was going to say. But then he spoke again, words bubbling from his mouth like the last breath of a drowning man. I understood none of it. He seemed to be arguing with the sea, arguing or pleading . . . The only word I thought I understood was "Mummy" and that made no sense at all. *Mummy?* No, that couldn't be right. But then he said it again: "Mummy, Mummy," like a small child crying to be picked up. It had to mean something else, but then "Mummy" is the same, or nearly the same, in so many different languages. Whatever it meant, I knew I shouldn't be hearing it, but I didn't move and so I crouched down and waited for it to stop. On and on it went, until at last the glutinous speech faded into silence.

The mist was beginning to burn off as the sun rose. I saw the first golden gleams of light find his wet arms and shoulders as he turned and walked along the beach, disappearing into the shadow of his black ships.

As soon as I was sure he'd gone, I ran as fast as I could through the dunes, but once inside the camp I was lost. I stood there, wet, bedraggled and terrified, with no idea of what to do or where to go. But then a girl came to the door of one of the huts and beckoned me inside. Her name, she said, was Iphis. She took care of me that morning, even filling a bath with hot water to wash the salt out of my hair. As I put my mantle to one side and prepared to step into the bath something fell onto the floor and I realized I'd brought the stone with me from the beach. My foot was still bleeding where it had cut me. It lay in the palm of my hand and I examined it minutely as people in shock will sometimes do, focusing their whole attention on a trifle. It was green, the bilious green of a stormy sea, but with one diagonal streak of white. Nothing remarkable about it, except that it was sharp. Very sharp. I raised it to my face and sniffed: seawater and dust. I licked it: felt grittiness, tasted salt. Then I ran my finger along the jagged edge: no wonder the cut was so deep. When I drew it across my wrist—exerting scarcely any pressure—it left a weal, beaded along its length with pinpricks of blood. There was a relief in that, making blood flow out of my numbed skin. But when I went to cut myself again, curious to know whether the relief would be repeated, something stopped me. I didn't know why the sea had given me this gift, but I knew it wasn't to hurt myself with. There were knives all over the camp if I wanted to do that. So I rested it again on the palm of my hand and looked at it, thinking of nothing else at all, just the colour and feel and weight of it. So many pebbles on that beach—*millions*—all of them worn smooth by the sea's relentless grinding, but not this one. This one had stayed sharp.

It mattered to me, that obstinate little stone, and it still does. I have it here now on the palm of my hand.

When Iphis brought me clean, dry clothes and I put them on— or rather she did, I was standing there with no more feeling than a block of wood—I slipped the stone inside my girdle where it would press against my skin every time I moved. It wasn't comfortable, but it was reassuring, reminding me of the sea and the beach—and the girl I'd once been and could never be again.

5

What I remember most—apart from the awful, straining, wide-eyed terror of the first few days—is the curious mixture of riches and squalor. Achilles dined off gold plates, rested his feet in the evenings on a footstool inlaid with ivory, slept under bedcovers embroidered with gold and silver thread. Every morning, as he combed and braided his hair—and no girl ever dressed more carefully for her wedding day than Achilles for the battlefield—he checked the effect in a bronze mirror that must have been worth a king's ransom. For all I know, it may have been a king's ransom. And yet, if he needed a shit after dinner, he took a square of coarse cloth from a pile in the corner of the hall and set off to a latrine that stank to high heaven and was covered in a pelt of black buzzing flies. And, on his way there and back, he would have to pass an enormous rubbish tip which was supposed to be burned off at regular intervals, but never was, and consequently had become a breeding ground for rats.

That's the other thing I remember: the rats. Rats everywhere. You could be walking along the path between two rows of huts and suddenly the ground ahead of you would get up and walk—oh, yes, as bad as that! The skinny, half-wild dogs that roamed the camp were meant to control the rats, but somehow they never did. Myron, who was in charge of the upkeep of Achilles's compound, used to organize the younger fighters into rat-hunting contests with prizes of strong wine for the winner. You'd see young men strutting about with rows of little corpses impaled on their spears: rat kebabs. But however many they killed, there always seemed to be plenty more.

I'm trying—rather desperately, perhaps—to convey my first impressions of the camp, though I was in no state to take anything in. In one way, it was a simple place: there was the sea, the beach, the sand dunes, a patch of scrubland and then the battlefield, which stretched all the way up to the walls of Troy. That's what I could see, but of course we—the captive women—were confined to the camp. Fifty thousand fighters and their attendant slaves were crammed onto that strip of land. The huts were small, the paths between them narrow, everything cramped—and yet that space seemed infinite, because the camp was our entire world.

Time played curious tricks too: expanding, contracting, burrowing back into itself in the form of memories that were more vivid than daily life. Particular moments—like the few minutes I'd spent staring at the stone—expanded till they felt like years, but that would be followed by whole days that drifted by in a haze of shock and grief. I couldn't tell you a single thing that happened on any one of those days.

Gradually, though, a routine began to emerge. My only real duty was to wait on Achilles and his captains at dinner. So I was on public view—not even veiled—every night, and that shocked me because I'd been used to leading a secluded life, away from the gaze of men. At first, I couldn't understand why he wanted me there, but then I remembered I was his prize of honour, his reward for killing sixty men in one day, so of course he wanted to show me off to his guests. Nobody wins a trophy and hides it at the back of a cupboard. You want it where it can be seen, so that other men will envy you.

I hated serving drinks at dinner, though of course it didn't matter to Achilles whether I hated it or not and, curiously, it soon stopped mattering to me. This is what free people never understand. A slave isn't a person who's being treated as a thing. A slave *is* a thing, as much in her own estimation as in anybody else's.

So, anyway, there I was, moving up and down the long trestle tables, pouring wine into men's cups—and smiling, always smiling. Every eye was on me, and yet as I leant over their shoulders there was no groping, no whispered, obscene remarks. I was as safe here as I would have been in my husband's palace; safer probably, because every man here knew if he overstepped the mark he'd have to answer to Achilles. To die, in other words.

Achilles sat at his table with Patroclus. They joined in the toasts and laughter until the conversation settled into a steady hum and then they spoke mainly to each other. If a quarrel broke out—and of course they did, frequently; these were men trained from earliest childhood to resent the slightest insult to their honour—Patroclus was on his feet at once, soothing, restraining, persuading the combatants to clasp hands, share a joke and, finally, sit down again as friends. Then he'd go back to Achilles and their conversation would start up again immediately. Theirs was not a relationship of equals, though Achilles always framed his orders courteously; always, at least in front of the men, he addressed Patroclus as "Prince" or "Lord." Nevertheless, Patroclus was clearly second in command, subordinate. Only that wasn't the whole story. Once, I saw them walking together on the beach, Patroclus resting his hand on the nape of Achilles's neck, the gesture a man will sometimes make to a younger brother or a son. Nobody else in the army could have done that to Achilles and lived.

You seem to have spent a lot of time watching him.

Yes, I watched him. Every waking minute—and there weren't many minutes I allowed myself to sleep in his presence. It's strange, but just then, when I said "I watched him" I very nearly added "like a hawk," because that's what people say, isn't it? That's how you describe an intent, unblinking stare. But it was nothing like that. Achilles was the hawk. I was his slave to do what he liked with; I was completely in his power. If he'd woken up one morning and decided to beat me to death, nobody would have intervened. Oh, I watched him all right, I watched him *like a mouse.*

The last part of the evening, after dinner, I spent in the company of Iphis, who was Patroclus's girl, given to him by Achilles. We used to sit on the bed in the cupboard and wait to be summoned. Patroclus sent for her most evenings, which was scarcely surprising, given her pale, delicate beauty. She was like a windflower trembling on its slender stem, so fragile you feel it can't possibly survive the blasts that shake it, though it survives them all. We talked a lot, but not about the past, not about the lives we'd led before we came to the camp, so in one sense I knew very little about her. That's the way it was—we were all born again on our first day in the camp. She knew she was lucky to have been given to Patroclus, who was always kind. I noticed how gentle he was with her, though I suspected he preferred her to the other girls largely because she was a present from Achilles.

In those early days, I distrusted Patroclus's kindness because I couldn't understand it. Achilles's brutal indifference made a lot more sense. He'd still barely addressed two words to me, though I often, as my wariness started to wear off, talked to Patroclus. I remember once, very early on, he found me crying and told me not to worry, he could make Achilles marry me. It was an extraordinary thing to say; I didn't know how to respond, so I just shook my head and looked away.

My solace was my pre-dawn walks to the sea. I'd wade in up to my waist, until I was standing on tiptoe, feeling the tug of every retreating wave. Often, mist would roll in from the sea, sometimes thick enough to blind you. Shrouded like that, invisible to anybody who happened to walk past, I was at peace, or as close to peace as I could get. My brothers, whose unburied bodies must, by now, have been reduced to fragments of gnawed bone, seemed to gather round me. That strip of shingle at the water's edge which, as the tides swept across it, belonged sometimes to the sea and sometimes to the land was our natural meeting ground. My brothers had become liminal in their very nature, since they belonged, now, neither with the living nor the dead. Which I felt was also true of me.

Though shrouded in mist and invisible, I was not alone. Achilles swam every morning before dawn, though there was never any contact between us. Either he didn't see me or he chose to ignore me. He had no curiosity about me, no sense of me as a person distinct from himself. When, at dinner, I put food or drink in front of him, he never once glanced up. I was invisible except in bed. In fact, I'm not sure how visible I was there, except as a collection of body parts. Body parts, he was familiar with: they were his stock-in-trade. I felt the only time he'd actually seen me was that one brief moment of scrutiny when I'd been paraded in front of him—he'd certainly looked at me then, though only long enough to make sure the army was awarding him a prize commensurate with his achievements.

He didn't speak to me, he didn't see me—but he sent for me every night. I bore it by telling myself that one day—and possibly quite soon—that would all change. He'd remember Diomede, the girl who'd been his favourite before I arrived, and send for her instead. Or better still, he'd sack another city—god knows, his appetite for sacking cities seemed to know no bounds—and the army would award him another prize, another shocked and shivering girl. And then, *she*'d be shown off to his men, flaunted in front of his guests, and I'd be allowed to sink into the obscurity of the women's huts.

Things did change—they always do—but not in the direction I'd been hoping for. I don't know how long I'd been in the camp, probably about three weeks. Like I say, it was almost impossible to keep track of time in that camp, I seemed to be living in a bubble, no past, no future, only an endless repetition of now and now and now. But I think perhaps the change started in me. The numbness began to wear off, to be replaced by a pain so intense I could neither stand nor sit still. Up to this point, I'd been both passive and abnormally vigilant, but curiously lacking in emotion. Now, there were frequent moments of desperation, even despair. When, on the citadel roof, my cousin Arianna had stretched out her hand to me, before leaping to her death, I'd chosen to live, but if I'd had that choice to make again, *now*, knowing what I knew *now* ... Would I still have made the same decision?

One night after dinner, instead of going to sit with Iphis in the cupboard, waiting to be summoned, I went down to the sea. Generally, once the men had finished eating, the women would snatch a quick bite, but I was sick to my stomach, I couldn't bear the thought of food. I walked down the path between the dunes, each step scattering soft sand. At times, as I thought of my brothers, I felt something like exhilaration. As long as I lived and remembered, they weren't entirely dead. And I wanted to live long enough to see Achilles sizzling on his funeral pyre. But such moments were brief and always followed by the realization that this was it, from now on this was my life. I'd share Achilles's bed at night until he grew tired of me and then I'd be demoted to carrying buckets of water or cutting rushes to spread across the floors. And when the war was over I'd be taken to Phthia—because the Greeks would win, I knew they would, I'd seen Achilles fight. Troy would be destroyed just as Lyrnessus had been destroyed. More widows, more shocked and bleeding girls. I didn't want to live to see any of it.

When I reached the beach, I walked straight into the sea as I usually did, but this time I kept on walking until the water closed over my head. Below me, shifting beams of moonlight gleamed fitfully on ribs of white sand. I tried to make myself take a breath, but it's amazing how the body struggles to survive even when the spirit's ready to depart. I couldn't force myself to take that breath and after a while the tightening of the iron band round my chest became intolerable. Involuntarily, I thrust upwards, breaking the surface with a shriek of indrawn air.

When I got back to Achilles's compound, bedraggled and downcast, Iphis was waiting for me. I was shaking as she pulled a clean, dry tunic over my head and twisted my hair into a knot at the back so its wetness wouldn't be too obvious. All the while, she was muttering with concern, patting my shoulders and stroking my face and doing everything she could to make me look presentable, but then Patroclus called for her and she had to go.

I went on sitting there. In the next room, Achilles was playing the lyre, as he always did at this time of night. There was one particular piece of music that finished in a sequence of notes like the last few raindrops at the end of a storm. It sounded familiar, as if I'd always known it, but I couldn't place it; I certainly couldn't remember any of the words. I listened, and then he stopped playing—the moment I always dreaded. I heard him put the lyre down on the table by his chair. A minute later, he opened the door and jerked his head for me to come in.

Letting my tunic drop to the floor, I stood for a moment chafing my wet arms and then slipped between the sheets. He was in no hurry, sipping the last of his wine, picking up the lyre and playing the same sequence of notes again. I lay and listened, hating the delicacy of his fingers as they moved across the strings. I knew every gesture of those beautifully manicured hands—which still, however, had blood embedded in the cuticles; even perfumed baths won't shift every stain. Because I'd been watching him so intently—from fear, not for any other reason—I felt I knew everything about him, more than his men, more than anybody, except Patroclus. Everything, and nothing. Because I couldn't for one moment imagine what it would be like to be him. And, during the same time, he'd learnt nothing at all about me. Which suited me, perfectly. I certainly didn't want to be understood.

He did, eventually, get into bed. I closed my eyes, wishing he'd turn the lamp down, though I knew he wouldn't; he never did. I felt him turn onto his side and cup those terrible hands round my breasts. I forced myself not to stiffen, not to pull away . . .

And then he stopped. "What's that smell?"

Those were almost the first words he'd spoken to me. I edged further away from him. I knew it was a mistake, but I couldn't stop myself. He leant forward, sniffing my skin and hair. I was aware of how it must appear to him, the crust of salt on my cheekbones, the smell of sea-rot in my hair. I fully expected him to kick me out of bed or hit me—the violence that was always simmering beneath the surface turned on me at last.

What he actually did was far more shocking.

Groaning, he buried his face in my hair, then moved across my skin, mouthing and licking till he reached my breasts. When he started sucking my nipples, I arched my back with the shock of it, because this wasn't a man making love to a woman—this was a starving baby, a baby who's sucking so desperately it loses the breast and works itself up into a towering rage. He pummelled my chest with his clenched fist and then, restraining himself, began stuffing wet strands of my hair into his mouth. Then down to my breasts again, taking the whole nipple into his mouth and clamping down hard with his jaws. You may be thinking: *Why did this shock you so much?* I can only say again: this wasn't a man, this was a child. By the time he let me go, he had that glazed, booby-drunk expression of a baby full of milk. An expression I'd never seen on a man's face before—or since.

When it was over, he looked down at me; he seemed bewildered, almost distraught. I tensed, expecting him to hit me, not because of anything I'd said or done, or not said or done, but simply because I'd witnessed this. I'd witnessed his need. Instead, he turned on his side away from me and pretended to be asleep.

6

Everything changed after that night—and not for the better. Instead of Achilles's brisk, efficient, matter-of-fact use of my body to get relief, there was immense passion; passion, but no tenderness. He made love—*huh!*—as if he hoped the next fuck would kill me. One moment, he was grinding me into the dust, the next, clinging onto me, as if afraid I might suddenly disappear. Some nights I thought he might actually strangle me.

Iphis kept asking me if I was all right. I just nodded and got on with whatever I was doing at the time. More and more, I was venturing further out from the women's huts, going first to the nearest campfires, where there were usually at least a couple of women I knew from Lyrnessus. I was outside, I had sunlight on my skin, I'd survived. We-ell, in a manner of speaking I'd survived. There were women in the camp, women who'd seen their sons killed, who still couldn't speak, who stumbled about dead-eyed with shock. Literally—you could clap your hands in front of their faces and they wouldn't blink.

But nothing's ever simple, is it? Incredibly, there were some women whose lives had changed for the better. One girl, who'd been a slave in Lyrnessus—and a kitchen slave at that, the lowest of the low— was now the concubine of a great lord, while her mistress, a plain, slack-bellied woman near the end of her childbearing years, had to scratch and scrape for food around the fires. Nothing mattered now except youth, beauty and fertility.

We all coped in different ways. There were two women I particularly remember—sisters, I think. They spent all day in the weaving sheds, never went out, except for one brief walk in the late afternoon and then they always went together, arm in arm, and so heavily veiled I'm surprised they could see where they were going. It was as if they hoped, by observing all the restrictions of a respectable woman's life, they could roll time back and undo what they'd become. I used to look at them and think: *You're mad.*

If anything, I went in the other direction. Every morning, alone and unveiled, I set out to walk around the camp. Some of these walks took me along the shoreline, past the various compounds, all the way up onto the promontory where the dead were burned. From there you could see for miles. On a clear day, you could see Lyrnessus's burnt and broken towers. There was another walk, inland, through the dunes and onto the scrubland where muddy and trampled tracks led, eventually, to the battlefield. From there, I could see right across the plain to Troy and, even, now and then, catch the glint of sunlight on King Priam's golden crown. He was almost always on the parapet, looking down on the battlefield, and beside him, leaning as far out as she dared, the white dot that was Helen.

Nobody could believe the war had dragged on as long as it had. For nine years they'd been fighting on the Trojan plain, the front line moving to and fro—never very far; neither side was able to break through. What had once been fertile farmland was now a waste of mud, for in autumn and winter the two rivers that meandered across the plain regularly overflowed. The trees had gone, cut down in the first winter of the war to build huts and repair the ships. The birds had gone too. It was startling how few of them there were, just a solitary buzzard sailing across the desolation.

I didn't do that walk very often. It was painful to see Troy, where I'd once spent two very happy years.

Gradually, I got to know the other "prizes"—women awarded by the army to the various kings. We met in Nestor's compound because it was closest to the central arena and therefore convenient for everybody. Hecamede, who'd been awarded to Nestor when Achilles sacked Tenedos, mixed dishes of strong wine and handed them round with platters of bread, cheese and olives. She was about nineteen, I suppose—more or less the same age as me—sleek-haired, brown-skinned, quick and deft in all her movements; she reminded me of a wren. She'd been presented to Nestor as his prize for "strategic thinking," since he was too old to take part in the actual raid.

"Too old for anything?" I ventured to hope.

Uza, also from Tenedos, hooted with laughter. "Don't you bloody well believe it! They're always the worst, old men, they think if you'd only do something—something *else*, something you're not doing already—it'd be rock-hard. Nah, give me the young 'uns anytime." Uza was Odysseus's prize. No problems there, apparently. All *very* straightforward. When it was over, he'd lie looking up at the ceiling and indulge in long, rambling reminiscences about his wife, Penelope, to whom he was utterly devoted. "They all talk about their wives," Uza said, stifling a yawn.

It was never made clear what Uza's profession had been before Tenedos fell, though I felt I could hazard a guess.

Ritsa turned to me. "What about Achilles? What's he like?"

"Fast," I said, and left it at that.

I was glad to see Ritsa again. She'd been awarded to Machaon, the army's chief physician, not so much for her looks—well, no, definitely not for her looks—but because of her skill in healing. She was a widow, older than the rest of us, and, in normal circumstances, wouldn't have approved of married women talking like this in front of young girls.

The youngest of us, Chryseis, was fifteen years old; the daughter of a priest, she'd still been living in her father's house when Tenedos fell. Agamemnon had picked her from a row of captured girls lined up for his inspection; as commander-in-chief, he always had first pick, though it was Achilles who bore the brunt of the fighting. Chryseis was lovely—as girls in that first flowering so often are. At first, she seemed very shy, though later I discovered it wasn't shyness at all but a formidable reserve. Her mother had died while Chryseis was still a child, so she'd been mistress of her father's house from an early age and she'd assisted him in the temple as well. The dual responsibility had given her a maturity beyond her years. She said very little the first time I met her—whether from shyness, reserve or prudishness I couldn't tell—but she was the focus of everybody's attention. When she left before the rest of us, the conversation immediately turned to her—and it wasn't malicious gossip either. They were all concerned for her. Though, in one respect, as Uza pointed out, she was better off than most of us: Agamemnon couldn't get enough of her. "Never sends for anybody else," she said. "I'm amazed she's not pregnant."

"He prefers the back door," Ritsa said.

She'd know. Ritsa had a jar of goose fat mixed with crushed roots and herbs that the common women round the campfires relied on if they'd had a particularly rough night. She was too discreet to reveal that Chryseis had been to see her, but the implication was obvious.

"Really?" Uza said. "Course, she is very skinny." And she leant back, clasping her hands behind her head to draw attention to her own opulent curves.

"He loves her," Hecamede said.

Uza snorted. "Yeah, till he gets tired of her. Do you remember what's-her-name—oh, hell. Begins with a 'W.' He was supposed to be in love with her but it didn't stop him handing her over to the men. And then there was—"

"Do they do that?" I asked.

"What?"

"Hand prize women over to the men."

Uza shrugged. "It's been known."

"It won't happen to her," Hecamede said. "He's besotted."

"No, well, I hope you're right," Uza said.

Ritsa stretched and yawned. "All she has to do is give him a son and that's it, made for life."

"Mightn't that be a bit difficult?" I asked. "If he prefers the back door?"

A ripple of laughter. It seems incredible to me now, looking back, that we laughed; but we often did. Crucially, perhaps, none of us had lost a child.

Another woman who came to these gatherings, though less regularly than the others, was Tecmessa, Ajax's prize. She'd been in the camp four years and had a baby son, whom Ajax was said to adore. Since Ajax's compound was next to Achilles's I'd often walk part of the way back with her. She was a big woman who found walking in the heat difficult so these were slow strolls with plenty of time to talk, but I found it hard to like Tecmessa or feel anything much for her except a kind of exasperated pity. Ajax had killed her father and her brothers and that same night raped her, and yet she'd grown to love him—or so she said. I wasn't sure I believed her. Admittedly, I didn't want to believe her. I found her adjustment to life in the camp threatening—and shameful. But then, she did have a son, and her whole life revolved around the child.

Her other passion was eating. There was a particular dish Hecamede often served, a mixture of dried fruit, nuts and honey, so cloyingly sweet that a mouthful or two at the end of a meal was as much as most of us could manage. Tecmessa could down a whole tray of it. The rest of us watched incredulously, now and then exchanging glances, but nobody said anything.

Once or twice, Tecmessa really annoyed me with well-meant but irritating advice on how to make the best of things. I should try to make Achilles love me, she said. "He's not married, you know, he's only got one son, that's nothing for a man in his position. He could've married her, but he didn't." The son was called Pyrrhus, apparently, and Achilles hadn't seen him since he was a baby. The boy was being brought up by his mother's family. "It's not the same," she insisted. "It's not like having a child and watching it grow up."

The message was clear: there was a vacancy and I was a fool if I didn't try to fill it. "Look at me—Ajax worships the ground I walk on."

I thought: *Well, yes, look at you. If your life's that bloody marvellous, why do your jaws never stop?*

One day, she appeared wrapped in a heavy mantle in spite of the heat. As she was bending down to pick up the little boy's toy battleship, the folds of cloth fell open to reveal black fingermarks round her throat. She knew we'd seen. For a long time, nobody spoke.

Then: "Trouble in Paradise?" Uza asked, addressing herself, apparently, to vacant air.

Ritsa shook her head, but it was too late. Tecmessa had turned an ugly, blotchy red. "It's not his fault," she said. "He has these awful nightmares, sometimes he wakes up, he thinks I'm a Trojan."

"You *are* a Trojan," I said.

"No, I mean a *fighter*," Tecmessa said.

On our way home—her word, not mine—that day, Tecmessa went over the events of the previous night, how she'd had to beat Ajax with her fists to make him stop. "He can't help it." Poor woman, she obviously needed to confide in somebody, but really I was the worst person ... "Does Achilles have nightmares?"

Silently, I shook my head.

"He will. Sooner or later, they all do. One night he'll wake up and think you're the enemy."

"Well, if he does, he'll be right."

"You won't say that when you've got a child."

When, I noticed. Not *if*.

Up to that point, I'd always believed I wouldn't get pregnant. After all, five years of marriage had failed to produce a much-needed son, but then it's a well-known fact that a barren mare will sometimes foal if she's covered by a different stallion. I started to wonder. There was Tecmessa with her little boy, and all over the camp women were pushing big bellies in front of them or carrying tiny, mewling babies in their arms. Those who'd been here longest had children already fending for themselves around the fires. And yet, I was convinced it wouldn't happen to me. Admittedly, I wasn't relying on conviction alone, I still washed him out of me every morning—against my own best interests, Ritsa would have said. And part of me understood perfectly well that what Nestor had said was true: *This is your life now.* There was nothing to be gained by clinging to a past that no longer existed. But I did cling to it, because in that lost world I'd been somebody, a person with a role in life. And I felt if I let that go, I'd be losing the last vestige of myself.

I parted from Tecmessa at the gate of Ajax's compound and walked the last few hundred yards alone. I was aware of the common women all around me, tending fires and carrying cooking pots, getting ready for the warriors' return. Of all the women in the camp these were the most wretched. Many of them carried the curious circular bruises that came from contact with the butt end of a spear. They lived around the fires, slept under the huts at night; the youngest of them were no more than nine or ten years old. I'd thought their lives were altogether separate from mine, but now I understood that Agamemnon at least would sometimes donate one of his concubines to his men for common use. When he was tired of her, perhaps, or she'd done something to displease him or simply because he thought his men deserved a treat. Had Achilles ever done that? I had no idea, I knew only that the camp had suddenly become an even more threatening place.

As I entered the compound gates—they were left open by day—my mind filled with dread of the coming night. There were baths to be prepared for Achilles and Patroclus, who both had a hot, perfumed bath at the end of each day's fighting, with the first of many drinks set ready to hand. There was no actual work involved in this for me—the common women boiled the water and carried the heavy cauldrons—but I always made sure Achilles's bath was ready on time because it made a difference to his mood, and Achilles's moods governed everything.

We all went quiet as his chariot approached. Always, even before removing his helmet, he'd go round to the stables and check to see his horses were properly rubbed down and watered. Only then would he strip off his armour and throw it to his squires to be cleaned. Often, instead of sinking into the hot bath that had been so carefully prepared, he'd plunge into the sea. Far out beyond the breakers, he'd turn on his back and float while in the camp behind him his bath water grew cold. Usually, Patroclus followed him down to the beach and stood on the shoreline, watching. He always looked anxious at these times, though I couldn't for the life of me see what there was to be anxious about—a man who swam like that was hardly going to drown.

At last, slowly, Achilles would wade ashore, striding unsteadily through waves that broke against his knees until he reached dry land. There, he'd stop and shake himself until his long hair, spiked black with blood, flailed around his head and drops of water puckered the surface of the sand, forming a circle all around him. Then, the blood washed off, he'd stand for a moment, wiping the spray from his eyes before he emerged, blinking, into the light. He seemed reborn. Then he'd throw his arm across Patroclus's shoulders and together they'd walk up the slopes of sand and shingle, take the cups of wine that were handed to them and enter the hut to prepare for dinner.

7

I was praying for something good to happen, anything—anything that would change the way I lived. At the time, it felt as though day followed day and night followed night with no sense of progression, but looking back, I can see there were changes, though they seemed trivial then. One evening, for instance, when Iphis and I were waiting in the cupboard, Patroclus came in to fetch more wine and, seeing us sitting there, said, "Why don't you come in?"

We glanced at each other. This was unexpected and any unexpected development was alarming, but we were conditioned to obey, so we got up and followed him into the other room. There, I sat on a chair as far away from Achilles as I could get, and sipped sweet wine from the cup Patroclus handed to me. I hardly dared breathe. Achilles looked momentarily surprised, but otherwise paid us no attention.

When Patroclus left, taking Iphis with him, I got into bed as usual. By now, I'd worked out that the alteration in Achilles's behaviour was connected to the smell of seawater in my hair. I tried to stay away from the beach, but I couldn't; I needed that immersion in the cold, salt, unforgiving depths and I seemed to need it more and more as time passed. So I went on coming to his bed with the stench of sea-rot in my hair and the tightness of salt on my skin, and braced myself to face his lust, his anger and his need, afraid—too afraid to talk to anybody. And understanding none of it.

That became the pattern of our evenings, Iphis and I being invited into Achilles's room before it was time for bed. Sometimes Achilles and Patroclus continued the conversation they'd been having over dinner, going over the day's fighting, deciding what needed to be emphasized in next morning's briefing. If the day had gone well, this conversation didn't last long. If it had gone badly, Achilles would erupt, spewing out contempt for Agamemnon. The man was incompetent, he cared nothing for his men—or anything, except his own greed. And worse than that, he was a coward, always staying behind "guarding the ships"—while other people bore the brunt of the fighting. "And"—here, Achilles raised his cup for more wine—"he drinks."

"We all drink."

"Not like he does." Achilles looked up at Patroclus. "Oh, c'mon, when have you ever seen me drunk?"

Eventually, after a good deal of soothing from Patroclus, Achilles would pick up his lyre and begin to play.

As soon as he was absorbed, I was free to look around. Rich tapestries, gold plates, a carved chest inlaid with ivory . . . Some of them, I suppose, he might have brought with him from home, but most had been looted from burning palaces. The full-length bronze mirror: I wondered where that had come from. I didn't wonder about the lyre, because I knew. He'd taken that from Eetion's palace, the day he'd sacked Thebe. Eetion killed, his eight sons killed, men and boys slaughtered, women and girls carried off into slavery—and only the lyre remained. I thought it was the most beautiful thing I'd ever seen.

As he played, the torchlight fell full on his face and I could see the strange markings on his skin. The areas covered by the forehead and cheek irons of his helmet were several shades lighter than the exposed skin around his eyes and mouth, almost as if the helmet had become part of him, had somehow embedded itself in his skin. Perhaps I exaggerate the effect. I remember mentioning it to Iphis and though she knew at once what I meant she said she hadn't noticed it particularly herself. For me, the tiger-stripes on his skin were the most noticeable thing about him. Somebody once said to me: *You never mention his looks.* And it's true, I don't, I find it difficult. At that time, he was probably the most beautiful man alive, as he was certainly the most violent, but that's the problem. How do you separate a tiger's beauty from its ferocity? Or a cheetah's elegance from the speed of its attack? Achilles was like that—the beauty and the terror were two sides of a single coin.

While Achilles played, Patroclus sat in silence, his chin resting on his clasped hands, sometimes absent-mindedly fondling the ears of his favourite hound, who sat gazing up at him or lay stretched out at his feet. Now and then, the sleeping dog would give a curious little yelp as it chased an imaginary rabbit and then Patroclus would smile and Achilles would look up and laugh, before turning his attention back to the lyre.

The songs were all about deathless glory, heroes dying on the battlefield or (rather less often) returning home in triumph. Many of these songs I remembered from my own childhood. As a small girl at home in my father's house, I used to creep down to the court-yard when I was supposed to be in bed asleep and listen to the bards playing and singing in the hall. Perhaps, at that age, I thought all the stirring tales of courage and adventure were opening a door into my own future, though a few years later—ten, eleven years old, perhaps—the world began to close in around me and I realized the songs belonged to my brothers, not to me.

The captive girls used to come out of the women's huts and sit on the veranda steps to hear Achilles sing. His voice carried; they'd be hearing snatches of these songs from end to end of the camp. At last, though, the song faded into stillness and for a moment nobody moved or spoke. Then, in a cascade of sparks, a log would collapse into the hollow fire and Achilles would look across at Patroclus and smile.

That was the signal. We would all rise, Patroclus and Iphis getting ready to leave. I would hear them whispering together in the hall and wonder how it was for her. She'd lost relatives, she'd lost her home, and Patroclus had been part of that. How was it possible for her to love him?

Achilles would then get undressed, but slowly, returning again and again to the lyre. I'd lie with my eyes closed and listen, breathing in the smell of resin from the wall beside me, till I knew from the darkening of my lids that he was scattering ashes on the fire. A moment later, I'd feel the bed sagging under his weight.

I don't know, perhaps if I'd been able to reach out to him, to speak, things might have been different. Though I think it's equally likely—*more* likely—that any reference to what was happening would have produced an explosion of anger. This was an intensely private ritual that had to be carried out in silence, in the dark. And so night after night I lay underneath this man, who was not a man at all but an angry child, and prayed for it to be over quickly. And afterwards, I'd stretch myself out as straight-legged as a corpse on a funeral pyre and wait for the moment when his sleeping breath would free me to turn onto my side and face the wall.

And I prayed for change. Every morning and every night, I prayed for my life to change.

8

I think I may have been the first person in the camp to see the priest.

I'd gone down to the beach, walking along the shoreline until I came to Odysseus's ships, which were hoisted up on cradles immediately behind the arena. I stopped and looked back the way I'd come, and there he was, the priest, striding towards me, his feet leaving a snail's trail in the gleaming sand. Grey-haired, travel-stained, he looked exhausted, as if he'd been on the road for days or even weeks. He veered from side to side as he approached, his robes flapping in the wind. At first, I took him for a sailor, but then, as he came closer, I saw that his staff was draped with the scarlet bands of Apollo and his clothes, though dirty and creased, were made of the finest wool.

When he was only a few feet away from me, he hesitated, as if he didn't know how to address me. I could see the problem. There I was, a young woman, richly dressed, unveiled and out walking alone . . . If he'd seen me in a city he'd have known exactly what I was. Immediately, I hardened against him, thinking: *Well, yes, old man, that's exactly what I am, but not by choice.*

"Daughter," he began, tentatively, "can you direct me to Agamemnon's lodging?"

I turned and pointed to my left, but at that moment one of Odysseus's men came out from between the ships and asked the priest what he was doing there. He'd come, he said, to ask Lord Agamemnon to accept a ransom for his daughter's return. I guessed he must be Chryseis's father. The man went into Odysseus's hut to report and shortly afterwards Odysseus himself appeared.

I ran as fast as I could to Nestor's compound and found Hecamede in one of the weaving sheds. Gradually, as I told her what I'd seen, loom after loom fell silent and women gathered round us to discuss the priest's arrival.

"He'll have to let her go," Hecamede said.

"Will he hell," I said. "He's Agamemnon—he doesn't *have* to do anything."

News of the priest's arrival spread from hut to hut. By the time I reached the arena, it was all over the camp; a crowd of jostling, gesticulating, excited men had already gathered.

This was the first time I'd been in the arena since the army had awarded me to Achilles and the memories of that day were so terrible I was tempted to turn back, but I stood my ground. I wasn't the only woman there; I saw Ritsa standing under the statue of Zeus, her brawny arms folded across her chest. I waved to her, but we weren't close enough to speak. All the time, men were crowding in as news of the priest's arrival spread, craning their necks to see what was going on and cheering loudly as Agamemnon arrived. All around the arena, the statues of the gods—paint cracked and flaking from the scouring winds that blew in off the sea—gazed down, blank-eyed and pitiless.

I looked around, trying to find a vantage point where I'd be able to see above the heads of the crowds. A movement caught my eye. It was Chryseis, standing right at the top of the dunes in the shadow of a stunted tree that the prevailing winds had bent into an arc. I ran to join her. As I came closer, I saw one side of her face was bright red, the eye on that side watering profusely; she kept raising the corner of her veil to dab at it, but she made no mention of the injury and neither did I. I just put my arms round her—and then we stood together looking down into the arena over the heads of the crowd.

She was gripping my arm and whimpered a little as she caught sight of her father waiting near the entrance.

Chryseis's fingers dug into my arm as the old man, her father, Apollo's priest, walked into the centre of the arena, holding aloft the staff and scarlet bands of the god. Immediately, the crowd fell silent. A wind was getting up, creating little dust devils in the sand that whirled a second or two then vanished as quickly as they came. A sharper gust lifted the priest's grey hair as he began to speak. First, he greeted Agamemnon courteously, praying that Apollo and all the gods would grant him victory, that he'd be able to sack Priam's city and carry the riches of Troy home in his ships . . .

"Only give me back my daughter."

After the formality of his opening words, the plea came as a shock. Suddenly, we were in another world, a world where the love of a father for his child mattered more than any amount of plundered wealth. But Agamemnon had sacrificed his own daughter to get a fair wind for Troy. I was afraid for the old man, and for Chryseis. For a long moment, after that, the priest seemed to be overwhelmed with grief, but then he forced himself to go on. He'd brought a great ransom with him, in the hold of the cargo ship they could all see anchored in the bay. Openly crying now, he begged Agamemnon to accept it.

"Please, Lord Agamemnon, please let me take her home."

Everybody in the arena was moved by the old man's tears—and by the size of the ransom he'd brought with him. Sentiment and greed—the Greeks love a sentimental story almost as much as they love gold. "Take it!" they shouted. "Give the poor old sod his daughter!" And then, as an afterthought, "Honour the gods!" Soon the crowd was in an uproar, fighters pushing and shoving and chanting: "Give her back! Give her back!"

After conferring briefly with his advisers, Agamemnon stood up. The hubbub continued for a moment or two, until the people on the fringes of the crowd realized he was on his feet, and then, apart from one or two isolated shouts, the chanting shrivelled into silence.

"Old man," Agamemnon said—no title, no respect—"old man, take your ransom and go. You've got away with your life this time, but if I catch you in the camp again the staff and bands of the god won't save you." He looked around the ranks of men—all silent now. "I'm not going to give her back. She'll spend the rest of her life in my palace, far from her native land, working at the looms by day, sleeping in my bed at night, bearing my children, until she's an old, old woman without a tooth in her head. Now get out. No more words, just *go*. Be thankful you're alive."

In silence, the priest turned away, letting his staff trail across the sand so that a sharp line followed him all the way to the exit. There, he turned for a last look at Agamemnon and his lips moved, but he was too frightened to speak. Agamemnon had already turned away. He was talking to the men behind him, smiling, even laughing, enjoying his little moment of triumph over a weak, frail, unhappy old man. Reluctantly, the crowd began to disperse, men walking away in groups of two or three, muttering. Nobody liked it. I thought I saw one or two men make the sign against the evil eye.

I almost didn't dare look at Chryseis, but I knew what she had to do. "Run." She gawped at me, too shocked to take it in. "Go on, *run*. Get back to the hut. He might send for you."

I knew he would. He wouldn't be able to resist a celebratory fuck. Her grief at the separation from her father would mean nothing to him.

She set off, running like a young hind between the huts, and I began to walk back to Achilles's compound. All the paths were crowded with men leaving the gathering, so I cut down onto the beach. And there was the priest, trudging across mats of dried-out seaweed, his shuffling feet raising clouds of sandflies that hovered all around him. He was making slow progress, crying and praying to Apollo as he went. I began following him—not intentionally, I was simply walking in the same direction. As he put more distance between himself and Agamemnon, he began to pray in a much louder voice, holding the staff and bands of the god high above his head, almost as if he were back inside his own temple, standing on the altar steps.

Lord of light, hear me!
Lord of the silver bow, hear me!

His chanting grew louder and louder until he was shouting at the sky.

I was moved by the old man, but exasperated too. If calling on the gods achieved anything, Lyrnessus would not have fallen. Goodness knows, no one could have prayed any harder than we did.

But I went on watching and listening as, still chanting prayers, he stumbled along the shore.

Lord of Tenedos, hear me!
Lord of Scylla, hear me!
If ever I sacrificed lambs and goats on your altar,
Revenge your priest!

I'd lost hope of my prayers being answered. No god I know of listens to the prayers of slaves, and yet I was transfixed by this old man. Sky and sea darkened around him and still the chanting went on, though the titles of the god were less familiar to me now.

Smintheus Apollo, hear me!
Lord whose arrows strike from afar, hear me!
Lord of mice, hear me!

Lord of *mice?* I'd forgotten—if I ever knew—that Apollo is the god of mice. And suddenly, I knew where all these prayers were leading. Apollo isn't the lord of mice because they're sweet, furry little creatures and he quite likes them . . . No, he's the lord of mice because mice, like rats, carry the plague; and Apollo, the lord of light, the lord of music, the lord of healing, is also the god of plague.

As the priest's great prayer for vengeance mounted to the skies, I found myself praying with him.

Lord of mice, hear me!
Lord of the silver bow, hear me!
Lord whose arrows strike from afar, hear me!

Until, finally, the forbidden words erupting from my mouth like blood or bile:

God of plague, hear me!

9

Nothing happened. Well, of course nothing happened! Isn't nothing what generally happens when you pray to the gods?

Next morning, the men mustered as usual before dawn. Amidst a great hammering of swords on shields Achilles sprang into his chariot and gave the signal to move off. After they'd gone, after the shouts and shield-banging had died away, the camp took on its habitual slightly surprised, dishevelled look, abandoned as it was to women and children and the handful of grey-haired men left behind to guard the ships.

I found Chryseis weaving, though she broke off when she saw me and offered me a cup of wine. Watching her move around the hut, I thought she was walking more stiffly than she had been the day before. Poor Chryseis, she knew none of the techniques women like Uza employ to control the appetites of men. I didn't know many of them, but she knew absolutely nothing, having gone to Agamemnon's bed a virgin and scarcely more than a child. Though, to be fair, she was managing, helped along by her devotion to Apollo and the occasional dip into the goose-fat jar.

When Ritsa expressed sympathy for Chryseis, Uza snorted with derision. "I've no sympathy," she said. "If a woman knows how to work it'll be over before he gets his dick anywhere near her."

"What do you mean, 'knows how to work'?" Ritsa said. "She's fifteen!"

"I was twelve."

Poor Chryseis, Agamemnon couldn't keep his hands off her. And how many girls, finding themselves loved, or at least lusted after, by the most powerful man in Greece, wouldn't have been puffed up with pride? Not Chryseis. She was utterly desolate, dreamt only of returning to her father. She told me she wanted to be a priestess, that her father was training her, and she'd have been a good one too. Very devout, prayed four times a day: sunrise, noon, sunset and up again before dawn pleading for the god's return. Apollo, the slayer of darkness, Apollo, the god of healing—who also happens to be the god of plague. She asked me once to join her in the noon prayers, but I made an excuse to get out of it. I did pray to Apollo—increasingly, I prayed—but mine were not the kind of prayers you share.

Lord of mice, hear me . . .

I walked back to Achilles's compound along the strip of hard sand between the cradled ships and the sea.

Lord of light, hear me!

The prayer rang hollow on my lips; I was spiralling down into darkness, too far gone already to be able to praise Apollo as the lord of light. Instead, my clenched fist beat a tattoo on the palm of my hand.

Lord of mice, hear me!
Lord of the silver bow, hear me!
Lord whose arrows strike from afar, hear me!

The sea that day was almost unnaturally flat and calm, with a smooth, milky sheen on the surface like the skin on a blister. The waves bulged against the confines of the bay, before breaking into overlapping arcs of yellowish foam that seethed briefly among the debris before vanishing into the sand. There was something menacing about this stillness, like the last few minutes before a storm. I looked at the cradled ships, at the huts and smouldering fires, and my skin felt bloated with anticipation.

Cutting across the arena, where the blank eyes of the gods followed me, I began walking along a path through the dunes that ran the whole length of the camp, at one point skirting the vast rubbish dump. Hardly the best place to be on a swelteringly hot day, for though the sky remained overcast the heat was increasing hour by hour. The stench, the myriad black, buzzing flies, the sweat trickling down my sides, all combined to produce a shudder of disgust. And yet something in me welcomed the contact with decay and decomposition. I actually thought this was where I belonged; *here*, among all the other rubbish. At that moment, I didn't blame Achilles or the Greek army or even the war for what I'd become. I blamed myself.

As I was passing the tip, I noticed a rat running between piles of rotting food. A lot of food got wasted in that camp, because nobody there had worked long hours to grow the crops or tend the cattle. No doubt that accounted for the size of the rats because I'd never seen rats as sleek and well fed as these. You were always catching glimpses of them, but normally they whisked away as you approached. This one didn't. In fact, it was behaving altogether oddly, staggering round in circles. As I got closer, I could see its fur was spiked and staring, nothing like the usual gleaming black. I walked past, but then something made me turn and look back and at that moment the rat screamed. Blood erupted from its mouth; it fell onto its side, rolled around in agony for a full minute, screamed again and died.

I noticed other rats then, all of them out in the open, none of them running away, and the more I looked, the more I saw. Bloated little corpses were scattered here and there among the rubbish. I nearly trod on one and, looking down, saw maggots busy underneath its skin. These were not recent deaths, the rats must have been dying for some time. I backed away and broke into a run, putting the rubbish tip behind me as fast as I could, gasping the last few hundred yards to the compound gate. I burst into the women's hut, full of what I'd seen and yet, once inside, told nobody, because, really, what was there to tell? A few dead rats? Not really worth mentioning, is it?

But I thought about them, as I got ready for dinner. I paid careful attention to my appearance, as I always did. Achilles's obsession with my hair and skin hadn't made me feel any more secure; rather the reverse, in fact. It had come on so suddenly, I felt it could turn equally quickly into revulsion. So I made sure that, in public at least, I was exactly what he wanted: visual confirmation that he was, as he'd always claimed to be, the greatest of the Greeks.

It was so hot in the hall at dinner, it actually hurt the inside of your nose to breathe. Body heat, burning torches, even the smell from platters of roast beef combined to thicken the air. The talk was still about Agamemnon's treatment of the priest. Nobody liked it. Nobody understood it. A ransom like that, *for a girl*, and he'd turned it down? Was he mad? Even Achilles, when I leant over to pour his wine, was talking about Agamemnon's refusal of the ransom. "*Why* didn't he take it? He's the greediest man alive."

"Perhaps he loves her," Patroclus said.

"*Love*, bloody old goat doesn't know what love is."

And you do? I thought, moving on.

I was starting to see some of the men as individuals—most of them tolerable, one or two of them definitely *not*. Myron was a middle-aged, corpulent man with a mass of curly, coarse black hair beginning to turn grey. I suppose he must have fought at some stage, but he wasn't fighting now. His job was to oversee the maintenance of the ships. It was an important position: Achilles carried out frequent raids on cities up and down the coast and needed his fleet to be kept seaworthy at all times. I'd noticed rotted rigging on the ships of some of the other kings—even, on one occasion, unrepaired damage to a hull—but you didn't see anything like that in Achilles's camp; his ships could have put to sea in a matter of hours. Myron carried out his duties meticulously. He was a man I disliked—personally disliked, I mean—though for no better reason than that the glances he directed at me were bolder, more crudely appreciative, than the other men's. He never said anything, of course—he wouldn't have dared—but he stared at my breasts as I bent over him and made little smacking noises with his lips, as if he were looking forward to the wine I was about to pour.

That night I poured his wine—quickly, as I always did, because I hated being near him—and then, stepping back, I noticed the tunic he was wearing. It was one I'd woven for my father. In fact, I'd finished it only a few days before I was carried on a litter to my new husband's house, the journey every girl must make. The embroidery on the back of the tunic wasn't particularly good—I've never claimed any great skill at weaving *or* sewing—but love had gone into every stitch. Of course this wasn't the first time I'd experienced that jolt of recognition; the day after my arrival, I'd noticed a gold serving dish from my husband's palace standing on a side table in the hall. But this was personal. I looked down at the fleshy folds in Myron's neck and once again the prayer sounded in my mind, involuntarily, almost as if the words were speaking me.

Lord of mice, hear me!
Lord of the silver bow, hear me!
Lord whose arrows strike from afar, hear me!
God of plague, hear me!

10

Everybody was unsettled by the heat. Quarrels broke out in the hall, one of them developing into a fight. Even Patroclus, normally so conciliatory, having dragged the combatants apart, hit one of them and rammed the other hard against the wall. There was a surly silence after that and the gathering broke up without the usual singing.

Even after dark, the sky retained a yellowish tinge, seeming to press down on the camp, trapping the heat inside like the lid on a cooking pot. After the dinner dishes had been cleared away, I sat alone in the cupboard waiting to be called. Iphis had been taken ill that morning with a stomach upset that was going round the camp. It was unusually quiet—no sound of music or conversation from the next room. After a while, tired of being cooped up in the hot, airless box, I went outside and found Patroclus sitting on the veranda steps, alone.

Immediately, I started to go back inside, but he motioned me to sit beside him. Achilles had gone for a swim, he said. Something in his voice made me turn to look at him. I could see the whites of his eyes and the gleam of his teeth when he smiled, but very little else. The camp was almost totally dark. No moon, no stars. Here and there, cooking fires still burned, but nobody wanted to sit around them in this heat. Far away in the distance, like a glimpse of another world, the lights of Troy glittered on the hill.

It should have been pleasant, sitting outdoors on a warm evening, but sweat prickled in every fold of skin and there was no cooling breeze to free you from it. Huge black insects—not moths, I don't know what they were—fluttered round our faces and had to be batted away. The rotten smell from the rubbish dump had spread into every corner of the camp—you could even *taste* it. I envied Achilles his plunge into the sea, but there was no way I could follow him down to the shore, not with Patroclus sitting there. Though I wondered a little why *he* didn't go. Perhaps Achilles had expressed a wish to be alone. Apart from one particularly vitriolic diatribe against Agamemnon, he'd been unusually quiet at dinner.

We went on sitting side by side. For a while, neither of us spoke—after all, what could we possibly have to say to each other, *Prince* Patroclus and Achilles's bed-girl? (That was by far the most flattering name for what I was.) But then, the heat, the silence, the darkness of the night seemed to bring the impossible within reach. I heard myself say: "Why are you always so nice to me?"

At first, I thought he wasn't going to reply, that I'd gone beyond what was permissible in a slave. But then he said: "Because I know what it's like to lose everything and be handed to Achilles as a toy."

His honesty winded me. But at the same time I was thinking: *How can you know? You, with all your privileges, all your power, how could you possibly know what it's like to be me?* Did I ask the question? I very much doubt it, but perhaps it shaped itself in the space between us. Either that, or he just needed to talk.

"When I was ten I killed a boy," he said. "I didn't mean to do it, he was my best friend, but we fell out over a game of dice. He said I was cheating, I said I wasn't, one thing led to another and I hit him. He fell down and I thought that was it, it was over—I'd actually started to walk away. But then he jumped up and head-butted me— broke my nose." He raised a hand to touch the flattened bridge. "I was in so much pain I couldn't think, I just grabbed a stone and hit him with it. I thought I'd only hit him once, I only remember doing it once, but that's not what happened because there were other boys there and they said I went on hitting him—and it must've been true because his face was smashed in. By the time they pulled me off him he was dead. Well, of course it was murder. His father was a powerful man. So I was sent into exile, shipped off to stay with Peleus, Achilles's father, not just for a few months either. For ever. And there was Achilles." He was staring straight ahead of him, without expression. "I don't think I'd ever seen a more miserable boy—well, except when I looked in the mirror. His mother had just left." He hesitated. "You know she's a sea goddess?"

I nodded.

"It wasn't a happy marriage. One day she just got up and walked into the sea. She'd done it before, she was always doing it, but this time she didn't come back. Achilles wouldn't eat, he wouldn't play with the other kids, I think he actually stopped growing. It's hard to believe but he was quite a little runt when I met him. Peleus was at his wits' end, so I came in very handy, because I *had* to be Achilles's friend." He laughed. "But it was good for me too."

"How?"

"He calmed me down."

"Peleus did?"

"No, Achilles. Yes, I know, hard to believe, isn't it?"

Some distance away, there was a burst of singing, ending in laughter. I felt rather than saw him turn towards me. "You watch us all, don't you?"

I shook my head.

"No, you do."

It wasn't a comfortable feeling, knowing my watchfulness had been observed.

"And I hear you crying sometimes . . ."

"You can't always help it. Well, women can't. I'm sure *you* never cried."

"Every night for a year."

This was said so lightly it was hard to tell if he was being serious or not. I nodded towards the beach. "A long swim."

"She might be there."

For a moment, I didn't understand. "You mean his mother?"

"Yes."

"She still comes to see him?"

"*Oh, yes.*"

Again, a note in his voice I couldn't place. Bitterness, perhaps? I remembered Achilles on the beach, the weird, bubbling, non-human speech, the repeated word—the only word I understood, or thought I understood: *Mummy, Mummy.* What would it be like to love such a man? "Do you regret it?"

"Growing up as Achilles's foster-brother? Not in the least. We-ell, obviously I regret killing my friend, but . . . No, they were very kind to me." He sat motionless for a minute or two, before suddenly slapping his knees. "I think I might have a walk down, see what he's up to."

"Why do you worry about him so much?"

"Habit." He stood up. "You do know, don't you, that he . . ."

I waited for him to go on, but he just smiled and turned away.

I was free to go now—I supposed—back to the women's huts, but after that conversation I couldn't settle. I decided to walk a little way along the path that led to the beach. My heart kept skipping beats and I didn't know why. I came out onto the beach at the place where the stream meandered over a pebbly bed towards the sea. Achilles and Patroclus were on the far side, close to the high-water mark. I was too far away to hear what they were saying, but I thought from their gestures they might be quarrelling. Once, Achilles turned his back and Patroclus grabbed his arm and wrenched him round again. For a moment, they stood facing each other, not speaking, then Achilles moved in closer till he was resting his head against Patroclus's forehead. They stayed like that without moving or speaking for a long time.

I stepped back into the shadows. I knew I'd stumbled on something too private to be witnessed. There were always those, then and later, who believed Achilles and Patroclus were lovers. Theirs was a relationship that invited speculation: Agamemnon, in particular, couldn't leave it alone, though Odysseus was nearly as bad. And perhaps they were lovers, or had been at some stage, but what I saw on the beach that night went beyond sex, and perhaps even beyond love. I didn't understand it then—and I'm not sure I do now—but I recognized its power.

11

Next morning, when I walked through the dunes to see Hecamede, there were forty-seven dead rats. I counted every one.

The punishing heat continued. The men came back from the battle-field one evening grey-skinned, exhausted—ready to lash out at each other or, more often, take it out on the slaves. Tepid baths, food and drink had to be provided immediately. My face shuttered, I waited at the table, loathing them all. I even avoided looking at Patroclus because I was ashamed of liking him. Instead, I concentrated on the men who bent over their plates like pigs guzzling in a trough. Myron was wearing my father's tunic again; he seemed to have grown fond of it. When I leant over his shoulder to pour his wine, his thick, pasty tongue came out and flicked around his lips and a pulse began to beat inside my brain: Lord of mice, *hear me,* lord of the silver bow, *hear me* . . . I don't know how I got through that night, but I did.

Next morning when I passed the rubbish dump there were too many dead rats to count.

We knew the camp was overrun with rats. How could it not be—so much meat and grain wasted, half-eaten food left lying around? You heard them at night under the floors, rustling and squeaking. Normally, during the day, the prowling dogs would keep them out of sight, but not now. Now, they seemed to have lost all fear, coming out from under the huts to die in the open air, and always with that terrible squealing, the sudden flowering of red blood at the end. The dogs couldn't believe their luck, so many rats, no need to hunt . . . But there were too many to eat, and soon the little black corpses dotted every path. Men walking along would kick them underneath the huts, where they swelled up and stank.

Myron hated it. He was responsible not only for the maintenance of the ships but also for the upkeep of the compound. Every rat that died in the open was dying on one of *his* paths or—worse yet—on one of *his* verandas. Of course, he had a whole squad of men to clear them away, but it was interesting to see how often he picked up the dead rats himself, as if he couldn't bear the sight of them a second longer. And always, after dropping them into the sack he carried around with him, he'd wipe his fingers fastidiously on my father's robe before drawing the back of his hand across his upper lip.

Not long after, the dogs and mules began to die. Unlike the rats, they couldn't just be piled up somewhere out of sight and left to rot; they had to be burned. And so the fires started. Round about this time, you noticed men darting quick glances at each other out of the corners of their eyes, though nothing was ever said. Over the evening meal, the laughter sounded a bit forced, perhaps, but then, as the dishes of wine were carried round, everybody relaxed. And, my god, how they drank! Every evening they staggered away from the table, flushed, boastful, bombastic, afraid . . . And Achilles, who drank less than anybody, flicked his gaze from face to face, watchful, assessing the mood.

On one particular evening, I'd just finished pouring wine into Myron's cup. Because I hated his lip-smacking, the carefully casual way he moved his arm so that it brushed against my breast, I always tried to pour his drink as quickly as possible—and without getting too close. This time, I misjudged the distance and some of his wine slopped over onto the table. It really shouldn't have mattered. Looking up and down the tables, you saw more than one pool of spilled wine. But it made Myron angry, to the point where there were veins standing out on his forehead; he was a man who became ridiculously upset over trifles. As soon as it happened, he was on his feet dabbing away with a cloth, muttering to himself. He was about to sit down again when a movement caught his eye. Standing immediately behind him, I could follow the direction of his gaze. A rat was running along the floor between the two long tables.

So far, nobody else had seen it. But then it began to stagger from side to side, letting out that terrible scream before finally toppling over onto its side and vomiting blood. By now, several people had turned to stare. A wave of silence ran along the tables as one by one the men stopped eating and craned to see what was going on. A dead rat? Well, one dead rat wasn't going to spoil the pleasure of food and drink. They'd already turned back to their plates when Myron staggered to his feet. He stood staring at me. "You," he said. "*You.*"

Evidently I was responsible for the dead rat as well as the spilled wine. He just couldn't bear it. The rat was half hidden in the rushes, but that didn't matter: he *knew* it was there and he kept glancing across the room to the small table where Achilles and Patroclus sat. Achilles didn't seem to have noticed the rat, but at any moment he might—and to Myron that prospect was intolerable. Grimacing with disgust, Myron walked a few paces, picked up the dead rat by its tail, took it to the door of the hall and threw it outside. Ironic cheers from the men, some of whom started drumming on the table as he walked back to his seat: *Why was he born so beautiful? . . .* Myron, sweating, wiped his hand on the side of my father's tunic, while the men went on bellowing the song, giving a final ironic cheer as he took his seat.

I moved on quickly, getting as far away from him as possible. And that day ended as every other day had done, listening to Achilles play the lyre, lying underneath him in his bed at night, gritting my teeth as he bit my breasts and tore at my hair. Afterwards, in the darkness, I closed my eyes and prayed: *Lord of the silver bow, lord whose arrows strike from afar, avenge your mice . . .*

———————

Next morning when I stepped out onto the veranda I trod on something soft. *Oh,* I thought, *the rat.* But when I looked down there were many rats, ten or twelve of them at least. I wondered what force drove them out of their dark, confined spaces to die like this in the open air.

They weren't the only rats I saw that day. I watched a group of Myron's men kicking a large rat around the beach. The narrow spaces between the ships were black with their bodies. All day long, Myron patrolled the paths, jabbing his spear as far underneath the huts as he could reach. The slave women kept out of his way as best they could. Somehow, in spite of this invasion, the camp and especially Achilles's hut had to be kept clean, tables scrubbed, fresh rushes gathered and laid on the hall floor, then baths prepared and food cooked—all this under the supervision of a man who seemed utterly distraught. I'd never seen a man work so hard and with such an air of desperation. But, in spite of all his efforts, the rats defeated him. Striding along the veranda, tugging at the buckles on his breastplate, Achilles stumbled over a dead rat and with an exclamation of disgust kicked it far out into the yard. The look on Myron's face at that moment would have melted any heart less cold than mine.

At dinner, the moment everybody was seated, Myron himself got up and barred the doors, an extraordinary thing to do in that heat, but nobody protested. I think everybody could see he was out of control. I carried round the wine as usual, though I asked Iphis to serve at Myron's end of the table. After pouring each cup, I straightened up and looked across at him. His eyes were darting from side to side: he obviously thought he hadn't got the door closed fast enough: the rats had got in, they were running around. Were they? I thought I could hear something, but that might've been my own feet rustling through the rushes as I walked up and down. Myron peered into the shadows, now and then seeming to focus on one particular spot. I thought: *He can see them,* though when I turned to follow the direction of his gaze there was nothing there.

Ten minutes into the meal, Myron, by this time streaming with sweat, began clawing at his throat and armpits. The other men teased him. "Got fleas, Myron?" This was a joke—everybody had fleas, the whole camp was crawling with them—but Myron was in no mood for jokes. He got to his feet and started for the door. Thinking he'd taken offence, one of the men shouted after him: "Oh, sit down, Myron, for fuck's sake, have a drink!"

I don't think Myron heard. He was tearing at his throat and armpits, he even put a hand up his tunic and started clawing at his groin. One or two of the men began to look uneasy; clearly something was wrong. "You all right?" somebody asked.

Myron slumped against the wall. "Look at the cheeky little sods," he kept saying. *"Look at them."*

Men at the far ends of the tables had fallen silent and were leaning forward to see what was happening.

"Look at them, *look!*"

Some men spun round, perhaps expecting to see Trojan fighters bursting through the doors. I knew he meant the rats, but there were no rats.

By now, Achilles was on his feet. Myron let go of the wall and set off in lumbering pursuit of something only he could see, though he'd taken no more than half a dozen steps when he fell headlong on the floor—not buckling at the knees, no graceful slide—crashing like a felled tree.

A moment's silence. Then Patroclus was kneeling beside him, turning him over onto his back, shouting at everybody to get back. "Give him some air."

The crowd parted to let Achilles through. He too knelt and pressed his fingers into the fleshy jowls round Myron's jaw. "Feel that," he said, in a whisper, to Patroclus.

Patroclus put his hand on Myron's neck and nodded. "Hard."

Achilles reached down the front of Myron's tunic to feel his armpits, then looked at Patroclus and, almost imperceptibly, shook his head. "Better get him across to the hut."

It took four men to lift Myron and another to support his head. As they staggered past me, I noticed a smell, like the water in a vase when lilies have been left to rot. Achilles went to the door and watched the little procession move across the yard. Meanwhile, Patroclus was walking up and down the tables, reassuring the men, telling them that, yes, Myron was ill, but he was in the best place, he'd be well looked after . . . Nothing to worry about, they all knew Myron, strong as an ox, take a lot more than this to keep *him* down, be on his feet again in no time, giving everybody hell.

Patroclus even took a jug from one of the girls and started filling the men's cups, urging them to drink to Myron's health. Every eye in the room followed him and gradually the talk and laughter started up again.

12

Early the following morning, I took Myron a pain-killing draught that had been mixed by Achilles himself. I'd watched him grinding the herbs and crushing roots for it the night before. One of the legends that grew up around Achilles was that he had remarkable powers of healing. Whether he actually had such powers or not, I don't know. The draught certainly didn't cure Myron, though it did, to be fair, relieve the pain.

I found Myron in the hospital hut propped up on pillows, tousle-haired and sweaty, still pawing at his neck, armpits and groin. His skin was hot to the touch and the swellings had begun to stink. When, gritting my teeth, I made myself feel his neck, he grasped my wrist and tried to pull me down onto the bed, which was when I knew his mind was gone. He kept staring into the shadows and muttering about rats, though there weren't any to be seen. Mixed in with his delirium, there were occasional moments of clarity. In one of them, I asked him how he felt.

"I'm not *ill*," he said, pettishly. "It's just the bloody rats, I've let it get to me."

"There weren't so many this morning."

That was just intended to soothe him. I realized only after I said it that it was true. He brightened slightly and finished off the dark, bitter-smelling draught. I made to leave, promising to bring him another cup. It did seem to be doing him some good, though I suspected that was mainly because he knew it came from Achilles. At the door, I turned to look back. He seemed considerably more comfortable, even sliding down the bed and pulling up the sheets to cover the black mat of hair on his chest.

A few hours later, I took another dose across to him and was shocked to see the deterioration. He'd thrown off the sheets and was lying half on the bed, half on the floor, his tunic rucked up round his waist. I could see the swellings in his groin bulging out of the fuzz of black hair like horrible, overripe figs. He'd vomited all over his chest and neck, a ropey mixture of mucus and bile. No solids, I noticed, but then he hadn't eaten anything that day and not much the day before. One hand was at his groin, the other at his neck—and his skin when I touched it was so hot I involuntarily snatched my hand back. He muttered something. I supposed it was about the rats, but then I caught the word "fire." "On fire" he seemed to be saying, but his throat was so clogged he couldn't get the words out. I offered him the cup, but he was obviously incapable of grasping it, so I bent over him and dribbled some of the dark brown liquid into his mouth. Almost at once, he vomited. I tried him on water and that came back too, though at least he'd been able to rinse his mouth and moisten his lips; he was burning up.

Even in his weakened state, he struggled to pull himself up when Achilles entered the room, sitting to attention, almost, and stretching his neck as if to distance himself from the sweating, stinking lump his body had become. "Sorry," he kept saying. "I'm so sorry."

"No need," Achilles said. "The rats have gone."

After a few minutes Achilles left, no doubt going down to the sea to swim before dinner. The door banged shut behind him, releasing a puff of cleaner air, but I'd no sooner felt it on my skin than it was gone. Still I lingered, managing to get a little more of the draught into Myron, whose eyes were starting to close. Shortly afterwards, he fell into a deep sleep and I was able to leave the hospital hut and go back across to the main hall, where the captains were starting to gather. I fetched a jug from the sideboard and was about to start my rounds, beginning, as always, with Achilles, when Patroclus took the jug from me and told me to go into the living quarters and get some rest.

That night, when I went to see Myron again, I really thought he was getting better—he seemed a lot brighter and was talking coherently again—but by the next morning he was worse, much worse, tossing and turning on sweat-soaked sheets, muttering constantly, though nothing he said made any sense. I called some of the other women and we bathed him, one girl turning aside to gag as the stench became too much for her.

Achilles, still in full armour, came in as soon as he got back from the fighting. He paused inside the doorway, obviously shocked. There were white crusts on Myron's lips like the fungus you sometimes see on fallen trees, and the corners of his mouth cracked when he tried to speak. Patroclus came in a few minutes later and looked across the bed at Achilles, who shook his head.

"I'll stay with him," Patroclus said.

"No, you won't," Achilles said. "You need something to eat."

"So do you. Go on, bugger off, I'll stay."

But Achilles sat down on the end of the bed and placed the palms of his hands on the soles of Myron's feet. It seemed to me a strange gesture of tenderness towards a man who had so little to recommend him, but obviously Achilles saw a different side to him. They were comrades, after all.

"Get some water, will you?" Achilles asked.

This seemed to be addressed to me so I went and fetched a jug of clean water from the vat near the door. Achilles took it from me and tried to force some into Myron's mouth. Myron was muttering, "Rats, rats . . ." and then again, as he seemed momentarily to recognize Achilles, "Sorry."

"It's not your fault."

But Myron was past caring whose fault it was. The end had come so quickly I think it took us all by surprise. We waited for the next breath. When it didn't come, Achilles felt for the pulse in Myron's neck, moving his fingers a little from side to side . . . "No, it's over." He closed Myron's eyelids, stood breathing deeply for a moment and then turned to Patroclus. "The sooner he's cremated, the better—burn everything belonging to him."

"Bit late for that."

"I know—but what else can we do?"

———

By long tradition, the laying-out of the dead is women's work—as much so in Greece as it was in Troy. Men carried Myron's body to the laundry hut and hoisted it onto a slab, but then they withdrew, leaving women to do the rest.

Because Myron had been Achilles's kinsman, I knew I had to be there. So I filled a bucket of water from a vat in the corner of the room, sprinkled a mixture of herbs—rosemary, sage, oregano and thyme—across the surface and set to work. Three of the women who worked in the laundry also filled buckets and carried them over to the slab, their bare feet *slap-slapping* on the wooden floor. The laundresses were heavy women, for the most part, slow-moving, with broad, shapeless feet, their faces pale, moist, open-pored, the skin on their fingertips permanently pleated from long immersion in water. I'd seen them standing in the troughs outside the laundry hut, their skirts bundled up round their waists, knee-deep in piss, treading garments hour after hour. Dried blood doesn't easily wash out and piss is one of the very few things that will shift it. As a result, the women's legs always stank; I could smell them, though I suspect they'd long since ceased to smell each other.

These women had no love for Myron, who'd always driven them hard *and* made use of them sexually too, but there was a job to be done. We stripped the sweat-stained clothes from his body, one woman exclaiming in disgust at the burst swellings in his groin. "The poor sod," she said, taking a step back.

But another woman muttered, "Serves the bugger right."

I was wringing out a cloth, about to start washing the body, when the door opened and Achilles walked in, closely followed by Patroclus. Achilles's chief aides, Alcimus and Automedon, crowded into the narrow space behind them. The women stayed where they were, so we ended up with Achilles and his men on one side of the slab and a row of silent, splay-footed women on the other.

I stepped forward and faced Achilles over the corpse. "We won't be long," I said. I couldn't for the life of me think what he was doing here.

He nodded, but showed no sign of leaving. Patroclus cleared his throat. "We brought some clothes to dress him in." He pushed them towards me over the damp marble. "Oh, and coins for his eyes."

Achilles was looking straight at me. Nobody moved or spoke. I think at that point he saw us, however briefly, as we really were. Not just women, not just slaves: but Trojans. The enemy. It satisfied something savage and unappeased in me that he should see us like that. That he should see *me* like that. At last, after a final, penetrating stare, he turned and strode out of the room, leaving the others to follow.

I knew what he was thinking: that Myron would be safe in our hands. If fear of earthly punishment didn't make us treat his body with respect, then obedience to the gods surely would. Women are, after all, renowned for their devotion to the gods.

We waited till the door had closed behind them. Then one of the women picked up Myron's poor limp penis between her thumb and forefinger and waggled it at the rest of us. The women hooted with laughter—and immediately clapped their hands over their mouths to silence themselves. But nothing could contain that laughter which rose in pitch and volume till it turned to whoops of hysteria that must have been clearly audible outside the hut. The woman waggling Myron's penis was shrieking as she gasped for breath. They must have heard us as they walked away, Achilles must have heard, but not one of them turned back and demanded to know what was going on. And so we were left alone with the dead.

13

As Achilles's kinsman, Myron was given a dignified funeral. His rotten carcass, oiled and perfumed and dressed in my father's tunic, was carried to the pyre with all the proper sacrifices, hymns, ceremonies, rituals and prayers. Before the kindling was lit, a priest poured libations to the gods. But when the fighters began to disperse, the talk was all of other men who'd fallen sick—five of them on the day Myron died.

Soon, the arrows of Apollo were striking thick and fast. The hospital hut filled with men tossing and turning in sweaty sheets. The few brave enough to visit their friends carried lemons stuck with twigs of rosemary and bay, but nothing could keep the noxious fumes out of your lungs. This was not the coughing plague so some of those who fell ill did survive, but many didn't. By the end of the first week, men were dying in such numbers that funerals could no longer be dignified rituals honouring the dead. Instead, bodies were transported under cover of darkness to a deserted part of the beach to be disposed of as swiftly and secretly as possible. Corpse fires were visible from Troy and nobody wanted the Trojans to know how many Greeks were dying, so often five or six bodies would be thrown onto a single pyre. The result, next morning, was a heap of charred and all too recognizable remains. Sometimes, the men following a dead comrade to his grave would sing loudly and clatter their swords on their shields, pretending they were on their way to a feast. In some of the worst incidents, rival groups of mourners fought each other to secure a place on the pyre for their dead friend.

At dinner, the singing and the table-banging still went on, but there were gaps on the benches that no amount of strong wine could make the men forget. Achilles himself went up and down the tables, joking and laughing, always with a cup of wine in his hand, though he did little more than moisten his lips. And I went on doing what I'd always done: smiled and poured, poured and smiled, till I wanted to vomit. I thought I detected a subtle change in the atmosphere, in the way the men looked at the women who were serving them. It was Iphis who worked it out. "It's because we're not dying," she said. That wasn't strictly true; several of the common women had died, crawling under the huts and dying alongside the dogs, but she was right in one respect: we weren't dying in anything like the same numbers as the Greek fighters. And the few deaths that did take place among the women went almost unremarked. After all, who's going to notice a few dead mice among so many squealing rats?

What did I feel during this time? Well, I was too exhausted from the nursing to feel anything very much. But that's evading the question. Yes. Yes, there were times when I watched a young man die and remembered my prayers for vengeance. Did I regret those prayers? No. My country was at war, my family had been killed—and remember, this wasn't a war that we'd chosen. So no, I didn't regret them; though, at the same time, I did grieve for the waste of so many young lives. But I never felt responsible for their deaths. Yes, I'd prayed for vengeance, but I wasn't vain enough to believe my prayers had carried any weight with the god. Apollo had been insulted and he was exacting a terrible revenge, as he was known to do.

On the ninth day, Achilles and Patroclus returned from a particularly distressing cremation, their hair and clothes reeking of woodsmoke and burnt fat. Achilles yelled for more wine, stronger wine, and I ran to fetch it. When I came back, Patroclus was slumped in his chair, his hands slack between his knees. Once I'd filled both their cups I started to relax a bit, but then Achilles leapt to his feet and began pacing up and down. "Why doesn't he call an assembly? What's he *doing?*"

Patroclus shrugged. "Perhaps he doesn't think it's enough of a crisis."

"So what else has to happen? Or perhaps *his* men aren't dying?"

"They are, the hospital's full, I asked."

"We might just as well pack up and go home." Achilles threw himself into his chair, then immediately jumped up again. "Well, if he won't call an assembly, I will."

Patroclus swished wine round the sides of his cup, raised it to his mouth and drank.

Achilles looked down at him. "What? *What?*"

"*He* hasn't called one."

"No—and we all know why not. He doesn't want to be told he's got to give the girl back."

"Perhaps he can't see the connection."

"Then he's the only one who can't. You insult Apollo's priest, you insult Apollo."

"He's going to need a lot of convincing."

"Well, I'm sure we can find a seer to tell him what everybody else knows already."

Decision taken. With some men, that might have been the end of it, but not Achilles; he ranted and raved, fists pumping, spit flying, working himself up into a state of near-insanity. Agamemnon was a total fucking disgrace, a king who cared nothing for his men, greedy, rapacious, cowardly, and as for clinging on to the girl . . . A cunt-sniffing dog would have shown more sense. Sometimes you see a toddler, purple with rage, screaming till he gasps for breath—and you know only a slap will shock him out of it. Achilles's rages were like that. But who was going to slap Achilles?

At last, the diatribe seemed to be coming to an end. When it was clear there'd be no more, Patroclus shifted in his chair. Up to that point, he'd neither moved nor spoken, just gone on staring into the fire. From a distance, he might have seemed relaxed; close to, you could see a muscle throbbing in his jaw.

After a brief silence, Achilles reached for his cloak. "I think I might go for a walk." He seemed to notice me for the first time. "I won't be needing you tonight." He touched Patroclus briefly on the shoulder as he passed his chair. Seconds later, the door banged shut behind him.

I got up to go. Patroclus caught the movement. "Oh, sit down, for god's sake! Have some wine. You look done in."

"Thanks."

We were easy with each other now. All those hours of grinding herbs together—and of observing Achilles, alert for any change in his mood—had forged a bond at last. I'd started to trust him, to the point where it was an effort to remember that he too had taken part in the sacking of Lyrnessus.

Now, he got up, refilled his cup and handed one to me.

"Will you wait up?" I asked.

"I expect so, I generally do."

I can't tell you why Patroclus dreaded the nights Achilles met his mother. I only know he did.

The fire had burned low. He threw on another log, which smoked for a time before the flames took hold. A silence fell, broken only by the sound of a dog scratching its neck. Further away, barely perceptible, came the murmur of waves creaming over on the beach. The unnatural stillness continued; even at high tide the sea barely encroached upon the land. I looked at the walls and sensed beyond them the straining immensity of sea and sky. I felt the hot darkness pressing in, and thought how easily all this could be swept away—this hut, so solidly built, a man and woman sitting together by the fire.

"I heard him once," I said. "Talking to her. I couldn't understand what he was saying." I waited. When he didn't comment, I said, "Does she talk back?"

"Oh, yes."

"Are they close?"

"Hard to say. She left when he was seven." A pause. "Apparently she looks younger than he does now."

I was feeling my way. "It must've been difficult leaving a child that age."

"I don't know, perhaps. The thing is, she hated the marriage, it wasn't her choice, nobody asked her . . . I think she found it all a bit disgusting. And she passed it on too." He glanced at me. "Well, you must've noticed? A certain . . . *distaste?*"

I had, more than a bit, but I was wary of pursuing the subject. I felt he was saying too much and might regret it later.

He was smiling. "You remind him of her."

"I remind him of his *mother?*"

"You should be flattered. She is a goddess."

"I'm trying."

He was still smiling. Somehow, when he smiled, his nose looked much more obviously broken. Every time he looked in a mirror, he must be reminded of the worst day of his life.

"You know I could make him marry you?"

I shook my head. "Men don't marry their slaves."

"It's been known."

"He could marry a king's daughter."

"He could—but equally he doesn't need to. Mother a goddess, father a king—he can please himself." A sigh—caught and held. "We could all sail home together."

I wanted to say: *You burned my home.*

That night, lying beside Iphis on a pallet bed in one of the women's huts, I went back over what he'd said. Men don't marry their slaves—oh, I suppose now and then they might, if she'd given birth to a son and there was no legitimate heir—but how often does that happen? No, it was ridiculous. But then I remembered the glimpse I'd had of Achilles leaning against Patroclus on the beach. I knew he wasn't exaggerating his influence.

Would you really have married the man who'd killed your brothers?

Well, first of all, I wouldn't have been given a choice. But yes, probably. Yes. I was a slave, and a slave will do anything, anything at all, to stop being a thing and become a person again.

I just don't know how you could do that.

Well, no, of course you don't. You've never been a slave.

14

Shortly after dawn, Achilles sent his heralds round the camp. He could, of course, have stood in the stern of his ship and simply bellowed the message. One shout from Achilles and the whole army would have heard, but like all the leaders he was meticulous in observing the correct forms. They were all hypersensitive to any failure to acknowledge their exalted status and meetings between them were generally conducted with elaborate courtesy.

I spent the first part of the day in the hospital hut, pouring pain-killing draughts into the mouths of dying men. Three new patients arrived while I was there, one of them so far gone his friends had to carry him in on a stretcher. They dumped him on the floor and left immediately, their battle shirts pulled up to cover their mouths. After attending to him as best I could, I went across to the hall, where Alcimus and Automedon were sitting with a group of Achilles's close companions, passing round a jug of wine. Here, the talk was all of the assembly, of how Achilles intended to demand—not ask, *demand*—that the girl Chryseis be sent back to her father. "And he'll not get a ransom for her this time," somebody said, with evident satisfaction. There was a rumble of agreement. "Be bloody lucky if he doesn't end up paying to be shot of her."

By mid-afternoon, the paths were crowded with men making their way to the arena. I was just about to set off when a little girl came running up to me. Breathless with the importance of her mission, she gabbled, "Hecamede says, 'Can you come to Lord Nestor's hut?'" Without waiting for an answer, she seized my hand and dragged me along the narrow path that led to Nestor's compound.

By the time we got there, Nestor, his son Antilochus and their attendant lords had already left for the assembly. Hecamede, carrying a jug of wine, came to the door to welcome me. As I stepped over the threshold, I saw Chryseis, chalk-white and shaking. Uza, who'd been trying to get her to eat something, looked up when I came in and shook her head. I went straight across and touched Chryseis's forehead if anybody looked ill in those days your first thought was: *Plague.* But she felt cool, although her skin was moist. No fresh injuries, I was glad to see.

Nestor's hut was very close to the arena. Standing on the veranda, we could see the statues of the gods and the kings' chairs clearly. A buzz of conversation rose from the assembled crowd, dying away to a respectful hush whenever one of the kings, preceded by his heralds and flanked by his advisers, took his seat. They sat in a huge semicircle facing Agamemnon's empty chair, which had been placed under the statue of Zeus from whom, ultimately, Agamemnon derived his authority. The sun was half hidden behind a gauze bandage of mist, as it had been every day since the plague began. The painted statues of the gods cast scarcely any shadows on the sand.

To the sound of drums and trumpets, Agamemnon entered, the last of the kings to arrive, and settled himself into his throne-like chair. Achilles was sitting directly opposite, apparently at ease— hands clasped lightly in his lap—though even at a distance I could sense the whole tormented, pent-up energy of the man. He was sharing a joke with Patroclus, laughing, or pretending to, but suddenly he stopped and turned to watch the last stragglers file into the back of the arena. He was outwardly placid, inwardly seething with rage—and when he stood up the tension showed, because he kept all his weight on the balls of his feet, as a man does when he's poised to fight or flee—though I doubt if fleeing often crossed Achilles's mind. Every eye in the arena was on him, though he addressed himself exclusively to Agamemnon.

"Well," he began, "Trojans on one side—plague on the other. We can't fight both, we may as well go home." A canine-baring grin. "That's true, isn't it?"

Agamemnon didn't reply.

"Or . . ." Achilles held up his hand to quell the murmurs of speculation. "We can try to work out why all this is happening. There must be somebody, a seer, who can tell us what we've done to offend Apollo? Because clearly it's Apollo who's sent the plague. And if we know what we've done—or not done—we can put it right."

He sat down. A confusion of movement in the front ranks subsided to reveal the seer Calchus, on his feet, looking distinctly nervous. Calchus was not, at the best of times, a prepossessing figure: pallid, etiolated, with a quite exceptionally long neck. His voice box, prominent enough to cast its own distinct shadow, was jerking spasmodically as he tried to speak, though when he finally succeeded the words came out in a croak. He seemed to be saying that should his prophecy implicate one man, one extremely powerful man, would Achilles undertake to protect him?

Achilles half rose. "Go ahead, tell us. Nobody's going to hurt you while I'm alive." He paused, but he couldn't resist. "Even if you mean Agamemnon, who claims to be the greatest of the Greeks."

There it was: the challenge to Agamemnon's authority flung down, in full view of gods and men, while thousands of Agamemnon's own fighters looked on.

Calchus then "prophesied," at considerable length, what everybody in the crowd already knew, that Apollo had sent the plague to punish Agamemnon for the insult to his priest—and that the only way, now, for Agamemnon to appease the god was to send the girl back to her father, with the sacrifice of a hundred bulls. And, obviously, without the ransom—

Before Calchus finished speaking, Agamemnon's finger was

jabbing at him. Pathetic, miserable, whining little runt, when had he ever prophesied anything good? And now here he was again, shouting—hardly an accurate description of Calchus's stumbling delivery—that Agamemnon was responsible for the plague, because he'd refused to send the girl Chryseis back to her father. "And it's absolutely true," he said. "I don't want to lose her."

In the room behind me, I heard Chryseis say, hopelessly, "There you are, you see?"

"I'll be honest, I prefer her to my wife. She's every bit as skilled at the loom and in other ways she's a whole lot better: height, beauty— build." I Iere a ripple of amused sympathy ran through the crowd. "But of course, as commander-in-chief, I accept full responsibility; I don't want to see my own men dying . . . So yes, obviously, yes, I'll send her back."

Hecamede whooped with joy. I turned, expecting to see Chryseis transformed, but she looked even paler than before.

"He doesn't mean it." Clenched fists, a small, fierce voice. "It's a trick."

"Well, I think he means it," Hecamede said.

Uza spread her hands, looking from face to face. "Am I the only one here with an ounce of sense? *He prefers her to his wife!* She should be begging him to let her stay."

"Shut up, Uza," I said. *"For god's sake."*

"Oooh, sorry I spoke."

I turned back to the arena. Agamemnon was still speaking, though his words were drowned by the cheering of the men. When, finally, the roar died down, he said, "But I'm afraid that leaves us with a bit of a problem. *I* have no prize. Everybody else keeps theirs, I'm left with nothing. I want a replacement."

Achilles stood up. "And where are we supposed to find you that? Does anybody know of a stock of undistributed treasure? *I* don't. Everything we got from Lyrnessus was shared out weeks ago. You'll just have to wait till we take Troy."

"No, Achilles, you don't treat me like that. I'm not going to be left with nothing—and if you don't *give* me a prize, all right, I'll take one. Perhaps your prize, Odysseus?"

Uza pumped her fist in the air. *"Yes!"* She wasn't pretending either. I liked Uza, but she didn't give a damn whose dick was up her so long as she had a comfortable life. And to be *Agamemnon's* prize . . . It didn't come more comfortable than that.

But Agamemnon was already moving on, pointing round the semicircle of kings lined up in front of him. "Or yours," he said. "Or yours." All this was pretence. His eyes were already fixed on one man and his jabbing finger soon followed. "Or yours, Achilles."

For one insane moment, I thought there was a mistake. *I* was Achilles's prize, he couldn't mean me. I didn't dare look at the other women, I just stood staring fixedly into the arena.

"But all that's for the future," Agamemnon said. "First, I have to send Chryseis back to her father and persuade him to use his influence with Apollo to lift the curse. Now, who can I trust with this delicate mission? Idomeneo, King of Crete, respected wherever he goes? Or Lord Nestor, renowned for his wisdom? Or Odysseus, perhaps, clever, eloquent, a skilled negotiator? Or you, Achilles—the most violent man on earth?"

I wasn't interested in their insults, their constant jostling for power, I only wanted to know what was going to happen to me.

Hecamede put a hand on my arm. "Don't worry," she whispered. "He won't do it."

I shook my head.

In the arena, Achilles took several steps towards Agamemnon; not far, but the space between them seemed to shrink to nothing. "I fought for that girl," he said. "She's my prize, awarded by the army in recognition of *my* services. You have no right to take her. But it's always the same; I bear the brunt of the fighting and you get the lion's share of everything we take. All I ever get's a scrap, a trifle—when I go back to my hut exhausted from the fighting—while you sit there on your fat arse 'guarding the ships.'"

Behind me, Uza burst out laughing. *"Scrap,"* she said. *"Trifle."* Even Hecamede was smiling, though her smile faded when she saw my face. Chryseis came running up and hugged me. "It won't happen," she said. "He does this, he sets traps for people, but it won't happen."

Agamemnon was shouting, "I'll fetch the bloody girl myself, I won't send anybody else, I'll go myself—and then you'll all see what happens to a man who dares to pretend he's my equal!"

"I won't fight for her," Achilles said. "The army gave her to me and the army's taking her away, because not one of you—" Here he looked round the semicircle of kings. "Not one of you has the courage to get up on your hind legs and tell him he's wrong. Well, all right, then—he gets the girl, but don't expect me to go on fighting. Why should I risk my life—or my men's lives—for that pile of steaming dog shit over there?"

After that, any pretence of mutual respect was abandoned. At one point, they very nearly came to blows; Achilles had his sword halfway out of its scabbard, but at the last moment he pulled back. After that, Nestor rose to his feet and tried to persuade them to make peace, but by then I'd stopped listening, I didn't care anymore. My hands were at my face, fingers trying to work the numb and rubbery flesh into a more acceptable expression, though I needn't have bothered. Silently, Hecamede wrapped her arms round me. I always remember that she wept for me when I couldn't weep for myself.

Only Uza tried to cheer me up. "You'll be all right," she said. "I know what he likes. Anyway, push comes to shove, there's always the goose-fat jar."

There wasn't much to say after that. The fighters were subdued as the meeting broke up: worried looks, muttered speech, more often, silence. Achilles had withdrawn from the fighting, the coalition was broken—and, for the moment, at least, nothing had been solved; the hospital huts were still full of men suffering from the plague.

The heralds had begun clearing a path for Agamemnon through

the crowd, but he lingered, talking to Odysseus, who'd been chosen to lead the delegation that took Chryseis home.

Hecamede grasped Chryseis's arm. "Run, go on, run. They'll be coming to get you."

Chryseis seemed dazed. She hadn't dared hope and she was afraid, even now, that it could all be snatched away from her. She got as far as the door, then turned and ran back to me. "Briseis, I'm so sorry."

"Don't be, I'll be all right. Go on, *go.*"

I dragged my way back to Achilles's compound. He wasn't going to fight for me, he'd made that perfectly clear. Oh, he'd fight to the death—Agamemnon's death—for any of his other possessions, but not for me. As I walked through the camp, I looked at the common women, noticing a split lip here, a bruise there. One girl, young and otherwise pretty, had a star-burst scar on her forehead where a spear butt had struck. Had she been one of Agamemnon's girls, one of those he'd tired of and thrown out of his huts?

Neither Patroclus nor Achilles had returned from the assembly. Somebody said they were walking along the beach, no doubt planning what they were going to do—or refrain from doing—when Agamemnon arrived to claim me. I wandered around the living quarters—not crying, I couldn't cry—just picking up things and putting them down again. I came to the mirror and leant in towards my reflection. For a moment, my breath misted the gleaming bronze and then it was gone—my existence in these rooms as fleeting, as insubstantial, as that. I retreated to the cupboard and sat on the bed. After a while, Iphis came in and held my hand. Neither of us spoke. At last, we heard footsteps in the hall: Achilles and Patroclus returning from their walk.

Achilles burst into the living quarters, still fighting the battle that had raged in the arena. "So have we got this straight? When he comes, you don't let him in. Stop him at the gate. You can take Briseis out to him there. I don't want to see him—if I see him, I'll kill him."

"He won't come."

"He said he would."

"I heard what he said."

"I'll kill him."

"Yes, I know, and he knows too. Which is precisely why he won't come."

Patroclus sounded tired. I guessed they'd been going round and round that particular circle for a long time. I could see them both so clearly, in my mind's eye, almost as if the wall between us had become transparent: Achilles pacing up and down, Patroclus sitting with clasped hands, outwardly calm, but with that muscle throbbing in his jaw.

"You might as well sit down," Patroclus said, after a pause. "They won't be here for hours yet."

"Ha! He won't be able to wait."

"He's got to get Chryseis back to her father first. And find a hundred bulls; I don't suppose they're just lying around. And then with any luck he might wait till the ship gets back. That's what he *ought* to do."

Listening, I felt myself begin to hope. The ship taking Chryseis home would have to stay overnight. The ritual slaughtering of a hundred bulls would take quite a long time and then there'd be prayers and hymns to Apollo followed by a great feast. That would go on all night—and then there was the journey back. They wouldn't set off early, they'd all have hangovers . . . Given all that time to reflect, wasn't it possible Agamemnon might change his mind? Was he really going to break up with Achilles and risk losing the war—*for a girl*?

More pacing from the next room. At last, I heard the creak of Achilles's chair as he threw himself into it.

Patroclus cleared his throat. "Would you like me to send for Briseis?"

"What, for a farewell fuck? No, thanks."

Silence. I imagined Achilles looking slightly ashamed.

"No, leave it," he said, at last. "She'll know soon enough."

15

Freed from the apprehension of being sent for, I seized the opportunity to slip away. I wanted to say goodbye to Chryseis and wish her well, because I felt her good news had been unfairly overshadowed by what was going to happen to me.

It was beginning to get dark as I ran along the curve of the bay to where Agamemnon's ships were being made ready to set sail. Small groups of women had already gathered on the shore and were watching the bulls swaying and lumbering on board. They were bellowing as they felt the ground shift and tilt beneath their feet and the decks were slippery with the green shit of their fear. The men driving them on board were singing hymns of praise to Apollo, though I thought there was a note of desperation in their singing. Suppose even this wasn't enough?

At the last moment, when everything else was ready, Chryseis was brought out from Agamemnon's hut. She was wearing a plain white mantle, no jewellery, her hair in tight braids round her head. She looked like a queen, pale, composed and suddenly a lot older. Agamemnon didn't appear. It was Odysseus who took her by the hand and led her up the gangplank onto the ship, where she stood in the stern, staring back at Agamemnon's compound and then along the bay at the rows of black ships. Her eyes, as she scanned the shore, were wide open, strained wide. I saw that underneath the surface composure she was terrified; terrified that at any moment Agamemnon would change his mind and all this would be snatched away.

We were jumping up and down shouting: "Good luck! Have a safe journey!"

At first, I thought she wasn't going to respond—she was so tense, so determined to stay calm—but then one small hand came up and, with a barely perceptible movement of her fingers, she waved goodbye.

Gazing around, I was filled with warmth—with love, in fact—for all these women who'd come to see her off. They didn't begrudge her her luck, though every one of us would've given her right arm to be allowed to go home—and to have a home to go to.

Suddenly, Odysseus appeared standing beside Chryseis in the stern. Immediately, everything was noise and bustle, sails hoisted, anchor weighed—and then the ship was pulling slowly away from the shore, her broad wake foaming brown with silt. To begin with, the men rowed—a drum beating time—but then as the ship moved further out the sails bellied and suddenly she was bounding away from us as if she shared Chryseis's own eagerness to be gone. We watched the ship dwindle into the distance and a disconsolate silence fell. I can't speak for the others but I know, at that moment, I was as desolate as I'd ever been.

As the crowd began to break up, I was aware of some of the other women glancing at me out of the corners of their eyes. By now, the news of what was going to happen to me would have spread all over the camp. One of them, a woman I didn't much care for, looked at me and smirked. "I suppose it'll be half a crown to speak to you now?"

I don't think any of the other women envied my promotion—if that's what it was.

I walked back along the shore, head down, seeing nothing but my own feet pressing moisture out of the damp sand. Once or twice I narrowly avoided bumping into people, so absorbed was I in my own thoughts, but then some instinct made me look up—and only just in time. Agamemnon was standing less than a hundred yards away watching his ship, with Chryseis on board, shrink to a black dot against the red glare of sunset.

I slipped into the space between two ships and waited. All along the shore, now, men were wading into the sea, scraping oil and dirt off their skins, plunging their heads beneath the waves, purifying themselves—and all of them, all without exception, chanting a hymn of praise to Apollo: *I will remember Apollo who shoots from afar. When he bends his silver bow even the gods tremble before him* . . . And prayers, countless prayers, all pleading with him to free them from the plague. Soon, the breaking waves were black with men, the land almost deserted. I knew I had witnessed something amazing: a whole army walking into the sea.

Some men, too sick to walk, had to be carried into the water on stretchers. Enough to kill them, you might think, that sudden immersion of heated bodies in the cold, salt, ravening sea. But, as far as I know, none of them died—and I did see one man, who looked desperately ill as he was carried in, walk back to shore.

The stars were beginning to prick through a greenish sky. All along the bay, cooking fires had been lit and, as the men came dripping wet out of the waves, cups of hot, mulled wine were pressed into their hands and every one of them poured a libation to Apollo before he drank. Soon, they were gathered, shivering, around the fires, passing jugs of strong wine from hand to hand. On Agamemnon's orders, goats and sheep had been slaughtered and soon platters of roast meat were set in front of them, but there was none of the laughter and joking that normally accompany a feast. Until Apollo had accepted the safe return of Chryseis and the sacrifice of bulls, the camp still lay under his curse, and the knowledge of that weighed heavily on them all.

From the shadows, I watched Agamemnon, who was still standing on the shore, an isolated, silent figure. Surely, with all this going on, he'd forget about me? Do what everybody else seemed intent on doing: get plastered and try to forget? That's what I told myself, though at the same time I knew he wouldn't. Even though it made no sense, to me or to anybody else, that the two most powerful men in the Greek army should fall out over a girl.

————————

When I got back to Achilles's hut I went at once to the cupboard where I sat alone, waiting to be sent for. Iphis didn't appear. Perhaps Patroclus had told her to stay away.

An hour dragged past. I spent a lot of the time pleating the hem of my tunic and smoothing it out again. You see old women do that. I remember my grandmother doing it—it's a sign they're starting to wear out. And there I was, only nineteen and doing it already. I forced myself to stop.

A jug of wine was standing on a table to the right of the door. I knew nobody would mind if I poured myself a cup, so I did, my hands shaking so much I spilled some and had to find a cloth to mop it up. I was still mopping when I heard voices in the hall. I thought at first it was Agamemnon come to get me and immediately felt betrayed. I'd been counting on a delay and now there was no delay. Achilles was right: Agamemnon couldn't wait to get his hands on me.

I stood up, smoothed my tunic and rubbed spit around my lips so there'd be no purple staining from the wine. I wasn't going to be dragged away, I'd keep my head up and not look back. I wouldn't give Agamemnon the satisfaction of seeing my fear.

But then, I heard Patroclus announcing Lord Nestor and his son Antilochus. Nestor. I thought at once this must be some kind of peace mission, that Agamemnon had relented, because Nestor was exactly the go-between he'd have chosen. I opened the door a crack so I could hear more clearly and see at least a little of what was going on.

Nestor stepped into the room: tall, silver-haired, richly dressed, and behind him, gawky and painfully shy, his youngest son, Antilochus, a boy so besotted with love for Achilles he seemed to find it difficult to breathe in his presence. They were both wearing cloaks, for although the night was warm a moist wind was blowing off the sea. Flecks of rain like tiny pinpricks of light lay scattered across their shoulders. Achilles had risen to greet them. Nestor took off his cloak and handed it to Patroclus, then smoothed down his ruffled hair. As he took the seat Achilles offered, I saw he was beginning to thin on the crown; you could see patches of pink scalp between the white strands. After seeing him settled, Achilles asked Patroclus to fetch better wine. "Virgins' pee, this stuff," he said, with an awkward laugh. Meanwhile, Antilochus looked around for somewhere to sit, saw the bed and stumbled towards it. Because he knew, or rather imagined, that Achilles was watching, he tripped over a rug and nearly fell.

Patroclus was mixing Nestor's wine; several shades of deep red swirling round the sides of a gold dish. When he'd finished, he walked across to the fire and poured a generous libation to Apollo; the fire irons sizzled and spat. Nestor raised his cup in a toast, then looked long and hard at Achilles. "I see you're not loading your ships yet?"

"He hasn't come for the girl. Yet."

Nestor smiled and shook his head. "You won't leave. Whatever else you are, you're not a deserter."

"I don't see it as desertion. This isn't my war."

"You were keen enough to get into it."

"I was *seventeen*." Achilles leant forward. "Look, what he did today was totally outrageous, everybody knew it, and there wasn't one voice raised against it."

"Mine was. Then, and later."

"So now, I just think: *Fuck it.* He wants Troy, he can take Troy—without me. Except we both know he can't."

Nestor was silent for a moment. Then: "I am usually listened to, Achilles."

"Go on, I'm listening."

"You can't let other men do the fighting while you sit here and sulk. Ye-es." Nestor raised one hand. *"Sulk."*

Achilles's reply was surprisingly measured. "What he did today broke all the rules. I fought for that girl. The army gave her to me—he has no right to take her. Well, OK—but that's it, I'm finished. I'm not going to risk my life, or my men's lives, for a weak, greedy, incompetent and cowardly king."

I was waiting for Nestor to leap to Agamemnon's defence, but he just smiled.

"He may be all those things—it doesn't matter. It doesn't matter that you're a better fighter, braver, stronger, whatever—that's not what it's about. He has more men than you, more ships than you, more land than you—and that's why he's commander-in-chief and you're not."

"None of that gives him the right to take another man's prize of honour. It doesn't belong to him; he hasn't *earnt* it."

There was a lot more, but I'd stopped listening. Honour, courage, loyalty, reputation—all those big words being bandied about—but for me there was only one word, one very small word: *it. It* doesn't belong to him, he hasn't earnt *it.*

When I was able to focus on the conversation again, Nestor was saying: "Well, I only hope—"

But we never did find out what Nestor hoped. There came a sound of running footsteps in the hall and, a second later, Alcimus, his pudgy face shining with sweat, burst into the room. "It's Agamemnon's heralds."

The cup I was holding slipped from my fingers, splashing red wine down the skirt of my tunic.

"Is Agamemnon with them?" Achilles asked.

Alcimus shook his head. I saw Achilles glance sideways at Nestor and flare his eyes, but when he spoke it was to Patroclus. "See if Briseis is ready, will you?"

Nestor was looking embarrassed. "I didn't know they were coming."

Achilles touched his arm in acknowledgement.

Agamemnon's heralds, resplendent in scarlet and black, with gold bands wound round their staffs of office, edged into the room. They were meant to look imposing, to stand tall and deliver Agamemnon's message in loud, clear, ringing tones. Instead, the elder of the two walked forward and fell on his knees. Immediately, Achilles stood up and helped the old man gently to his feet. "Don't worry," he said. "I'm not going to take it out on you. It's not your fault."

The cupboard door opened wide. Patroclus came in and tried to put his arm round my shoulders, but I brushed him off. "Do you still think you can make him marry me?"

He didn't have time to reply. Achilles called, "Patroclus? Is she ready?"

Patroclus offered me his hand. I took it because I knew I had to, and let myself be led into the other room. The heralds were already backing out. I risked a glance at Achilles and to my amazement saw tears coursing down his cheeks. No sobs, nothing like that, just this silent stream that he wouldn't acknowledge even to the extent of wiping it away.

Achilles cried as I was taken away. *He* cried; *I* didn't. Now, years later, when none of it matters anymore, I'm still proud of that.

———

But I cried that night.

PART TWO

16

Ever since he came to Troy, he's known—intermittently, at least—that he won't be going home. Not for him the joyful greetings, the embraces, the feasts. Not for him the long, tedious aftermath, breeding dull children from a boring wife, spending long hours listening to peasant farmers complain about their neighbours, adjudicating in petty lawsuits, until with the passing of the years come physical weakness, old age, frailty and death. Death in a comfortable room with a fire blazing, children and grandchildren gathered round his bed. And then, for a few years more, his name on everybody's lips, people who'd known him all his life, men who'd fought with him at Troy. But human memory doesn't last long—three generations, at best—and then the slow, unnumbered centuries begin, grass growing tall on his burial mound, and people driving past in chariots he can't imagine will pause and say: "What do you suppose that is? It looks man-made."

None of that. And he really doesn't mind; in fact, it's actually easier to accept that soon there'll come a time, whether at dawn or dusk or in the white heat of noon, when a sword or spear will cut him down, and he'll die, as he's lived, in a shadowless glare of light. There'll be no end, then, to his story—because that's it, that's the bargain, that's what the tricky gods have promised him: everlasting glory in return for an early death under the walls of Troy.

———

He knows all the moods of this sea, or at least, until the past two weeks, he would have said he did, but the movement of the tides recently has been so strange—like nothing he's ever experienced before. Every day under the sullen sky, the waves swelled and swelled, never breaking into foam, just a long, continuous, menacing bloat. He'd felt the god's anger in the tightening of his skin, days before the first plague-arrows struck.

During the plague, there'd been no high tides, but now the sea's reclaiming lost ground. Each wave, slavering up the beach, leaves a fan of dirty foam that seethes gently for a second before sinking into the sand, and then the next wave flings itself higher, and the next higher still. The tide's reaching parts of the beach that have been dry for years, lifting thick mats of bladderwrack, carrying broken shells and the white bones of seagulls high above the shore.

The night they took Briseis away, one of the anchored ships broke loose from her moorings. Patroclus shook him awake and together they raced down to the beach, shouting orders, organizing teams of men to haul the ship clear of the tide. When dawn came, she lay listing to one side, the pale barnacles on her hull giving her the look of an ancient, warty sea-monster. No tide since then has reached as high as that, but still, it was a warning. Since then, they've checked the moorings of every anchored ship and carried some of the cradled ships further inland.

He's dwarfed by the immensity of sea and sky. The dunes rise up behind him, their tall, waving grasses casting spikes of black shadow on the pale sand. But now a mist's beginning to roll in, as it often does around this time. Within minutes, it's enveloped him and he doesn't have to see anything, only listen to the crash of waves breaking, only feel the ripples of water trickling between his toes. As a child, he'd slept with his mother in a bedroom facing the sea. After she left, he used to wake up in the darkness and pretend the waves were her voice soothing him back to sleep.

Memory plays strange tricks. One of his most vivid memories is of standing at the bedroom window and watching his mother wade into the sea, her long black hair fanning out across the water like strands of seaweed before the next wave swallowed her up. And yet he knows he can't possibly have seen that: the sea wasn't visible from the room he slept in as a child. No later imaginings, though, can distort his memory of the lonely bedroom, the ache of her absence. His father had tried everything: tempting him to eat; buying him expensive toys; every night, at bedtime, offering his own arms for comfort, only to have him turn away or, worse, tolerate the embrace but, like his mother before him, lie stiff and unresponsive within it. Priests, soothsayers, female relations, nurses—all were consulted and none of them knew what to do. The sons of the nobility were ferried in to be his "friends"—though they recognized instantly, as children do, that he wasn't "right," and, after a few desultory attempts, played only with each other. He stopped growing. And then, one day, when he'd become a pallid, silver-haired little shrimp, every rib in his chest showing, Patroclus came. Patroclus, who'd killed another child, a boy two years older than himself, in a quarrel over a game of dice.

The day Patroclus arrived, Achilles heard a commotion and, hoping it might be his mother back for one of her infrequent visits, burst into the hall, only to skid to a halt when he saw his father talking to a stranger. Close by stood a big, ungainly boy with a bruised face and a broken nose, though the injuries weren't recent because the bruises had a yellow centre and a purple rim. Another "friend"?

The two boys stared at each other, Patroclus peering round Achilles's father's side. What Achilles felt at that moment was not the familiar awkwardness of meeting yet another "friend," but something infinitely more disturbing: a long, cool shiver of recognition. But he'd been hurt too much and too often to make friends easily, so when the other boy, prompted by his father, held out his hand, Achilles just shrugged and turned away.

As soon as it became known that Patroclus had killed somebody, had actually done what they were all being trained to do, the other boys were queueing up to take him on. He became the one to beat. And so he was always fighting, like a chained bear that can't escape the baiting, but must go on and on, whimpering and licking its wounds at night, dragged out to face the dogs again by day. By the time Achilles finally plucked up the courage to approach Patroclus, he was well on the way to becoming the violent little thug everybody believed he was.

How did they come together? He can't remember—but then he remembers almost nothing about the two years after his mother left. He knows they fought, played, quarrelled, laughed, trapped rabbits, picked blackberries, came home with purple stains round their mouths, inspected the scabs on each other's knees, fell into bed and slept—as naked and sexless as two beans in a pod. Patroclus had saved his life, long before they got anywhere near a battlefield. But then, Achilles did the same for him, fighting beside him whenever one of the other boys attacked, until they stopped attacking and recognized a natural leader. By the time Achilles was seventeen, he and Patroclus were more than ready for war, ready to take on the whole world.

Comrades-in-arms: commendably virile.

The truth: Patroclus had taken his mother's place.

He'll be back at the hut now, waiting for him. For some reason, Patroclus has always hated these nocturnal visits of his to the sea. Perhaps he's afraid that one night Achilles might walk straight into it, as his mother did, when breathing the thick air had become intolerable.

Well, worried or not, Patroclus is going to have to wait. He's not ready to go back yet, not ready to face the empty bed. Which needn't be empty—god knows, he's got plenty of girls. But that's not the problem. The problem is, he doesn't *want* the other girls, he wants *that* girl—and he can't have her. And so he turns the pain of loss over and over in his mind, trying to grind it smooth, like the pebbles he's standing on, every one of them smooth. The fact is, he misses her.

He shouldn't, but he does. And why? Because, one night, she came into his bed with the smell of sea-rot in her hair? Because her skin tastes of salt? Well, if that's all it takes, he can have the whole bloody lot of them thrown into the sea—they'll all come back smelling of salt.

She's his prize, that's all, his prize of honour, no more, no less. It's nothing to do with the actual girl. And the pain he feels is merely the humiliation of having his prize stolen from him—yes, *stolen*—by a man who's his inferior in every way that matters. The cities besieged and sacked, the fighters killed, the whole unrelenting bloody grind of war ... And he takes her, just like that That's what hurts—not the girl—the insult, the blow to his pride. Well, that's it. He's out of it now. Let them try to take Troy without him—they'll soon come crawling for help when they find out they can't. He tries to squeeze pleasure out of the thought, but it doesn't work. Perhaps he should have followed his original instinct and gone home? Patroclus was in favour of it, and Patroclus, though it pains him to admit it, is almost always right.

There are no answers, or none to be found on this mist-shrouded beach. His mother won't come tonight. And so he wraps his cloak round him and sets off back to the hut where he knows Patroclus will be waiting.

As he walks between the cradled ships, his mind fills with small tasks, lists of things he has to do. If the next spring tide's as high as the last, they perhaps ought to think about moving some of the storage huts further inland. They were built eight, nine years ago after that first dreadful winter under canvas. The wood's pearly-grey now from long exposure to wind and rain and no doubt if you looked underneath you'd find plenty of rotten planks. A rebuilding programme, then? Give the men something to do and at the same time demonstrate his commitment to seeing it through—whatever "it" turns out to be. *Yes, keep them busy*, he thinks—practical, earth-bound, a fighter again, nothing wishy-washy, nothing liminal, about him— as he slips like a shadow along the sides of his spectral ships.

17

But I cried that night.

So what did he do that was so terrible? Nothing much, I suppose, nothing I hadn't been expecting. But then, when I thought it was over and I was at last free to go, he took my chin between his thumb and forefinger and tilted my face up to his. For one insane moment I actually thought he was going to kiss me—but then, inserting a finger between my teeth to prise my jaws apart, he worked up a big gob of phlegm—leisurely, taking his time about it—and spat it into my open mouth.

"There," he said. "Now you can go."

Floundering around an unknown compound in the dark, I stumbled eventually on the women's huts. I was all the time frantically trying to scrub my mouth out with the hem of my tunic and the effort made me retch so badly I threw up on the sand. I was still wiping my mouth when a door opened and Ritsa's face peered out. I fell into her arms. For a long time I couldn't speak. She rocked me, murmuring reassurances—the sort of things you say to children who've had a bad dream—and some of the other women gathered round and stroked my back. I couldn't tell them what had happened, but perhaps I didn't need to, perhaps they already knew, or guessed.

Most of them would have slept with Agamemnon at one time or another, before his obsession with Chryseis had relieved them of the duty. Ritsa was very kind, but even with all her soothing it was a long time before I was calm enough to sleep.

I woke in the early hours and lay staring into the half-darkness, petrified. I knew that as soon as Agamemnon got tired of me—and that wouldn't take long, he'd already told me I was a poor substitute for Chryseis—he'd hand me over to his men for common use. Though next morning, when I mentioned my fears to Ritsa, she said, "No, he won't do that, he can't, you're Achilles's prize." I just shook my head. I thought that was precisely why he would do it: the ultimate insult to a man who'd dared to challenge his authority. No, I reckoned a few more nights of inventive humiliation and I'd be crawling under the huts to find a place to sleep.

None of that happened; after the first night, he never wanted me again—or not for a long time. But still every evening I was required to pour wine for his guests. Why, you may ask, would he want me to do that, when he so obviously couldn't bear the sight of me? I was useful, I suppose; I served a particular purpose. Men carve meaning into women's faces; messages addressed to other men. In Achilles's compound, the message had been: *Look at her. My prize awarded by the army, proof that I am what I've always claimed to be: the greatest of the Greeks.* Here, in Agamemnon's compound, it was: *Look at her, Achilles's prize. I took her away from him just as I can take your prize away from you. I can take everything you have.*

So I smiled and poured, poured and smiled, until my cheeks ached. And then, after they'd all gone, I would creep back to the women's hut, pull a blanket over my head and try to sleep. The hut was crowded with sleeping bodies, fuggy with the smell of sweat. I'd found a place near the wall, where a gap between two planks let in a breeze from off the sea. Some nights, I lay with my mouth pressed against that narrow crack sucking in cold salt air.

We slept on pallet beds lined up between the looms. The beds were stored under the huts by day and dragged out in the early evening when it became too dark to go on working. Above us were the squares of cloth we'd been weaving, rich reds and greens and blues, though even the brightest colours looked dark in the rush lights that were dotted here and there across the floor. Women's faces, clustering round the lights, shone like the pale wings of moths. Even in bright sunlight, the women looked pallid, and many of them had hacking coughs caused by breathing in minute particles of wool. Some days the air was so full of tiny floating threads of cloth it looked like soup. In my husband's palace, the weaving rooms had opened directly on to the inner courtyard, so there was always fresh air and the sight of people passing. These huts were completely enclosed; we worked long hours and it was rare for us to go outside. As we worked, we sang songs we'd known from childhood, the songs our mothers had taught us. But by late afternoon we were exhausted and the singing died away. Then a quick meal, bread and cheese, a cup of wine so diluted it was barely pink, and, if we were lucky, a brief glimpse of the outside world, before darkness fell.

And so it went on. Usually, I got back to my hut late, sometimes very late. I'd tell Ritsa any little scrap of information I'd managed to glean from the conversation at dinner, then strip off my finery and lie down on the hard bed. One by one, the lamps would be extinguished, though even in the semi-darkness you could sense the presence of the looms. Gradually, as our eyes became accustomed to the gloom, we could make out the elaborate patterns we'd been spinning all day. So we spent the nights curled up like spiders at the centre of our webs. Only we weren't the spiders; we were the flies.

———

Sometimes, before dinner, I would seize a moment to walk down to the beach and catch a glimpse of the sea, though I was no sooner there than I had to run back and get dressed to serve wine. On one of these brief excursions, I saw Achilles running in full armour along the shore, his bare feet flashing in and out of the shallow waves. He hadn't seen me. After a while, he stopped and bent over, his hands resting against his knees as he struggled to catch his breath. Then he looked up and saw me. He didn't speak, didn't wave, didn't acknowledge me in any way, just turned and started running back the way he'd come, a small figure dwarfed by the vast expanse of sea and sky.

———

The first few evenings after his quarrel with Achilles, Agamemnon was jubilant. The plague was clearly over; there'd been no new cases since the return of Chryseis to her father, though the ritual of prayers and sacrifices to Apollo at sunrise and sunset was still meticulously observed. Even more gratifying, Agamemnon's army had advanced several hundred yards across the muddy plain, so that treacherous little shit had already been proved wrong—of course they could take Troy without him, could and would. All the way through dinner on those nights Agamemnon kept jumping to his feet proposing toasts until by the end of the meal he could barely stand.

Later, in his living quarters, surrounded by the few men he almost trusted, the talk became more scurrilous. What on earth was Achilles finding to do with himself? Sulking in his hut, of course, eating his heart out because he couldn't fight—*and whose fault was that?* Getting drunk, stuffing his face till he had to throw up to make room for more and then falling into bed with Patroclus and lying there till noon. A few more weeks of that, and they'd both be as flabby as eunuchs. His guests laughed, sycophantically, though they must have known that none of it was true. Every one of them, at some time or another, must have seen Achilles running in full armour round the bay, or heard Patroclus marshalling the Myrmidons for yet another gruelling session at the training grounds; and yet nobody contradicted him. The only real friend Achilles had left was Ajax, and Ajax stayed away.

But then, gradually, evening by evening, the mood began to darken. The ground they'd won in days of hard and bitter fighting was soon lost again and the casualty figures were beginning to creep up. Oh, there were still toasts and songs, but there weren't quite so many jokes about Achilles. One evening, Agamemnon pointed out that Achilles's armour had been a gift from the gods to his father, Peleus, on the occasion of his marriage to Thetis. "Divine armour," Agamemnon said. "Which does rather raise the question: is it the armour or is it the man?"

"Well," said Odysseus, smoothly, "I suppose you could always challenge him to a bare-knuckle fight. You'd soon find out . . ."

There was a slightly shocked silence after he'd finished speaking. The mere fact that he'd dared, however subtly, to challenge Agamemnon revealed how drastically the atmosphere had changed.

I was beginning to dread the nightly drinking parties; I sensed that my presence—walking round the table, pouring wine into their cups—had begun to evoke a different response. I was no longer the outward and visible sign of Agamemnon's power and Achilles's humiliation. No, I'd become something altogether more sinister: I was the girl who'd caused the quarrel. Oh, yes, I'd caused it—in much the same way, I suppose, as a bone is responsible for a dog-fight. And because of that quarrel, *because of me*, many souls of young, brave Greek fighters had gone down to Hades—martyred youth and manhood overthrown. Or was it the gods who'd done that? I don't know, I get confused. I only know when they weren't blaming the gods, they were blaming me.

I was aware of glances following me around the room, and they were not, as they'd once been, discreetly admiring. I remembered an incident I'd once witnessed when I was a girl in Troy. A man had stepped forward and greeted Helen with every sign of respect, chatting, smiling and then bowing as he took his leave. Only I happened to turn round as we walked past and I saw him spit on her shadow.

I could feel the same hostility, the same contempt, beginning to gather around me. I was Helen now.

18

When I was a young girl—too old for dolls, not yet ripe for marriage—I was sent to stay with my married sister in Troy. My mother was dead, I hated the young concubine who'd taken her place and my father had become exasperated by the sound of quarrelling issuing from the women's quarters. It seemed better for everybody if I went away.

My sister, Ianthe, and I had never been close. By the time I was born, she was already preparing for her marriage to Leander, one of King Priam's sons. The marriage was not happy. Leander had soon tired of her and taken a concubine by whom he now had three sons, so my sister was not much called upon to perform her marital duties. She'd become a plain, dumpy little woman, her disgruntled expression making her seem much older than her years. How such a woman could have become Helen's friend was a mystery—and yet they were, genuinely, friends. They used to gossip for hours over a dish or two of wine. Both of them, I think, very lonely women.

Ianthe used to take me with her on these visits and I sat and listened, though I never took much part in the conversation. But then, one day, my sister was called away to attend to some domestic crisis and I was left alone with Helen. For a time she talked—rather shyly, as normally confident people sometimes are shy with children—and then she suggested a walk. I was twelve, the prison walls had already started to close in. Girls approaching marriageable age didn't go out except—closely veiled and chaperoned—to visit female relatives. And yet Helen seemed to think a walk to the battlements was nothing out of the ordinary. She was lighthearted, suddenly, pinning on her white veil and taking me by the hand as if we were setting out on a great adventure. We walked straight through the marketplace, accompanied only by a single maid. I must've looked surprised, I suppose, because she said, "Well, why not?" There was no point in her worrying what people might think. The Trojan women—"the ladies," as she always called them—couldn't think any worse of her than they did already, and as for the men . . . We-ell, she had a pretty good idea what they were thinking—the same thing they'd been thinking since she was ten years old. Oh, yes, I got that story too. Poor Helen, raped on a riverbank when she was only ten. Of course I believed her. It was quite a shock to me, later, to discover nobody else did.

––––––––

From the ramparts you could look down on the battlefield, the once-fertile plain so churned up with horses' hooves and chariot wheels it had become a wasteland in which nothing grew. Two or three carrion crows circled low above our heads. I remember thinking their wing feathers looked exactly like outstretched fingers. Helen walked right up to the parapet. I had no choice but to follow, though I was careful not to look down. Instead, I gazed up at the sky, and then, cautiously, further down to where sunlight glittered on a calm sea.

Immediately below us, all was violence and confusion. I heard a horse scream, I heard the cries of wounded men, but I was determined not to look. I noticed how Helen's breathing quickened as she leant over the parapet; she seemed desperate—no, not desperate, *avid*—to see as much as she could. I didn't know then—and can't imagine now—what she was thinking. To hear her talk, she felt nothing but guilt and misery at being the cause of all this carnage, but was that really all she felt? Did she never look down and think: this is about *me*?

We'd been there half an hour, perhaps, when Priam arrived. Somebody placed a chair for him and he summoned Helen to sit beside him. He always treated her with the greatest courtesy, though he must have known that the people of Troy—and particularly the women of his own household—hated her.

"Who's this?" he said, looking down at me.

I blushed miserably as Helen explained. But then, in the midst of all his worries, the war going badly, Hector publicly accusing his brother, Paris, of cowardice, the death toll mounting, his coffers emptying, Priam took out a silver coin and put it on the palm of his hand. He passed the other hand quickly across it, muttered some magic words, and the coin vanished. I stared, knowing it was a trick, but not being able to see how he'd done it. He pretended to search inside his robes, patting himself all over. "Where's it gone? Oh, don't tell me I've lost it. Have *you* got it?" I shook my head. Then he reached forward, felt behind my left ear and produced the coin. I was rather inclined to stand on my twelve-year-old dignity, I was too old for magic tricks, and yet at the same time I was fascinated because I still couldn't see how it was done. He presented me with the coin and then turned to watch the battle, the lines of his face immediately settling into an expression of deep sadness.

Afterwards, we walked back to Helen's house. She unpinned her veil and ordered wine and cake, a sweet lemony cake they make only in Troy. In public, Helen was forever beating her breast, blaming herself for the part she'd played in starting this ruinous war. Perhaps she thought if *she* used the word "whore" frequently enough, others would be less likely to use it. If so, she was wrong. In private, it was quite a different story. She ridiculed the Trojan women—"the ladies"—and, god knows, they gave her plenty of material. The stupid way they copied her hairstyles, her makeup, her clothes ... It was astonishing the way really quite intelligent women seemed to believe that if they carried their eyeliner beyond the outer corner of the lid and gave it a little upward flick, they'd have Helen's eyes. Or if they fastened their cinctures the same way she did hers, they'd have Helen's breasts. All this mindless imitation of a woman they affected to despise . . . No wonder she laughed at them.

So we sat there gossiping and drinking wine—rather too much wine—and I felt very grown-up, very flattered. When my sister came to collect me, she was absolutely horrified, but then that only added to the fun.

After that, I often used to visit Helen on my own, though chaperoned of course by one of my sister's maids. Almost always, Helen took me with her to the battlements and, while she hung over the parapet drinking in every detail of the fighting, Priam would discover sweets and coins behind my ears. Sometimes Hecuba, the queen, would be there too, always with her youngest child, Polyxena, clinging to her skirt and bristling with a little girl's pride in her mother. Helen tried to make friends with her, but Polyxena wasn't having it; she'd absorbed her mother's hatred of Helen. I used to see her sometimes in the palace grounds, charging along behind her older sisters, shouting: "Wait for me! Wait for me!" The cry of youngest children everywhere.

Hecuba and Helen would exchange a few stilted words, but I noticed we never stayed long if she was there. Helen preferred to get Priam on his own. One final searching glance over the parapet and then it was back to her house for wine and lemon cakes. Every visit ended the same way—she'd suddenly stop smiling and say, "Ah, well, back to work." And that was my signal to put on my mantle and wait for the maid to chaperone me home.

Sometimes, Helen would go into the inner room even before I left and then I'd hear the chattering of the loom, the rattle as the shuttle flew to and fro. There was a legend—it tells you everything, really—that whenever Helen cut a thread in her weaving, a man died on the battlefield. She was responsible for every death.

And then, one day, she showed me her work. I've known some great weavers in my life, including some of the women in the camp.

The seven girls Achilles captured when he took Lesbos—they were brilliant, no other word for it, they were *brilliant*. But even they weren't as good as Helen. I wandered round the room looking at the tapestries while Helen sat at the loom and sipped her wine. Half a dozen huge battle scenes covered the walls, a sequence that taken together told the whole story of the war so far. Hand-to-hand combat, men decapitated, gutted, skewered, filleted, disembowelled; and, riding high above the carnage in their glittering chariots, the kings: Menelaus, Agamemnon, Odysseus, Diomedes, Idomeneo, Ajax, Nestor. I knew Menelaus had been her husband, before she ran away with Paris, but her voice didn't change when she said his name. Did she point to Achilles that day? I think she must've done, but I really don't remember.

The Trojans were there too, of course, Priam looking down from the battlements, and below him, on the battlefield, his eldest son, Hector, defending the gates. No Paris, though. Paris seemed to be fighting the war from his bed. On the rare occasions I saw them together, it was obvious even to a child that Helen preferred Hector to Paris, whom I think she'd grown to despise. His reluctance to go anywhere near the battlefield was notorious, as was Hector's contempt for his brother's cowardice.

When I'd finished walking round the tapestries, I went round again because I wanted to check something I didn't understand.

"She's not there," I said to my sister that night after dinner. "She's not in the tapestries. Priam's there—but she isn't."

"No, well, of course she isn't. She won't know where to put herself till she knows who's won."

There was so much bitterness in that remark, and it wasn't the routine malice of the other Trojan women, but something altogether deeper. Looking back, I wonder whether my dumpy, plain sister wasn't slightly in love with Helen. I was probably a little in love with her myself.

That night, I lay in bed wishing I'd said more to Helen, that I'd at least tried to express my admiration of her work. Why hadn't I?

Struck dumb, I suppose. Oh, but it was more than that . . . I think I was groping after something I wasn't old enough to understand. What I came away with was a sense of Helen seizing control of her own story. She was so isolated in that city, so powerless—even at my age, I could see that—and those tapestries were a way of saying: I'm here. *Me*. A person, not just an object to be looked at and fought over.

There was a story that dates back to the first year of the war. Menelaus and Paris, the two rivals, had agreed to meet in single combat, the outcome to decide which of them would get Helen. Both armies gathered to watch, the battlements were crammed with spectators eager to see the fight, but Helen wasn't there. Nobody had bothered to tell her what was happening. So her fate was decided without her knowledge. I think the tapestries were a way of fighting back from that moment. Oh, I know she wasn't in them, I know she deliberately made herself invisible, but in another way, perhaps the only way that matters, she was present in every stitch.

I don't know how much good it did me, dwelling on those memories of Troy. Really, what use is it to a slave, trying to get to sleep on a hard bed in a smelly hut, to remember that once the King of Troy did conjuring tricks to amuse her? Wouldn't it be better, easier, to accept the joyless grind your life has become?

But then I think: *No. Of course it isn't better.* That night, remembering the hostility I'd felt being directed at me in Agamemnon's hut and tasting, as I always did, the slime-gob of his phlegm in my mouth, I wrapped King Priam's kindness round me like a blanket and it helped me drift off to sleep.

19

One evening, after dinner, Achilles and Patroclus went to see the great fortifications Agamemnon had started building between the camp and the battlefield. From the stern of his ship, Achilles had greeted the success of the Trojan counter-attack with whoops of joy, apparently untroubled by the growing number of Greek casualties. Now, he was curious to see Agamemnon's attempts to shore up his defences.

By the time they reached the building site, it was beginning to get dark, but they could still just about see what was going on. A great trench had been dug in the scrubland that divided the sand dunes from the battlefield. Hundreds of men, so thickly caked in mud they seemed to be made of it, were pushing wheelbarrows full of soil away from the site, while others dug deeper into the water-logged clay. It had never been more brutally apparent that this land was a floodplain bisected by two great rivers that regularly burst their banks during the autumn storms. The trench was filling with water as fast as the men could dig. A short distance away another group of men was piling up sandbags to try to keep the water out. Duckboards had been laid along the bottom of the trench, but even so, in places, the labourers were well above their knees in water. A vast parapet towered over their heads, sentry posts set at intervals along its length from which pale faces gazed down on the chaos below.

"Well," Achilles said, "he obviously thinks they're on the verge of breaking through."

Patroclus turned to look back at the beach with its long row of ships pulled up onto the sand. Black, beaked, predatory ships, designed to produce terror wherever they sailed—but now, in this changed situation, just so many heaps of dry wood. A few blazing arrows shot onto the decks, enough of a wind to carry sparks and the entire fleet would be on fire—*in minutes.*

It was intolerable to him to stand there doing nothing. "You know we could help with this. You only said you wouldn't fight, you didn't say you wouldn't do *anything.*"

"I mightn't have said it, but I certainly meant it. Whose fault is it he's in this mess? *His.*"

"But everybody else is in it as well." Patroclus jabbed his finger at the struggling men. "It's not *their* fault."

"No, and it's not *mine* either."

A tense silence. Looking down, Patroclus remembered a colony of ants he'd watched when he was a child, the kind that carry snipped-off triangles of green leaves and look like tiny ships in sail. He tried to place the memory but he couldn't. Slowly, in this wordless pause, he and Achilles were working their way together again. When he sensed it was safe to speak, he said, "Do you think it'll keep them out?"

Achilles shook his head. "No, if anything it'll slow down his retreat." He pointed to the area of scrubland on the other side of the trench. "*That* is a killing field."

Patroclus took a deep breath. "So this is it, then?"

"Depends what you mean by 'it.' I don't expect to hear from him just yet."

This isn't about you.

They knew each other so well that the unspoken words hung in the air between them. Then Patroclus said, "You know, if they break through you're going to have to fight anyway. They won't spare your ships just because you're not fighting."

Achilles shrugged. "If I'm attacked, I'll fight." He turned to go. "C'mon, I've seen enough."

20

We knew the war was going badly for the Greeks. The battle was no longer a distant rumble you could just about manage to ignore, but a deafening roar clearly audible above the clacking of the looms. We knew from the noise that the Trojans were getting close, though even if we'd been deaf the grim faces of our captors would have told the same story. They were, to a man, vile-tempered, inclined to kick anything or anybody that got in their way. We were careful to pretend indifference to the outcome, not that they gave a damn what we thought, anyway. Some of the girls, mainly those who'd been slaves in their previous lives, were genuinely indifferent. No likely end would bring them loss or leave them happier than before. But those of us who'd once been free, who'd had security and status, were torn between hope and fear. Some managed to convince themselves that if—*if*—the Trojans broke through they'd greet us as their long-lost sisters. But would they? Or would they see us as the enemy's slave girls, theirs to do what they liked with? I knew which outcome I thought more probable. And even that was assuming we survived the battle. They were likely to attack at night and shoot blazing arrows into the camp to create the maximum amount of chaos and confusion. Within minutes, the huts would be on fire, and at night the women were locked in.

So we waited in a tide race of hope and fear as day by day the

Trojans advanced. Every morning, the camp emptied of men—everybody who could stand up and walk had to fight—so at least we were free of the constant supervision that had been one of the most irksome features of life in Agamemnon's compound. We still worked all day, but we took regular breaks, sitting in the sunshine to eat our bread and olives, listening to the battle, trying to decide if it was closer now or a little further away.

One morning, we were sitting on the steps when I saw Ritsa approaching. I hadn't seen her for several days because she was working so hard she had to sleep in the hospital. She looked haggard, I thought, and I felt a stab of fear. I couldn't afford to lose Ritsa.

"I'm all right," she said. "Last couple of days have been hard . . . Fact, that's why I'm here; I asked Machaon if I could have you to help—and he said yes."

I was overjoyed, but immediately thought: *No, it won't happen.* "He'll never let me go."

"He will, Machaon's already asked."

The main hospital was close to the arena, a twenty-minute walk from Agamemnon's compound. I didn't dare look back or relax till I was outside the gate, but then I slowed down, gazing around me as if I were seeing everything for the first time: the heat shimmer over a cooking fire, the iridescent sheen on the neck of a cockerel pecking for grain, the sharp tang of urine from the laundry hut as we walked past. It was all new and miraculous and for no reason other than that I'd left the weaving huts behind.

As we turned the corner into Nestor's compound, I was surprised to see that several large tents had been erected in front of the hospital huts. Their canvas was stained and foul-smelling from long storage in the holds of the ships. These must be some of the tents the Greeks had lived in during the first winter of the war when they were still arrogant enough to believe it would be over in months or weeks. Now, nine years later, the tents were being pressed into service again to shelter the wounded. Ducking my head, I followed Ritsa through a flap into the nearest tent. Despite the din of battle and the gloomy conversations I'd overheard every night at dinner, I don't think I'd realized till then how badly the war was going. The place reeked of blood.

I followed Ritsa down the narrow space between two rows of beds to where Machaon was sitting on a bale of straw, stitching a wound. He glanced up. "You took your time," he said, curtly, to Ritsa. And then, to me, "Welcome on board."

I liked Machaon, whom I'd got to know, slightly, when he came to Achilles's compound to advise us on the treatment of plague. I've forgotten a lot of the men I met in that camp, but I remember Machaon clearly. He was a portly man in late middle age—though I've a feeling he may have been younger than he looked. White hair receding from a high forehead, grape-green eyes meshed in a net of wrinkles, a sardonic sense of humour—and a profound scepticism about the power of medicine to alter the course of nature; a scepticism which, in my experience, all the best physicians share. Standing there, watching the movement of his fingers as he pulled the thread, I felt safe for the first time since I'd arrived in the camp. I don't know why. He finished tying the knot, congratulated the sweating man on his courage and set off down the aisle to attend to his next patient. Ritsa gave the man a drink of water—he wasn't allowed wine—and settled him to sleep. He turned cautiously over on to his uninjured side, closed his eyes and was asleep in minutes. I wondered how anybody could sleep there. There was a constant buzzing of blue-bottles in the green gloom and shouts and screams from some of the patients: men who were trying to claw their bandages off—as, in delirium, many did—and had to be forcibly restrained.

Ritsa took me to the back of the tent and sat me down at a long table. It felt good to be sitting beside her on the bench with a pestle and mortar in front of me and several jars of dried herbs close at hand. Above our heads, swaying slightly in the draught, hung a laundry rack with bunches of dried herbs suspended from it. Fresh herbs, those that could be gathered locally, lay in swathes across the table, giving off their sharp, sweet, penetrating scents and attracting bees that flew in through the open tent flap. Many of the herbs—those I could identify—were for pain relief, but others were used to clean wounds. More men died of infection, Ritsa said, than from loss of blood. "Watch Machaon when he's examining a patient, you'll see he doesn't just look at the wound, he listens to it."

Later that day, I watched Machaon bending over a man who'd been brought in that morning. At first, he just looked long and carefully at the wound but then his fingertips began to probe, pressing down gently, again, and again, and, yes, Ritsa was right, I could tell from his face he was listening. And then—faint, but unmistakable— I heard it too: a crackling underneath the skin. Machaon smiled and said something reassuring, but less than an hour later the patient was transferred to a hut on the promontory where the dead were burned. It was known as "the stink hut" because the stench grabbed you by the throat whenever the door opened or closed. Nobody who went into the stink hut ever returned.

"It's the soil," Ritsa said. "It gets into the wound—and as soon as you hear that crackle . . ." She shook her head.

I have to confess that something about that pleased me, that it was the rich earth of Troy that was killing the invaders. But I was torn too, as I had been during the plague, because so many of these men were very young, some of them hardly more than boys—and for every one who was going ho and desperate to fight there was another who didn't want to be there at all. But though I sympathized, almost involuntarily, with men having their wounds stitched up or clawing at their bandages in the intolerable heat, I still hated and despised them all. I said as much to Ritsa, who just shrugged— "Yes, yes"—and continued spreading paste onto a poultice.

I sensed her impatience with me, but at the same time I thought it was important to keep some things clear. It would have been easier, in many ways, to slip into thinking we were all in this together, equally imprisoned on this narrow strip of land between the sand dunes and the sea; easier, but false. They were men, and free. I was a woman, and a slave. And that's a chasm no amount of sentimental chit-chat about shared imprisonment should be allowed to obscure.

Every evening, before dinner, the kings and captains came to visit the wounded, walking from bed to bed, jollying the men along: *Don't worry, we'll soon have you out of here.* The men always laughed and cheered and went along with it, though as soon as the top brass departed the grumbling started up again. As far as I know, none of the kings ever visited the stink hut, and even in the main hospital tents they concentrated on the slightly wounded.

In spite of all this, I remember the days I spent in that hospital working alongside Ritsa as a happy time. *Happy?* Yes, it surprised me too. But the fact is, I loved the work, I loved everything about it. There's a saying: *If any man love the instruments of any craft, the gods have called him.* Well, I loved that pestle and mortar, I loved the smooth hollow of the cup, I loved the way the pestle fitted into the palm of my hand as if it had always been there. I loved the jars and dishes on the table in front of me, I loved the smell of fresh herbs, I loved the laundry rack above my head with its scraggy little bunches of dried herbs swaying in the breeze. Hours would pass, and I couldn't have told you where the time had gone. I lost myself in that work—and I found myself too. I was learning so much, from Ritsa, but also from Machaon who, once he saw I was interested and already had a little knowledge and skill, was generous with his time. I really started to think: *I can do this.* And that belief took me a step further away from being just Achilles's bed-girl—or Agamemnon's spittoon.

––––––

A day came when the battle got so loud everybody in the hospital tent looked up, startled, thinking that at any moment the Trojans were going to burst in. There was an influx of wounded, followed almost immediately—only half an hour later—by another. I took pain-killing draughts from bed to bed and, as the pressure of work grew, helped wash and bandage wounds. Machaon made us bathe

the wounds in salt water—not seawater, fresh water from the wells with salt added—and the process was extraordinarily painful, though the men always laughed and joked while we were doing it. It was a point of honour with them not to cry out. These were the lightly wounded, of course. Those brought in semi-conscious or on the point of death didn't care what we did.

After their wounds had been dressed, those who could walk went to sit outside in the cool air. I passed round jugs of diluted wine and went from group to group handing out plates of cold meat and bread. All the talk was of defeat. They were angry with Achilles for refusing to fight, but they blamed Agamemnon for letting it happen. "He should give him the bloody girl back," one man said, as I helped him pour his wine. "That's what started it all." "It's all right for them," another man said. "How many generals do you see in here?" A rumble of agreement. "*No*, they're all too bloody busy leading from the rear."

But that was about to change. First, Odysseus came in wounded, followed, almost immediately, by Ajax, and then, a couple of hours later, by Agamemnon himself. He might have avoided taking part in the raids, but he couldn't avoid the fighting now. Too much was at stake. His own survival was at stake. Machaon himself cleaned and dressed his wound, though it was hardly more than a scratch. Strange, though, to see Agamemnon sitting there, looking pale and pinched under his tan, though, from a distance, he still cut an impressive figure. I realized, suddenly, what he reminded me of: the statue of Zeus in the arena (though I subsequently found out the statue had been modelled on him, which made the resemblance rather less surprising).

A lot of false cheeriness while he was there, but the minute he swept out, down the path that had been cleared for him between two rows of beds, the muttering started up again. You heard the same grumbling from men coming to visit their friends, but mainly from the wounded who had to lie there, hour after hour, tossing and turning in the heat, trying not to scratch at the itching skin underneath their bandages. Gradually, as I listened, the muttering began to resolve itself into a single name. From all ranks, foot soldiers, officers, right up to some of Agamemnon's closest aides, you heard the same thing: *Bribe him, plead with him, kiss his sodding arse if you've got to, but for god's sake, make the bugger* fight!

I hung around, listening, as long as I dared, but then I had to go back to the bench to make more poultices ready for the next influx of wounded. But even from that end of the tent, you heard the same name, whispered at first, but then, increasingly, spoken aloud. Over and over, as the day wore on and still more wounded men crammed into the already overcrowded tent, you heard it: Achilles, Achilles, and again: *Achilles!*

21

"No, no, and again, *no!*"

As he spun round to confront Nestor, Agamemnon's sleeve caught a jug of wine, which toppled over, sending a dark red flood across the table. I crept up and began dabbing ineffectually only to be waved impatiently away. Wine dripped steadily over the edge of the table and formed a red puddle on the floor while the silence that had followed Agamemnon's outburst lengthened and congealed.

Then, speaking with great precision, Agamemnon said, "I am not going to crawl on my hands and knees to that shitting bastard."

"So send somebody else," Nestor said. "Let *them* crawl. He won't expect you to go yourself."

"Oh, I think you underestimate his arrogance."

Feet thumped on the boards of the veranda and, a second later, Odysseus half fell into the room, gasping for breath and with a strip of bloody rag tied round one arm.

"This had better not be bad news . . ." Agamemnon said.

"For god's sake, man . . ." Nestor turned and beckoned me. "Give him some wine."

I poured a cup and took it to Odysseus, who tossed it back. It was strong wine, the strongest Agamemnon had, and might well increase the bleeding, but it wasn't my place to say so. I could see the rag was already sodden.

Nestor bent over him. "No hurry, take your time."

"We don't have *time.*" Agamemnon ground the word out.

Odysseus wiped his mouth on the back of his hand. "It *is* bad news, I'm afraid. They're camped just the other side of the trench, you can hear them talking. No, I mean actual conversations—that's how close they are. Nine years, *nine bloody years,* and it ends like this."

Nestor straightened up. "It hasn't ended yet."

"Good as."

"Well, *I'll* fight tomorrow."

"Nestor, with respect, you're too old. Sorry, but you are."

Nestor looked affronted. "We need every man we can get."

"*No-o,* we need *one* man."

"Save your breath," Agamemnon said. "Nestor's said it all already." He sat down heavily. "So—let's get down to brass tacks. How much do you think it'll take?"

Odysseus's mouth twisted, whether with pain or distaste it was hard to tell. "He won't come cheap."

"If he comes at all," Nestor said.

Agamemnon waved that aside. "Look, here's what I'm prepared to do." Checking off the items on his fingers, he began: "Seven tripods, never fired, ten bars of gold, twenty cauldrons, a dozen stallions—every one of them a winner—oh, and the seven women I got when we took Lesbos." He pointed his finger at Odysseus. "*My privilege*—"

Nestor had taken a seat by the fire and was twisting the thumb ring on his left hand round and round. It was a ruby, I remember, big enough to cast a red light over his hand. He lifted his head. "And the girl?"

"Well, yes, obviously . . . *The girl.*"

They all turned to look at me and I shrank back into the shadows.

"*If* he still wants her," Odysseus said. He looked from one to the other. "Well, isn't she a bit shop-soiled? I'd have thought she was."

Agamemnon said, stiffly, "No more soiled than she was when she arrived. *I've* never laid a finger on her."

Nestor and Odysseus glanced across at me. I felt the blood rush to my face, but went on staring stubbornly at the floor.

"And would you swear that under oath?" Nestor asked. His face was expressionless.

"Of course."

In the silence that followed a log collapsed into the fire, sending a shower of sparks into the air.

"*Good*," Nestor said.

"And wait, no, wait—that's not all. If—no, no, not *if*, when—*when* we take Troy, he can choose whichever one of my daughters he wants, I'll make him my son-in-law—equal in every respect to my own son. Now that's generous, you can't say that's not generous. But of course there's a price. In return, he has to acknowledge my authority as commander-in-chief. In the end, he has to obey *me*."

"It is generous," Odysseus said, carefully. "Will you go yourself?"

"Course I bloody won't, I'm not going to plead with the little prick. I'll send . . . Oh, I don't know . . . *You*, I suppose."

"He needs that wound seen to," Nestor said.

"Nah, it's just a scratch. Course I'll go."

"Who else?" Agamemnon said. "You, Nestor?"

"No, I don't think so. If I'm there he'll feel he's got to be polite—and I don't think we want that. I think he'll need to rant and rave a bit, before he gives in. *If* he gives in. What about Ajax?"

"*Ajax?*" Odysseus said. "He can barely string three words together."

"No, but Achilles respects him. As a fighter, I mean. And they are cousins."

"That's true."

Suddenly nervous, Agamemnon looked from face to face. "Is that settled, then?"

"He's got to get that wound seen to," Nestor insisted. "It's still bleeding."

"*Good*," Agamemnon said. "If he gets a bit of blood on his carpet it might make him realize how bad things are."

"He knows how bad they are," Nestor said.

I could understand why Nestor didn't want to be part of the embassy. He was too wily an old bird to risk association with failure—and it *would* fail. I didn't dare let myself hope for any other outcome. The prospect of returning to Achilles's compound was . . . I don't know. Miraculous. I don't think I'd ever known till then how much I missed the kindness of Patroclus.

"Oh, and the girl," Agamemnon said. "Take her with you." He cupped both hands against his chest and hoisted them up. "Show him what he's been missing."

Odysseus forced a smile. "All right. You never know, it might just make a difference."

"And tell him I never . . . you know."

"Fucked her?"

"But that's as far as it goes, mind. No apology." He pointed his finger. *"No apology."*

Nestor turned to me. "Go and get your cloak."

Dismissed, I ran across to the women's huts, where I found Ritsa sitting on the floor with a blanket wrapped round her shoulders. I stopped on the threshold, so agitated I couldn't remember what I'd come for, just staring stupidly around the hut. Rush lamps guttered in the draught from the open door, sending grey shadows wriggling across the floor.

Ritsa gazed up at me, pupils big and black as she strained to see my face. "What's wrong?"

"He's sending me back." Even as I spoke, I was smoothing my hair, biting my lips, pinching my cheeks. I thrust my feet into a sturdier pair of sandals, more suited to a walk along the beach, then crawled on my hands and knees to a chest in the corner. I opened the lid and, trusting to touch alone, dragged out my best mantle.

Ritsa whispered, "What's going on?"

Keeping my voice low, I said, "They're trying to bribe Achilles, get him to start fighting again. The girls from Lesbos—" I nodded at the far corner. "They're part of it too, but don't tell them, it mightn't come off."

I wrapped the mantle round me, swaddling myself as tightly as mothers do their babies to stop them crying. I heard men's voices, coming closer. Ritsa shoved me towards the door. "Go on, *go*."

Ten or fifteen feet away, Ajax and Odysseus were standing side by side, Odysseus ferret-thin and dark; great, blond, raw-boned Ajax towering over him. Agamemnon's heralds were there too, their ceremonial robes the colour of ox blood in the dim light. I heard Odysseus talking as I approached, laughing at the idea that Agamemnon hadn't laid a finger on me. "It's not his finger I'm worried about," he sniggered. Then he caught sight of me and snapped, "Where's your veil?"

Ritsa ran into the hut and returned, a minute later, carrying a long glistening white veil, which she threw over my head and shoulders. I shivered, remembering Helen. Surrounded, as I was, by men with blazing torches, I must have looked like a young girl leaving her father's house for the last time. Instead, I felt like a corpse on its way to burial. I was still refusing to hope. I gazed round me, though I could see virtually nothing because of the veil, except, when I looked straight down, my feet.

Odysseus took something from inside his robe: "Here, put this on."

Pulling the veil away from my face, I saw he was holding a necklace of opals, five big stones, milky-looking at first, but with a fire in their depths that stirred whenever his hand moved. My heart thumped against my ribs, because this was my mother's necklace, her bride-gift from my father on their wedding day. Agamemnon must have claimed it as his share of the plunder when Lyrnessus fell. I took it with trembling hands and put it round my neck; Ritsa hurried forward to help me with the catch. I felt sick with shock—this was worse, if anything, than seeing Myron in my father's tunic—but then, as the necklace warmed against my skin, I started to feel better. The five stones felt like my mother's fingers touching me.

We set off, the heralds with their gold staffs leading the way. I trailed along behind, adjusting the folds of my veil so that I could see where I was walking. Glancing over my shoulder, I saw Ritsa standing on the steps to wave me goodbye, but she was dwindling fast into the dark. I turned and walked on.

In Agamemnon's compound, the sand was black, impacted hard with the weight of trampling feet, but on the shoreline it was cleaner, softer and damp. I watched Odysseus and Ajax striding ahead of me, water oozing out of their footprints. Nobody turned to look at me, so after a few minutes I felt free to raise my veil and gaze out over the sea. Briefly, the moon appeared, just long enough to create a path of light over the water before racing black clouds gobbled it up again.

The heralds set a dignified and stately pace. I sensed Odysseus's impatience; he wanted to be there, get it over with, whatever "it" might turn out to be. I don't think he believed this mission stood much chance of success, but I don't know, perhaps he did. He was talking to Ajax, but I couldn't hear what he was saying—gusts of wind snatched the words from his mouth and carried them away. On my left, huge breakers crashed onto the rocks, sending clouds of white spray high into the air. On my right, drifting across the roofs, came the sound of Trojan voices singing. Amazingly close; they might almost have been inside the camp. I saw Odysseus and Ajax turn to look in that direction, their faces in the moonlight sharp and pale.

The walls of Achilles's compound were higher than I remembered and surmounted by sharp stakes. This was no longer a mere convenient demarcation of the Myrmidon section of the beach, but a serious fortification—and it was not facing Troy. Odysseus flared his eyes at Ajax, as if to say: *You see that?* Guards had been posted at the gate, but there was no problem: Odysseus and Ajax were recognized immediately and waved through.

It was an emotional moment for me, walking through that gate. Music floated out onto the night air; Achilles singing and playing the lyre. And, as always, many of the captive women had come out onto the verandas to listen. I looked for Iphis, but I couldn't see her.

When we reached Achilles's hut, Odysseus told me to wait outside. There was some discussion over how they should enter. The heralds wanted a formal procession through the hall, but Odysseus overruled them. He wanted this to be a friendly, informal visit, two old friends happening to drop by ... The heralds looked faintly scandalized, but Odysseus outranked them and they had to back down. So it was decided; they would all go to Achilles's private entrance, the one that led directly into his living quarters, and then the heralds would leave. "Leave, or wait at the gate," Odysseus said. "I really don't mind. But you are not going in there."

Not knowing what else to do, I sat on the steps to wait, putting my hands inside my sleeves to warm them. I heard Achilles's voice, sounding surprised, I thought, but courteous, welcoming—perhaps a little bit wary, but I may have been imagining that. I listened for Patroclus's voice, but I knew he'd be sitting there in silence, as he so often did. A cold wind whistled between the huts. I thought of trying to find Iphis, but I was afraid of being summoned. Presumably, I *was* going to be summoned, at some stage.

I looked along the veranda. Here and there, a few torches still burned, though they were near the guttering end of their lives. A smell of cold beef fat lay heavy on the air. Inside the hut, the rumble of voices went on. I'd have liked to go down to the sea, perhaps walk straight into it, as I used to do when I lived here, but of course I didn't dare. I just sat there like a tethered goat, knowing my fate was being decided on the other side of that door. I put my hand on my mother's necklace, cradling the opals delicately, one by one. They felt like eggs still warm from the laying. Deliberately, I went back to Lyrnessus, I sat on the bed in my mother's room, watching her get ready for a feast. It must've been something special, my eldest brother's wedding day, perhaps, because she was putting on the opal necklace. Sometimes, if she wasn't in too much of a hurry, she let me brush her hair ...

Breathing in the warmth of the memory, I'd forgotten where I was, until suddenly the door was thrown open and Odysseus stood there, beckoning me to come inside.

22

For hours, Achilles had stood in the stern of his ship watching the progress of the battle, divided between exasperation and triumph. The trench was a fucking disaster—as he'd known it would be; the fighting was now quite literally *bogged* down, the men floundering in mud. You might just as well have sent a messenger to Priam saying: *Don't worry, old man, we know we can't win.*

Well, then: wine, food, celebration . . . ! Fat chance. The atmosphere at dinner was positively funereal. It turned out he wasn't the only one who'd been watching the battle, but not everybody was equally happy with the prospect of a Greek defeat. Patroclus hardly spoke. In fact, he'd said scarcely anything all week, which might suggest the situation was static. Huh! It wasn't static at all. His silences were getting steadily louder.

After dinner, Achilles made a few attempts at conversation, got no response, so he picked up his lyre and started to play. As always, after the first few notes, he lost himself in the music. The fire roared, the dog resting its head on Patroclus's knee sighed with contentment, the last few notes of the song wound down into stillness . . . Achilles was about to speak, but Patroclus held up his hand. Sounds on the veranda: the slapping of sandalled feet on bare boards. They exchanged glances. Nobody came to see them at this hour; in fact, nobody came at all. Achilles put the lyre aside, just as the door burst open, letting in a blast of cold air. The torches shuddered, sending shadows leaping across the walls. The dogs bared their teeth and began circling, until Patroclus, recognizing the men hesitating on the threshold, said, "Friends!"—and reluctantly, grumbling deep in their throats, the dogs fell back.

Odysseus stepped into the firelight, closely followed by Ajax. Odysseus: short, lean, muscular; Ajax: immensely tall, freckles dotting his nose like gnat bites, grinning to reveal a mouthful of large white uneven teeth.

"Come in, come in." Achilles jumped up and started pulling chairs closer to the fire. "Sit down, Ajax, you'll crack your head."

Patroclus forced the door shut against the wind. Instantly, the flames grew tall again, the tapestries stopped flapping and in the pause that followed Achilles's greeting, the oddity of Odysseus and Ajax being there at all began to sink in.

"Something to eat?" Achilles said, still smiling, but wary now, as he hadn't been a moment before.

Ajax rubbed his knees. "No, thanks, I'm fine."

"Not for me," Odysseus said, lowering himself carefully into a chair.

"You're wounded," Achilles said.

"Just a scratch."

Achilles looked from the bandaged arm to Odysseus's face. "A bit more than that, here ..."

He reached out as if to remove the bandage, but Odysseus pulled away. "No, really, it's nothing." He draped his cloak across the injured arm. "Have you been watching the battle?"

"Off and on."

"They're camped on the other side of the trench."

"Really? As close as that ... ?"

"Fuck's sake, man, you can hear them!"

"Now you come to mention it, I think I did hear something— a while back."

Patroclus finished handing round cups of wine. Achilles raised his, Odysseus and Ajax raised theirs ... And nobody could think of a toast.

After a moment's hesitation, Odysseus put his cup on the table beside him. "Come on, Achilles, you know why I'm here."

"I don't, I'm afraid. You're the clever one, Odysseus. Ajax and me, we just muddle on as best we can."

Hearing his name, Ajax looked up, but couldn't think of anything to say. Odysseus braced himself against the back of the chair—he was in a lot more pain than he was letting on—and forced a laugh. "Have you put on weight?"

Achilles shrugged. "Don't think so."

"Are you sure?" Odysseus bunched his fingers at his waist. "I'd have said half a stone at least."

"My armour still fits."

"Oh, you try it on, do you?" He flicked a glance at Patroclus. "Well, a quiet life obviously suits you. You both look *very* well."

"And you look like shit, so why don't you get to the point?"

"I'm here on behalf of Agamemnon."

"Who's wounded in both legs and can't walk?"

"Do you really expect him to come himself?"

"*Yes.*"

Odysseus shook his head. "What I don't understand is how you can sit there and do nothing while literally a few hundred yards away the whole bloody Trojan army's getting ready to attack. All right, perhaps you *don't* watch the fighting—perhaps your conscience won't let you—but you can't tell me you don't know what's going on."

"My conscience is fine, thank you."

Patroclus leant forward. "I hope—"

Achilles waved his hand. "Oh, don't worry, we're not quarrelling. Odysseus and I go back a long way, we understand each other very well." He glanced at Odysseus. "Don't we?"

"I used to think so."

Achilles reached for the wine. "Go on, then, let's hear it."

"I'm authorized to make you an offer. In return for you leading your Myrmidons into battle tomorrow morning—"

"*Tomorrow morning?*"

"Afternoon might be a bit late! Look, do you want to hear what he's offering or not?"

Pausing at times to ease his back, Odysseus embarked on a long list of the objects Agamemnon was prepared to give: tripods, textiles, gold, racehorses, women . . . Achilles listened intently, though when Odysseus finished speaking, he seemed to be waiting for something else. Something more.

"We-ell?" Odysseus said at last.

"That's it?"

"I think that's quite a lot."

"None of it's worth my life."

Odysseus looked taken aback. "No, I know . . . But then, when have you ever fought for *things*? You fight for glory, for reputation."

"Not anymore. I've had a lot of time to think, Odysseus. This isn't my war, I don't want any part of it. What have the Trojans ever done against me? Have they stolen my cattle, burned my crops—taken my prize of honour? No. Nothing, that's the answer. They've done nothing."

"Oh, come on, you're gagging for it."

"What? I'm sorry—what am I '*gagging* for'?"

"Fighting. You know you can't get enough of it. It's who you are. You live, breathe, eat, sleep war."

"Not anymore."

Odysseus sat back. Beads of sweat gleamed on his upper lip; he was finding it hard to control his temper. "Look, you agreed to fight, you signed up for it . . . You couldn't bloody well wait."

"I was seventeen."

"I don't care. You agreed to be part of this coalition—and you can't back out now just because you've changed your mind. It's not honourable, Achilles."

"I didn't back out because I changed my mind. I did it because his behaviour was outrageous. And don't talk to me about honour when you come here representing a dog turd."

In the silence that followed, Patroclus cleared his throat. "And Briseis?"

"*Ah!*" Odysseus said.

He struggled to his feet. Achilles reached out to help him, but then let his hand drop. Odysseus staggered to the door and, using his full body weight, pushed it open against the wind. Once again, the torches guttered and sent shadows fleeing across the walls. A few muffled words and he was back, dragging behind him a woman so heavily shrouded in white she might have been a corpse. He pushed her into the circle of light round the fire and, with all the panache of a conjurer, pulled off the veils. "Here she is!"

Dazed as a rabbit in the sudden glare, the girl stared from face to face. Achilles's knuckles whitened round his cup, but he said nothing. Odysseus looked baffled, obviously expecting a much more dramatic response, because after all this was *the* moment: Achilles's prize of honour, the girl, the bloody girl, the cause of all the trouble, *returned.* With a king's ransom thrown in. What more could he possibly want? And yet he sat there and said nothing.

Odysseus made himself go on. "And he's prepared to swear a solemn oath in front of the entire army that he never touched her. She's been living in his huts with the other women unmolested."

"He never touched her?"

"That's right. And he will swear to it."

Achilles got up and went across to Briseis. They were so close now he could feel her breath on his face, but she wouldn't look at him. He picked up one of the opals—warm from her skin—and cradled it in the palm of his hand, turning it this way and that until glints of fire shone through the milky haze. Abruptly, he let the stone drop, put his forefinger under her chin and gently raised her head until she was forced to meet his eyes . . .

A moment later, he turned to Odysseus. "Tell him he can fuck her till her back breaks. Why would I care?"

Briseis clapped a hand over her mouth. Immediately, Patroclus was by her side, putting his arm round her shoulders and leading her out into the corridor and towards the hall.

"All right," Odysseus said, breathing deeply. "Perhaps that wasn't such a good idea, but at least hear me out."

"You mean there's *more*?"

"When we take Troy—"

"'*When?*'"

"Twenty women, your choice—well, obviously not Helen, but anybody else—seven fortified cities, as much gold and bronze as your ships can carry and—no, *wait*—Agamemnon's own daughter as your wife. He'll accept you as his son-in-law, equal in every respect to his own son—"

"Hang on a minute, let's just see if I've got this right. I'm going to be equal in every respect to his own son?"

"That's what he said."

"Equal *in every respect* to a fifteen-year-old boy who's never yet lifted a sword in anger?" Achilles leant in to Odysseus until their faces were only an inch apart. "And I'm supposed to be flattered?"

"And the daughter brings a huge dowry with her—and that's on top of everything else. You can't say it's not generous."

"Where's it all coming from?"

"Well, from his stores, of course."

"Yes—but how much of that comes from the cities I took? While he sat on his fat arse and did nothing."

Odysseus sat down again and passed a hand across his eyes. "What do you *want*, Achilles?"

"*Him. Here.* I want an apology, I want him to admit he was wrong."

Odysseus turned to Ajax. "Come on, we're wasting our time." He picked up his cloak and then, as if the thought had only just occurred to him, turned back. "Are you holding out for something else? Because if you are, for god's sake, man, spit it out—we don't have time to play games."

"I want an apology. It's quite simple. And cheap."

"And I'm supposed to go back and tell him that?"

"Oh, I think *we* can do better than *that*. Tell him, if I was given the choice of either marrying his daughter or fucking a dead pig, I'd choose the pig every time. There, that should do it."

Odysseus had already turned to go, when, unexpectedly, Ajax spoke. "Men are dying out there, not Trojans, not the enemy, your own side, men who looked up to you—men who bloody near worshipped you—but you don't care, do you? You don't care about anything except your honour—and getting an apology. They're *dying*, Achilles. You could save them—and you won't. Where's the honour in that?" He was on the verge of tears. "I'm ashamed of being your cousin. I'm ashamed I ever called you a friend."

He snatched up his cloak and, wiping tears and snot away on the back of his hand, plunged out into the night.

23

Patroclus said: "I think I'd better go back in."

I nodded, and went on sitting at the small table where he'd placed me. After a few minutes, I was able to look around. The dinner plates had been cleared away and fresh rushes spread on the floor, but there were still some platters and wine jugs lined up on the sideboard at the far end of the hall. I walked down between the two long tables and peered into the jugs until I found one still half full and poured myself a cup. The wine had been standing too long and had a vinegary edge to it, but it would have to do. I drank long and deep, wiped my mouth, poured another cup.

It had all happened so quickly: hauled from darkness into light, stripped of my veil, displayed barefaced like a whore in the marketplace . . . Like being in the arena that first day all over again. And, at the end, that one moment of disturbing intimacy when Achilles had looked straight into my eyes and suddenly there was nobody else in the room and I knew I couldn't lie.

Tell him he can fuck her till her back breaks.

More wine. I found another jug and poured the dregs into my cup. A door banged and immediately I froze, the cup an inch from my lips. I was expecting Odysseus to appear, but when I went out onto the veranda, it was Ajax I saw—pacing up and down twenty or thirty yards away, thumping one clenched fist repeatedly into the palm of his other hand. Patroclus came out and tried to talk to him, but Ajax just shook his head and went on pacing. After a while, Patroclus gave up and came back towards the hut. When he saw me standing there, he took the cup from me and sniffed: "*Ugh*, god, I think we can do better than that."

He led me back into the hall and, from a cupboard under the sideboard, brought out a flagon of wine—the best—the wine I used to serve to Achilles at dinner. He poured two generous cups and handed one to me. We sat at the small table looking down the length of the hall. I said: "You gave me wine the first night I was here. I was sitting in the back room, absolutely terrified." I glanced sideways at him. "I couldn't think why you'd do that for a slave."

"You know why."

I didn't, unless he was referring to the time he'd been alone and frightened in Achilles's father's palace, with no future, no hope and no friends. I hoped he meant that—anything else would have been too difficult.

"I'm sorry," he said.

"Why? *You* haven't done anything."

"Odysseus shouldn't have brought you."

No, I thought, *it could all have been decided without me.* Would that have been better? Perhaps. If I hadn't given the game away, Achilles might have believed Agamemnon. It was a big thing to undertake: the swearing of a solemn oath in front of the gods. He might well have thought Agamemnon couldn't be lying.

Voices from the other room. "What's going on, do you know?"

"Well, they're still talking ... I thought Odysseus was going to leave a while back, but he didn't."

The voices were coming closer. We stood up as Odysseus, looking suddenly much older, came into the hall.

"I'll see you to the gate," Patroclus said.

"No need." Curt, dismissive.

"No, Achilles would want me to."

Odysseus came closer. Letting his contempt show, he said: "Do you do *everything* Achilles wants?" Without waiting for an answer, he turned on his heel and strode off down the hall. I knew I had to follow him.

It had begun to rain, that very fine rain that looks like mist, but soaks you to the skin in seconds. Odysseus and Ajax set off to the gate, carrying the torches—Agamemnon's heralds had long since returned to his compound—leaving Patroclus and me to stumble along behind as best we could. Patroclus grabbed a torch from a sconce outside one of the huts and held it high above our heads. Occasionally, as we walked, his cloak would brush against mine, but apart from that there was no physical contact. We didn't talk much either. In fact, I'm not sure we spoke at all. I suppose some people would have attempted easy consolation: *It won't be for long, don't worry, we'll sort something out* . . . And so on. But he didn't, and for that I was grateful.

We left him at the gate of the compound. I turned and looked back at his tall figure circled in light, but Odysseus called my name, sharply, like somebody bringing a dog to heel, so I knew I had to look forward again. It was a very subdued, bedraggled little group that straggled on around the curve of the bay. Waves racing in fast, breaking in overlapping arcs of foam around our feet, and always that steady, fine rain falling. I floundered through wet sand until, in the end, I simply took my sandals off and walked barefoot. After all, it scarcely mattered what I looked like now. Neither Odysseus nor Ajax showed any interest in me. I had simply ceased to exist.

I was afraid. I'd been afraid since Lyrnessus fell. No, longer than that—*years*. I'd been afraid ever since the cities of the Trojan plain started falling to Achilles; every burning, every sacking, brought the war closer. But my fear that night was of an altogether different order, more sharply focused than it had ever been before. I knew my presence in his compound no longer reflected well on Agamemnon. Rather the opposite, in fact; I was a constant reminder of the quarrel that had brought the Greek army to the brink of defeat. My only potential use, my only value to him—since he certainly didn't want me in his bed—had been as a possible bargaining chip in future negotiations with Achilles. Now, even that was gone.

Tell him he can fuck her till her back breaks . . .

There was nothing, now, to stop Agamemnon handing me over to his soldiers for common use. I'd seen the lives of those women. Once, I'd watched a couple of the older women at the rubbish tip scavenging for food among the rats. Patroclus's dogs lived better.

Back inside Agamemnon's compound, I didn't know what to do. I'd have liked to slip into the women's huts, but I didn't dare, until Odysseus told me I could. Apart from anything else, I was still wearing the opal necklace. The problem was solved when Odysseus ordered me to fetch a pain-killing draught from Machaon's stores. I ran all the way to the hospital, mixed a ready-made draught with fresh herbs in a jug of strong wine and raced all the way back.

Odysseus was sitting in a chair by Agamemnon's fire. He snatched the jug from my hand and downed half the draught in one go. Ajax was kneeling beside him peeling the bandage off his wound. Agamemnon was silent, pacing up and down. I guessed Nestor had called a halt to further questioning until Odysseus had been attended to. I went to see if I could help, but Agamemnon called for me to refill his cup. He'd flushed a mottled red and there were two deep frown lines between his brows as if he couldn't believe what was happening . . .

At last, Ajax finished tying a fresh bandage and stood up.

Immediately, Agamemnon said, "Does he actually understand what I'm offering?"

"Yes," Odysseus said, wearily.

"Marriage to my daughter?"

"Yes." A stark silence. "Of course he said how honoured he was . . ."

Nestor darted a glance at Ajax, who shrugged.

"And he still said no? Did he favour you with a reason?"

"This isn't his war, he's got nothing against the Trojans, they've never raided his cattle, they've never burned his crops, they've ... never stolen his wife."

"He's not bloody well married!"

Odysseus jerked his head at me. "He referred to her as his wife."

"*Did he?*" said Nestor. "Ah."

"Oh, and he used to believe in honour and glory and all that stuff and now he doesn't. Nothing is worth his life."

"That doesn't sound like Achilles," Nestor said. "You sure you went to the right hut?"

"And he's going home."

"*Again?*" Nestor snorted.

"He won't go," Agamemnon said. "Not till he's seen me on my knees in front of Priam."

Odysseus grunted. "In front of *him*, I think."

"And he doesn't care how many Greeks die?" Nestor asked.

"No."

"He's not human," Ajax blurted out.

"Well, of course he bloody isn't," Agamemnon said. "His mother's a fish."

Nestor smiled, thinly. "A sea goddess, I believe."

"Huh." Agamemnon seized the jug from me and poured himself another cup. "What the hell's he on about? *Nothing's worth his life.* This is what happens when a thug like Achilles starts trying to think."

"No point going over it," Nestor said. "He's given us his answer and he's not going to change it. The question is: what do we do?"

"Could we launch the ships tonight?" Agamemnon asked.

Ajax gaped at him. "What, run away?"

Nestor ignored him. "No—they'd attack. We'd be trying to launch the ships and fight them off as well. No, there's no choice, we've just got to stay and see it out."

"*Fight,*" Ajax said.

"Yes," Nestor said, wearily. "*Fight.*"

A long silence. Agamemnon looked from face to face, waiting for somebody to come up with a solution.

"There's always the Myrmidons," Nestor said.

Agamemnon stared at him as if he thought the old man had finally taken leave of his senses. "I think you'll find they come with Achilles attached."

"I don't know," Nestor said. "They don't like what's happening. I mean, when Achilles said, *I've been insulted, we're going home,* they were fine with that, but they don't understand this. Hundreds of miles away from their families and they're stuck here doing *nothing*?"

"They worship Achilles," Ajax said. "They won't do anything without him."

"He's right," Odysseus said. "Achilles leads them."

"No," Nestor said. "Achilles *inspires* them."

Agamemnon looked thoughtful. "Would they follow Patroclus?"

"I can't see it," Odysseus said.

"No, they would," Nestor said. "He's not a bad fighter—he's a bloody good charioteer, he could drive me any day. And they respect him."

"Yeah, but there's a bit of a drawback, isn't there?" Odysseus said. "He can't wipe his own arse without getting Achilles's permission first."

"How do you know?" Nestor said. "We don't know what goes on behind closed doors—nobody does."

Odysseus grinned. "I think we all know what goes on behind *that* door."

"Anyway," Agamemnon said, "it might just work in our favour. He's a king's son, Patroclus. Does he really want to go down in history as Achilles's bum-boy? Because that's the way it's heading . . ."

Ajax had flushed to the roots of his hair. "I don't know anything about that. But I do know Patroclus wouldn't do anything to hurt Achilles."

"Yes, but don't you see?" Nestor said. "He wouldn't be hurting him. He might be helping, because I don't think Achilles wants this situation, I don't think he's happy with it, he's just backed himself into a corner."

"Yes, I'm inclined to agree," Odysseus said. "In fact, the more I think about it, the more I think it's worth a try."

"I suppose so," Agamemnon said, grudgingly. "Nestor, why don't you sound him out?"

"That's if you can get him on his own," Odysseus said. "They're more or less joined at the hip."

"Well," Nestor said, "I'll do my best."

Agamemnon clapped him on the back. "Good man. Well"—he looked around him—"I don't think we can do any more tonight—and we've got a hard day ahead of us tomorrow."

I was standing directly behind his chair, looking for an opportunity to escape. I'd taken off my mother's opals and put them on the carved chest beside his bed. My skin where the warm stones had rested felt bereft. As Agamemnon's guests lingered over their good nights, I began to edge closer to the door; but then, at the very last moment, just as the door closed behind Odysseus, Agamemnon said, "No. You stay."

Carefully wiping all expression from my face, I turned back into the room.

24

Patroclus had been gone a long time; much longer than could be accounted for by his escorting Odysseus and Ajax to the gate.

Achilles picked up the lyre, put it down again, poured himself a cup of wine, didn't drink it. The dogs, ears pricked for the sound of footsteps in the hall, had begun to whine. He bent down and fondled their heads, thinking: *Yeah, you and me both.*

When, at last, Patroclus came in, wet hair straggling across his face, he looked like a wild animal, something you might glimpse in the dunes at night, red eyes stitched on darkness. The draughty, wind-warped hut seemed to shrink around him as he came towards the hearth, chafing his arms, pretending to be colder than he was so he could lean in closer to the fire and not have to look at Achilles.

"You took your time."

Patroclus was trying and failing to disguise his anger.

"Well," he said, at last, "that was brutal."

"The dead-pig bit? Aah, don't worry, he won't repeat it."

"No, Achilles. Briseis. *That* was brutal."

Achilles shifted in his chair. "At least she didn't lie."

"She didn't speak!" Patroclus pushed the dogs away from him. "Achilles, what is it you *want*?"

"I want him to admit he was wrong."

"But he can't. Odysseus knew you wanted an apology, he just couldn't offer it."

"Then it's a pity he didn't save himself the walk."

Patroclus sat down and the dogs settled at his feet. "I suppose it was quite funny in a way."

"Was it? I must've missed that bit."

"*Yes*—Odysseus, so clever, so articulate, so—"

"Devious."

"But it was Ajax who really got to you."

"He didn't. Get to me."

Patroclus looked at him. "Yes, he did."

Achilles selected an unnecessary log and threw it onto the fire. "How was she?"

"How d'you think?"

"I couldn't have done anything else."

Patroclus remained stubbornly silent.

"All right, let's have it."

"We should've gone home. No, listen. *List-en.* Not so long ago, you criticized Agamemnon when he told his men the war was over and they were going home—"

"Well, of course I did, I've never heard anything so bloody stupid."

"But don't you see, you did exactly the same thing? *I've been insulted, that's it, we're finished here—we're going home.* Everybody understood. Only then, suddenly, we're not going home. They'd started looking forward to seeing their wives and kids. It's not been easy. It's not easy to get them out there morning after morning training to do something they're not allowed to do."

"I know it's not easy—and you're doing a marvellous job. Do you think I don't know that?" Achilles reached behind his head and tugged his hair out of the band that was tying it back. "C'mon, then, what are they saying?"

"Oh, just the usual—that you're impossible. That your mother suckled you on bile."

"Well, that's true."

"No, *listen*. They don't know what they're doing here. Sitting around like a load of poky old women while the *men* go off to fight."

"He'll come crawling in the end."

"No, Achilles. He won't."

"He will if he's faced with losing the war."

Patroclus puffed out his cheeks. "I give up."

"More wine?"

"No thanks." He stood up and reached for his cloak.

"Now what?"

"What do you mean: 'Now what?' I'm going out . . ."

"You've just been out." He watched Patroclus wrap the damp cloak round him. "Do you want company?"

A fractional hesitation? "No, but you can come if you want to."

I don't know who's more delighted, Achilles thought. *Me or the dogs.*

––––––––––

Walking through the camp, Achilles saw men lingering by the fires, postponing the moment when they'd have to go into the huts to try to sleep. Agamemnon ought to be going round from fire to fire, trying to instill some fighting spirit into the men, but there was no sign of him. No, he'd be skulking in his hut, getting legless, or else in bed with Briseis—lying, shitting, cheating, fucking bastard.

Patroclus hadn't said a word since they'd left their hut. Achilles glanced sideways at him and, in a clumsy attempt at reconciliation, threw an arm across his friend's shoulders. Patroclus let it lie there, but not before Achilles had felt a moment's involuntary recoil.

They left the camp and began walking along the path through the dunes, their elongated shadows stretching ahead of them over the pale sand. They could hear Trojan fighters singing around their campfires, but it was only when they'd left the dunes behind and were looking out over the scrubland towards the battlefield that they saw the full extent of the Trojan encampment. Leaning his back against a knobbly olive tree, Achilles gazed out over the vast Trojan plain and thought: *My god.* They were so close; closer than they'd seemed from the stern of his ship. He could actually hear the horses champing on their feed. And so many fires! Like the stars on a moonless night when you lie in the long grass and look up at the sky till your head swims. Peering into the flame-studded darkness, he saw firelight red on sweaty faces, glints of eye white, the occasional gleam of bronze and then—so near he could smell the smoke—a great shower of sparks flying upwards as one of the Trojan fighters poked his fire.

"Seen enough?" Patroclus said, grimly.

He nodded, but couldn't find the words to reply.

They walked back through the gates and across the yard to their hut, Patroclus continuing silent and remote. When Achilles suggested a final drink, he shook his head. "No, I think I'll turn in. You never know, we might be fighting tomorrow."

"*No-o,* we will *not* be fighting tomorrow."

"We will if your ships are on fire."

Nettled by what sounded remarkably like insubordination, Achilles opened his mouth to deliver a stinging rebuke, but the door had already closed.

25

Next morning, knowing there was no hope of getting the Myrmidons to concentrate on training, Patroclus set them free to watch the battle. They crowded together in the sterns of the ships, jostling heads and shoulders black against the skyline, waiting in tense silence for the fighting to start. When, at last, the clanging of swords on shields began, they started jumping up and down, cheering on the Greek fighters, for all the world like spectators at a chariot race. Sickened, Patroclus turned away. Since when had war been a game for fit young men to stand and watch?

When he could bear it no longer, he climbed down from the stern and went inside the hut, where he plunged his head into a vat of cold water. Coming up, dripping wet, he stared at his reflection in the bronze mirror, trying to ground himself in some external reality—if only the sight of his own face. At least, here, away from the men, he didn't have to guard his expression.

He lay down on Achilles's bed—he hadn't slept more than two hours last night—but as soon as his head touched the pillow he caught the smell of Achilles's skin and hair—not unpleasant, but strong, almost feral. Outside, the roars and cheers went on. Closing his eyes, he felt the undertow of sleep and soon was drifting just beneath the surface, rocking lights above his head, shadows sliding across the white sea floor.

"Patroclus!"

Groggy from his abrupt awakening, Patroclus swung his legs over the side of the bed. Achilles yelled again. For a moment, he actually contemplated not going to him, but that was out of the question, of course, so he heaved himself onto his feet and went outside. Even in the short time he'd been asleep, the ships' huge shadows had lengthened on the sand. Shading his eyes, he saw Achilles, gold and black against the dazzling light.

"What do you want?" Too abrupt, but he couldn't help that.

"I think Machaon's wounded. I saw him just now in Nestor's chariot—at least, I think it was him. Would you mind going to ask?"

Would you mind . . . ? Whenever others were present, Achilles's orders were always framed as requests and generally with a title added. *Prince* Patroclus . . . *Lord* Patroclus . . . *Would you mind?* None of it quite disguised the fact that Achilles was using a king's son as a messenger boy, but it had been like this so long Patroclus hardly knew how to resent it.

And so he set off at a run, weaving his way between groups of wounded men limping back to the hospital tents. Others, more seriously injured, were being carried along on carts, every lurch, every jolt of the wheels, producing groans and cries of pain. He'd seen it all before, of course, many times. What was shocking, today, was the atmosphere of defeat. Defeat was there in the drooping shoulders and the shambling walk; above all, defeat was in the dead-eyed, incurious stares that followed him as he ran past.

As soon as he could, he got off the path, slipping down narrow passageways till he reached Nestor's hut. There, on the steps, he stopped to get his breath back, before going into the hall. At the far end, lying on a couch, was Machaon, with Hecamede pressing a white cloth to his shoulder. A portly, white-haired man, with a cynical, fleshy, self-indulgent face, Machaon had no business on a battlefield, and yet he'd turned out to fight. Patroclus fell on his knees beside him. "How are you?"

Machaon winced. "I'll live. Looks a good bit worse than it is."
He looked up at Hecamede. "*Harder*, get your weight behind it, girl."

"Shall I have a go?"

"Bloody hell, no, I'd have no shoulder left. You could pass me that
cup though . . ."

Patroclus sniffed the cup. "Strong. You sure it's a good idea?"

"No, of course it isn't *A. Good. Idea.* I need something to take the
edge off." A flash of his eyes as he lifted the cup. "*Cheers.*"

After sneaking a quick look at Machaon's wound—a flesh wound,
quite deep, but it looked clean—Patroclus went through into the
living quarters, where he found Nestor sitting by the hearth, surrounded by pieces of armour he'd unbuckled and let drop. God,
how old was he? Seventy? Bit more than that, perhaps. Patroclus,
young, strong and fit, hovered in the doorway praying for the earth
to swallow him.

"Patroclus! Come in!"

Nestor levered himself out of his chair and, clasping Patroclus by
the hand, dragged him across to another chair next to his.

"No, I can't stay. Achilles sent me to ask after Machaon, but I can
see he's being well looked after." He lowered his voice to a whisper.
"Will he be all right?"

"Oh, I should think so, he's got the best doctor in the world.
Himself. We just do as he says. Come on, sit down."

"No, he'll be wondering where I am."

Nestor smiled. "He can't be that much of a tyrant . . ."

"Can't he?"

"You've only just got here."

Patroclus hesitated. "Oh, all right, then."

Relaxing a little, Patroclus accepted the cup Nestor held out
to him. Nestor raised his own cup to his lips and drank deeply.
His nose was sharper and the red veins in his cheeks more prominent than Patroclus remembered. He was starting to look a bit . . .
threadbare.

"So," Nestor said. "Achilles cares about Machaon?"

"Well, yes, of course he does, he—"

"*One* man? And suddenly Achilles cares? Do you know how many men died today? While he stood on his ship and watched?"

Patroclus opened his mouth.

"And *don't* tell me you agree with it, I know you don't."

"I think I should be going."

"No, please." Nestor patted the chair beside him. "I'm an old man, humour me."

Reluctantly, Patroclus sat down.

"*You* could do it, you know."

"Do what?"

"Lead the Myrmidons."

"You mean, without Achilles?"

"Yes, why not?"

Patroclus shook his head. "That's never going to happen."

"It won't if you don't suggest it."

"There's no point, he'd never agree."

"How do you know? You've never asked him. I've known Achilles a long time, not as long as you have—but long enough. I don't believe he's easy with this, I don't believe he sleeps at night—"

"Oh, he does."

"I think he's backed himself into a corner and he can't see a way out."

"You're saying it's his fault and—"

"I'm saying it doesn't matter whose fault it is. We've gone well beyond that. I think he's looking for a way out. You never know, you might just be doing him a favour."

"I might just get his knife in my guts."

Nestor smiled. "Not you."

"You're sure about that, are you? I wish I was. But, then, I know what it's like to kill a friend and spend the rest of your life regretting it."

"I know, I remember. And yet you turned out well."

In the next room, Machaon cried out. Both men looked at the door and Nestor half rose from his chair.

A second later, Machaon called, "Apologies. She just put the poultice on."

"Now you know what your patients suffer." Grimacing, Nestor lowered himself back into his chair. "Old bones," he said, tapping his knees.

"I don't know what to say."

"It might just be enough to push them back. I don't know what else is going to do it. You know they've already set fire to one of Agamemnon's ships?"

"No, I didn't know."

"It's . . ." Nestor held up his thumb and forefinger so close they were almost touching. "They're that close." He waited, then abruptly lost patience. *What do they have to do before he'll fight?*"

"Burn one of his ships."

"Well, that might be leaving it a little bit late. Of course, that's the trouble with ratting on your comrades, you end up fighting alone."

"He'd still fancy the odds."

Nestor smiled. "Yes, I know he would."

Patroclus drew a hand down across his eyes. When he looked up again, he found Nestor watching him, his expression not calculating or manipulative now—simply curious.

"Don't you ever want to get out of his shadow?"

"I grew up in his shadow, I'm used to it."

"But that's not really an answer, is it?"

Patroclus shrugged.

"This could be your chance to—"

"No. *No*, stop right there. If I do this I'm doing it *for him*."

A long silence. Only Nestor's arthritic fingers twisting together betrayed his tension. Finally, Patroclus said: "All right, you win, I'll suggest it. I can't promise more than that. And now I really ought to be getting back."

Barely able to disguise his triumph, Nestor accompanied him to the door. "Oh, just one more thing," he said. "Ask him to lend you his armour."

"*What?* Now I know you're mad."

"If they see *him* on the battlefield—or *think* they see him—it's worth a thousand men."

Nestor stood back, watching the possibilities work like maggots under the young man's skin. He'd said enough. "Well, do your best." He rested his hand briefly on Patroclus's shoulder. "Nobody can do more."

26

On his way back to Achilles's compound, Patroclus heard his name called and looked up to see an old friend, Eurypylus, limping along the path towards him with an arrowhead embedded in his thigh. Patroclus ran towards him and they embraced, cautiously, since Eurypylus was unsteady on his feet.

"That looks nasty," Patroclus said, stepping back.

"Plenty worse."

"Come on, let's get you seen to . . ." Bracing himself to take the weight, Patroclus draped Eurypylus's arm across his shoulders and set off in the direction of the hospital. "The sooner you get that cleaned up the better."

Hobbled together like that, their progress was slow. When, finally, they reached the hospital tents, Patroclus found Eurypylus a space right up against the canvas and lowered him carefully onto a blanket. Looking around for something to use as a tourniquet, he found a strip of bloody cloth and, kneeling down, grasped the arrow shaft and started to pull. Eurypylus screamed. Patroclus ignored him—it was false kindness to put off doing what had to be done. Tightening his grip, he pulled the arrow steadily out, checked he'd left nothing inside, then twisted the cloth tightly round Eurypylus's leg a couple of inches above the wound. Eurypylus turned his head to one side and vomited. By now, a lightly wounded man had limped across to see what was happening. He was short, with a shock of red, curly hair brushed straight up off his forehead, perhaps to give the impression of greater height. Patroclus knew he knew the man, but he couldn't for the life of him remember his name. "Can you take over?" he said.

The man took the ends of the cloth from Patroclus. "You all right, mate?" he asked the wounded man. Eurypylus attempted a reply, but his teeth were chattering so much he couldn't speak.

"I'll get you some water," Patroclus said.

Cupping a hand over his nose and mouth to keep out the stench, he stood up and looked around. Many of the wounded men were crying out for water, others were asleep or unconscious. One, several beds away to his left, was very obviously dead. He saw a middle-aged woman giving a drink of water to a man who'd lost an eye. "Water?" he asked, miming the act of drinking. Not all the slaves understood Greek. She pointed behind her, to a table at the far end.

The tent was so crowded he had to step over inert bodies to reach the back. As he got closer, he saw a vat of water with half a dozen jugs lined up beside it, several sacks full of roots—strong, earth-smelling—and a rack of dried herbs swaying in the breeze from an open flap. A dozen or so women were sitting at a long table, some grinding herbs, others spreading a thick, greenish-brown paste onto squares of linen cloth. This was an island of calm efficiency, though a high tide of blood and pain was lapping at the rocks. Walking along the rack, he selected several bunches of dried herbs, picked up sprigs of fresh coriander and thyme and sat down to begin grinding. Dishes of water, honey, milk and wine were ranged at intervals along the table, everything within reach. He needed to clean and bandage the wound, pour a pain-killing draught into Eurypylus's mouth—and then get back to Achilles, preferably before he'd started foaming at the mouth. There'd been no time to think about Nestor's suggestion, but perhaps that was just as well. If he'd had time to think, his nerve might have failed him by now.

Intent on finishing quickly, he didn't immediately recognize the girl sitting opposite him, but then, reaching for a jug of milk, he glanced across the table and there she was: Briseis. "What on earth are *you* doing here?"

"I work here."

As she lifted her head, he saw she had a split lip. Her face and neck were covered in bruises. None of this had been there the previous night when Odysseus had pulled off her veil. "How are you?"

"All right. Surviving."

"I've just seen Machaon."

"Yes, we heard he was wounded. How is he?"

"Not bad. It's a flesh wound—clean as far as I could tell." He was trying not to stare too obviously at the bruises. "He's a dreadful patient ..."

She smiled. "I can imagine." She raised a hand and touched her lip.

After that they worked in silence. When he'd finished grinding the herbs, he said, "Can you find me some vinegar?"

Carefully, he transferred the ground herbs to the dish, with honey and milk, crushed several roots between the heels of his hands and stirred them into the mixture, then added wine and salt. He was aware of her watching him. Almost without looking, he could see the red veins in the whites of her eyes, the fingermarks still developing on her neck.

"Who's it for?"

"Friend—I just bumped into him. Fact, he's some sort of cousin, I think. I don't know, I lose track."

"I'll bring a poultice too, if you like."

Going back, he found it easier to edge along the side of the tent, feeling the thick, stained canvas scrape across his back. He found Eurypylus white and drained, though at least the tourniquet seemed to be working: the flow of blood had slowed to a trickle. He thanked the ginger-haired man, who was probably glad to get off and nurse his own wound, and started dribbling the pain-killer into Eurypylus's mouth. The wound had almost stopped bleeding. He was reluctant to disturb any clots that might have begun to form, but on the other hand the wound needed to be cleaned . . . He wished Machaon was there to advise. In the end, he decided cleaning the wound mattered more than anything else. He'd seen too many men die of gangrene; there was nothing worse, not even the plague.

Briseis came up behind him. "Can I help?"

"You could start washing him."

He lifted the cup again and trickled more of the draught into Eurypylus's mouth. Slow, painstaking work: Eurypylus kept choking on the mixture and had to rest between mouthfuls. Briseis began washing the leg, gentle, thorough, sweeping movements, bending at intervals to make a minute examination of the wound. She pressed her fingers round the edges, probing delicately, listening to the skin. Patroclus looked a question. She said, "All right, I think. Clean."

Hearing her, Eurypylus seemed to find fresh strength and gulped down the remainder of the draught. Patroclus wiped his friend's mouth and lowered his head gently onto the blanket. "There—you'll feel better now."

Eurypylus's eyes were already rolling back in his head. A few seconds later, he was asleep.

Immediately, Patroclus turned to Briseis. "You're sure it was clean?"

"Far as I can tell, yes."

She walked with him to the entrance. At one point, they had to step aside to let four men carrying a stretcher edge past—and found themselves face to face with nothing to say. Or nothing that could be said. He reached out and gently touched her face. "What's all this about?"

"Apparently I didn't try hard enough to make Achilles want me back. And it's true, I didn't. I should've lied."

He shook his head. "It won't always be like this."

"Oh, I think it might."

"No—honestly it won't. Things do change. And if they don't you bloody well *make* them."

"Spoken like a man."

"You'll get your chance. One day. And when you do grab it with both hands."

"Odysseus said Achilles referred to me as his 'wife.'"

"He did. I was there."

She shrugged. "Probably another reason I got this."

And so they parted. A hundred yards further on, he turned to look back and saw her standing at the entrance to the tent, one hand raised, watching him go.

27

Waiting on the steps of his hut, Achilles snapped: "Where've you *been*?"

No time for this now, no patience. Patroclus pushed past, throwing over his shoulder: "Machaon *is* wounded."

"Badly?"

"No, not badly. Nestor's looking after him."

Achilles followed him in. "And it's taken you all this time to find that out?"

Patroclus pulled a chair out and sat down, burying his face in his hands.

"What's wrong?"

"Nothing. What could possibly be wrong?"

"Something is. You don't usually come back bawling your head off like a little girl."

Patroclus wiped the heel of his hand across his cheek. "I'm not."

"Well, you could've fooled me. Ooh, Mummy, kiss it better, Mummy, Mummy—"

Enough. Patroclus sprang out of the chair, got his hands round Achilles's neck, thumbs pressed against the larynx, and squeezed. Achilles's face purpled, his eyes started to bulge ... His hands came up and seized Patroclus's wrists—but then, suddenly and deliberately, he let them drop—and simply hung there, unfazed and unafraid, watching as Patroclus struggled to bring himself under control. At last, shuddering, he pushed Achilles away. Silence. Achilles grasped his neck, coughed, swallowed hard several times and, finally, managed to speak. "I'd forgotten what a temper you have."

The words were casual, though his voice was hoarse and pinpricks of red had appeared in the whites of his eyes.

Patroclus sat down. "Machaon's fine."

"*Good.*"

Another silence.

"Which does rather bring us back to the question: why are you crying?"

"Because I'm not made of stone—and apparently you are."

Achilles took a deep breath. "What—"

"No, Achilles, *no.* Just for once you listen to me. *You* listen. I've been to the hospital, it's so overcrowded there's no room to walk between the beds. And they're putting up another tent because people are still pouring in. As I walked back, I could hear the Trojans cheering. And tonight, Achilles, while they're roasting meat on their campfires, we'll be up there burning the dead. And you know you could stop it."

"What do you want me to do?"

"*Fight!*"

"You know I can't."

"How do you live with yourself? How do you *sleep*?"

"I didn't start this, Aga—"

"Oh god, not again—"

"Yes, I know, you've heard it all before. Doesn't mean it's stopped being true."

"So this is how you want to be remembered, is it? The man who sat in his hut and sulked while his comrades fought and died? You sure about that?"

"I can't do it."

"Then let me."

"*You?*"

"Why not? Is it so very hard to imagine?"

Achilles shook his head. "No, of course not."

"Or perhaps you think the men wouldn't follow me?"

"No, I know they would."

"Well, then?"

Achilles was silent, thinking hard.

"If I wore your armour, they'd think it was you. The Trojans, I mean." Patroclus waited. "It would fit me—well, just about."

A measuring look. That objective assessment, where he'd been used to seeing only affection, struck a chill. He had to force himself to go on. "It might be enough to push them back."

"Yes, at the expense of making you a target!"

"I know, but—"

"And not just anybody's target—the best. *Hector.*"

"You're saying I'm rubbish."

"No, you're not rubbish. But you're not me either."

A deflating silence. "I don't care what happens to me."

"No, but I do!" Unable to keep still, Achilles walked the length of the room and back again, coming to a halt in front of Patroclus. "I suppose it might work."

"No, it *would.* I know it would. Once they see the armour, they won't be able to see past it—"

"All right." Achilles sank into a chair. He looked winded, as if somebody had landed a punch in his gut. "But with conditions. *One,* the minute they fall back from the ships, you stop. I don't care how well it's going, you STOP. And *two,* you don't fight Hector."

"I'm not going to run away from him—"

"You do *not* fight Hector. *Agreed?*"

Silence.

"Look, that's it, that's the deal."

"All right, agreed." Patroclus stood up and took a deep breath. The walls seemed to be closing in on him. He needed to be outside, moving, doing things—but he knew he had to stay put. "When do we tell the men?"

"Before dinner. Before they get completely paralytic. Do you want a planning session?"

"Nah—plan is get out of the trench and fight like hell." Suddenly, Patroclus laughed out loud. "I can't wait to tell them, there'll be no holding them. They've been pawing the ground for weeks."

Achilles was looking at him, rather sadly. "You know one of my dreams was that you and I would take Troy together."

"What, just the two of us?"

"Why not?"

"I'd have thought that was fairly obvious."

"Not to me."

Achilles *was* laughing at himself, though only just.

"So, in this dream of yours everybody else is dead?"

"Yes, I suppose so."

"Your own men? *All* of them?"

Achilles gave a little shrug.

"You're a monster, do you know that?"

"Yes, oddly enough, I do." He threw his arm across Patroclus's shoulders. "Come on, let's eat."

28

The rules had changed. Once, not so long ago, Agamemnon's women had been strictly confined to the huts; now, we were required to get out and cheer the Greek army as it set off for the battlefield.

An hour before dawn, the weaving sheds emptied; even women in the hospital tents had to go. I left it as late as I dared and then dragged myself to the mustering ground. I couldn't think why Agamemnon insisted on our presence, since we raised, at best, only a few bedraggled cheers. Though I noticed that, on this occasion, men carrying spears were walking up and down the lines of women, encouraging more vociferous support.

But everything about that day was different. It was all over the camp that Achilles had relented, that he was going to fight at last. I didn't believe it. I'd heard him unequivocally reject Agamemnon's bribes. What could possibly have happened in the interim to make him change his mind? Unless, of course, there'd been another, secret, offer ... A deal. And if there had, did it include me? Nobody would have bothered to tell me.

I looked around, trying to assess the mood. In the hospital, the rumour that Achilles had put aside his anger and was going to fight again had not been enough to lift the gloom. Too little, too late, was the general verdict, but those were sick men. Once I got away from the hospital, I saw nothing but joy and relief.

Nowhere more so than in Achilles's own compound. Unable to stay away, I walked through the gates with a veil wound tight round my head and shoulders. Ritsa, I knew, would cover for me as long as she could. Already fully armed, the Myrmidons were circling the marshalling yard, as restless as a wolf pack that's scented blood. Behind them, in the stables, I could see Achilles's horses being groomed till their coats shone. And when Achilles himself came out of the hut and climbed into the stern of his ship to speak, there was a full-throated roar of approval—though it must have seemed strange to the men, as it did to me, to see him standing there, unarmed and alone. Why wasn't he armed? Everybody else was. And I couldn't see Patroclus anywhere, though by now he ought to have been in the chariot with the reins wrapped round his waist.

Then, as Achilles finished speaking, the door of the hut was thrown open—and Achilles came out. Dead silence; where there should have been cheers, silence. I don't think the men were surprised, they knew what was happening—but that moment, when the two versions of Achilles met and stood face to face, was chilling, as if a shadow had passed over the sun. Oh, they made up for the silence later, with cheers, stamping feet, banging of swords on shields, drums, pipes, trumpets ... but the first reaction was fear, that quite specific dread people feel in the presence of the uncanny. Standing there, identical to Achilles in every respect, Patroclus had become his fetch, the double that appears to herald a man's death. Achilles felt it, I know he did, I saw his expression change, but he recovered quickly. In fact, he was the first to cheer, running up the steps to clasp Patroclus in his arms.

They crossed the yard together, the crowd parting to let them through. Patroclus even walked like Achilles. Perhaps the change was forced upon him by the armour, which was, after all, tailored to fit Achilles, or it may have been a deliberate attempt to mimic his movements, but I think it was more than either of those things. He'd become Achilles. Isn't that love's highest aim? Not the interchange of two free minds, but a single, fused identity? I remembered seeing them on the beach the night I'd followed Patroclus down to the sea. This was what I'd glimpsed then.

Automedon, who was taking Patroclus's role as charioteer, braced himself to steady the chariot as Patroclus leapt on board. After a further brief conversation—Patroclus bending down to listen, Achilles looking up to speak—Automedon slapped the reins against the horses' necks and the chariot rolled forward. Drums beat, trumpets blared—men kept time with the banging of their swords on their shields—and slowly the column moved off. The Myrmidons were to lead the attack, because they were fresh, and because everybody knew the sight of Achilles would strike terror into the Trojan ranks. Oh, I could imagine it, the consternation, the alarm, as Priam on the battlements and Hector in the field recognized the shining helmet with its dancing horsehair plumes. Hector was no coward, he wouldn't hold back, he'd be carving his way towards that helmet. And every Trojan fighter with a reputation to make or defend would be trying to get there before him. The man who killed Achilles was guaranteed immortal glory.

But it wasn't Achilles inside the armour; it was Patroclus. That morning, I found out what it was like to have divided loyalties. I didn't dare pray, because I didn't know what to pray for.

After the drums and shield-banging had faded into the distance, the camp fell eerily silent. Iphis, who'd also watched Patroclus leave, invited me to share a dish of wine with her, but I said no, I had to be getting back. And I did set off immediately, walking purposefully down a path between two rows of huts, but the minute I knew I wasn't being observed, I slowed down.

I just wanted a few minutes to enjoy the silence. Nobody groaning, nobody crying out for water; no sound at all except for a door banging loose on its hinges and the cries of seagulls circling overhead. All the paths were deserted. The men gone, the women inside the huts, where a great chattering of looms had already begun. I closed my eyes for a moment, listening to the constant thrum of the wind in the ships' rigging—that mind-at-the-end-of-its-tether sound I'd grown to hate—and when I opened them again, he was there.

He hadn't seen me. He was standing at the corner between two rows of huts, looking inland towards the battlefield. For the first time since I'd heard his battle cry ringing round the walls of Lyrnessus, I thought he seemed vulnerable. I drew back into the shadows. I wondered how it felt to be the only unwounded man left in the camp, because he was the *only* one, everybody else had gone, even the older men who normally remained behind to guard the ships. I stayed still, hardly daring to breathe, and after a while he walked off in the direction of his hut.

Freed from the oppression of his presence, I slipped down onto the beach, where immediately I kicked off my sandals and started wandering along the shore, scuffling through mats of dry seaweed, my feet releasing clouds of tiny stinging sandflies. Now and then I stooped to pick up a razor shell, a mermaid's purse, the partially articulated wing of a seagull: all the detritus the sea offloads onto the land. Occasionally, I'd pick up a pebble, but none was as beautiful as the sharp-edged, green stone I'd discovered on my first night in the camp. I was so absorbed I didn't know where I was going until I felt a sudden chill and looked up to see the first of the black ships towering over me, her dark underbelly encrusted with grey barnacles. I walked along her side trying to prise one loose with my fingernails, but they were stuck fast. Deep shadow between the ships, a dank, green, underwater smell that after a while became unpleasant. Wanting to get away from it, I started to walk faster and, then, just as I reached the stern, there he was, coming full pelt round the corner.

We almost collided. Pulling up just in time, he took a step back. I noticed he'd gone very pale and at first I couldn't think why, and then I realized that in this murky, submarine light he'd mistaken me for Thetis. Though why a meeting with his mother should have that effect on him, I didn't know. I do know the shock made him angry, but that was no surprise. All Achilles's emotions seemed to be varying shades of anger.

"You," he said. "What on earth are *you* doing here?"

Backing away from him, I said, "I came to see them off." Angry though I knew he was, I had to ask, "Will he be all right?"

"If he does as he's told, he will."

"It was amazing, they'll all think it's you."

"It should be me."

I could see he was still angry. I tried to edge past him, but he caught my arm, his nails digging deep into my skin. "I wish I'd never met you." Said very quietly. "I wish you'd died that day at Lyrnessus."

He rammed me hard against the side of the ship. I raised my arms to shield my face, but he just seized the end of a rope ladder and with a few powerful steps climbed onto the deck. I waited till I was sure he was gone, then ran towards the huts. When I turned to look back, there he was in the stern of the ship: a tall figure, black against moving grey clouds. He wasn't looking at me, he was looking straight over my head towards the battlefield.

With a sense of having escaped, I lowered my eyes and ran all the way back to the hospital, and Ritsa—and safety.

29

Putting his encounter with the girl behind him, Achilles concentrates his whole attention on the battlefield. The sun's directly above his head now, hard and white, a spear point boring into his skull. He keeps having to brush sweat out of his stinging eyes. He's trying to follow the progress of his own plumed helmet through knots of grappling men and it's beginning to unsettle him, this unblinking focus on a distant figure who's indistinguishable from himself.

Below the stern of his ship, the compound's deserted: women nattering away behind the closed doors of the weaving sheds, dogs—all lolling pink tongues and misery—sprawled in the shadows of the huts. He has a jug of water beside him, but it's warm and tastes brackish, though the girl who brought it swore she'd got it straight from the well. He takes a gulp, swishes it round his mouth and spits it out onto the deck. Even that small break in concentration's enough to disorientate him. When he looks back at the battlefield, he can't immediately see the helmet and tenses up in expectation of the worst. But no, there it is—*thank god*. Patroclus is carving his way through the Trojan ranks on towards Troy and the inevitable meeting with Hector. *What's he doing?* The ships have been safe for the last hour at least. *"Turn back."*

He realizes he's said it aloud. There's nothing around him but the empty deck and the empty camp, nobody to hear, and yet the hot, affronted silence makes him feel self-conscious. *Well, sod that . . .* He yells at the top of his voice: "Turn back, you fucking idiot. For god's sake!"

The fighting's thick and fast around the helmet now. He can't bear to watch, but neither can he bear to skulk in his hut and not know. Four hours, bareheaded in the hot sun, four, then five, and counting . . .

At first, it's easy to ignore the strangeness, the not-rightness, till suddenly he's inside the helmet, head bouncing off the bronze sides as blows from a sword come crashing down. For a moment the sky's black, then he's up again and running, yelling his great battle cry as he sees the gates of Troy. All around him the ground's wormy with wounded men. And then, glimpsed through a wall of struggling backs, Hector. But the shield's so heavy, it's nearly wrenching his arm out of the socket, his body's slick with sweat all over and when he tries to grip the spear his fingers slip and—

Achilles wipes his eyes, eases his shoulders back, turns his head cautiously from side to side, makes himself focus on details: the jug of water at his feet, the precise grain of the wood in the plank it's standing on. He needs to reconnect with his surroundings, get back into the real world, adjust to a view not framed by the cheek irons of a helmet.

Gradually, his breathing steadies, but still he's not fully present to himself. He keeps looking down at his hands, stealing furtive glances, as if he thought they belonged to somebody else. Surely they can't be as big as that? He grasps the rail tighter, tighter again, trying to squeeze the delusion out of his brain, and slowly his hands return to their normal size. But it's shaken him, no doubt about that. He needs a drink of cold water, really cold, not this tepid muck, or better still, perhaps, a cup of cool wine. Feeling weaker than he can ever remember feeling, he climbs halfway down the rope ladder and then lets himself drop to the ground. A few minutes out of the hot sun, he'll soon be himself again.

He'll be himself again. He notices, as if hearing it for the first time, the oddity of that expression. Spot on, though. He hasn't been *himself* all day, not since early morning when he woke to find Patroclus standing, naked, in front of the bronze mirror. He'd already braided his hair and the long thick plait hanging down his back looked like a second spine.

Catching a movement in the mirror, he turned to Achilles and smiled.

"Did you sleep?" Achilles asked.

"Eventually."

"Was I snoring?"

"What do you mean: 'Was I snoring?' After what you had to drink?"

"I didn't drink a lot." It's true. He never drinks too much, never eats too much either—and he certainly never misses his run in full armour round the bay. He has all the minor virtues, and only one—*colossal*—vice. "How do you feel?"

Patroclus turned back to the mirror. "I'm fine."

A tap on the door and Alcimus came in carrying greaves so highly polished it hurt your eyes to look at them. Achilles swung his legs over the side of the bed, telling Alcimus he wasn't needed, that he'd help Patroclus fit the armour. He sounded confident, as if he and he alone knew how to adapt his armour for use by another man, though in fact the possibility of somebody else wearing his armour had never occurred to him before. The fact was, he needed these few minutes alone with Patroclus.

Working quickly and silently, he helped him buckle on the cuirass. Nothing could be done about the hinge, but at least the straps could be adjusted, though the all-important area under the right arm took a dozen attempts before they got it right. "There, how does that feel?"

Patroclus circled his arm again. "Fine."

"Here, try the helmet."

Staring at his reflection, Patroclus lowered the helmet gingerly onto his head, adjusted the cheek irons and only then turned away from the mirror to face Achilles. Now, with the bronze crest and horsehair plumes tossing around his head, he looked suddenly a foot taller. With forehead and nose covered and the cheek irons jutting out along the line of his jaw, his face had almost vanished.

"Well? Do you think they'll believe it's you?"

"God, yes, even *I* believe it."

Achilles laughed as he said it, but he knew his voice sounded shaky. Turning aside, he looked down at the remaining armour: shoulder guards, arm guards, neck guard, greaves . . . He pretended to find a speck of dirt on one of the greaves and started rubbing it with a soft cloth, pulling back to inspect the area, then breathing on it and rubbing again. With each sweep of the cloth, his face reappeared, features brutalized by the curve of metal. "Do you want my spear?"

"No, I'll take my own, they won't be looking at the spear. Well, not if it's inside them, anyway." He turned back to the mirror. He seemed to be mesmerized by his own reflection—or was it Achilles's reflection he was looking at? "I'll take your sword though."

Achilles went to fetch it, but then, instead of handing it over, he started slicing the air, coming steadily closer and closer to Patroclus, the blade flashing so fast he seemed to be wielding half a dozen swords. Patroclus stood his ground, though he looked taken aback and Achilles could see the first faint glimmering of fear in his eyes. At last, laughing, Achilles lowered the sword and held it out, but even then couldn't bring himself to relinquish it. Instead, he pointed it at Patroclus's naked throat, a blade so sharp even resting it lightly against the skin could produce a cut. The tip was quivering with the pulse in Achilles's hand. "Remember what I said? Doesn't matter how well it's going, you turn back the minute the ships are safe. And you do not fight Hector. Hector's mine."

"All right." Patroclus smiled, though you could see him wanting the sword point to be lifted. "I've said: *All right.*"

For a long moment, they stared at each other. Then, with a slight, self-mocking bow, Achilles handed the sword over. "And remember, I expect you back in time for lunch!"

Patroclus laughed, but he wasn't paying much attention, he was too eager to be gone. Wearing Achilles's armour had changed him, and changed the relationship between them. He was Achilles's equal now—in his own estimation, at least. The increased confidence showed in his walk, his gestures, even in the way he held his head—and it made him utterly convincing.

"You know," Achilles said, "I'm beginning to think this might work."

Patroclus was once again circling his right arm, only this time holding the sword. "It will."

"You're sure that's all right?"

"It's fine."

"I wish you'd stop saying everything's fine."

Patroclus pulled him into an embrace. "But it *is*."

"I'll talk to the men first."

Patroclus went ahead of him into the dark hall, but stopped just inside the door. They embraced again—a private embrace, more intimate than the public embrace that would follow it, though even then, Achilles could feel the tension in Patroclus's shoulders, his eagerness to be gone.

Achilles shook him. "Just come back."

And then, fixing a smile on his face, he stepped out into the blinding light.

Hours later, stepping from light into the near-darkness of the hall, he pauses to get his bearings. When he can see again, he goes to the vat of water in the corner of the hall and plunges his head under the surface, running his fingers through his sweaty hair, staying under long enough for his lungs to start to hurt. Coming up, dripping wet, drops of water scattered like grey pearls across his skin, he finds himself shivering uncontrollably. Definitely caught the sun—but he does feel better. At least his mind's clear.

Better, but livid. *Stop the minute the ships are safe. Don't press on to the gates. Don't fight Hector. Hector's mine.* Could he have made it any clearer? Though, to be fair, Patroclus hasn't fought Hector—not yet, at any rate—but the rest of it he's just ignored. Achilles paces up and down, kicking anything that gets in his way, and everything does, of course—except the dogs, who know better and slink out into the yard. It's not as if he doesn't understand *why* Patroclus has disobeyed his orders. Sometimes, in the heat of battle, there's a moment of calm, when time slows and the shouting and the clamour fade away and you see the red veins in the whites of an enemy's eyes and you know—not believe, not hope—*know* you can't miss. They're rare, those moments. The other ninety-five percent of the time, war's just a tedious, bloody grind, composed in equal parts of boredom and terror, but then it comes again, that shining moment, when the din of battle fades and your body's a rod connecting earth and sky.

Nobody in that state could possibly stop and turn back. And he suspects Patroclus has been in that state—or somewhere near it—all morning.

Nevertheless. Orders are orders and have to be obeyed. Oh, he'll congratulate him, slap him on the back in front of the men, pour him a cup of the finest wine, serve him the best cuts of meat at dinner, sing his praises, give thanks to the gods—all that; but later, when they're alone, he'll really cut the little bastard down to size. Has to, he can't possibly let this go. But obviously he'll wait till he's got him on his own and then he'll say . . . What will he say?

Abruptly, Achilles stops pacing and stares into the bronze mirror, where his face, looking back at him, shows no anger at all, but only fear—the fear he'll never say anything to Patroclus ever again. It breaks him. He curls up on the bed where the sheets still hold the smell of Patroclus's skin and says his name over and over again, as if just saying it might be a charm against disaster. "Patroclus." And again, louder: *"Patroclus."*

————————

On the battlefield, Patroclus hears Achilles calling his name and for a second his concentration falters. A second, but long enough, because suddenly there's Hector straight in front of him. He tries to raise Achilles's sword but already it's too late. Hector drives the spear hard into his side—it goes in so easily—and suddenly he's on the ground, thrashing like a fish in a pool that's drying out. Dark shapes of Trojan fighters crowd in, blocking off the light. "Achilles!" he shouts. And again, as the red blood spurts out of him and his spirit begins to slip away into the dark: *"Achilles . . ."*

————————

A mile away, Achilles lifts his head. Just for a moment there he'd thought he heard Patroclus calling his name. Patroclus? Well, no, it can't be. A man's voice, though, which is strange because the men are all out there fighting. There are only women left in the camp. The bitterness of that realization bites into him.

He knows whose voice it was, but he's afraid to let himself think what that could mean. So he tells himself, *No, it was a gull.* Their cries sound amazingly human sometimes . . .

Lifting his gaze to the rafters, he tries to pray, but prayer never comes easily to him—he's his mother's son, he knows too much about the gods—and after a few stumbling words he abandons the attempt. No point sitting here. Time he was back on the ship, though if the advance continues at that rate, they'll soon be out of sight.

He's barely reached the door when he hears his name being called again, and this time there's no mistaking it. So they are back! Somehow or other—god knows how—*they're back.*

He throws the door open and steps onto the veranda, expecting to see the yard teeming with men and horses, but there's nobody there. Only silence, and somewhere in the distance a door banging loose on its hinges.

Back onto the ship, see what's happening. Halfway up the rope ladder, he stops, because something's caught his eye. A movement. And then he sees it: a chariot being driven hard and fast, the horses emerging from a cloud of dust. Somehow—and he knows this immediately—he has to stop that chariot getting here, because when it does, he's going to hear the worst words he's ever heard. And so he exerts the full force of his will to push it back, but not even his power can stop time or solidify air.

He takes a deep breath, lets himself drop to the ground and walks into the centre of the yard to wait for what he knows is coming. Nothing moves in the huts around him. Not a breath of wind stirs.

White sun. Black shadows, knife-edged. Silence.

30

All that long day I'd sat on the bench grinding herbs while the sound of battle, clamorous at first, moved steadily further away until, by mid-afternoon, it was no more than a muffled clash on the horizon. A few wounded men straggled in—none seriously hurt—and the news they brought back was good—good, if you were Greek. The Trojans had been pushed back, Patroclus and the Myrmidons had reached the gates of Troy. It even seemed possible the city would fall that night.

The news spread rapidly from tent to tent and soon all but the most seriously injured were laughing and singing. Marching songs, sentimental songs about mothers and home, romantic songs about wives and sweethearts and—increasingly, as the day wore on—songs about Helen.

The eyes, the hair, the tits, the lips
That launched a thousand battleships . . .

They all believed that Menelaus, her husband, Agamemnon's brother, would kill her when he got her back—he'd said so, many times. Some of them were inclined to think that was a waste. Fuck her first, *then* kill her.

Fuck her standing,
Fuck her lying,
Cut her throat and fuck her dying.
When she's dead but not forgotten
Dig her up and fuck her rotten.

They sang themselves hoarse, calling for jugs of stronger wine, which, on Machaon's instructions, we had to refuse. Then came a lull. I took round jugs of water; the heat in the tent was stifling, the stench of stale blood from bandages and sheets a physical barrier you had to force your way through. By late afternoon, the sound of battle was starting to grow louder again. The men kept looking at each other. Why? Were the Greeks being forced back? Shortly afterwards, an influx of wounded men brought up-to-date and dreadful news. Patroclus was dead, killed by Hector. They were fighting over his body now, Trojans trying to drag him inside the walls of Troy, Greeks standing astride his body to hold them off. One man said he'd seen Hector grab Patroclus's legs while Automedon and Alcimus hung on to his arms. "I thought they were going to tear him apart."

Dead. I couldn't believe it, though I'd known from the moment he came out of the hut wearing Achilles's armour that the day would end in his death. I felt I had to go to Iphis—it was easier to think about her grief than my own—but I saw no way of escaping from the hospital, now that so many wounded men were streaming in.

So I wasn't there when Achilles got the news, but Iphis, watching from the doorway of one of the women's huts, saw and heard it all. It was Antilochus, Nestor's son, the boy who worshipped Achilles, who told him Patroclus was dead. As soon as the words were out, Achilles let out a great cry and fell to the ground, his hands clawing at the filthy sand, scooping it up and throwing it over his face and hair. Afraid he might draw his dagger and slash his throat, Antilochus caught and held his wrists. Hearing his cry, the women came pouring out of the huts and surrounded him, where he lay collapsed on the ground, powerless now for all his power.

Suddenly, a high wind started blowing. It came from nowhere, Iphis said, whistling under the doors, lifting horses' manes and tails, creating little whirling dervishes of sand that subsided as quickly as they came. The sky darkened; thick black clouds extinguished the sun.

Antilochus stared from face to face. "What's happening?"

And then they saw her, striding up the beach, silver-grey storm-light casting a metallic gleam over her face and hair. A whisper ran round the crowd. "Thetis."

The name leapt from mouth to mouth and immediately they began to back away. Some knelt, foreheads touching the damp sand, while others cowered in doorways or ran inside the huts and slammed the doors. All of them, desperate to get away, desperate not to have to witness this meeting. Even Antilochus let go of Achilles's wrists and crawled away into the shadow of a hut.

A silence fell as she approached. Those who were still out in the open covered their eyes or turned away, leaving the goddess alone with her son.

31

What's wrong?
  What's the matter?
  Where does it hurt?

———

The old questions. The ones she used to ask whenever he came home crying with a scrape on his knee or a bruise on his head. Every slight abrasion seemed to remind her of his mortality. Not that he didn't lap it up, of course he did, her constant fussing, her murmurs of *Mummy, kiss it better;* but he resented it too, because what sort of mother starts to grieve for her son at the moment of his birth? He'd grown up saturated in her grief. He was strong, he was healthy—or at least he was until she left—but none of that mattered. Nothing could console her for his mortal birth.

  What's wrong?

That keening cry, the fishy smell of her fingertips as she cradles his head in her hands. And so it floods out of him: the death of Patroclus, his guilt—because none of this should have happened. It should have been him inside that armour—and even now, men far less skilled in the art of war than he is are fighting to stop Hector dragging Patroclus's body inside the gates of Troy. Other men are dying to save his friend from mutilation and dishonour, while he still sits here, a useless weight on the good green earth.

But enough of that. That's past, it can't be changed. Now, all that matters is finding and killing Hector.

But if you kill Hector your own death follows at once.

"Do you think I care? It's the only thing keeping me alive—the thought of killing him. Once he's dead, my own death can't come soon enough."

You can't fight without armour.

"Why not? If I'm going to die anyway?"

But she's right, of course. Without armour he won't live long enough to reach Hector.

Stay away from the battlefield for now. Tomorrow at dawn I'll bring you armour fit for a god.

And so she walks back into the sea, sinking beneath a swelling wave, her black hair fanning out across the water, there for a second, then gone.

He waits for the familiar ache of loss, but this time nothing happens; perhaps the agony of losing Patroclus has swallowed every lesser grief.

———

Mainly, in the next few hours, he feels numb. It's a physical sensation. He looks at his hand lying on the tabletop and can't tell where flesh ends and wood begins. Again and again, he half imagines, half hallucinates, the moment when he'll thrust his sword into Hector's throat. He hauls himself back into the present, shaking his head like a bewildered ox. He's always had a good memory, right from childhood, but for the rest of his short life these first hours after Patroclus's death will be a blank.

Without armour, he's a snail without a shell. *Useless.* But then he thinks perhaps there *is* something he can do. And so he climbs onto the parapet above the trench and, standing there outlined against the sky, sends his terrible war cry ringing across the battlefield all the way up to the gates of Troy. Women at their looms stop to listen, wounded men lying in the hospital tents look at each other with renewed hope, and Briseis, sitting at the long table grinding herbs, shudders, remembering the first time she heard that cry, the day Lyrnessus fell.

On the battlefield, the Greeks fighting to save Patroclus's corpse recognize the cry and turn towards it. What do they see? A tall man standing on a parapet with the golden light of early evening catching his hair? No, of course they don't. They see the goddess Athena wrap her glittering aegis round his shoulders; they see flames thirty feet high springing from the top of his head. What the Trojans saw isn't recorded. The defeated go down in history and disappear, and their stories die with them. Three times Achilles shouts and three times the Trojans fall back, the last time long enough for the Greeks to pull Patroclus's body clear and carry it back to their camp.

Now at last there's something he can do. He can wash the body—the poor, ruined body, so slashed about with swords it's a miracle it's held together; he can pour oil into the wounds. Somebody binds up the jaw with a strip of linen and he doesn't like that because it makes Patroclus look too dead; but he doesn't protest. He knows it has to be done. He takes Patroclus in his arms and rocks him, feeling the last warmth deep in his chest and belly, though his arms and legs are already cold. A priest arrives and intones prayers; women cry and beat their breasts; his friends try to put their arms round him, but he pushes them away. None of it helps.

When he can bear it no longer, he walks down to the sea, but, for perhaps the first time in his life, doesn't wade straight into it. He wants to preserve the filth that covers him. He won't wash or comb his hair—he's not even going to bury Patroclus—not until he sees Hector lying dead at his feet.

———

That night he spends with Patroclus, curled up against his side, as he lies stretched out, cold and rigid, on the bed.

Well before dawn, he's up and waiting on the beach. He doesn't recognize the burning in his eyes as tiredness, nor identify the aching underneath his ribs as hunger. This is the way it is now. He paces up and down. Sometimes she's late, often very late; he's never been able to rely on her coming. Sometimes, when he was a child, she promised and then didn't come at all. Perhaps this will be one of those times.

But then, suddenly, there she is, striding out of the sea, carrying his new and glittering armour. Slung across one slender arm, there's a shield that later in the day Alcimus and Automedon, both strong young men, will struggle to lift. For her sake, he pretends to admire the shield and all the other pieces, though in reality he scarcely sees them. He needs this armour to get onto the battlefield, that's all. It means no more to him than that. Sobbing, she embraces him and he forces himself to return the pressure of her arms, but the truth is, he can't wait to be shot of her. The tears of women—even the tears of a goddess—are of no use to him now.

War. Hector. That's all he cares about. He won't rest now till Hector's dead.

32

I heard him before I saw him: his battle cry ringing around the camp as he strode along the beach summoning the men to war.

The wounded in their sweaty beds looked from one to another and those who could walk at all insisted on getting up and hobbling to the arena. I slipped through the open flap at the back of the tent and ran down to the sea, where already hundreds of men had gathered to watch Achilles as he walked towards them. The sun shone, the wind lifted that great mane of hair, and yes, he did look, for one brief moment, as if his head were on fire.

Soon, the entire camp was converging on the arena. Everybody went, even the men who normally stayed behind to guard the ships. Odysseus, who'd been wounded yet again, this time in the leg, limped in, leaning heavily on his spear. Last of all came Agamemnon, his wounded arm held stiffly by his side. As he entered, silence fell.

One of his heralds had seen me standing at the back among the other women and—presumably obeying orders—grabbed me by the arm and bundled me to the front. I stood there, shivering, for the dawn wind was cold, and gazed down at my sandals, trying to shut out awareness of the staring eyes. Somewhere close by, a horse whinnied. Suddenly, I understood what was happening: Agamemnon was trying to assemble, as best he could at such short notice, the goods he'd promised Achilles. That promise still had to be kept, though it was obvious to everybody that Achilles would have fought for nothing.

I tried not to hear their voices, but short of sticking my fingers in my ears it was impossible. These men had been trained in oratory from childhood; their voices carried—and with no apparent effort—to every part of the arena. I risked a glance behind and saw Hecamede watching from the steps of Nestor's hut. I saw her raise her hand, but I didn't dare wave back. I hardly dared breathe. I was under Agamemnon's paw.

Achilles got up and stood at the centre of the ring. He felt nothing but shame, he said, that he and his dear comrade Agamemnon had quarrelled over a girl, had nearly come to blows over her for all the world like a couple of drunken sailors in a bar. Better the girl had died when he took her city, better if a stray arrow had caught her then and ended her life. How much grief and suffering the Greeks would have been spared. How many brave men, now dead, would still be alive . . .

He was blaming me for Patroclus.

That's when I knew there was no hope.

But enough of that, Achilles went on. That's past. He was ready now, more than ready, to fight—and this time there'd be no stopping till he brought Hector's head back to the camp on the point of his spear.

Uproar. Every man on his feet shouting. It was a long time before Agamemnon could make himself heard—and what he said was hardly worth the hearing. A long, rambling, self-justifying tirade followed by a recital of the goods he was still prepared to bestow upon Achilles—though now, of course, that wasn't, strictly speaking, necessary. I glanced at Achilles and saw him struggling to hide his impatience as Agamemnon went through the list. When, finally, he stopped speaking, Achilles's reply was crisp. The goods Agamemnon had promised could be delivered now, or later, or not at all: Agamemnon's choice. He couldn't have said it more clearly: *This isn't about* things; things *don't matter now.*

I thought that was it, it was over, I could go, but then Odysseus stood up and reminded Agamemnon he'd promised to swear a solemn oath that he'd never touched me. It was only right, he said, that Achilles should know he hadn't been wronged. Odysseus sounded pious, even a little priggish; you had to look closely to catch the glint of mischief in his eyes.

This was followed by a long silence during which I felt every eye in the arena turn on me. Agamemnon heaved himself to his feet. Yes, of course he'd swear the oath, of course, why not? A boar was dragged, squealing, into the ring. I smelled the stink of its fear-shit and closed my eyes. Intoning a prayer to Zeus and all the gods, Agamemnon cut its throat and swore that he'd never once lain with me "in the manner of men with women." I felt an absurd desire to giggle; that was so very nearly true. Agamemnon went on to say that I had lived, unmolested, among the other women in his huts and he called upon the gods to punish him if he lied.

Achilles's dirt-streaked face remained expressionless. Did he believe Agamemnon? I have absolutely no idea. Perhaps—it's a terrible thing to lie under oath, he might have doubted that even Agamemnon would do that, but the truth is I don't think he cared. Patroclus was dead; nothing else mattered.

And with that oath, the deal was done. Agamemnon invited all the other kings to a great feast where he and Achilles would once more sit down and eat as brothers. Meanwhile, the Myrmidons would gather up the stuff and take it to Achilles's compound. They set to work at once. The tripods, the cauldrons, the bales of rich, embroidered cloth, the gold dishes and plates were carried from Agamemnon's storage huts and loaded onto mule-drawn carts. Prayers and libations were offered to the statues of the gods, then the drivers cracked their whips and the procession moved slowly off. Four great prancing stallions headed the column, followed by a long line of overladen carts, jolting and swaying over the rough tracks.

And I brought up the rear, along with the seven girls from Lesbos, and all the other things.

33

The first thing I saw when I returned to Achilles's compound was Patroclus's body laid out on a bier. He'd been a living man when I left. I fell on my knees and clasped his cold feet in my hands. I think at that moment I felt more alone, more abandoned, than I'd ever felt. I wept without restraint and the other women, hearing my cries, came running out of the huts to mourn with me.

I think we were all, to some extent, using Patroclus's death as a cover to mourn our own losses. I thought about my brothers as I wept. I even thought about poor, silly Mynes, who'd have been perfectly happy, I think, with another wife. But I wouldn't like it to be thought our grief for Patroclus was in any way staged, or insincere. I held his cold feet in my hands and remembered how he'd once told me not to cry, that he'd promised to make Achilles marry me.

Oh, I've no doubt that on the battlefield, in the thick of the fighting, he was every bit as ferocious as the rest of them, but here in the camp, among the captive women and their children, he had always been kind.

———

Ah, yes, I hear you say. *But that's not the whole truth, is it? You didn't just "remember" he'd promised to make Achilles marry you, you made bloody certain everybody else remembered it as well. Especially Achilles. A dead man's wishes carry enormous weight with the living, particularly when the dead man has been as deeply loved as Patroclus. Go on, admit it! You were trying to arrange your marriage.*

Hardly! Achilles had just told everybody he wished I was dead!

No, but you gave it a go, didn't you? How could you do that? This man killed your brothers, he killed your husband, he burned your city, he destroyed every single thing you'd ever loved—and you were prepared to marry him? I don't understand how you could do that.

Perhaps that's because you've never been a slave. No, if you want to pick at something, why don't you ask me why I'm telling this as if it were a communal event? "Our" grief, "our" losses. There was no "our." I knelt at Patroclus's feet and I knew I'd lost one of the dearest friends I ever had.

———————

Sometimes at night I lie awake and quarrel with the voices in my head.

34

The feasting in Agamemnon's hall went on far into the night, but Achilles was back before midnight. That night, he spent with Patroclus again, curled up on the bare boards beside his bier.

Already, I'd noticed a certain uneasiness among the men. Patroclus should have been cremated by now, his bones raked out of the ashes of his funeral pyre and buried with prayers and chanting and libations to the gods. Among the Greeks—and it was the same among the Trojans—the custom was to hold the cremation before sunset on the day following the death, but for some reason Achilles had decided the funeral rites for Patroclus must wait. Perhaps he was hoping that after he killed Hector—and I don't think he ever doubted he would—his own death would follow so fast he could be burned with Patroclus on a single fire. He'd have liked that.

Before dawn the next day, he was up and armed. The new armour was so miraculously wrought, so perfectly fitted to his body, that he moved as if he were wearing nothing more constricting than a tunic. I met him in the narrow passage between his living quarters and the hall and his eyes were bloodshot, but he was perfectly calm, coiled as tightly as a hawk in the last few seconds before it stoops onto its prey.

There was only one moment when I saw him falter. As he was about to climb into the chariot, he looked up and saw Automedon standing there, where for so many years Patroclus had stood, and he took an involuntary step back. But he recovered at once. Automedon held out his hand, but Achilles ignored it, leaping into the chariot unaided, and turned to take his shield from Alcimus, who was staggering under its weight.

And then, yelling his great battle cry, Achilles raised his spear and signalled the advance.

And so began the greatest killing spree of the war.

As it happens, I know the names of all the men he killed that day. I could recite them to you, if I thought there was any point.

We-ell . . . I don't know. Perhaps there is a point.

Iphition. Eighteen when he died. Achilles killed him with a sword cut straight down the middle of his head, the two sides falling neatly apart, like a split walnut, to expose the convoluted brain. Dropping to the ground, he fell under the hooves of Achilles's trampling horses and the chariot wheels ground him deep into the mud.

And then—

Demoleon. A spear thrust to the temple, straight through the cheek iron—his armour was nowhere near as good as Achilles's—piercing the bone and turning his brain to pulp.

And then—

Hippodamas. A spear between the shoulder blades as he tried to run away. He rolled over and the light faded from his eyes.

And then—

Polydorus. Priam's youngest son, fifteen years old, too young to fight, but in the closing months and weeks of war underage boys were routinely sent into the field. Another spear thrust, and again into the back, though Polydorus wasn't running away. Quite the reverse, in fact. He was showing off, charging the Greek lines without looking to see who was coming up behind. Achilles's spear came out below the navel. Polydorus screamed and fell forward onto his knees, clutching his steaming guts in his cupped hands.

And then—

Dryops. A sword swipe to the neck that very nearly took off his head. And then—

Demuchus. A spear in his right knee. As he stood there helpless, waiting, Achilles finished him off with a sword thrust to his neck. And then—

Laogonus and *Dardanus*, brothers. They clung to the sides of their chariot, but Achilles hooked them out of it, as easily as picking out winkles with a pin. And then he killed them, quickly, efficiently, one with a spear thrust, the other with his sword. And then—

Tros. He died clutching Achilles's knees, pleading for his life. Achilles sank his sword into the upper belly, inflicting a wound so deep the liver slid out of the gap, and blood gushed and puddled at his feet. And then—

Mulius. A spear thrust to the ear delivered with such force the tip jutted out of his other ear. And then—

Echeclus. A sword thrust to the head. And then—

Deucalion. A spear thrust, slicing through the sinews at his elbow. Sword arm dangling useless by his side, he waited for death. Achilles swung his sword, Deucalion's head and helmet flew off together and fluid oozed out of the severed backbone as his body lay spread-eagled in the dirt. And then—

————

But you see the problem, don't you? How on earth can you feel any pity or concern confronted by this list of intolerably nameless names?

In later life, wherever I went, I always looked for the women of Troy who'd been scattered all over the Greek world. That skinny old woman with brown-spotted hands shuffling to answer her master's door, can that really be Queen Hecuba, who, as a young and beautiful girl, newly married, had led the dancing in King Priam's hall? Or that girl in the torn and shabby dress, hurrying to fetch water from the well, can that be one of Priam's daughters? Or the ageing concubine, face paint flaking over the wrinkles in her skin, can that really be Andromache, who once, as Hector's wife, stood proudly on the battlements of Troy with her baby son in her arms?

I met a lot of the women, many of them common women whose names you won't have heard. And so I can tell you that the brothers Laogonus and Dardanus weren't just brothers, they were twins. When they were little, Dardanus's speech was so bad his own mother couldn't understand him. "What's he saying?" she'd ask his brother. "He says he wants a slice of bread," Laogonus would reply. "You've got to make him talk," the boys' grandmother said. "Make him ask for it himself." "But I was busy," the mother told me. "I'd have been stood there hours if I'd listened to her."

And Dryops, whose mother's labour lasted two full days. "Me mam sent the midwife downstairs in the end. 'You go and get yourself a cup of wine,' she says. 'I'll stop with her.' And the minute the midwife was out the room, she whipped the covers off and I don't know what she did, but oh my god, the relief. Ten minutes later he was born. 'Oh,' the midwife says, 'I didn't think she was as close as that.' Me mam just smiled."

And then there was Mulius, the one with Achilles's spear point sticking out of his ear. "Six months old he was when he walked—never crawled, never shuffled around on his bum or anything like that, he just straight stood up. I used to walk him around, holding on to his hands, bent double—hours, *hours*—and the minute he sat down he wanted to be up again. Me back was broke."

Or Iphition's mother, remembering the first time his dad took him fishing, the frown of concentration on his face as he tried to get the worm onto the hook . . . "Oh, and the minute he stood up, it fell off again. I didn't dare laugh. Poor little soul. But give him his due, he went on trying. He was like that—he wouldn't give in."

Some of the younger women had since had children by their

Greek owners, and I'm sure they loved those children too—as women do—but when I spoke to them, it was the Trojan children they remembered, the boys who'd died fighting to save Troy.

———

And then—

Rhigmus. Achilles's spear point struck him in the chest and bubbles of blood gargled from his pierced lung.

And then—

Areithous. Achilles killed him with a spear thrust to his back as he was struggling to turn his chariot round. He fell to the ground, and the frantic horses galloped off, the empty chariot bouncing over the rutted ground.

And then—

But it really doesn't matter who came next—he forgets the men he kills. Even as he pulls the spear out, he's turning to look for the next man, and the next. So why, out of all this red blur of killing, should one man's death stand out? "Man," he says, but "boy" would be more appropriate: bum fluff on his chin instead of hair—his presence on the battlefield proof of Trojan desperation, or else of his own desire to fight and prove himself a man. Either way, there he is, crawling out of the river . . .

Lycaon, son of Priam. The one he won't be able to forget.

No funeral rites for any of these men, no cleansing fire. He's not going to stop fighting to let the Trojans bury their dead while Patroclus lies, unburied, in his camp. He doesn't take prisoners either, not now, not anymore. Everyone who crosses his path he kills. Their bodies go down under his chariot wheels; blood, shit and brains fly up until his armour's caked in filth. He doesn't stop to look down or back, but stares straight ahead, urging the horses forward, always forward, every death bringing him closer to the gates of Troy, closer to the moment when he will fight and kill Hector.

Blood, shit and brains—and there he is, the son of Peleus, half beast, half god, driving on to glory.

35

Five days it lasted, and during all that time he scarcely slept. It was difficult to look at him, his eyes so raw with weeping and his face, under the streaks of dirt, white and drawn.

Each day began before dawn with a visit to Patroclus's bier. I'd unwind the linen cloth we'd wrapped tightly round his head to keep the flies out and then I'd stand well back, sick to my stomach with the smell of rancid meat. *Burn him, for god's sake*, I wanted to say, and I wasn't the only one wanting to say it. But Achilles didn't seem to notice any change in Patroclus. Before leaving, he always bent down and kissed him on the mouth, though the lips had darkened and begun to retract. Even with linen strips wound round his head it was difficult to keep the mouth closed. After Achilles left, the laundresses gathered round the bier, muttering to themselves, but I didn't stop to hear what they had to say.

After dinner, he went to see Patroclus again, but at night nobody was allowed to go into the room with him. Once, I thought I heard him say "Not yet," meaning, I suppose, that Hector was still alive. Alcimus lingered outside the half-open door, peering round it, now and then, to see Achilles standing by the slab, his bowed head resting on Patroclus's chest. Late one night, he groaned aloud and Alcimus put his hand on the door.

I grabbed his arm. *"No."*

"He shouldn't be left alone."

"He *is* alone."

After a while, he nodded and stepped back.

———

The Trojans were fighting now right under the walls of Troy. As soon as the Myrmidons marched off to the battlefield, I'd climb into the stern of Achilles's ship and watch. I was there when, on the morning of the fifth day, the Trojan line finally broke. Even then, I expected them to regroup, but the huge gates swung open and the Trojan fighters ran inside. Priam was leaning over the parapet beckoning Hector to take refuge inside the walls. Hecuba even bared her old woman's wrinkled dugs, pleading with her son to save himself, but Hector wouldn't. Instead, he turned his back on home and safety and walked out to face Achilles, alone.

I couldn't bear to go on watching. I went back to the hut and told the other women what I'd seen. We knew we were witnessing the last days of Troy and with the city's death would go our last hope of being freed. Yet still the endless routine of weaving went on, the shuttles flew to and fro, inch by inch the cloth grew, perhaps because the women were afraid that if they stopped, if they broke the thread, the world would break too and carry them away.

But then, above the relentless rattle of the shuttles, we heard a new sound. We had to strain to hear it above the clacking of the looms and no doubt some of us managed to convince ourselves it was the cry of gulls we heard—that hysterical, yapping call they sometimes make—but no, these were women's voices and the noise went on and on. Gradually, one by one, the looms stopped and, in the silence that washed over us, we heard the cry of lamentation more clearly than before; and we knew that Hector, the last and greatest defender of Troy, was dead.

PART THREE

36

At first, I couldn't think what it was. When, finally, Achilles drove his chariot into the stable yard I could see something fastened to the back, bumping over the rutted ground, but it must have been five minutes before I realized the torn and bloody lump was Hector. The Myrmidons were buzzing with excitement. Not only had Achilles killed Hector, he'd driven his corpse three times round the walls of Troy, while Priam, Hector's father, stood on the battlements looking down, watching his strong and handsome son reduced to a bag of leaking guts.

That was the moment the Greeks won the war. And everybody knew it. I expected singing and dancing, but instead Achilles had Patroclus's bier carried to the training ground, where he ordered his Myrmidons to drive their chariots in a circle round it. Faster and faster they went, horses snorting, whips cracking, clouds of dust rising from under the churning wheels . . . Only when horses and men were sweating and exhausted did Achilles get down from his own chariot, walk across to the bier and place his hands, red with Hector's blood, side by side on Patroclus's chest. "Hector's dead," he told him. "Everything I promised you, I've done. You can sleep now."

It was a solemn moment after the tumult of battle. The Myrmidons fell silent and many of them wept.

But if Achilles was content to mark the moment of his greatest triumph with a renewed outpouring of grief, Agamemnon was definitely not. Not only did he announce a great feast in Achilles's honour, but actually came in person to escort Achilles to his compound, attended by many of the other kings. There was a good deal of drinking, back-slapping and laughter as they strolled up and down the yard. Achilles did his best to laugh with the rest of them, but he seemed dazed, as if he didn't know who these people were or why he was expected to talk to them.

He looked hollow, I thought. All that killing, all that revenge . . . Perhaps he'd managed to convince himself that if he did all that—killed Hector, defeated the Trojan army, broke Priam—Patroclus would keep his side of the bargain and stop being dead. We all try to make crazy deals with the gods, often without really knowing we're doing it. And so there he was—he'd done it all, kept every promise—but Patroclus's body was still just a body. An absence.

But he had to go to the feast. Any "invitation" from Agamemnon had the force of a command. And besides, they were, officially, friends.

After Achilles departed with the other kings, the Myrmidons settled down to their own celebration. Iphis and I were kept busy carrying round jugs of wine, until Automedon abruptly ordered us back to the safety of the women's huts and told us to bar the doors. He knew there was a wild night ahead.

I couldn't sleep. Partly, I suppose, it was the noise, the cheers, the singing . . . but also the thought of Hector lying out there on the muddy ground, mutilated and alone.

After a while I got up, selected a sheet of pure white linen, pulled my mantle close round my face and crept out to the stables. Though I'd made scarcely any sound, the horses knew at once I was there. One kicked its stable door, others started weaving and turning; I saw glints of eye white here and there along the rows of tossing heads. The corpse was lying in the middle of the yard—so badly broken, it hardly retained the shape of a man. I made myself go closer. There was just enough light to see by, though after one quick glance I was glad to look away. I spread the linen sheet gently over his poor ruined face and tiptoed away, leaving him alone under the indifferent stars.

37

Yet more wine; with much stamping of feet and cheering, the cups are raised again.

Why was he born so beautiful?
Why was he born at all?
He's no fucking use to anyone!
He's no fucking use at all!

Men at the surrounding tables bang on the boards with cups and fists, but those sitting close by beat time on *him*, slapping his arms, his shoulders, his head, his thighs—any bit of him they can reach. They can't get enough of him, they can't stop touching him, but his whole body aches from the fighting. There isn't an inch of him that doesn't hurt.

And the feast seems to go on for ever. He wants to go home—or what passes for home now Patroclus isn't in it. He needs darkness and silence at least. But still huge jugs of strong wine are carried from table to table and every few minutes somebody else jumps up and proposes a toast. Achilles drinks and drinks again, because he has to, because there's no choice. Laughing, sweating faces dissolve into a blur . . . There's some sort of joke doing the rounds, people keep nudging each other, whispering . . . Can they persuade him to have a bath? That seems to be the gist of it. *Look at him! Look at the state of him, look at his* hair . . . ! He forces a grin to show he doesn't mind, he's taking it in good part. But then, abruptly, he stands up. "Need a piss," he says, when somebody asks where he's going, but all the way to the door he's surrounded by men wanting to slap him on the back and congratulate him. They buzz around him like hornets, landing playful punches on his arms and chest. All of this hurts, and deep inside, where there should be joy and laughter, there's only a sunless pit.

Outside, he leans on the wall of a stable block and watches his piss trickle over the flagstones at his feet. The lighted hall's a little over to his right, but he knows he doesn't want to go back in. It's nearly dawn, for god's sake, surely he's done enough? Anyway, they're all so drunk there's a good chance he won't be missed. So he sets off to walk back to his own compound along the beach. Waves seethe and fret around his feet, the sea's ragged breathing echoes his own. Inland, campfires are blazing all around the curve of the bay. He knows he'd be welcome at any one of those fires, and yet he's never felt more completely excluded, more alone, in his life.

Agamemnon, just now, pretending to share his grief for Patroclus . . . Bastard was over the moon when Patroclus was killed, because he knew it would bring Achilles back into the war . . . Nothing else would have done it. No, if he wants to be with anybody tonight, it's his own Myrmidons, who at least share his sense of loss, but then, as he gets closer to his ships, he realizes he doesn't want them either. No, he's better off out here on his own . . . Might even sleep here, on the beach. Why not? He's done it before.

Swim first? Everybody seems to think he's overdue for a bath. Perhaps they have a point? He lifts his fingers to his face and smells the fish-scale stink of dried blood, then raises his arms and sniffs his armpits. Oh my god, yes, they have a point. Without bothering to undress, he walks straight into the sea. Waves slap against his thighs, groin, belly, chest, each swell lifting him up and letting him drop until, at last, a wave bigger than the rest closes over his head.

He lets it drag him down; down, down, into a green, silent world, *his* world—or it might be, if it wasn't for the searing pain in his lungs. Surfacing with a shriek of indrawn breath, he turns on his back and floats, letting himself drift to and fro with the tide.

There's a sprinkling of stars, fading fast as the sun's power starts to gather on the rim of the world. He's crying, salt water trickling into salt water, pissing again too—he feels the stream briefly warm at the top of his thigh—everything streaming out of him, the grief, the pain, the loss, until finally he achieves a kind of hollow peace.

Back on dry land, the grind of his feet climbing the shingle shuts off every other sound. He seems to be weaving from side to side. Drunk? Is he drunk? No idea, can't remember how much he had to drink—certainly didn't eat—only something's wrong, he feels ... weird, as if he's being stretched out very tight and thin. Never mind, whatever it is it'll pass. Hector's dead, that's the main thing. It's *over.* He repeats the word every time his right foot hits the pebbles. O-ver, o-ver, o-ver. Hector's dead; Troy can't survive without Hector—and the decisive blow in the entire war has been struck *by him.*

He scrabbles about in the corners of his mind for some faint echo of the praise heaped on him by the other kings, but it's not there. Killing Hector isn't enough. He knew that the minute he did it. What he really wanted to do was eat him—there aren't many people he'd say that to, but it's the truth. He'd wanted to rip Hector's throat out with his teeth. That's why he'd dragged the corpse three times round the walls of Troy, knowing Priam was watching, and even that was no more than a pale substitute for the taste of Hector's flesh on his tongue.

Sleep. He sits down, feeling the sand silky under his fingertips and then—digging deeper—hard, damp and cold. His eyes are sore, his lids scrape painfully across the iris every time he blinks. Even this far away from the camp, he can hear drunken singing, his own men, carefree around the campfires, stuffing themselves with food and drink. He could still join them—drink till he can't stand up, among men he loves and trusts. Or, if not, there's a soft bed waiting for him, fires lit, bread and olives on the table, a jug of wine set ready to pour . . . But no Patroclus. No, he's better off out here, with the sting of salt water sharp on his cracked lips and his chest rising and falling to the rhythm of the sea.

He lies back, wiggling his shoulder blades to make hollows in the sand. Black spikes of marram grass score the sky like the strings of a broken lyre and immediately he thinks of *his* lyre that he can't play anymore—hasn't played once since Patroclus died. Leave it, *leave it*. He blinks several times, a big baby fighting to stay awake, and abruptly falls into a sleep that's as sparse and threadbare as the light.

A few minutes later, gagging, mouth wide open, tongue dry, struggling to speak, he's awake again. Or is he? He can see the slopes of shingle and the clumps of marram grass waving above his head, but the dream hasn't stopped. Patroclus is bending over him—and not some etiolated ghost either, but the man himself, as strong and vigorous as he'd been in life. But antagonistic, almost hostile, as in life he'd never been.

You're neglecting me, Achilles.

No, he tries to say, but can't. Can't speak. Can't move either. He tries to reach out to Patroclus, but his hands won't work.

You never neglected me when I was alive but you do now.

He wants to say: *I fought Hector for you!*

You haven't even buried me! Do you know what it feels like to have flies laying eggs in your skin?

Who's speaking here? Is it this . . . thing kneeling beside him, this image that looks achingly like Patroclus, or are these thoughts his own? And yet Patroclus looks so *real*; he's even wearing one of the robes he used to wear. Tall, strong . . . The light's changing on his face, as the sun begins to rise.

Burn me, Achilles. The dead won't let me in, they won't let me cross the river, they say I don't belong there, but I don't belong here either. Give my body to the fire, bury my bones in the golden urn your mother gave you. It's big enough for two. Let's lie together in death as we did in life.

Fuck "lie together in death," he wants Patroclus in his arms right now. He tries again to reach out, but his hands still won't move.

Remember how we used to sit together after dinner and make plans? I can't think of it now without crying . . .

So let's cry together, he wants to say. *Let's sit down and howl like wolves over everything we've lost.*

And suddenly, the bonds that have kept him dumb and paralysed drop away. With a cry he reaches out for the living man he sees in front of him, but Patroclus's spirit slips between his fingers and vanishes, with a little, squeaking cry, into the ground.

There's nothing left. Nothing at all. But he *was* there. To the end of his life, he'll believe Patroclus came back and spoke to him. Rolling onto his knees, he quickly scoops out a hole in the silvery sand, clawing his way down to the dark, moist layer underneath. Then, with both hands, working feverishly, he builds a miniature burial mound to mark the place where Patroclus was. He knows once the body has been burned, the spirit can't return.

But Hector's dead. He clings to that—that's a real, solid achievement. And yet, in this strange, liminal space, caught between sea and land, between life and death, he actually begins to doubt it. If Patroclus is alive—and he's just seen him, he's just heard him speak—is Hector really dead?

That's what he needs to do now: see Hector, piss on whatever's left of him, and then give Patroclus funeral games fit for a king.

Slowly, he walks back to the camp. The darkness is thinning fast, but still the feasting goes on, men with glazed eyes staggering about too drunk to recognize their own mothers. Wrapping his damp cloak round him, he slips silently between the huts, making for the stable yard. Once there, he stops. Hector's body lies in the filth where he left him, only now it's covered up. Somebody's thrown a sheet over it. He can't believe any of his men would do that, and yet who else? A slave wouldn't dare.

As he moves closer, he's caught in a tide race of impressions. What he left here was a bag of broken bones, but the body under the white sheet has the length and shape of a man. His eyes see the change, but his brain can't accept it. Somebody's been playing tricks; this isn't Hector's body. It can't be. Slowly, very slowly—he's ashamed of how much courage it takes—he bends down and pulls the sheet away.

Hector's face, flawless, as if he were alive, gazes up at him. The eyes are open, but apart from that one detail he might be asleep, at home in a royal bed with his wife, Andromache, by his side. Achilles can't stop staring at the eyes. His fingers itch to close the lids, not to have to go on looking into that blank vacancy, but closing them would be a mark of respect—he won't do that, he'd sooner gouge them out. In fact, he does neither, simply straightens up and looks around the yard as if expecting to see the culprit lurking there.

Nobody. The stables are deserted, everybody's feasting round the fires. But in any case, he's being stupid, because no human being could have done this. It has to be the work of the gods. Well, then—*FUCK THE GODS*. He throws back his head and yells his defiance. All around the yard, horses' heads toss, hooves trample, shadows chase each other across the walls . . . Achilles shouts and shouts again, his war cry ringing round the yard. He won't be beaten, not even by the gods. As soon as the sun's up, he'll tie Hector's body even more tightly to his chariot and drive full tilt round the camp, and this time he won't stop till every bone's broken, every feature smashed . . . Nobody's going to cheat him out of his revenge, not even a god.

38

Women don't attend cremations, so I wasn't there when Patroclus was burned, though I heard about it later from Alcimus. Alcimus had started talking non-stop, stammering over the words, almost as if he daren't pause long enough to think. He loved Achilles, but he was afraid of him too, and—increasingly, I think—afraid *for* him.

Achilles kept his word, everything he'd promised Patroclus he did. He cut the throats of twelve Trojan youths, dragging their heads back by the hair and pulling his knife across their throats as quickly and cleanly as if they'd been goats. He killed Patroclus's horses too and threw them on the fire, followed by his favourite dogs, the two that had lived with them in their hut. So much blood, Alcimus said, he wondered how they'd ever get the pyre to burn, but burn it did in the end.

From the doorways of the women's huts, we saw flames and sparks leaping high into the night sky. I put my arms round Iphis, who was standing beside me, and led her back inside. "What's going to happen to me now?" she kept saying. And I couldn't answer because I didn't know. Iphis had been kind to me when I first arrived in the camp. At least, now, I could repay some of her kindness.

During the funeral games, the women were kept busy behind the scenes, preparing food and wine, but we didn't serve drinks at dinner. It's the Greek custom for young men to wait on their elders at such times. Nor were we officially present at the games, though we crept out of the huts now and then to watch some of the contests. Achilles was everywhere, judging races, awarding prizes, so tactful, so adept at resolving minor disputes before they escalated into full-blown quarrels that I scarcely knew him. He seemed to be turning into Patroclus. Only the eyes were still Achilles's eyes, inflamed and difficult to meet.

Mainly, I stayed in the women's huts in Achilles's compound. Sometimes, I'd invite the other "prizes" over to share a meal and a jug of wine. I remember, on one of those occcasions, looking across the room and seeing Tecmessa deep in conversation with Iphis. You could hardly imagine a greater contrast: Iphis, so pale and delicate; Tecmessa, red-faced, sweating profusely as she attacked a dish of lamb and herbs. No two women could have been more different and yet, in one crucial respect, they were alike: they'd each grown to love their captors. That raised an uncomfortable question for me. I'll be honest, I despised Tecmessa, and yet it would never for a second have occurred to me to despise Iphis. I wondered whether my contempt for Tecmessa was anything other than blind prejudice against a woman who'd so often patronized me. I didn't think so, but I couldn't be sure. I only knew I liked Iphis, even loved her, and perhaps it was easy for me to understand why she'd loved Patroclus because I'd grown to love him too.

I've said Achilles awarded prizes—oh, and what prizes they were! Nothing was too much for him to give in memory of Patroclus: armour, tripods, horses, dogs, women ... Iphis. He made her first prize in the chariot race. We had no warning. When Automedon came to fetch her, we were sitting in one of the women's huts, mending clothes. She tried to hold on to me, but relentlessly Automedon worked her fingers loose and dragged her out into the yard. All the women followed and watched as she stood there, shivering in a cold wind off the sea, waiting to find out who her new owner would be.

It was a thrilling finish. All the men shouted and cheered as Diomedes crossed the line and, laughing in triumph, reined his horses in. Face streaked with dirt from the track, he jumped down and walked across the yard to greet Achilles, who pointed to Iphis as the prize. Diomedes tilted Iphis's head from side to side, exactly as Achilles had done to me, then nodded, satisfied, and turned to embrace Achilles. They stayed like that for a long time, their hands on each other's shoulders, talking and laughing together, while in the background one of Diomedes's aides took Iphis by the arm and led her away.

As the crowd opened up before them, she turned and looked back, straight at me: one last, agonized glance, and she was gone.

————

The funeral games ended with the chariot race, the captains and the kings departed and Achilles was back to presiding over dinner, alone. Once, I'd followed every move he made, registered every minute change in his expression; now, I was afraid to look at him. This man had twice said, once to my face and once in front of the entire army, that he wished me dead. I didn't think he'd kill me, but I did think he might sell me on to a slave trader. Any importance I'd once had as his prize of honour was long gone. So I kept my head down, filling first one cup and then another, up and down the long tables, till I could escape and go to bed.

The men were subdued; Achilles's grief cast a pall over the gathering. I didn't feel sorry for him. And though I grieved for Patroclus, even my grief for him was marinated in bitterness. Yes, he'd been a good man, yes, he'd been kind to me, but he'd been cremated with all the honours due to a king's son. My brothers had been left to rot.

Although, as I say, I avoided looking at Achilles, I was always aware of him, sitting at the table he'd once shared with Patroclus, in this crowded hall, surrounded by men who adored him, utterly alone.

As was I. With Patroclus dead and Iphis gone, I was more alone than I'd ever been. Up to the moment Iphis was taken away, I'd have said I was inured to loss, but evidently I wasn't, because I missed her desperately. I was friendly with most of the women in Achilles's compound, but there was nobody else I was close to, or wanted to be close to. I just sat, blankly, at the loom, served the wine at dinner, trudged mile after mile along the beach; expected nothing. After each meal, I went back to the women's hut, climbed into the bed I'd once shared with Iphis and pulled the covers over my head.

———————

Then —I suppose it must've been four or five nights after the funeral games were over—this period of bleak peace came to an end. At dinner, just as I'd finished serving the first round of drinks, Automedon beckoned me across to him and said, "Achilles wants you tonight."

My legs turned to sand. I didn't know if I should continue serving drinks or put the jug down and go at once. Automedon gave me no guidance; he'd already turned away. Not knowing what else to do, I just went on pouring wine till the meal was over and then slipped out of the hall. I combed my hair, bit my lips, pinched my cheeks and went to sit in the cupboard where I'd been put on my first night in the camp. I remembered how I'd stroked the woollen coverlet on the bed, tracing the pattern with my fingertips, as if by escaping into its loops and whorls I might never have to think or feel again. Then Patroclus had come in and given me a cup of wine. And the next night, and most of the other nights after that, Iphis had been there.

No such comfort now. Shivering, I sat on the bed until I heard voices in the passage outside: Automedon and Alcimus on their way to share a last cup of wine with Achilles. I peered through a crack in the door and saw Patroclus's empty chair. No dogs, and that surprised me, I was so used to seeing them stretched out by the fire, but then I remembered Achilles had sacrificed them on Patroclus's funeral pyre. Oh, I could see it happening. He'd have called them to him, slapping his thighs, saying, "Here, boy! Here!" And they'd have crawled to him on their bellies, tails wagging, nervously licking their

PAT BARKER

lips, knowing something bad was going to happen, but compelled to go to him anyway. Perhaps, after all, Iphis had been lucky, awarded as first prize in a chariot race. He'd cut the dogs' throats.

Finally the conversation in the other room ended; Automedon and Alcimus were taking their leave. After they'd gone, there was a long silence, or it seemed long to me. Then, heavy footsteps approached the door. Slowly, Achilles pushed it open, the slit of light widening to cover the floor. He looked at me and jerked his head towards the other room.

I followed him in, taking a seat as far away from him as I could get. Patroclus's empty chair dominated the room. Compared with that compelling absence, even Achilles seemed insubstantial. The lyre in its cocoon of oiled cloth lay on the table by his chair, but he didn't pick it up. I hadn't heard him play once since I'd returned to his compound.

The silence was choking the breath out of me. When I could bear it no longer, I said, "Why don't you play?"

"Can't. Won't work."

In bed, in the dark, I was the lyre. He fumbled about, sucking my breasts hard as if trying to remember what it was that had once excited him. This went on for a few minutes, then he climbed on top and tried to stuff his limp cock inside me. I put my hand down, squeezing and stroking, meaning to help, and not helping, making everything worse. I was afraid of what failure would mean—not for *him*, for *me*. When it became clear nothing was going to happen, he groaned and rolled over onto his back. I slid down the bed and took his cock in my mouth, shlurping away as if I'd just discovered a particularly juicy pear; but however hard I tried it stayed as soft as a baby's.

After a while I gave up and lay on my back beside him. I knew anything I said would be dangerous, so I said nothing. He was so quiet he might have been asleep, but I could tell from his breathing he wasn't. I said: "Would you like me to go?"

In reply, he turned on his side away from me. I slipped out of bed and groped about for my clothes. The fire was almost dead, the lamps had all burned low. I found my tunic and pulled it on quickly—back to front, as I discovered later—and felt my way to the door. I couldn't remember where I'd put my sandals and I was too frightened to stay and look for them. On the veranda, I stood for a moment, taking long, deep breaths. Returning to the women's huts, as early as this, would let everybody know I'd fallen from favour—*if* they didn't know already. Nobody would be nasty, but everybody would take note. I could think of at least two girls who'd be fancying their chances of taking my place.

I didn't care if another girl became the favourite. Only I thought the slave market had just moved a step closer—and I cared a great deal about that. I told myself it wasn't too bad. He hadn't hit me, hadn't lashed out in frustration—in fact, he hadn't done any of the things he might well have done. So I wrapped my arms round myself for comfort and rocked from side to side. Then, when I was more or less calm again, I set off across the hard sand to the women's huts, barefoot, in the dark.

39

He can't sleep. Can't eat, can't sleep, can't play the lyre—and now, apparently, can't fuck ... *Useless.* He turns first one way, then the other, pulls the bedclothes up to his chin, pushes them down again, throws his arms and legs across the full width of the bed, curls up into a ball—and all the time thinking about Patroclus. Not thinking, *craving.* The shape of his head, that little dent just below the bridge of his nose, the lopsided grin, broad shoulders, narrow waist, the biscuity-brown smell of his skin. The way they were together.

He hadn't known grief was like this, so much like physical pain. He can't keep still. Surely he ought to be better than this by now? He's done everything he promised, killed Hector, cut the throats of twelve Trojan youths and used their bodies as kindling for Patroclus's funeral pyre. He's raked about among the hot ashes and collected his friend's charred bones, right down to the knuckle bones and the small bones of the feet, and buried them in a golden urn—big enough to hold his bones too, when the time comes—which, please god, will not be long.

Now, he can see what he's been trying to do: to bargain with grief. Behind all this frenetic activity there's been the hope that if he keeps his promises there'll be no more pain. But he's beginning to understand that grief doesn't strike bargains. There's no way of avoiding the agony—or even of getting through it faster. It's got him in its claws and it won't let go till he's learnt every lesson it has to teach.

When, eventually, he sleeps, he slides at once into the same dream, the one he dreams every night. He's in a dark tunnel. As he gropes his way along it, he stumbles repeatedly over bulky shapes barely visible in the gloom. As he treads on one, its distended belly squelches under his feet. Since he can't see them, he has no way of telling whether the faces he steps on are Trojan or Greek, and in this place, this funereal place, bereft of light and colour, it scarcely seems to matter. He'd like to believe he's in the cellars of a palace—Priam's palace, perhaps. Which means they've taken Troy and, in spite of all his mother's dire warnings, he's lived to see it, to be part of it—and now he's down here in the cellars searching for frightened women who've hidden themselves away. He knows they're here, now and then he thinks he hears the rustle of a skirt; and he can smell their fear.

He desperately wants to believe this, though at the same time every stiffening hair on his head is telling him that this is Hades and the shapes that surround him are the dead.

So he concentrates hard on the life inside his own body, tensing his arms, flexing his muscles, taking deep, painfully deep, breaths. Gradually, as he inches forward, the murk begins to clear. Soon there's light enough to make the desolation visible. The dead lie like bundles of old rags, bloated inside their battle shirts. Trojan or Greek? He still can't tell. He looks more closely, drawing back folds of cloaks and blankets—even begins shaking shoulders and arms, trying to make them wake up, because it's lonely down here, it's lonely being the last man left alive. No response. Blackened faces look up at him, eyes as dull as dead fish in their lidless sockets. Oh, they need the fire, these men, the cleansing fire, and he'd give it to them if he could. Trojan or Greek—nobody should be left to rot like this, unburied and unmourned. Then, as he probes them, one springs up and stares with piteous recognition in fixed eyes . . .

Friend, it says.

And immediately he knows who it is. Lycaon, Priam's son. The one he hasn't been able to forget.

I don't know you, he tries to say, and the effort of moving his lips wakes him.

He sits up and gazes wildly around him, terrified he might have brought that undead, unclean thing back with him. Only when he's sure there's nothing lurking in the shadows does he let himself flop back against the pillows. He can smell his own fear-sweat; his groin's a swamp. For one horrible moment, he thinks he might have wet the bed, as he sometimes used to do, that first dreadful winter after his mother left, but no—feeling the sheet underneath him—no, it's all right, it's only sweat. Throwing off the covers, he lets the air get to his skin.

Why Lycaon? He's killed dozens of men since Patroclus died, hundreds since the beginning of the war—so why, out of all that welter of blood and slaughter, should this one man emerge? It's that word "friend." It incensed him at the time and it's haunted him ever since. Certainly, there was nothing memorable about Lycaon himself, who looked like a drowned rat when Achilles first saw him, crawling out of the river, his armour pulled off in the struggle to stay afloat. The river was in full spate, greedily snatching every corpse Achilles threw into it and chuckling as it carried them away.

For Achilles, those few minutes were a brief respite from the battle, barely long enough to draw breath. But long or short, the break was over now, because there he was, or there *it* was, this worm, this maggot, this drowned rat of a man with no helmet, no shield, no spear because he'd thrown them all away in his desperation to live. He—*it*—was crawling up the muddy bank on its hands and knees. Achilles said nothing, merely waited with a predator's cruel poise for the sodden wretch to recognize him and be afraid.

To be fair, Lycaon didn't try to run, but then he had nowhere to run to, the river behind him and Achilles in front. Instead, he—*it*—

ran forward, clasped his knees and began pleading for its life. Achilles looked and listened, felt nothing, no glimmer of awareness that he and this thing were men breathing the same air. And god, how it talked, betraying everything in its desperation to escape death. It wasn't Hector's *brother*, he said, not really, oh, well, yes, admittedly, yes, the same father, but not the same mother, and as for Hector— well, he hardly knew him! And he'd had nothing to do with the death of Patroclus. Have mercy, Achilles. Think what your friend would do—your good, kind, brave, *gentle* friend.

That word.

So die *friend*, he'd said. Why make such a fuss about it? Patroclus is dead and he was a far better man than you.

Raising his sword, he stabbed the firm young throat just beside the collarbone, driving the blade in as far as it would go. Lycaon fell forward, his red blood gushing and puddling on the muddy ground. Even before he finished twitching, Achilles picked him up by the ankle and hurled him into the river, where he floated for several minutes, his war shirt ballooning out around him, before the current caught him and carried him away. Achilles stood on the bank and watched until the body vanished from sight. The fishes would have glutted themselves on his glistening kidney fat long before he reached the sea. No funeral rites for him, no cleansing fire. No mercy at all for Trojans now.

And now he dreams about the bastard every night! Why, *why*, in god's name, since he's apparently condemned to spend his nights with the dead, does he never dream of Patroclus? Thrusting the covers aside, he levers himself to his full height and pads across to the mirror, where he stares long and hard at his reflection, while, in the room behind him, the spirit of Patroclus begins to gather. He feels its presence, but he doesn't bother to turn round, because he knows from repeated disappointments there'll be nothing there. Nothing to see, anyway—and certainly no warm, living body to hold.

He leans in closer to his reflection, so close his breath mists the mirror.

So die, friend. Why make such a fuss about it? Patroclus is dead and he was a far better man than you.

Nothing and nobody replies. Defeated, he shambles back to the bed. Oh, yes. Swift-footed Achilles, who once seemed made of air and fire, shambles now. Plods. Lumbers. Trudges. His body, leaden with the death inside him, weighs heavily on the earth.

It must be near dawn. Giving up any idea of sleep, he pulls on his tunic and leaves the hut, going straight to the stables where Hector lies face down in the dirt. Nobody dares cover him up or show any other mark of respect. That one small act of rebellion—throwing a sheet across his body—has never been repeated. Heavy-footed, Achilles walks across the yard, his toes slipping inside his sandals. Despite the pre-dawn cold, his body's still slick with sweat. He scarcely seems human, even to himself, so it's no surprise when the horses shift uneasily from side to side.

He takes long, deep, experimental breaths. Why do his lungs hurt when he breathes? Perhaps they've decided to close down a week or two before the rest of him? Or is he starting to develop gills? That's one of the things the men say about him behind his back. Gills, webbed feet ... Well, with a sea goddess for a mother, what do you expect? In fact, his toes *are* webbed, as indeed his mother's are; though on her the extra skin's translucent. On him, it's thick and yellow; he's ashamed of it. Another thing Patroclus knew about him that nobody else knows: that he's ashamed of his feet. A lot of him went on to the fire with Patroclus, because what isn't shared ceases to seem quite real, perhaps even ceases to *be* real.

The grooms look up as he approaches, clear their throats, nod respectfully, though with no hint of servility. The Myrmidons are like that. Renowned throughout the world for their courage, dedication to duty and unquestioning obedience. Well, the courage and dedication are real enough ... Unquestioning obedience? Forget it. They're not impressed by royal blood—or even divine blood—their respect has to be earned. He knows he's earned it a thousand times over in the last nine years and yet, just recently, he's noticed ... Not withdrawal, exactly, but a degree of wariness. It's not his anger that bothers them—under a generally taciturn exterior these men are often angry—no, it's his ability to hold a grudge. *All right*, they probably wanted to say, *he took your girl, your prize of honour, he's insulted you—so bloody well fuck off home, then!* They've never understood why he kept them here, on this shithole of a beach, sitting around like a load of old grannies while, less than a mile away, men who'd once been their comrades fought and died.

But that's the past, they should have forgotten it by now. Perhaps they have. Perhaps it's what he does now, every morning, that sticks in their throats.

He lays his hand on the chariot rail where, for so many years, Patroclus stood, the reins strapped round his waist. Every morning, the same memory; every morning, the same stab of pain, sharp enough to make him catch his breath. But it's second nature to him to conceal any sign of weakness. And so he walks round the chariot, scanning every inch, bending down now and then to inspect the underside of the carriage. By the end of a hard day's fighting, there's so much blood and filth it clogs his chariot wheels. And the grooms are lazy—if they think they can get away with a shortcut they will. Oh, they don't neglect the horses—they'll feed the horses before they feed themselves—but they're perfectly capable of nipping down the beach to fill their buckets with seawater, though they must know that, over the years, salt will corrode even the finest metal. He keeps telling them: water from the well. *Not* seawater. Kneeling down, he licks his finger, runs it along one of the spokes and tests it on his tongue. No, it's all right.

Standing up, he feels exhausted. Every bit of energy seems to have drained out of him. Perhaps not this morning? Perhaps just this once he can give it a miss, go back to bed and sleep? But no, his anger whips him on, the unappeasable rage he has to go on trying to appease, like a beggar covered in sores who scratches till his nails draw blood and still can't find the itch.

The men won't look at him. All the time he's here they keep

busy, carrying buckets of water, polishing, rubbing, breathing on the metal, checking the gloss, rubbing again. Nervous, because he's watching them; making mistakes, because he's watching them. And so he forces himself to turn away. Nobody looks him in the face now, it's as if his grief frightens them. What are they afraid of? That one day they'll have to endure pain like this? Or that they never will, that they're incapable of it, because grief's only ever as deep as the love it's replaced.

The work goes a lot quicker once his back's turned. So he leaves the yard altogether, letting them get on with it, and when he returns, ten minutes later, it's all done. The bronze guard rails glitter, the horses' coats shine. The men are tense till he inspects the work. They're expecting, at best, a terse nod, a grunt of approval, but he surprises them, flashing a smile, making eye contact, thanking them, individually, before he takes the reins. They nod and mumble and back away. People always back out of his presence, they've been doing it since he was seventeen. Perhaps it's a tribute to his prowess on the battlefield, or fear of his anger, or for some other darker reason he doesn't want to have to think about. Instead, he rests his forehead against a horse's muzzle, feeling its breath warm on his skin, and this contact with a non-human creature makes him feel almost human again.

Now for Hector. His ankles are still roped together and fastened to the axle bar. He checks the knots, jerks them tighter and only then kicks the corpse over onto its back. Last night, he'd dumped a torn and bloody mess of broken bones into the filth of the stable yard; this morning, yet again, Hector looks like he's asleep, a deep, calm, peaceful sleep—the sleep that every night eludes Achilles. He'd like to throw back his head and howl. Instead, he climbs into the chariot and begins to turn the horses round. Behind him, Hector's body bumps over the rutted ground, slowly at first, then faster, as he drives out of the yard, out of the compound, away from the beach, away from the battlefield, up the stony track that leads to the promontory where the dead are burned.

How high the flames shot into the sky the night he burned Patroclus, how the blood of the Trojan captives jumped and sizzled on the burning logs. Twelve youths he'd promised Patroclus and twelve he got: tall, strong, young men, the pride of their families, but passive at the end, resigned, as bulls sometimes are before the sacrifice.

At the very last moment, before lighting the fire, he'd cut his own hair, hacking through the thick braids and twining them round Patroclus's fingers. Before setting sail for Troy, he'd vowed not to cut his hair until he returned home. Standing on the windswept promontory, he watched the thick ropes of hair shrivel, seeming almost to melt before they vanished in a spurt of blue flame. With the breaking of that vow, he'd abandoned all hope of seeing his father again. Like his mother said, his death follows hard upon Hector's. He feels it. He knows he won't be going home. A few days, weeks at the most, and then—nothing.

The urn is invisible beneath the great mound the Myrmidons raised for Patroclus, though as clear and present to his mind as the day he placed Patroclus's bones, one by one, inside it. Knuckle bones— recalling the games of dice they'd played as children; long thigh bones—bringing back other memories of summer nights on this beach, nine years ago, when they first came to Troy; and finally the skull. He'd run his scorched fingertips over the cranium and around the empty eye sockets, remembering flesh, remembering hair.

Now, with a great shout, he slaps the reins against the horses' necks and sets off at full gallop round the grave.

Below him, in the camp, men polishing armour stop what they're doing and look up, grooms glance at each other, thinking what state the horses will be in when they get back, focusing on that because they're too frightened to think of anything else. Again and again, Achilles's war cry drifts across the camp, as he drives his sweating horses faster and faster round the burial mound.

By the time he returns, Hector's body has been reduced to a mass of red pulp and splintered bone. The face is flayed—beyond recognition. Achilles jumps to the ground, throws his reins at a tight-lipped groom and strides down the narrow passage that leads from the stables to his hut. Briseis is coming towards him—seeing her startles him, in the half-light she looks like Thetis. He smells her fear as she flattens herself against the wall.

Once inside his living quarters, he returns to the mirror. He does this every morning now, it's become part of the routine. He knows what he's going to see, but he needs to make himself see it, to prove he's not afraid. Reflected back from the shining metal, the injuries he's just inflicted on Hector lie like shadows on his own skin. Is this why they won't look at him, the grooms who run to take his reins?

But then he moves a little to the right, the shadows lift and it's his own face looking back at him again. They're illusions, those marks on his skin, but he sees them every morning and every night and it's difficult not to believe they're real.

Shivering, he goes in search of the sun. Standing on the veranda steps, he looks around him at the waking camp. Fires are burning, the preparations for his dinner already well under way. Herbs are being ground to flavour his meat. Looms are clattering, making clothes for his back and covers for his bed. Round the corner in the stable yard, men are grooming his horses and polishing his chariot and soon Alcimus will arrive to put the finishing touches to his armour. He's in control of everything he sees.

But every morning, he's compelled to drive his chariot round and round Patroclus's grave, to defile Hector's body, and, in the process—as he understands perfectly well—to dishonour himself. And he has no idea how to make any of it stop.

40

After that disastrous night, I didn't expect Achilles to send for me again, but he did. Only two nights later, in fact.

He came into the living quarters, having eaten scarcely anything at dinner, and called for more wine, only to sit staring into the fire, not drinking from the cup I'd poured. Automedon and Alcimus cleared their throats and shifted from side to side in their chairs. Patroclus's empty chair continued to dominate the room.

Achilles let them go early, but he didn't dismiss me. Dreading the night, I sat on the bed and waited. But when, eventually, he stood up it wasn't to get undressed but to fetch a pair of scissors from a carved chest in the corner of the room. He turned his chair round and dragged it across to the mirror, handed me the scissors and held up the hacked-off ends of his hair. "Here," he said. "See what you can do with that."

This was unexpected. I took the scissors and looked about for something to wrap round his shoulders. He'd thrown his battle shirt on the floor by the bed so I used that. Then, pulling a strand of his hair straight between my fingers, I started to cut. A strange feeling, touching him like that; in a way, more intimate than sex. I didn't like it, but after the first few fumbles I was making a pretty good job of his hair. It helped that the scissors were sharp. *Very* sharp. I ran my fingers through his hair to check that the ends were even, and suddenly—no warning—saw him lying on the floor in a pool of blood with the scissors sticking out of his neck. The vision, if that's what it was, brought me to a halt. I just stood there, feeling slightly sick. When I raised my head, I saw him watching me.

"Go on," he said. "Why don't you?"

We stared at each other, or rather we stared at each other's reflections in the mirror. I wanted to say: *Because your precious Myrmidons would torture me to death if I did.* But I knew it would be dangerous to say anything, so I just lowered my head and went on cutting, and this time I was careful not to stop until I'd finished.

From that day, he told me to stay behind every evening after dinner, though he never again asked me to stay the night. *Asked,* I say. Force of habit—there was never any question of asking.

Usually, Automedon and Alcimus would be there too, though he never kept them long. At some point between their departure and bedtime, he'd pick up a torch, tell me to bring another and go out to where Hector's body lay in the filth. Usually he'd kick it over onto its back, lower the torch and examine the face. In the twelve hours that had passed since the last time he'd dragged it round Patroclus's grave, the features had been completely restored. Even the eyes were back in their sockets—he always pushed the lids up to make sure. When he straightened up—and this was the moment I feared most—the injuries he'd inflicted on Hector were stamped on his own face.

Sometimes, it ended there. At other times, he'd check the rope that tied Hector's ankles to his chariot and set off again, driving round and round Patroclus's burial mound in the dark. On those nights, I used to cower in the living quarters, listening for his return, in a state of absolute terror—not for myself, particularly, but because there seemed to be no humanity left in him at all. He'd become an object of . . . I was going to say of pity and terror. But he never inspired pity—and he certainly didn't feel it. Terror, yes. I wasn't the only one to feel that. Automedon and Alcimus, who loved him and would've helped him if they could, even they were afraid.

But they were as trapped as he was in a never-ending cycle of hatred and revenge. And if they couldn't free themselves from it, with all the advantages they had, what hope was there for me?

41

Every night at dinner he sits alone at the table he used to share with Patroclus. Mealtimes are difficult because nobody can eat anything until he does, and his appetite's deserted him. But he does the best he can, forcing himself to chew away with apparent enthusiasm, though he doesn't always manage to swallow what he chews. Instead, he spits little balls of mashed-up meat discreetly into the palm of his hand and secretes them under the edge of his plate. Alcimus and Automedon wait on him and have a drink with him afterwards, though he senses a little impatience as the evening drags on. No doubt they're wanting to get it over with so they can have a drink with their friends or go to bed with a favourite girl. Do either of them have a favourite girl? He has no idea. Patroclus would have known.

Once the last dish has been served, he waves Automedon and Alcimus away. Their constant hovering's beginning to get on his nerves, though to be fair, there's nothing wrong with either of them, apart from the one great, irredeemable flaw of not being Patroclus. Alcimus, particularly, is a good lad, kind-hearted, loyal—brave too, a good fighter. A bit of a fool, perhaps, but then time could sort that out. Automedon's a different matter: tall, lean, a first-rate chari-oteer, but thin-lipped, humourless, full of conscious rectitude. He was there when Patroclus died. He, not Achilles, held the dying man in his arms; he, not Achilles, witnessed the passing of his last breath. He, not Achilles, fought off the Trojans who were trying to drag the body back to Troy—and, because of this, Achilles must be eternally grateful to Automedon and not let him suspect, even for a second, how bitterly he resents him. *Why him? Why not me?* He asks the questions over and over, as if one day they might have a different answer, and the burden of guilt be lifted at last.

Alcimus and Automedon: they're his closest companions now. Thanks to them, he's never alone, and because they're not Patroclus he's never more alone than when he's with them.

He clasps the carved arms of his chair—two snarling heads of mountain lions, finely wrought—and tries to snap out of his torpor, to force himself to rise and thereby give permission for everybody else to leave. But just as he's about to stand up, he notices—not a commotion, exactly—a disturbance of some kind, at the far end of the hall. Somebody's opened the outside door and let in a draught of night air. Torches gutter, smoke swirls, he feels cooler air on his eyelids—and there, suddenly, is an old man, white-haired but not stooped, leaning on a staff, walking towards him. *Father*, he thinks. Though why his father should brave a dangerous sea voyage to visit him here is beyond comprehension; he's never done it before. And, anyway, as the old man comes closer, it's obvious he's nothing like Peleus.

Nobody else seems to have noticed him, which makes the moment feel strange, even a little uncanny—outside the normal order of things.

The old man takes a long time to reach him. It's obvious who he's come to see: his eyes are fixed on Achilles. A peasant farmer, judging by the coarse cloth of his tunic and the rough-hewn staff he's leaning on, though he certainly doesn't carry himself like a peasant. A suspicion's already started to form at the back of Achilles's mind, but faintly, because it's even more improbable than the unheralded arrival of his father. No, not improbable. Impossible.

The man reaches him—he's only two or three feet away now—

and then, with an audible clicking of arthritic joints, lowers himself
to the floor and clasps Achilles's knees—the position of a suppli-
cant. For a moment, everything stays still, though one or two of the
men have begun to exchange puzzled glances. And then the old man
speaks, face to face, not raising his voice, as if there's nobody else
in the room except himself and Achilles, nobody else in the world,
perhaps. Achilles feels the shorn hair at the nape of his neck rise. It's
as if he's looking back from sometime in the unimaginably distant
future and seeing himself seated in a throne-like chair with a tall,
white-haired man kneeling at his feet. There they are, *fixed*, not for
this moment only, but for all time.

A voice jerks him back to the present.

"Achilles." The old man's gasping for breath, as if saying the name
exhausts him: "Achilles."

Just the name, Achilles notices; no title. Despite this abject kneeling at his feet, there's an assumption of equality here. He feels his
hands bunch into fists, but it's just a reflex—he doesn't feel threatened. He could pull this old man apart with his bare hands, as easily
as an overcooked chicken. And yet he *is* afraid . . .

"Priam."

He whispers the name, so the men around him won't hear, and
somehow just saying the word hardens suspicion into fact. Instant
rage. "How the bloody hell did you get in?"

By now, his closest aides are on their feet, guilt and consternation
writ large on every face. They still don't know who this is, but they
know he shouldn't be here. He should never have been able to get
into the compound, let alone walk straight into the hall and reach
Achilles, unchallenged, close enough to touch him, close enough to
kill him, for that matter . . .

Achilles holds up his hand and reluctantly, grumbling like circling dogs, they fall back.

Priam's weeping now, swift, silent tears coursing down his cheeks
and disappearing into the white beard. "Achilles."

"You don't need to keep saying that. I know who I am." Does he?

He's so thrown by this, he's not sure he does anymore. "I asked you a question. How did you get in?"

"I don't know. Guided, I suppose."

"By a god?"

"I believe so."

"*Huh!* Really? You didn't bribe the guards?"

"No, nothing like that." Priam sounds surprised he should even think it. "I heard what you said when I came in."

"I didn't say anything."

"You did; you said: 'Father.'"

Achilles tries to think, but his mind's gone blank. He certainly thought, *Father*, but he's virtually certain he didn't say it aloud; and Priam's reading of his mind only underlines the strangeness of this meeting.

"He'll be an old man now, your father—he can't be a lot younger than me."

"He's nothing like you, he's . . . strong."

"You've been away *nine years*, Achilles . . . You'll see a difference when you get back."

I'm not going back.

He has to stop himself speaking the words aloud, and, oddly, it's not the presence of the old man, his enemy, that restrains him, but the faces crowding round them, red and sweaty in the torchlight: the faces of his friends. He can't bring himself to tell the truth to *them*.

"He'll be missing you. Though at least he's got the consolation of knowing you're still alive . . . My son's dead."

Achilles twists in his chair. "What do you *want*?"

"Hector. I want to take Hector's body home."

The words drop like stones into a well so deep you could spend the rest of your life listening for the *plop* as they hit the water. It's not intentional; if Achilles could speak, he would.

"I've brought a ransom." Priam's visibly forcing himself to press on against the wall of Achilles's silence. "You can see for yourself, it's outside in the cart . . . or send one of your men . . ." Priam looks round the circle of hostile faces and for a moment his voice falters, but then he lifts his head. "Give me my son, Achilles. Think of your father, who's an old man, like me. Honour the gods."

Still, silence.

"You have a son, Achilles. How old is he?"

"Fifteen."

"So, nearly old enough to fight, then?"

"Not yet—he's at home with his mother's father."

"I bet he can't wait to get to Troy. Fight beside his father, prove himself worthy . . . He'll be here soon. How would you feel, Achilles, if it was *your* son's body lying unburied inside *my* gates?"

Achilles shakes his head. Priam grips his knees harder, his fingers digging in: "I do what no man before me has ever done, I kiss the hands of the man who killed my son."

Achilles feels the thin, dry lips brush the back of his hand and the sensation provokes an immediate burst of rage. He wants to lash out, to send this bag of old bones skittering across the floor. He's twitching all over, every muscle tense, but he manages to keep his hands still. Only, when he looks down, he sees there's something wrong with them. They're big at the best of times, a fighter's hands, trained from childhood to wield a sword and spear, but surely they've never been as big as this? He remembers the same thing happening the day Patroclus died. He tries flexing his fingers, but that only makes it worse. Every individual nail's embedded in a red cuticle. Why won't the blood wash out?

Then suddenly his hands belong to him again. He pushes Priam away, but gently, feeling the sharpness of the collarbones under the thin tunic. Then he covers his face and weeps for his father and for Patroclus, for the living and the dead. And Priam, still holding on to the arm of Achilles's chair, weeps for Hector, and for all his other sons who've died in this interminable war.

They're close, these men, so close they're almost touching, but their griefs are parallel, not shared.

All around them, men shift their feet and cough. By now, it's obvious to everybody who the old man is; obvious, but no less incredible for that. Automedon goes to the door, convinced he'll find a contingent of Trojan guards outside, because it's simply not possible that Priam's here, unarmed and alone. The King of Troy driving under cover of darkness into the heart of the Greek camp? No flag of truce, no guaranteed safe passage? No, it's not possible, he'll have brought guards with him at least . . .

But Automedon returns a moment later, shaking his head. There's nobody out there, only a covered farm cart and a pair of mules.

The ring of men around Achilles is becoming tighter, but then Achilles glances at Automedon and jerks his head, meaning *Keep them back.* Instantly, Automedon spreads his arms, pushing everybody away, and Alcimus, who's been rooted to the ground till now, slack-mouthed with shock, does the same, so they create a space around Achilles and Priam. Everybody else is reduced to a circle of muttering faces, with the torchlight casting their shadows over walls and ceiling, but still that's not enough. Achilles makes pushing movements with both hands. At once, Automedon breaks the circle and starts ushering everybody out. "It's all right," he keeps saying, as he herds them towards the door. "You can see it's all right . . ." A few linger and look back, still unable to credit what they've seen, but Automedon half persuades, half pushes them over the threshold. Outside, as they begin to disperse, a voice can be heard asking: *"Is it him?"* Then other voices: *"Yeah, it's all very well, though, isn't it? He could've had a knife." "Still could—nobody's searched the bugger." "What the FUCK were the sentries doing?" "They must've been bribed."*

Gradually, the voices fade away.

Inside the hall, silence. Achilles holds out his hand and raises Priam gently to his feet. Priam's knees click as he struggles to stand up, and he smiles, as old men do, ruefully accepting the slight humiliation.

Achilles pulls up a chair. "Come on, sit down. It's all right, you can have your son. Tomorrow, though, not now."

But Priam doesn't *want* to sit down. Quite suddenly, he's at the end of his tether, as out of control and petulant as a toddler past its bedtime. He wants to see Hector's body and, no, not tomorrow—NOW. He wants to touch him, wrap him lovingly in whatever covering he can find and take him home. He wants to give Hector's mother the only consolation she can have now: to prepare her son's body for cremation. There's a hectic flush on his cheeks, he's elated, even reckless—because he's survived, he's walked into the enemy camp, right into Achilles's hall, and survived. He never expected to—yes, the laws of hospitality are sacred, but they don't apply to him, he's an interloper, not a guest. But even if he had been a guest, what can the laws of hospitality possibly mean to a man like Achilles, who's broken every other law there is?

Somewhere, in the back of Priam's mind, is the fear that Hector's body has long since gone to feed the dogs, and Achilles is playing with him, Priam, for some cruel purpose of his own. So: No, *no*, he won't sit down. Why should he sit and chat to his son's killer, while somewhere in this compound Hector's body lies, dishonoured at best, at worst reduced to a pile of bones surrounded by dogs licking their chops? *No, no, NO!* "Don't ask me to sit down, Achilles, when my son's out there, unburied. Fed to your dogs for all I know."

For the first time, in his petulance, he sounds like what he is: a weak old man.

Instant fury. "I said: *SIT DOWN.*" A vein in Achilles's temple stands out like a worm under the skin. "If I'd fed him to the dogs there'd be nothing left for you to take home. *And* I'd have been fully justified, because that's what he had planned for Patroclus. *And* you'd have let him do it. Don't tell me you wouldn't, *I* know you would."

Even the two young men who seem to be Achilles's closest companions are backing away from him now. Shaking, Priam falls into the chair. Meanwhile, Achilles strides up and down, punching his clenched fist into the palm of his other hand, bringing himself gradually, by slow degrees, under control. At last he stops pacing and looks down at Priam. "Come on, let's go through there and have

a drink. It's more private, anybody could walk in here." Unexpectedly, he smiles. "Well, I don't need to tell *you* that, do I?"

They go through to the living quarters, Achilles leading the way.
As always, there's a fire burning, a jug of wine ready to pour, plates
of sliced figs, cheese, bread and honey set out on the table.

"Sit down," Achilles says.

Still shaking, Priam sits in what he does not know to be Achilles's
chair.

"Briseis!" Achilles yells at the top of his voice. And then, to
Automedon, "Tell her to bring something stronger, it's virgins' piss,
this stuff." He turns to Priam. "You'll have a cup of wine."

Priam's got one hand pressed against his mouth to keep his lips
still. He looks like a frightened old man. But that's on the surface.
Underneath, where it really matters, he's indomitable. Achilles sees
both the fear and the courage—and Priam has his absolute respect.

Alcimus and Automedon are still hovering. "You can go now,"
Achilles says. "I'll be all right."

Involuntarily, Automedon shakes his head.

"Oh, and keep the men quiet. I don't care what you have to do,
just *shut them up.* We don't want this all over the camp."

Reluctantly, Automedon bows and backs out. Still gaping at
Priam, Alcimus follows.

Priam stares into the fire, as motionless as a mouse under a cat's
paw. He's thinking: *Well, what's the worst that can happen?* He's going to
die soon, anyway. Even without the war, he's . . . Well, who knows?
Somewhere near the end. And mightn't it be better to die now—one
quick thrust of Achilles's dagger—than have to endure weeks of
further torment? And yet he wants to live, he wants to kiss Hecuba
again and tell her he's brought their son home.

A girl comes in, carrying a jug of wine, and hesitates in the doorway, obviously not knowing who to serve first. Achilles indicates
Priam. When both cups are full the girl withdraws, silently, into the
shadows, but not before Priam's noticed how beautiful she is. Even
here, at life's end, in the presence of his enemy, he can't stop himself

wondering what it would be like to be young again and hold *that* girl in his arms . . .

Achilles sits down and takes a sip of wine, but he seems restless and soon jumps up again. "I've got a few things I need to see to. If there's anything you want, ask Briseis. I won't be long."

I know that name, Priam thinks. He's pretty sure he's seen the girl before—she's not the kind of girl you forget seeing—but he can't for the life of him remember where.

"Would you like more wine, sir?" she asks.

And he thinks: *Yes, why not?*

Achilles returns a few minutes later. Probably he's been checking the ransom's big enough, something like that. He comes straight to the fire, rubbing his hands. "I've told them to bring us some food."

"I'm not hungry."

"No, but you'll have something . . . When did you last eat?"

Achilles turns to Briseis, but she's a step ahead of him. The table's already being laid.

42

Once the platters of roast meat had been carried in and set down on the table, Automedon and Alcimus were again told to withdraw. Automedon, I could plainly see, was furious; as Achilles's chief aide he'd normally have been the one to wait on a royal guest, and he obviously found the thought of me taking his place intolerable. He needn't have worried. Achilles himself waited on Priam, selecting the juiciest cuts of meat and transferring them deftly to his plate.

I'd put a lamp on the table and the light glinted on gold cups and plates. Usually, when entertaining a king, Achilles would have worn one of his richest robes, but tonight he'd changed into the coarsest and plainest tunic he possessed, obviously not wanting to outshine his guest. Nothing would have pleased me more than to be able to think of Achilles as a thug with no redeeming characteristics or grace of manner; but he was never that.

I set another jug of wine on the table by his elbow and withdrew into the shadows.

First problem: Priam had no knife. Quickly remedied; Achilles simply polished his own dagger on a linen cloth and handed it across the table, while I scurried around to find him a replacement. Oh, it sounds trivial, I know—but that trifling little incident changed everything. Achilles's face had gone smooth with shock. He'd known

Priam was unarmed—no sword, no spear, no posse of Trojan fighters waiting outside the door—but to come into the hall of his worst
enemy without even a dagger . . . Nobody left home without a knife,
not even a slave. Achilles was a connoisseur of courage on the battlefield, but this was a kind of courage he'd never encountered before.
And because he was fiercely, almost insanely, competitive, I knew
he'd be wondering: *Could I do that? Could I do what Priam's just done?*

Achilles ate remarkably well, considering this was his second
dinner of the evening, but then he'd eaten virtually nothing at the
first. Juices and blood ran glistening down his wrists as he cut and
tore the meat. Priam merely picked at his, though he was careful to
taste and praise every dish. But I could sense his relief when, his
duty as a guest done, he was able to push the plate away.

I couldn't hear much of the conversation, and in fact they spoke
very little, seeming content just to stare at each other—like lovers,
or a mother with her newborn baby. Generally, an unblinking stare,
particularly when directed by one man at another, will be seen as
threatening, but neither of them seemed to be made uncomfortable
by it. They were meeting for the first time. Nine years before, when
Achilles came to Troy, Priam was already too old to fight. Almost
every day since then, he'd watched Achilles on the battlefield and
no doubt, from time to time, Achilles had looked up and seen a
white-haired old man looking down, and known, or guessed, that
it was Priam. But, crucially, they'd never tested each other's strength
in combat, and so perhaps this prolonged scrutiny was a substitute
for that. Though I think it went deeper. They seemed to be standing
at opposite ends of a time tunnel: Priam seeing the young warrior
he'd once been; Achilles the old and revered king he would never be.

I'm sure Achilles thought of this as a meeting of equals. That
wasn't the way I saw it. For more than forty years, Priam had ruled
over a great and prosperous city; Achilles was the leader of a wolf
pack. But that made it all the more strange to see the two of them
dipping bread into the same dish. In fact, everything about that
evening seemed unreal, dreamlike—and infinitely fragile, like the

bubbles that form on a breaking wave, there a moment and gone for ever.

Towards the end of the meal, I brought in a platter of sliced figs drizzled with honey and was pleased to see that Priam did eat a little of that. Perhaps he'd reached the stage of exhaustion where all you crave is sweetness. When I thought he'd finished, I offered him a bowl of warm water scented with lemon juice and herbs and he washed his fingers and dabbed them dry on a square of fine linen.

After the meal, he went back to Achilles's chair and sat staring into his wine. Nothing had changed, and yet suddenly the atmosphere was tense again.

"Please," Priam said. "I want to see Hector now."

I could see Achilles's mind racing: he'd be thinking of Hector's body lying on the cobbles of the stable yard, naked and caked in shit. If Priam were to see that, his grief might well flare into anger and that in turn would reignite Achilles's grief for Patroclus and with it his own rage. You could see Achilles pacing himself, reining himself in, like a rider on a half-broken horse. Beneath the courtesy—and the occasional flicker of something remotely resembling compassion—I don't believe he was ever more than one breath away from killing Priam.

"Of course you can," he said, standing up. "But not tonight. Tomorrow, first thing. I promise."

He refilled Priam's cup and beckoned me to follow him. Alcimus and Automedon were waiting on the veranda. I held the torch while they unloaded the ransom from Priam's cart and carried it into the storage huts. A lot of it was textiles, clothes and bedding made from the rich embroidered cloth for which Troy was famous. Achilles set aside a particularly fine tunic to clothe Hector's body. Then he told me to make a bed up for Priam on the veranda, but round the side of the building, where it couldn't be seen from the main entrance, and to make it as warm and comfortable as possible.

"Take anything you need," he said. "Take the furs from my bed if you like, I don't want him to be cold."

I went to one of the storage huts and collected ox-hide rugs to form the base of the bed. The smell of ox hides, no matter how carefully they've been cured, is not pleasant and normally I'd have been in and out of there as fast as I could. But I needed these few minutes alone. Like everybody else, I'd been shaken by the sudden appearance of Priam in Achilles's hall. I'd felt blank and at the same time abnormally attentive. I could still hear him pleading with Achilles, begging him to remember his own father—and then the silence, as he bent his head and kissed Achilles's hands.

I do what no man before me has ever done, I kiss the hands of the man who killed my son.

Those words echoed round me, as I stood in the storage hut, surrounded on all sides by the wealth Achilles had plundered from burning cities. I thought: *And I do what countless women before me have been forced to do. I spread my legs for the man who killed my husband and my brothers.*

That was the lowest point for me, worse than standing in the arena half naked in front of a baying mob, worse even than the hours I'd spent in Agamemnon's bed, and yet that moment of despair strengthened my resolve. I knew I had to seize this opportunity, minuscule though it might be. I had to get away. So, almost at random, I selected a couple more hides and asked Alcimus to carry them to Achilles's hut. They were good, strong, thick hides, far too heavy for me to lift.

It didn't take me long to make up the bed. I used only the finest linen sheets, the softest pillows, the warmest blankets, and spread over it all a coverlet of purple wool lavishly embroidered with gold and silver thread. Then I put a cup of well-diluted wine on a table by the bed, and a bucket, discreetly covered, a few yards away. As a girl, I'd helped my mother care for my grandfather; I knew the ways of old men in the night. By the time I'd finished, it really did look like a royal bed, and I hoped it would comfort Priam, here, in the midst of his enemies, to be accorded the honour due to a king.

When I returned to the living quarters, I found Priam, exhausted after his dangerous journey, dozing over his wine, though he jerked awake a minute later when Achilles came in. "I want to see Hector," Priam said again, apparently forgetting that he'd asked for this already.

"Tomorrow," Achilles said. "Sleep first."

Priam passed a hand over his eyes. "Yes, I'll be glad to be in bed."

He bade Achilles a courteous good night and managed to get as far as the door without stumbling, but once outside on the veranda he was weaving from side to side. I guided him round the corner of the hut and he almost fell onto the bed. He sat on the edge for a moment, stroking the coverlet with both hands, appreciating the beauty of the cloth. Then he let out a small, contented sigh. "I don't think I've ever been so glad to see a bed in my life."

I asked if there was anything else he needed. He looked up at me then, and said, "Don't I know you?"

"We have met, sir, but it was a long time ago."

"Where?"

"In Troy. I lived there for two years. Helen used to bring me with her to the battlements."

"*Yes!* I knew I'd seen you before, you're Helen's little friend." His face was flooded with an old man's pleasure at identifying a figure from the past. "Well. Who'd have thought *you'd* grow to be a beauty?"

"I'm not Helen's friend anymore. I'm Achilles's slave."

His expression changed. "Yes, I know, I heard. It's hard on the women when a city falls."

I knew he was thinking of his own daughters, who'd be shared out among the conquerors when Troy fell. And it would fall. I looked at the frail old man sitting there—no strong sons left to defend him—and I knew there was no hope.

When I went back inside, Achilles was standing by the table staring down—rather vacantly, I thought—at the empty plates. He looked round when I came in. "Is he in bed?"

"Yes."

"Asleep?"

"Not yet, but I don't think it'll be long."

He was tapping his fingers on the table, clearly thinking hard. "What a thing for him to do. Did you notice, he didn't have a knife?" He shook his head. "Come on, we've got to get the body washed—and there isn't much time. He's got to be out of here before dawn. If they find him here they'll kill him."

43

Taking a torch from a sconce by the door, Achilles led the way to the stables, Automedon and Alcimus following along behind. I could see Hector's body, spread-eagled on the filthy ground. Dirty, yes—every inch coated in mud and shit—but still the length and shape of a man. I shivered with relief. Because it had crossed my mind that the gods might play one final trick and Achilles would find what he should have been finding for the last week at least: a pile of greasy, partially articulated bones.

Looking down, he nodded grimly, then knelt and slid his hands underneath the corpse. Without needing to be told, Alcimus knelt on the other side and did the same. Very slowly, they lifted Hector until he was shoulder height, Automedon supporting the legs. All around us, horses stamped and whinnied. I held the torch high, as the three men shuffled slowly out of the yard and down the narrow passage that led to the laundry hut, where the dead were prepared for cremation.

When they reached the door, Automedon changed position, cradling Hector's head in his hands to see it safely across the threshold. Unexpectedly, I found myself wanting to laugh: the care they were taking now was so ludicrous after all the abuse Achilles had inflicted on that body day after day. I followed them inside and found a sconce for the torch. Grunting with effort, they lowered Hector onto the slab and stepped back.

I was facing Achilles across the slab, as I'd done three months before when Myron died. Then, Achilles had been reluctant to leave, asserting his authority over the washerwomen, his slaves, who'd stood their ground, mutely affirming their own authority, their right to lay out the dead. And amazingly, in the end—not a word spoken—they'd forced him to back down. I felt their shadowy presence in the space behind me, but their nameless authority was of no use to me now.

Achilles had begun to remove a clump of straw that had stuck to Hector's skin. He was having to scrape hard to get it loose and I tensed, expecting to see strips of skin come away with the straw. I was still finding it difficult to believe in the miraculous preservation of Hector's body. I bent down over the slab and sniffed, expecting the dark, rancid, meat-going-off stench that once encountered is never forgotten, but there was nothing like that, only the pervasive smell of wet wool from the huge cauldrons where bloodstained garments were left to soak overnight. Hector lay stretched out as if asleep. Even the eye whites—you could just see them under the half-closed lids—were clear. And, gradually, my nose taught my brain to believe the evidence of my eyes.

The silence had gone on too long. Achilles looked over the full length of the corpse and made a little disgusted clicking sound with his tongue. "See how the gods defy me?"

The gods defy you?

For one horrible moment, I thought I'd spoken the words aloud, but of course I hadn't. I was aware, suddenly, of the silence in the camp. The drunken fighters would have nodded off to sleep; the guards on the parapet would be struggling to stay awake, staring into the shifting darkness where stumps of trees take on the shapes of men and start to creep closer . . . Not a sound in this room either, except for the rise and fall of our breathing. I looked at Hector—so alive, so *present*—and half expected to see his chest rising and falling in time with my own.

Abruptly, Achilles ordered Automedon and Alcimus out of the room. They looked surprised, in fact more than surprised—shocked. Automedon actually turned round when he got to the door, as if to check Achilles meant what he said. I'd been assuming all three of them would go and leave me to it, though I'd no idea how I was supposed to turn the body on my own. Instead, there was Achilles, facing me across the slab.

"I could fetch the women . . ." I said.

"And have it all over the camp? I don't think so."

Somehow it was obvious he wasn't going to just stand and watch, so I filled two buckets with water and handed him a cloth. I worked on the left side, Achilles on the right. With every sweep of our hands, bands of white flesh became visible, almost as if we were bringing Hector to life—creating him. After a while, I refilled the buckets, found more clean cloths and we went on working, up and down, side to side, performing a kind of silent dance around the slab. At one point, I was washing Hector's feet, rubbing the rag between his long, straight toes, while Achilles worked on his hands, finger by finger, using his dagger point to clean under the nails. I knew he wouldn't be able to do the face, so I fetched a jug of water and poured it over the head, working my fingers through the hair to clear the tangles and loosen clods of earth. I remember it took eight jugs for the water to run clear. Only then did I start on the face. Once I'd wiped away the filth from Hector's eyes and nostrils and cleaned inside his ears, I stepped back and looked down. This was the man who would have been king of Troy after Priam died, and yet here he was, his flesh as white and dense as dead cod.

I was struggling not to cry. When I felt my tears were becoming too obvious, I bent down and pretended to rinse the cloth. As I straightened up again, I saw Achilles watching me.

"I don't have to send him back, you know."

My heart thumped. "But you've taken the ransom . . ."

"Not Hector, *Priam*."

I was afraid to speak, terrified for Priam and for myself. If he didn't let Priam go, I—

"How much do you think the Trojans would pay to get their king back?"

I just shook my head.

"Anything. Absolutely *anything*."

"But you've already got . . ."

He waited. "No, go on."

"You've already got a king's ransom. For Hector."

"No, you don't understand. I could ask for Helen."

"For *Helen*?"

"Well, why not? They can't wait to be shot of the bitch."

He was right, of course. The Trojans would exchange Helen for Priam any day, not a second thought, and then . . . My mind was racing ahead. Helen restored to her husband, no need to go on fighting, no reason to sack Troy . . . The war would be over. *The war would be over*. Everybody could go home. Well, not me, of course—and not any of the other slaves either. But everybody else. The armies, the armies could go home. The possibilities were immense, dizzying.

But then I looked at him. "You won't do it."

"He's a guest."

"Not invited."

"No, but accepted."

A strange conversation, you might think, to be taking place between owner and slave, but remember the darkness of night surrounded us, and we had no witness but the dead.

After that, the work went on in silence, though the quality of the silence had changed.

When the time came to seal the orifices, Achilles stepped back, leaving me to work alone. I wound a fine linen cloth round the head to keep the jaw in place and looked about for coins to put on Hector's lids. No coins in sight, but I found a bowl full of small, flat pebbles, kept for just this purpose. I selected two—I remember they were a pale blueish-grey with thin white lines running across—and felt how light and smooth they were. My brothers used to skim stones like these across the river, as no doubt Hector would have done when he was a boy. I placed the pebbles on his lids and then, carefully, lifted his head—you always forget how heavy the human head is, no matter how often you lift one it always comes as a shock—and wound a strip of cloth across the eyes to keep the stones in place. Then I stood back. Hector was gone now. I felt, in some way, that he hadn't been dead till then.

We dressed him in the tunic Achilles had set aside, then wrapped him in a sheet of fine linen. I put sprigs of thyme and rosemary between each layer of cloth: I wanted the women who unwrapped him, his mother and his wife, to know that some care and reverence had gone into this, that he hadn't just been sluiced down and bundled up by indifferent hands. Lastly, I laid a linen cloth, so thin it was almost transparent, over his face.

Then Achilles lifted him off the slab, while I ran ahead to open the door. Immediately, Alcimus and Automedon were at his side, ready to help, but Achilles insisted on carrying Hector to the cart himself—a considerable feat of strength even by his standards. Alcimus leapt into the cart to receive the head and shoulders. Achilles climbed in after him and began fastening the body to the sides with thick woollen bands so that there'd be no unseemly sliding and slithering about when the wheels jolted over rough ground. By the time they'd finished, all three of them were out of breath.

Achilles jumped down and stood with one hand resting on the tailgate. I thought he looked desolate, though I was judging his mood more from posture than expression because I couldn't see his face. At last, he said, turning to Automedon, "I just hope Patroclus understands."

I thought—and, who knows, perhaps Automedon did too—that Patroclus would never have wanted Hector's body to be dishonoured in the first place. Only the mercy of the gods had prevented

Priam from coming out this morning to find a heap of pullulat-ing maggots in his cart. And then his grief and horror would have reignited Achilles's rage, and . . . And where would that have ended? Quite possibly, with Priam lying dead in the cart beside his son.

"I think we need a drink," Achilles said.

So the three of us followed him through the hall into his living quarters, where I set to work mixing dishes of strong wine. Achilles, most unusually for him, sank his cup in seconds. Alcimus, who was young and had hollow legs, was eyeing the cuts of cold roast lamb that had been left lying on a platter.

"Go on, help yourself," Achilles said, taking another cup of wine from me. Then he asked: "Where's yours?"

So I poured myself a cup and sat down on the bed. Now and then, barely distinguishable from the ebb and flow of the sea, came the sound of Priam's snores. It was peaceful, staring at the fire, though my face felt numb. After they'd finished the wine—and Alcimus had put away an incredible amount of meat in a short time—Achilles rose and wished them good night.

I could see neither of them wanted to go. As they saw it, they were leaving Achilles alone with a Trojan—yes, an old man and apparently unarmed—but a Trojan nevertheless.

"He didn't even have a knife," Achilles said, wearily. "I had to lend him mine."

"And the girl?" Automedon said.

"She stays."

Achilles sounded amused rather than irritated, but Automedon knew better than to press the point. Alcimus, his lips shining with grease, glanced sideways at me as they backed out. When I looked round, Achilles was smiling. "They think you're in league with Priam," he said. "They think you're going to murder me in my sleep."

His mood seemed to have lightened. That brief moment of desolation when he'd wondered what Patroclus would have thought seemed to have been forgotten. And his movements were lighter too. I'd noticed it earlier when he jumped down from the cart, landing as noiselessly as a cat, but I'd thought I might be imagining it. Here, in the firelight, the change was unmistakable. I watched him kick off his sandals, first one, then the other, and catch them in mid-air.

He was pulling his tunic over his head. I started to get undressed too, since I was evidently staying. Really, this was the last thing I needed. I needed to be outside talking to Priam, but there was no way of avoiding it. I lay on my back with my eyes closed, waiting for the bed to sag under his weight. I was praying he'd fall asleep quickly, but he was as full of energy as I'd ever known him. Something else too. There were times he seemed almost tentative, not unsure of himself, he was never that, but more as if he were wanting a response. When, at last, he closed his eyes, his breathing was quick, light and shallow. Still worse, he'd thrown his arm across my chest and the weight of it pinned me down. I felt his sweat cooling on my skin, but I knew I didn't dare move, not yet.

44

I think I must have nodded off to sleep, because the next time I became aware of my surroundings, I was staring into the darkness, feeling disorientated and dazed. Gradually, as the sleep-fog cleared, I remembered that Priam was out there on the veranda— *Priam, here!*—just on the other side of that door. I had to get to him. I lay and listened. When I was sure Achilles was asleep, I breathed out, flattened myself against the bed and tried to wriggle out from under his arm, but it was too heavy. I was pinned.

The oil lamps were almost out. Shadows cast by the last guttering flames seemed to gather round the bed, breeding more shadows as the light died. I looked at the gap under the door and tried to judge how close we were to dawn.

Achilles's body was hot and heavy. Cautiously, I moved my thigh, and my skin unpeeled from his. I felt sticky, full of him. On any other night, I'd have been longing for the cold slap of waves as I walked into the sea, but not tonight. My mouth was dry, foul-tasting— the grim aftermath of drinking two cups of strong wine. Achilles's sweat actually smelled of wine, but then he'd drunk more than me.

Somewhere outside, a dog barked, or perhaps a fox—there were always foxes on the beach, prowling the tideline for dead seagulls— and the sound must have reached him for he muttered in his sleep and turned on his side away from me. The weight of his arm was gone, but even then I didn't dare slide to the foot of the bed. Not yet, let him settle first.

Pushing back the covers, I looked down at my body. I put both hands on my belly and thought how totally this flesh, this intricate mesh of bone and nerve and muscle, belonged *to me.* In spite of Achilles, in spite of my aching hips and thighs. My skin goose-pimpled in the draught from the door, but I didn't pull the covers up again. I needed to feel the cold, the shock of the outside world.

Gingerly, inch by inch, I began to work my way down the bed. I knew I didn't dare risk crawling over him. Every time the bed creaked, I lay still and listened again. Once, he stirred and seemed about to wake and I froze for several minutes, afraid even to think in case my thoughts woke him. A third attempt brought me to the foot of the bed, where I sat for a minute, flexing my toes on the sheepskin rug. How long had I slept? Ten minutes? Half an hour? Not long. I listened for noises, voices, anything that might tell me what time it was, but no, the camp was completely quiet. Even the sea was so calm I could scarcely hear its breathing. The fire had burned low, the logs reduced to a heap of blackened wood and white ash. I reached for my mantle and wrapped it tightly around me. Achilles was sleeping heavily now, his lips puckering on every out-breath. Very slowly, alert for any movement from the bed, I stood up—and the movement seemed to loosen the knot of fear inside me. Really, I thought, what was there to be frightened of? If he woke and found me gone, I could always say I'd thought I heard Priam calling. He couldn't find fault with me for waiting on his royal guest.

I lifted the latch and opened the door a crack. The night air struck cold on my face, the eye closest to the gap began to water. Taking a deep breath, I slipped out, making sure the latch fell noiselessly into place behind me. It was deep night; nothing stirred. I edged along the veranda. I knew every creaking board, I'd walked this way so many times, escaping for my few precious moments by the sea.

Priam was asleep, stretched out straight and still—not even his ankles crossed—like a body on a funeral pyre, except that he was making snuffly sounds as he breathed, rather pleasant, like a horse inside its feedbag. I could see his feet sticking up, twin peaks, folds of purple cloth falling away on either side. He looked so like my grandfather as he slept, I knew I couldn't just shake him awake, so I fetched a bowl and went off in search of warm water for him to wash.

A fire was kept banked up and burning in the yard so Achilles could have a hot bath every morning; no matter how often he chose to swim instead, that bath still had to be prepared. I poured fresh water into a metal bowl, set it among the embers and hunkered down to wait. Under the nearest hut, I could see the huddled shapes of women too old or ugly to rate a bed inside. All the doors were closed. Even the dogs were asleep, though now and then I saw a rat run from hut to hut, trailing its naked tail along the ground. Oh, yes, the rats were back, though in much smaller numbers than before. The water was slow to heat up, but I didn't mind, I needed time to think, to plan what I was going to say. But then I heard a footstep behind me and wheeled around, expecting—dreading— to see Achilles, but it was Alcimus and, immediately behind him, Automedon. Neither of them would have closed their eyes for a second knowing Achilles was asleep in his hut with a Trojan only a few yards away, even if he was an old man and—allegedly—unarmed.

Alcimus bent down and said something, but I was too startled to take it in. I said: "I'm getting water for Priam to wash."

"Is he awake?" Automedon asked.

"Yes. No, well, I thought I heard him . . ."

"And Achilles?"

"Asleep."

Leaning across me, Alcimus dipped a finger in the bowl. "It's warm enough."

Wrapping the hem of my mantle round my hands in case the handles were hot, I lifted the bowl from the fire and prepared to stand up.

"I'll carry it," Alcimus said.

I stared at him. One of Achilles's chief aides, carrying water for a slave? No, not for me—well, of course not for me!—for Priam, who, although an enemy—*the* enemy—was still a king and had to be treated with the honour due to a royal guest. But then I saw Alcimus's expression, and thought: *No, for me.*

The offer was a nuisance. I needed Priam alone, not being danced attendance on by Achilles's aides. I might persuade Alcimus to go away and let me get on with it, but Automedon was a different matter. In fact, he led the way, striding ahead confidently, as perfectly groomed and alert after his wakeful night as he would have been after the things he has as always

When we reached the steps, I said as firmly as I could, "I'll take it to him." I looked straight into Automedon's eyes. "He knows me. My sister's married to one of his sons."

Automedon blinked, forced, for a moment—and I honestly think it was for the first time—to see me as a human being, somebody who had a sister, and a sister, moreover, who was King Priam's daughter-in-law. He hesitated, then nodded, and the two of them watched me set off along the veranda. I sensed rather than saw them settle down on the steps, waiting for Achilles to wake. Once, I thought I heard him moving about inside the hut and stopped to listen, but it was only a creaking board; the walls and floors creaked all the time. All the same, it was a shock. I had such a narrow crack of opportunity and it seemed to be getting narrower all the time.

Priam was still lying stretched out on his back, his position unchanged, though as I came closer I noticed a tension in the small muscles around his eyes that hadn't been there before. So I wasn't surprised when, as I approached the bed, his lids suddenly flashed open. His eyes, which might once have been a vivid blue, were bleached with age, with a rim of silver-grey around the iris that I remembered seeing in my grandfather's eyes. Just for a second, he looked frightened. Then I realized he couldn't see me, so I stepped into the circle of light around the lamp. Immediately, he relaxed. He'd thought I was Achilles.

"Lord Priam," I said gently, emphasizing the "lord." "I've brought you some water to get washed."

"Well, my dear, that's very kind."

He rolled over onto his elbow. I soaked a cloth in the warm water and handed it to him. He ran it over his face and into his ears and then lifted his hair and beard and scrubbed as much of his neck and chest as he could reach. I saw, with a stab of love and pity, that he was totally absorbed in the task, like a small boy who's being trusted to wash himself for the first time. For those few minutes, he forgot the war, the last nine dreadful years—forgot even the death of Hector. It all fell away from him, the lifetime he'd ruled Troy, fifty years of happy marriage, all gone, wiped away on a square of warm, damp cloth. It seemed perfectly natural to me, witnessing that transformation, to run my wetted fingers through his hair, brushing it back from his forehead and tweaking stray strands into place behind his ears. He watched me, and then suddenly said, "Yes, that's right, Briseis, isn't it? Helen's little friend?"

I could see him gathering himself together, assuming the burden of memory. The carefree little boy had vanished, his place taken by an old man, an old man who'd seen and suffered too much; but still a king. He pushed back the covers, swung his legs over the side of the bed and paused there for a moment. Obviously, standing up was a bit of a challenge. He tried several times to straighten his painful knees, then I put my arm through his and grasped his hand. When he was upright and the worst of the pain seemed to have subsided, I couldn't hold back any longer. "Take me with you," I said.

He looked astonished.

"My sister's in Troy. You remember her? She's married to Leander, and she's the only family I've got left."

"Yes, I remember. Your husband was killed, wasn't he?"

"And my brothers, all four of them. I've only got her."

"I'm sorry."

"Achilles killed my brothers and now I sleep in his bed."

"Well, then, you know what happens to women when a city falls.

There isn't a day goes by I don't think of it. I look at my daughters . . ." He shook his head as if trying to dislodge the images that had gathered there. "At least I won't live to see it. With any luck I'll be dead by then."

"*Please?*"

He put his hand on my shoulder. "My dear, you're not thinking straight. Yes, your sister'll give you a home, I'm sure she'd be glad to—and Leander. But what then? A few weeks of freedom and then Troy falls and you're a slave again—and perhaps to a worse man than Achilles."

"*Worse?*"

"Why, is he unkind to you?"

"He killed my family."

"But that's *war*." He was standing tall again now, Priam, the king, the weakness that had needed my help forgotten. "No, I can't do it. How do you think Achilles would feel if I stole his woman? My son Paris seduced Helen while he was her husband's guest—and look where that got us."

"If it's any help, I don't think he'd mind."

"Are you sure? He broke with Agamemnon over you."

"Yes, but that was just hurt pride."

"And this wouldn't hurt his pride? After he took me in, accepted me as his guest? He could've killed me. No, I'm sorry." He shook his head. "I can't do it."

I heard a movement behind me and turned to see Achilles standing in the shadows. My heart jumped a beat. How long had he been there?

"I see Briseis is looking after you."

Long enough.

"Yes, she's been very kind."

Priam touched my face, resting the palm of his hand gently against my cheek, but I couldn't bear to look at him.

"It's time to go," Achilles said. "It'll be light soon and we daren't risk Agamemnon finding you here."

"What do you think he'd do?"

Achilles shrugged. "I think I'd rather not find out."

"But you'd fight for me?"

"Oh, yes, I'd fight. I don't need a Trojan to teach me my duty to a guest."

Priam dropped the cloth he was holding with a soft *plop* into the bowl. "All right, I'm ready."

Achilles was not only dressed, but armed, his clasped hands resting on the hilt of his sword. Obviously he'd meant it when he said he was prepared to fight. Afraid to look at his face, I looked instead at his hands and noticed Priam staring at them too. Achilles took a step back, wrapping his cloak more closely round him, so that his hands, those terrible manslaughtering hands, disappeared into the folds. I don't think he was ashamed of anything those hands had done—proud of it, in fact—but all the same they were a problem, because they shaped other people's perceptions of him in ways he couldn't control.

I picked up Priam's cloak and followed them along the veranda. I was invisible now; the ties of host and guest, the ties that bind men together, had reasserted themselves. But then I noticed how daunted Priam was by the steps. Achilles offered his arm, but Priam brushed it aside—one of those sudden spasms of anger that had punctuated this meeting. Already, I could see Priam regretting that moment of involuntary recoil, trying to *make* himself take Achilles's arm ... It was Achilles who stepped aside and indicated to me that I should help Priam. Priam rested his hand on my shoulder and managed the steps very well, wincing only a little as he reached the ground. Achilles had gone on ahead and was speaking to Automedon, perhaps not wanting to draw attention to the contrast between Priam's weakness and his own strength. I thought how wise Priam had been to appeal to Achilles through his father. Achilles always showed great tact and delicacy in his dealings with old men and that sensitivity could only have sprung from his love for his own father.

Priam was now leaning his full weight on me. He seemed to have aged ten years in the night, to have moved in a few short hours from vigorous old age into frailty. I felt his veins throbbing under my hand like the heartbeat of a fledgling you know can't possibly survive. Achilles was waiting for us to catch up. "Everything's ready," he said. "I'll go with you as far as the gate."

By the time we reached the stable yard, Automedon and Alcimus were already harnessing the mules to the cart. I felt Priam shaking as we approached. So far he'd held himself together, but now—mules champing on their bits, harness bells jingling—he turned towards the cart.

At a gesture from Achilles, Alcimus held the torch higher so that a circle of light fell onto Hector's body. I lifted the linen cloth so Priam could see his son's face. Priam made a little noise deep in his throat, then almost timidly reached out and touched his son's hair. "Oh, my boy, my poor boy." He was crying now; he put a hand up to his mouth and tried to hold the lips together, but the sobs couldn't be kept in.

We waited. At last, he turned to Achilles.

"How long do you need to bury him?" Achilles asked.

The brutality of the question jarred. But then I saw that by focusing on the practicalities Achilles had averted what might easily have become a confrontation. Grief was what united them, but it divided them as well.

"Oh ..." Breathless now, Priam held on to the side of the cart and tried to think. "It's a long trek to the woods to get timber—our trees were all cut down to build your huts—and the people are afraid to go ... We'll need a ceasefire."

"I'll make sure you get it."

"Then I'd say ... eleven days? Eleven days for the funeral games. And then on the twelfth day we'll fight again. If fight we must ..."

That was almost a question. *And why not?* I thought. *Why not?* If he and Achilles could so easily agree to a ceasefire, why not go on and make a permanent peace ... ?

"I'll see you to the gate," Achilles said.

Unexpectedly, Priam looked amused. "Are you sure? What are the sentries supposed to make of that? Great Achilles, godlike Achilles, escorting a farmer's cart?"

Achilles shrugged. "It doesn't matter what they think as long as they do as they're told. But I take the point, we certainly don't want a guard of honour." He turned to Automedon and Alcimus. "You stay here, wait for me in the hut."

"I think it would be better if we said goodbye here," Priam said.

"No—until you go through that gate you're still my guest. It wouldn't be good if you were recognized."

Priam nodded assent. I could see him wanting all this to stop so he could look at Hector again.

"But first," Achilles said, "let's drink the parting cup."

So thin a veneer of civility hid the anger raging underneath, I thought Priam might refuse, but no, he consented readily enough, even took Achilles's arm as they walked back to the hut. Automedon and Alcimus glanced at each other, obviously exasperated by the delay, but they followed on behind. I didn't understand it either, after all that talk of needing to get Priam out of the camp as soon as possible, but it suited me well enough. Nobody noticed what I was doing. To begin with, I just went on standing by the cart, only edging a little to my left so the high sides would hide me should anybody happen to look round.

The dawn wind was freshening. The torches in their sconces all around the yard guttered and burned pale. I rested my hand on the tailgate and waited for the sound of their footsteps to die away. It was now or never; I knew I'd never have a chance like this again. There was no time to think, no time to wonder if I was doing the right thing. As soon as I was sure I wasn't being observed, I climbed into the cart and lay down beside Hector, my hot body flattened against his cold side. I pulled the linen sheet loose so its folds would cover me too. His body felt clammy against my skin, the smells of thyme and rosemary not strong enough to hide a whiff of decay. His appearance hadn't changed at all, but my nose told me the inevitable

process of decomposition had begun. I didn't look out to watch for
their return, but kept my face pressed hard against Hector's arm so
no movement of my breath would disturb the cloth. It only needed
Priam to stop for one more look at his son's body—and what could
be more natural than that?—and there'd be all hell to pay, for me,
and perhaps for Priam too, whose assurances that he hadn't known
I was there might not be believed.

I tensed as I heard their footsteps returning. Achilles and Priam
were talking in low voices, I couldn't hear the words. After a while
they fell silent—and that silence was more frightening than speech.
I thought I heard Priam coming to look at Hector's body again, but
then I felt the cart tilt as he climbed into the driving seat. A jingle
of bells, the slap of leather against a mule's neck, and we lurched
forward, Hector's cold flesh rubbing against my cheek.

Ruts in the stable yard; even out on the path the wheels kept jolting over holes in the ground. I held on to Hector's body, which was
kept more or less stable by the bands tying it to the sides of the cart.
I was cold now, almost as cold as the corpse, every muscle clenched
in fear. But my mind was racing, I saw my sister, my brother-in-law,
the warmth and safety of their home—and above and beyond all
that, the great prize of freedom. Me—myself again, a person with
family, friends, a role in life. A woman, not a thing. Wasn't that a
prize worth risking everything for, however short a time I might
have to enjoy it?

But the more I thought about it, the more insane this bid for
freedom seemed. If Priam discovered me before we got to Troy, he
might well tip me out of his cart, even while we were crossing the
battlefield, perhaps. A few sentimental memories of a little girl he'd
once done conjuring tricks for would count for nothing against the
duty he owed to Achilles as his host. He wasn't going to jeopardize
that eleven-day ceasefire for my sake.

And even if I got as far as Troy and succeeded in reaching my sister, what did the future hold? A few weeks of happiness, shadowed
by fear, and then I'd be hiding in another citadel, surrounded by

another group of terrified women, waiting for another city to fall. Waiting for Agamemnon to unleash thousands of drunken fighters onto the streets. I'd heard his plans for Troy, his and Nestor's. Every man and boy killed—and that would include my brother-in-law—pregnant women to be speared in the belly on the off chance their child would be a boy, and for the other women, gang rape, beatings, mutilation, slavery. A few women—or rather a few very young girls, mainly of royal or aristocratic birth—would be shared out among the kings, but as a former slave I'd have no such status. I might easily end up living the life of the common women, dodging blows by day and sleeping under the huts at night. Or worse still, come face to face with Achilles and endure the punishments that were invariably inflicted on runaway slaves. No hope of mercy there, I'd seen how vengeful Achilles could be ...

Priam's right, I thought. *This is mad.*

Squeezing my eyes tight shut, I tried to think. I was trapped. All I could do now was lie beside Hector's corpse and wait for the cart to stop. *If* it stopped ... There was always the possibility that the guards, recognizing Achilles, would wave it through. Carts leaving the camp weren't usually stopped and searched, anyway.

At last, the lurching stopped. I'd felt Achilles's presence walking beside the cart every moment, but now the sense of him was lifted and, a few minutes later, I heard him talking to the sentries. The mules' harness jingled. Priam sighed and coughed, from tension, I suppose. I wanted to cough too. Desperately, I imagined the sharp taste of lemons, gathering saliva and swallowing hard to soothe the tickle in my throat. I heard Achilles and the guards laughing together.

At any moment, the cart would move forward again. It had to be now. I freed myself from the sheet, wriggled to the end of the cart and slid down to the ground. Immediately, I began to walk: cold, frightened, damp, desperate, my skin smelling of Hector's skin ... I felt Achilles's gaze stitched to my back, but didn't dare turn round to see if he was really watching me. My instinct was to run, but I knew that would attract too much attention, so I simply wrapped my mantle tightly round me and set off at a fast but steady pace. I wasn't looking where I was going, I kept tripping over the hem of my tunic. At every moment, I expected to hear my name called.

All around me the camp was awakening: men who'd been drunk the night before yawning and shouting for food; women carrying kindling to revive the overnight fires. The dawn wind ruffled my skirt and hair. I made straight for a group of women and tried to blend in with them, even picking up an empty bucket and carrying it, leaning a little to one side, pretending it was full. Finally, I plucked up the courage to look back and realized none of this play-acting had been necessary. Priam's cart was already trundling through the gate. Achilles stayed to watch it go, one hand raised in a final salute, then he turned and strode rapidly away in the direction of his hut.

Only then did I take a deep breath. I gave it another few minutes and then followed him, my mind filling with a jumble of routine cares. He'd want hot water to bathe. I spoke to the women whose duty it was to prepare his bath and then went into the hut. He was sitting at the table, staring into space, but glanced up as I came in. I thought he looked surprised.

"Would you like something to eat?" I asked.

He nodded and sat in silence while I prepared bread and olives and a crumbly, white goat's cheese that they used to make in Lyrnessus. The smell always took me back to my childhood. It had been my mother's favourite; she used to eat it with some of the small, hard apricots that grew on a tree behind our house. I broke off a few crumbs, put them on my tongue, and the sharp, sour taste brought her back to me. Tears prickled in my eyes, but I didn't let myself cry. I set the platter down on the table in front of Achilles and stood back.

He seemed to be hungry, tearing off pieces of bread and dipping them in oil, spearing squares of cheese on the point of his dagger and popping them into his mouth. I poured diluted wine into his cup and set it down beside his plate.

Then he said, casually—only it wasn't casual—"Why did you come back?"

So he'd known all along. My mouth went dry. Then I thought: *No. He just thinks I went to the women's hut and he's wondering why I came back without waiting to be summoned.* So I turned to face him—and saw I'd been right the first time. He did know. For a moment, the shock made my mind go blank, but then I thought: *If you knew I was in the cart, why didn't you stop me?*

I said, slowly, "I don't know."

He pushed the platter of bread and cheese towards me. Thinking he'd finished, I made to pick it up, but stopped myself. *He was offering me food.* It wasn't exactly a gracious invitation: he simply pointed at my chest and then at a chair. So I sat down, facing him, and we ate and drank together.

I'd said *I don't know* because I couldn't think of anything else to say. All that stuff about Troy falling and becoming a slave again and being hauled in front of Achilles—it was all true. But I'd known all that before I got into the cart. Something else, something I couldn't put my finger on, had made me turn back. Perhaps no more than a feeling that this was my place now, that I had to make my life work *here.*

We ate and drank in silence, but I sensed the atmosphere had changed. I'd tried to escape, but then—*for whatever reason*—I'd come back. He'd known I was in the cart and—again, *for whatever reason*—had been prepared to let me go. So this was no longer, straight-forwardly, a meeting of owner and slave. There was an element of choice. Or was there? I don't know, probably a lot of it was wishful thinking—and I don't suppose for a second any of this crossed his mind.

Suddenly, he pushed his plate away and stood up. "I've got to see Agamemnon."

"He won't be up yet."

He looked amused. "No, that's true."

So he sat down again and we finished the wine.

45

After nine long years of blood and conflict, these eleven shining days of peace.

I remember it as a strange time; a time out of time. We seemed to be living in the hollow of a breaking wave. Every day was punctuated by shouts and cheers from inside the walls of Troy, as another fighter won a race and received his prize from Priam's depleted stores, though none of them would be able to enjoy his prize for long.

On the second day, Ajax came to dinner, bringing with him Tecmessa and their little son. We women sat on the veranda eating a tray of the sweetmeats Tecmessa loved—or rather, she ate them; I watched. The child was playing with a wooden horse his father had carved for him, clicking his tongue as he made it gallop along the veranda. I sat, shading my eyes, watching Achilles and Ajax play dice. They were sitting at a table in the centre of the yard, laughing, teasing each other with the freedom of long familiarity, groaning loudly and clapping their hands to their foreheads whenever the dice didn't fall their way. All their gestures seemed slightly exaggerated, like people miming playing a game of dice.

Suddenly, Ajax leapt to his feet. Thinking he'd seen somebody inside the hut, I turned to follow his gaze, but there was nobody there and when I looked back Ajax was on the ground. He lay there, knees drawn up to his chin, wailing like a newborn baby. Achilles sat motionless, letting the outburst run its course, until, at last, Ajax regained control of himself and sat down again. Neither of them spoke, just went on with their game as if nothing had happened. The whole incident, from beginning to end, couldn't have lasted longer than ten minutes.

Tecmessa, who'd started to stand up, settled again into her chair and reached for another square of honey-coated nuts.

"He's not sleeping," she said. "He has these awful nightmares; the other night he dreamt he was being eaten by a spider, he could hear its jaws moving and everything, woke up screaming. Oh, and if I ask him what's wrong . . ."

"He won't tell you?"

"Course he bloody won't! I'm supposed to just put up with it and say nothing, and if I do try to talk about it, it's: 'Silence becomes a woman.'"

Every woman I've ever known was brought up on that saying. We sat on the shady veranda and contemplated it for a moment and then suddenly burst out laughing, both of us together—not just laughing either, whooping, screeching, gasping for breath, until, finally, the men turned to stare at us and Tecmessa stuffed the hem of her tunic into her mouth to gag herself. The laughter ended as abruptly as it had begun. We sat drying our eyes and wiping our noses on the backs of our hands. I picked up the tray and offered her another slice . . . On the surface, we were back to being our normal selves—apart from the occasional, subversive hiccup—but something had changed. I'd never liked Tecmessa all that much, but after that moment of shared laughter we were friends.

I said: "How soon can you tell if you're pregnant?"

She stared at me. "Depends—I knew straightaway, sick as a dog from day one, but, you know . . . Everybody's different, some women say they don't know till they're in labour, though I don't know how they don't know; I mean, even if you were still seeing your periods, you'd think being head-butted in the bladder every five minutes might be a clue." All this time, although she'd been careful to speak in general terms, she'd been looking at me shrewdly. "Is it his?"

"Yes," I said.

"Are you sure?"

"Yes."

"Not Agamemnon's?"

"Not possible. The back gate, remember?"

She was overjoyed for me; a good deal more overjoyed than I was for myself.

The shadows were lengthening. In a moment, the men would get up and go into dinner, but for those last few minutes—the sun hanging on the lip of the horizon—nobody stirred. Ajax had twisted round in his chair and was looking in our direction. At first, I thought he was watching the little boy, who was now jumping down the veranda steps, shouting: "Look at me, Mummy! Look at me!" But then I saw with a shiver that his eyes were perfectly blank. Achilles shifted in his chair; he seemed to be desperate to distract Ajax with another drink, another game, anything, but that terrible blank stare went on and on, through the hut, through the stable yard and out across the battlefield to the gates of Troy and far beyond. He wasn't looking at any one particular thing; he was staring at nothing. *Into* nothing, perhaps.

———————

After dinner, the drinking and the music carried on in Achilles's living quarters. Alcimus played the lyre, Automedon revealed an unexpected talent for the double flute, though when he tried to sing he sounded so much like a bull calf newly separated from its mother that everybody begged him to stop. All the songs were about battles, about the exploits of great men. These were the songs Achilles loved, the songs that had made him. He was happier that night than I'd seen him since Patroclus had died.

Later in the evening, the little boy became fractious. Tecmessa picked him up and took him outside, where she walked up and down the yard with the heavy child in her arms, singing him to sleep. The lullaby was one I remembered from my own childhood. My mother used to sing it to my youngest brother while I snuggled into her side, allowed, for those few precious moments, to be a baby again myself. As Tecmessa went on singing, the men gradually fell silent and listened. She had a sweet voice. I looked around the group. There they were: battle-hardened fighters every one, listening to a slave sing a Trojan lullaby to her Greek baby. And suddenly I understood something—glimpsed, rather; I don't think I understood it till much later. I thought: *We're going to survive—our songs, our stories. They'll never be able to forget us. Decades after the last man who fought at Troy is dead, their sons will remember the songs their Trojan mothers sang to them. We'll be in their dreams—and in their worst nightmares too.*

The song came to an end in a flurry of cooing from Tecmessa and a deep sigh of contentment from the sleeping child.

"Ah, well, then," Ajax said, slapping his thighs. "Best be off."

He and Achilles hugged each other long and hard, but wordlessly, and then we stood on the veranda together, watching the little family disappear into the night.

I went back into the hut with Achilles and we settled by the fire. The short time that had passed since Priam's visit had confirmed my first impression of a change between us. Achilles no longer sent for me. He just assumed I'd be there. I thought a lot about that night. Looking back, it seemed to me I'd been trying to escape not just from the camp, but from Achilles's story; and I'd failed. Because, make no mistake, this was his story—*his* anger, *his* grief, *his* story. *I* was angry, *I* was grieving, but somehow that didn't matter. Here I was, again, waiting for Achilles to decide when it was time for bed, still trapped, still stuck inside his story, and yet with no real part to play in it.

Though that might be about to change. I stared into the fire and I knew I had to tell him. I don't know what kept me silent. All the other women were saying: *Go on, tell him, for god's sake, what are you waiting for?* This was my chance of security, or as close to security as I was ever likely to get. I remembered what Ritsa had said about Chryseis: that if she gave Agamemnon a son she'd be made for life. And yet I held back, because from the moment I spoke the words, I knew my life would change again. I'd be the mother—the prospective mother—of a child who was both Trojan and Greek. The old loyalties, the old certainties—the very few I had left—would drop away. So I sat by the fire and sipped my wine, and said nothing.

46

He had to fight long and hard to get the ceasefire Priam wanted. The negotiation was a complex, time-consuming business because he had to convince not only Agamemnon but all the other kings as well. And, in fact, the case for pressing on with the assault now that Troy had been fatally weakened by Hector's death was unanswerable. But somehow, he managed to bring them round at last. Patroclus would have been proud of him. Even Odysseus, who'd blocked him every inch of the way, said, "*Well,* that *was* a surprise. We might make a diplomat of you—one day."

Achilles just laughed and shook his head.

There is no "one day."

Every morning, he goes to stand on the beach, on the strip of hard sand, and strains his eyes for the first glimpse of his mother.

At first, she's no more than a dark stain on the white gauze of mist, but then, as she wades towards him through the shallows, he catches the silvery gleam of her skin. He both longs for and dreads that moment, because every meeting now is a prolonged goodbye. He's tired of this, he wants it to be over. He's spent his entire life saturated in her tears. So when, at last, she disappears into a swelling wave, he's secretly relieved. The mist she brings with her immediately begins to clear and there's the sea, stretched out in front of him, a thin, glistening transparency like the first film of skin on a healing wound.

By the time he gets back to the hut, the sun's burned off the last shreds of mist and the camp's bursting into life. A woman's kneeling by a fire, blowing on the underside of a log and feeding a handful of dry grass into the flame. Horses snuffle inside their feed bags and men bend over them, running gentle, calloused hands down every leg, lifting hooves to check for stones. Nothing new, nothing special, he's seen this every morning for the last nine years, but he's never seen it so clearly, never loved it as it deserves to be loved, till now.

Every morning, Alcimus sits on the veranda steps polishing his armour. Sometimes Achilles picks up a cloth and joins Alcimus in this task—ignoring Automedon's scandalized expression. Great Achilles, godlike Achilles, is not supposed to polish his own armour. But he enjoys the work: the rhythm of the strokes; the challenge of digging out a particularly recalcitrant bit of dirt; the simple, achievable reward of shining bronze. When his mother gave him this armour, he'd hardly bothered to look at it, he was so intent on finding and killing Hector. Now, he has all the time in the world to appreciate the beauty of the shield: herds of oxen grazing by a river, young men and girls circling a dance floor, sun, moon and stars, earth and sky, a quarrel, a lawsuit, a marriage feast ... Though he can't help wondering what his mother meant by the gift. This is the strongest, the best-made, the most beautiful shield in the world, but it can't save him. His death's determined by the gods. Instead, every morning, it reminds him of the richness of the life he's about to lose.

He thinks a lot about his mother as he polishes the shield. Somehow, here at life's end, it seems natural to go back to the beginning, to close the circle if you can. As a small boy, allowed to stay up late in the hall after dinner, heavy-lidded, fighting sleep, he used to look at her and notice how inflamed her eyes were. "It's the fire," she used to say. "The smoke." But he knew it wasn't. Some nights she could hardly breathe. And then her skin would begin to crack—always, the corners of her mouth went first—and then the cracks would deepen and spread till they began to ooze. Not long after, she'd disappear and he'd be left to wander, listless and bereft, along the shore until suddenly there she was again, sweeping him up into her arms and kissing him, eyes clear, skin glowing, her shining black hair smelling of salt.

But the bad times became more frequent. Often, his father would reach out and stroke her arm—and she always let him, she never once pulled away, though, cuddled close into her side, Achilles felt the suppressed violence of her recoil. She was an angry woman, his mother, angry with the gods who'd condemned her to a mortal's marriage bed. And how she hated it: the slime mould of human copulation and birth. Even breast-feeding her child ... He imagines her—is it imagination, or memory?—every muscle in her neck tense, trying not to pull away from the little sea-anemone mouth clamped to her nipple, sucking milk, sucking blood and hope and life, binding her ever more closely to the land. Oh, it's left its mark on him, that imagined, or remembered, revulsion. He's never found much joy in sex, whether with man or woman. Physical relief, yes ... But no more than that. Even Patroclus was made to pay a high price for such pleasure as he gave or got.

All his love, all his tenderness, is for his father. He is, first and foremost, "the son of Peleus"—the name he's known by throughout the army; his original, and always his most important, title. But that's his public self. When he's alone, and especially on those early-morning visits to the sea, he knows himself to be, inescapably, his mother's son. She left when he was not quite seven, the age at which a boy leaves the women's quarters and enters the world of men. Perhaps that's why he never quite managed to make the transition, though it would astonish the men who've fought beside him to hear him say that. But of course he doesn't say it. It's a flaw, a weakness; he knows to keep it well hidden from the world. Only at night, drifting between sleep and waking, he finds himself back in the briny darkness of her womb, the long mistake of mortal life erased at last.

————

Even his grief for Patroclus grows easier with the approach of his own death. It's not the tearing, rending agony of amputation it used to be, but an almost peaceful feeling, as if Patroclus had gone ahead of him into the next room. He talks about him often, telling Alcimus and Automedon, who are both too young to remember the first years of the war, about the battles and sea voyages of that now-distant time. But alone with Briseis, he goes back beyond the battles, beyond Troy, to the childhood he and Patroclus shared, all the way back to their first meeting. "I'd never seen him before in my life and yet when I looked at him my first thought was: *I know you*."

"It was a stroke of luck, wasn't it? Meeting him."

"For me, it was. I don't know how lucky it was for him. Let's face it, if he hadn't met me, he'd probably still be alive."

"I don't think he'd have chosen a different life."

"No—but I would *for* him." Achilles shrugged. "He had a lot of patience, he'd have been a good farmer. A good king. He'd have been good at the really tedious stuff, court cases, all that."

Whenever he's alone with Briseis, there's a sense of Patroclus's presence, sometimes so strong it's actually quite difficult not to speak to him. He's never asked Briseis whether she feels it, because he knows she does. It's been like this from the beginning, their relationship—if you can call it a relationship—filtered through their shared love for Patroclus.

Achilles lives in the present. He remembers the past, not without regret, but increasingly without resentment. He rarely, if ever, thinks about the future, because there is no future. It's amazing how easily he's come to accept that. His life rests like a dandelion clock on the palm of his open hand, a thing so light the merest breath of wind can carry it away. From somewhere—perhaps from Priam—he seems to have acquired an old man's acceptance of death. He knows there's no future and he really doesn't mind.

And then one morning, he wakes to find the bed empty. He's grown used to Briseis always being there and so he gets up and goes in search of her. He finds her outside, bent double, retching into the sand.

"What's the matter?"

"Nothing."

"Well, *something* is . . ."

"I'm pregnant."

It takes a moment to sink in. He says: "Are you sure?" He has a dim memory of somebody saying a woman doesn't know she's pregnant till the baby kicks. Is that true? He knows nothing of such matters.

She looks him steadily in the eye. "Yes."

He believes her. She's not a woman who tells lies. She didn't even lie about Agamemnon not sleeping with her when it would've been in her own best interests to do so. So immediately, in the space of a few seconds, there *is* a future, though not a future he can be part of, but still, one he has to reckon with.

The idea of this new life worms itself into his mind. And with that comes a renewed fear of dying. He wakes in the darkness, drenched in sweat, wondering how, precisely, his life will end. There isn't much he doesn't know about death in battle: he's seen the worst, because he's inflicted the worst. And then, afterwards, to be naked and helpless in the hands of women . . . Though god alone knows why he's worrying about that. It's not as if he's going to be *there*, in any meaningful sense.

But he does worry about it—in the long hours of darkness. And then, in the morning, he forgets the weakness of the night.

———

All this time, his lyre's been wrapped in oiled cloth and stowed away in a carved oak chest. Now and then, he takes it out and touches the strings, though he always ends by setting it aside.

But then, one evening, towards the end of the eleven-day truce, he catches himself thinking: *How do I know I can't do it?* The truth is, he doesn't know; he can't know until he tries. So he sits down, cradles the instrument in his arms and picks out the simplest tune he knows: a child's lullaby. After playing it through several times, he jumps to his feet and paces up and down, too excited to sit still.

After that, the lyre's never out of his hands. Next night in the hall, after dinner, he plays duets with Alcimus. Song follows song, the lyrics becoming steadily more obscene as the evening wears on, until at last everybody's helpless with laughter. Afterwards, in his own quarters, he plays the music he loved as a boy, songs of battle, sea voyages, adventure, the glorious deaths of heroes ... It's such a joy to be able to play again, not just sit empty-handed and listen to others play.

Briseis is watching him from the bed. It's late, very late. "I've just remembered, there's something I've got to do," he says, and gets up and goes out into the hall.

On the veranda steps, he yells for Alcimus, who comes running, white-faced, breathless, clearly afraid he's done something wrong, that something calamitous has happened, like Achilles finding a speck of dirt on the miraculous shield. He pours the lad a drink, sits him down—in the hall, because it wouldn't be kind to do this in front of Briseis—and tries to explain. So great is Alcimus's relief at not being in trouble, that he simply goggles at Achilles. It's obvious he's not taken in a word.

"If I die ..." Achilles says, again.

At least that bit seems to get through, though at first Alcimus says nothing, just makes fending-off movements with both hands, as if these were the worst words he's ever heard. *Well, if I can face it, surely you can?* Achilles thinks, beginning to lose patience. "*If* I die ... I'm not saying I will, *if ...*" Alcimus looks terrified. "Look, I haven't had a premonition or anything like that ..." It's not a premonition, it's knowledge. "I just want to make a few sensible plans for the future."

Alcimus gapes at him.

"Briseis is pregnant." Ah, *that* went in. "If I die, I want you to marry her and ..." He holds up his hand. "If. *If.* I want you to take her to my father. I want the child to grow up in my father's house." Silence. "Is that all right?"

Alcimus says, miserably, "It's an honour I don't deserve."

"But you'll do it?"

"Yes."

"Swear?"

"Yes, of course. I swear." And then: "Does she know?"

Achilles shakes his head. "No, there's no need to tell her yet. As long as you and I know what's happening."

He says good night and goes back to his living quarters, where he finds Briseis sitting up in bed waiting for him. For a moment, he's tempted to give in and join her, but his mood's changed now, darkening as the shadows fall.

So he sits by the fire and picks up the lyre again, remembering the song he'd been working on before Patroclus died. It had been so much a part of their last evenings together, he's not sure he can bear to play it, even now. And indeed the first few notes reduce him to tears. But after a few minutes, he tries again and this time plays it through to the end. Except there *is* no end. *Yes,* he remembers now, *that was always the problem, wasn't it?* He has never been able to finish the bloody thing. And Patroclus was no help. "I don't see what's wrong with it—sounds all right to me."

He plays it through again, aware of Briseis watching him, and aware too—undeniably, powerfully aware—of Patroclus sitting in his chair by the fire. Because Patroclus has relented in the last few days, really ever since Achilles started playing the lyre again, and comes now every evening. It's really quite difficult not to ask him what he thinks—but he knows what Patroclus thinks. He's always known. "For god's sake, can't you play something a bit more cheer-ful? It's a bloody *lament*."

Smiling at the memory, Achilles plays the song again only to arrive at the same tormenting sequence of notes. The aftermath of a great storm: raindrops dripping from an overhanging bough, *pick-pocking* into the swirling river underneath . . . *Yes*, yes, *but what next?*

And suddenly he knows: nothing, nothing comes next, because that's it, that is the end—it's been there all along, only he wasn't ready to see it. Wanting to make sure—because all this seems a little bit too simple, too convenient—he plays the song again, right through from the beginning. No, he's right, that's it, that's the ending. He looks across at Briseis. "That's it," he says, patting the still-vibrating strings. "Finished."

47

The final notes faded into silence. Achilles wrapped the lyre back in its oiled cloth and set it gently to one side. It seemed in those few moments as if time had been suspended, that the wave curling over us might never break.

Pure delusion, of course. The future was hurtling towards us, Achilles's life measured now in days not weeks.

On the morning of the day he went back to war, Achilles stood on the veranda steps and yelled for Alcimus, who came running as he always did, his round, honest face shining with sweat. He looked terrified. I was still in bed, gnawing on a piece of dry bread. Ritsa had told me that if you can manage to eat something before you even move your head, it stops the morning sickness developing. Well, it didn't do that, but it did seem to help a bit, so now I kept a crust under the pillow. I didn't think whatever Achilles wanted Alcimus for could possibly involve me, so I forced down the last mouthful and turned, cautiously, on my side, away from them.

At that moment, the door opened and a priest walked in. No warning. No greater ceremony than that. There can hardly have been a scruffier or more badly dressed bride, standing there still dishevelled from Achilles's bed, wrapped in a semen-stained sheet, with breadcrumbs in my hair. Alcimus, blotches of red all over his face and neck, kept darting agonized glances at me. Had he even been asked if he wanted this? When the brief ceremony was over, he backed out of the room, leaving me alone with Achilles, who said, brusquely, "It's for the best. He's a good man." And then, perhaps noticing how shocked I was, he relented a little, taking my chin between his thumb and forefinger and tilting my head. "He'll be kind to you. And he'll take care of the child."

————

Hours later: news of Achilles's death, and the great roar of absence in his empty rooms.

————

Achilles would not have approved of the manner of his death: an arrow between the shoulder blades, shot by Paris, Helen's husband, in revenge for the death of Hector. There's an even nastier version of the story: that the arrow was poisoned. Others say Paris shot him in the heel, the only part of his body that was vulnerable to wounds. Pinned to the ground and helpless, he was hacked to death. Either way, a coward's weapon in a coward's hands: that's the way Achilles would have seen it, though I suppose he might have taken some consolation from the fact that he died undefeated in hand-to-hand combat.

Achilles's heel. Of all the legends that grew up around him that was by far the silliest. His mother, in a desperate attempt to make him immortal, is supposed to have dipped him in the waters of Lethe, but she held him by the heel, making that the only part of his body that was not invulnerable to mortal wounds. Invulnerable to wounds? His whole body was a mass of scars. Believe me, I *do* know.

Another legend: that his horses were immortal, a gift from the gods on the occasion of his mother's marriage to Peleus—a guilt offering, you might say. The horses are supposed to have vanished after his death. I think about them sometimes, lazily cropping the grass in a green field, far away from the din of battle, being tended by a groom too fuddled in his wits to marvel why his horses never grow old. I like that story.

———

I spent the first days after his death sitting in his living quarters listening to the shouts of spectators at his funeral games. The room was quiet, two unoccupied chairs facing each other across the empty grate. Without turning round, I was aware of the bronze mirror behind me; and aware, as you sometimes are, of being watched by a person you can't see. There's a belief that mirrors are a threshold between our world and the land of the dead. That's why they're usually kept covered between a death and the cremation. More than once, I was tempted to get up and throw a sheet over that mirror, because if ever a spirit was strong enough to make the journey back from Hades it was Achilles's. But in the end I decided to leave it uncovered. Even if he did come back, I knew he wouldn't hurt me.

———

On the night they finally set fire to Troy—it had taken three whole days of looting to strip the city bare—Agamemnon gave a feast. One of the guests of honour was Achilles's son, Pyrrhus, who'd killed Priam—or butchered him, rather. He'd arrived in the camp eager to fight alongside his father: the moment he'd been training for ever since he was old enough to lift a sword, but by the time he reached Troy, Achilles was already dead. A burial mound, an empty hut, but no living father to greet him. At dinner in the hall, I watched him stagger across the floor, his fresh, young face slack with booze and shock, staring from one man to another, desperate for these men who'd known his father, who'd fought beside his father, to say how like Achilles he was. *Oh, isn't he like him? Honest to god, you'd think it was Achilles back again* . . . But nobody did.

At the feast, Agamemnon got so drunk he fell over twice. The second fall seemed to shake something loose inside his fuddled brain.

Alcimus, who'd been invited to sit at the top table—having done rather well in the fighting, whatever "doing well" in a sacked city means—heard him rambling on to Odysseus. "Achilles," he kept saying. "Achilles."

"What about him?" Odysseus was also drunk, but as sharp as ever.

"You know the time I sent you to see him?"

"Ye-es?"

"I promised him the twenty most beautiful women in Troy . . ."

Odysseus waited for clarification. "Ye-es?"

"Well, don't you see, he's got to have them, hasn't he?"

"Hmm, no, not really, he *is* dead. He certainly doesn't need twenty women—even one would be a bit of a waste."

But Agamemnon was adamant: Achilles had to have his share. Of course, Agamemnon was frightened—and I could scarcely blame him for that. I'd sat with my back to the bronze mirror and felt how powerful a force Achilles could still be. But Agamemnon's fear went beyond reason. He was leaning in towards Odysseus, shaking his shoulder. Look at the trouble Achilles caused over that girl. One girl, and he wouldn't go on fighting because he couldn't have her. "Bloody near lost us the war."

Odysseus waved his hand, dismissively. "Well, he can't lose you the war *now*, can he? You've won."

"No, but he could stop us getting home."

"I really don't see how." Odysseus was already looking forward to seeing his wife again. "All we need's a change of wind. Then it's three days, that's all."

But gradually, as the evening wore on, Agamemnon's jitters hardened into certainty. Achilles had to have a girl, and not just any girl either. The absolute best—"the pick of the crop."

And so Polyxena, Priam's virgin daughter, fifteen years old, was selected for sacrifice. I remembered her from my time in Troy, a sturdy little girl, built like one of those mountain ponies, short legs, a mane of dark brown hair. She was the youngest of Hecuba's large family, always running to keep up with her sisters, wailing the great cry of youngest children everywhere, "Wait for me! Wait for me!"

I kept waking up during that night, thinking about her. In the morning I dragged myself out of bed, feeling something of her dread of the coming day. But I certainly didn't expect to be involved in her fate.

Before breakfast, the little girl who was Hecamede's messenger came tearing into the yard. "Hecamede wants you," she said, breathlessly. "She says, can you come at once?" I thought perhaps Hecamede had been taken ill, I couldn't think what else it might be, and so I ran all the way to Nestor's hut, or as close to running as I could get by then. My pregnancy was just beginning to show. None of the men I passed was properly awake, they were all still sleeping off the drunkenness of the night before and Nestor's guards were no exception. Nestor himself, though, was up and dressed. Hecamede gestured to me to follow her into the hall.

"Have you heard about Polyxena?"

I nodded. I didn't say anything more: there was no point, so we just stood in the half-darkness and looked at each other. Then Hecamede said: "Nestor wants me to go with her, he says her mother and sisters won't be allowed to go and . . . well. She can't go on her own." She was twisting the end of her veil between her fingers. "Will you come with me?"

I stared at her. I saw how white and sick and terrified she looked—and this was a woman who'd been kind to me when it really mattered. I said: "Yes, of course I'll come."

She nodded. Then, turning to the table beside her, began arranging small honey cakes on a tray. "They've had nothing to eat." Her voice was shaking, she was making herself keep busy so she wouldn't have time to think. I helped her set out the cakes and she handed the trays to two of Nestor's servants to take to the arena. I doubted very much if any of it would get eaten, but I could see she needed to be doing something. We finished loading a second batch of cakes and then braced ourselves for what we knew we had to face.

The women of the royal household—Priam's widow, daughters and daughters-in-law—were being held in the same small hut I'd been put in, on the night I arrived. It was horribly overcrowded, worse now than it had been then, and some of the women had spilled out and were sitting or lying on the sand. Hair stringy, faces bruised, eyes bloodshot, tunics torn: their own families would have struggled to recognize them. Helen had been given a hut to herself. Probably just as well—if she'd been housed with the Trojan women, I doubt she'd have lasted the night. Menelaus was still saying he was going to kill her, though he'd amended the plan. Now, he was going to allow his fellow countrymen to kill her—by stoning, presumably—but only after he'd got her back home. Nobody believed a word of it. They all thought she'd worm her way into his bed again, long before then.

We threaded our way through the crowd of women. Here and there, you saw a girl baby being given the breast, or a small girl playing listlessly in the sand. From force of habit, I looked from face to face, though I no longer expected to find my sister. I'd searched for her among the women I'd seen being forced down the muddy track that led from the battlefield into the camp, slipping and slithering like cattle being driven to the slaughter. Those who fell were encouraged to stand up again by blows from the butt ends of spears. No pregnant women among them, I noticed. And no mothers leading small boys by the hand. Agamemnon had been as good as his word. I stared from one terrified face to the next, but fear made them look alike. It took me a long time to be certain she wasn't there. Later, somebody told me a small group of women had thrown themselves from the citadel when they saw Greek fighters streaming through the gates. I'd no way of knowing, but I thought instantly my sister would have been among them. It was in Ianthe to do that—as it was not in me.

Inside the hut, we found Hecuba with Polyxena kneeling at her feet. Beside them, Andromache, Hector's widow, sat staring into space. The woman standing next to me said Andromache had just been told she'd been allocated to Pyrrhus, Achilles's son, the boy who'd killed Priam. Looking at her face, you could see how little it mattered to her. Less than an hour ago, Odysseus had picked up her small son by one of his chubby legs and hurled him from the battlements of Troy. Her only child dead, and tonight she was expected to spread her legs for her new owner, a pimply adolescent boy, the son of the man who'd killed her husband.

As I looked at her, I heard again, as I'd been hearing for months, the last notes of Achilles's lament. The words seemed to have got trapped inside my brain, an infestation rather than a song, and I resented it. Yes, the death of young men in battle is a tragedy—I'd lost four brothers, I didn't need anybody to tell me that. A tragedy worthy of any number of laments—but theirs is not the worst fate. I looked at Andromache, who'd have to live the rest of her amputated life as a slave, and I thought: *We need a new song.*

Nothing worse could happen to Andromache now, but there at Hecuba's feet was Polyxena—fifteen years old, her whole life ahead of her—and she was actually trying to console her mother, begging her not to grieve. "Better to die on Achilles's burial mound," I heard her say, "than live and be a slave."

Oh, these fierce young women.

Hecamede pushed her way to the front and spoke briefly to Hecuba, then we went to sit in the corner, in the shadows. We weren't needed yet.

Roaming around the fringes of the crowd, Cassandra, another daughter of Priam, grimaced and muttered and let out the occasional shriek. I thought perhaps one of her sisters might try to restrain her, but even her own relatives seemed to withdraw from her. She was a virgin priestess of Apollo, who'd once kissed her to give her the gift of true prophecy, and then, when she still refused to have sex with him, spat in her mouth to ensure her prophecies would never be believed. Incredibly, Agamemnon had chosen her as his prize. God knows why, perhaps he felt he hadn't offended Apollo enough. She was a disruptive, jangling presence; still wearing the scarlet bands of the god, though the garlands round her neck were withered now, she ran up and down the hut, shoving aside anybody who got in her way. It was a relief when Agamemnon's aides came to take her away. At the last, she clung to her mother, babbling something about nets and axes, prophesying that she and Agamemnon would die together, that in choosing her he'd chosen death. Nobody believed her. And so, still raving, she let herself be dragged away, the god's curse pursuing her to the end.

As they passed me, I heard one of the guards say, "Bloody hell, I wouldn't want that in my bed." "Nah," said the other, "you'd never dare sleep."

Next, it was Andromache's turn to be taken away. She was too dazed with grief to feel the parting, though it was a bad moment for me, because it was Alcimus who came to get her. I suppose I should have expected it—he'd served Achilles, now he served Achilles's son—of course he'd be sent to fetch her. I hadn't seen much of Alcimus recently. The truth is, in the last few days, I'd been avoiding him, as far as I could. I had to spend the rest of my life with this man, and that wouldn't be made any easier by knowing what he'd done in the final days and hours of Troy. Now I did know, or at least I knew one thing: that he was the man who took Andromache away.

Holding her by the arm, he stopped close by me. I whispered, "How close are we to leaving?"

"Not very, nobody's up yet." He jerked his head towards Polyxena. "And there's that . . ."

Oh, yes, I thought. *There's that.*

The hours dragged past, as, very slowly, the Greek camp came to life around us. Everything that needed to be said had been said, everybody was worn out with grief and fear. They wanted it to be over, but at the same time they were ashamed of wanting it, because these were the last few precious minutes of Polyxena's life.

"He might change his mind," Hecamede said.

I knew he wouldn't. Unless of course he'd forgotten what he'd said, which was possible, given how drunk he'd been at the time.

Though if he had, there were others to remind him: Odysseus, who'd argued so eloquently for Hector's little son to be killed. And besides, Agamemnon was genuinely afraid of Achilles, more frightened of him now, probably, than he'd been when he was alive. Alive, you could at least bribe the sod, or try to—but then, I supposed Polyxena's death could be seen as a bribe. No, he'd go through with it, all right. He'd do whatever it took to keep that turbulent spirit underground.

It was past noon when the men came. They tried to seize Polyxena by the arms and drag her out, but Hecuba stood up and confronted them, staring first into one man's eyes and then another's until, whether from fear or shame, they dropped their gaze. In her creased and mud-stained tunic, she was still Hecuba, the queen. And in fact no force was necessary: Polyxena was more than ready to go. Wearing a clean white tunic that had belonged to Cassandra, her hair brushed and braided, she looked if anything younger than her age, but she was calm as she embraced her mother and sisters for the last time. Hecamede and I took our places by her side and slowly, preceded by the guards, shuffled to the door.

As we left the hut, we heard Hecuba howling like a wolf who'd just seen the last of her cubs killed. At the sound, Polyxena tried to turn back, and one of the men caught her roughly by the arm. Stepping in front of him, I said, "There's no need for that." And—I must say, to my surprise—he let her go.

It was a long, uphill walk to the promontory. We positioned ourselves a step behind her, ready to support her if she needed it. I couldn't stop remembering the stocky little girl who'd raced after her big sisters, shouting: "Wait for me!"

A whole army was waiting for her now.

She walked on steadily until she came to the foot of the burial mound where Agamemnon stood with Pyrrhus by his side. Pyrrhus, still very much the favourite because he'd killed Priam, had been awarded the honour of sacrificing her on his father's grave, though you might be forgiven for wondering how many honours a teenage boy deserves for having hacked one frail old man to death. When she saw the two of them standing there, Polyxena faltered.

Nestor stepped forward, whispered something to Hecamede and handed her a pair of scissors. Then, not meeting my eyes, he gave me a knife. Hecamede, her hands shaking uncontrollably, began trying to cut the girl's plaits; but the scissors weren't sharp enough and the blades merely mouthed the thick ropes of hair. So we had to stop and unfasten the braids, a fiddly job in the hot sun with thousands of fighters looking on. At last, her hair, curly from its long confinement, snaked all the way down her back as far as her waist. Somehow, holding thick clumps in our hands, we managed to get it cut off, though by the time we'd finished I was dry-mouthed, and trembling almost as badly as Polyxena herself. I had to keep swallowing to stop myself being sick. I remember black shadows on trampled soil, the searing white heat of the sun on the back of my neck. And then, without warning, Polyxena got up, staggered forward a few steps and began to speak. Instant consternation. Perhaps they thought she was going to curse them—and the curse of a person about to die is always powerful—because she'd got no further than Agamemnon's name when a guard seized and held her while another forced a strip of black cloth between her teeth and knotted it tightly at the back of her head. Her arms were pulled behind her and bound at the wrists. Shorn and trussed like that, unable to speak, she began to scream deep down in her throat, the sound a bull will sometimes make before the sacrifice.

Directly in front of us, standing in two long rows behind Agamemnon, priests dressed in scarlet and black began chanting hymns to the gods.

Polyxena was dragged forward and forced to her knees in the shadow of the burial mound. Looking green and sick, Pyrrhus stepped forward and began shouting his father's name: "Achilles! Achilles!" And then, his voice breaking, "Father!" I thought he sounded like a little boy afraid of the dark. Grasping Polyxena by what little remained of her hair, he pulled her head back and raised the knife.

One quick clean cut—I honestly believe she was dead before she hit the ground. Or at least I have to hope she was—though we still had to witness the jerks and spasms of her body after death.

No further ceremony. Everybody, including Agamemnon— perhaps especially Agamemnon—was eager to get away. Though on second thoughts I doubt if Polyxena's death affected him much. This was a man who'd sacrificed his own daughter to get a fair wind for Troy. I looked at him as he turned and walked away and I saw a man who'd learnt nothing and forgotten nothing, a coward without dignity or honour or respect. I saw him as Achilles saw him, I suppose.

Hecamede and I stood to one side, waiting for the men to disperse, before walking down the hill together. We didn't talk much. I think we were both holding ourselves in, determined *not to feel*. At one point, we stopped and looked back at the burning city. A huge ball of black smoke, shot through with jets of red and orange flame, billowed into the sky above the citadel. I was shaking, worse now than I had been when Polyxena died. Why had I watched it? I could have looked away or down at the ground and not seen the actual moment of her death. But I wanted to be able to say I'd been with her to the end. I wanted to bear witness.

At the bottom of the hill, we stopped. We could have gone back to Nestor's hut, raided his wine stores and spent the rest of the day getting determinedly drunk—I don't think anybody would have blamed us—but instead, without even needing to consult each other, we returned to the hut where the Trojan women were being kept. The interior now was even hotter and smellier than it had been earlier: that distinctive female smell of nursing mothers and menstruating girls. Hecuba looked dazed. We knelt before her and told her how bravely and quickly and cleanly and easily Polyxena had died. She nodded, twisting her hands around a scrap of cloth in her lap. How much she understood, I don't know. One of the women was trying to persuade her to drink, but after moistening her lips Hecuba waved the cup away.

After nearly an hour inside the overcrowded hut, I was beginning to feel faint and had to go outside into the arena. Even here the air smelled scorched and tasted of dust. In the distance, the long rows of black ships shimmered in the heat. Out of the haze, I saw a man walking towards me, his shape wavering as he came: Alcimus. He was carrying a huge, glittering shield—not his own—and, in the crook of his other arm, what looked at first like a bundle of rags. As he got closer, I saw it was a dead child. I backed away, thinking I should run into the hut and warn them, because I knew at once this must be Hector's little son; I didn't see who else it could be. But, instead, I waited for Alcimus beside the door.

We met over the body of the dead child, man and woman, Greek and Trojan, and he told me what had happened. Brought face to face with Pyrrhus, the boy who was now her master, Andromache had fallen to her knees and begged him not to leave her son's body to rot under the battlements of Troy, but to let him be buried beside Hector and cradled on his father's shield. She was asking a great deal—not so much the burial, which would take a couple of men under an hour, but the giving of the shield. This was the shield Achilles had taken from Hector on the day he'd killed him, and it was possibly the most precious thing Pyrrhus had inherited from his father. Hector's shield would have had pride of place in Peleus's hall for generations to come.

Nevertheless, to do Pyrrhus justice, he agreed, though he wouldn't allow Andromache herself to prepare the child for burial, he needed her to go on board immediately; he was planning to sail as soon as the wind turned.

"So . . ." Alcimus said. "Here he is. I washed him in the river on the way up, there won't be time for them to do it."

Kneeling, he transferred the little body from his arms to the inside of the shield and carried it into the hut.

At first, nobody paid him any attention, he was just another Greek fighter shouldering his way through the crowd, but then somebody caught sight of what he was carrying. The knowledge leapt from tongue to tongue to be followed, immediately, by the first ululation of grief. The sound rose to a crescendo, and then petered out, gradually, as Alcimus laid his burden at Hecuba's feet.

Nothing could have prepared Hecuba for this. She knew, of course, that her grandson was dead, but knowing was one thing— seeing his body lying on the ground before her, with his little arms and legs broken and a gash in his head deep enough to expose the brain, that was quite another. She fell to her knees beside him and began touching him all over. At one point, she seemed about to pick him up, but she drew back and left him lying where he was, in the hollow of his father's shield. At times, I don't think she knew who she was crying for. More than once, she called him "son," as if she thought it was Hector lying there—Hector, as he'd been at the beginning when she first held him in her arms.

Alcimus whispered, "I'm off to dig the grave. We're almost ready to sail, he's only waiting for the wind. I know it's hard but they've got to get a move on."

Hecamede ran across the arena to fetch a clean linen cloth from Nestor's hut and together we helped prepare the child for burial. One or two of the women produced small trinkets they'd managed to save—whatever hadn't been ripped off their necks by the guards—and we put them round the baby's neck so that at least he was given some faint semblance of a royal burial.

Hecuba was calmer by the end, though the wound in the boy's scalp distressed her. "I can't hide this," she kept saying. Hecamede tweaked a fold of cloth to cover the child's head, but it made no difference, Hecuba just went on saying, "I can't hide this, I can't hide this." She was scrunching folds of her tunic in her hands and staring vacantly from face to face. "I can't hide this."

No, I thought. *None of us can.*

Abruptly, she sat back on her heels, seeming suddenly to be almost indifferent, saying we'd done everything we could and we had to leave the child now, Hector would take care of him in the next world. There was a collective sigh of relief as she let him go. I hadn't known till then that I was holding my breath.

Alcimus came back with Automedon, who'd helped him dig the grave, and together they carried the little body away.

Hecuba went on kneeling, rocking backwards and forwards, rubbing her empty hands up and down her thighs. "It doesn't matter to them," she said, meaning the dead. "It doesn't matter to them if they have a big funeral or not. It's just for the living, all that. The dead don't care."

She was quiet after that. We all were, though the mood changed as soon as Alcimus and Automedon returned.

"You've got to go now," Automedon told her, speaking very loudly and clearly, as if he thought she might be deaf or demented. "Odysseus is ready to sail."

Odysseus had killed her grandson and now she was Odysseus's slave. I watched as two of the women helped her to her feet. She looked so frail, so thin—like a leaf in winter that storms have stripped all the way down to its shrivelled veins. I honestly thought she mightn't live long enough to reach the ships. I hoped not, for her sake.

More guards arrived. No gentleness now, no consideration for age and infirmity. The women were herded roughly into the arena and lined up for the march to the ships. I started walking the other way, determined to take one last look at the burial mound, but one of the guards raised his spear and I had to step back.

"*Oi!*" somebody said. "What do you think you're doing? That's Alcimus's *wife*." And, immediately, the spear was lowered.

So I was free to return to the burial mound. There was one thing more I knew I had to do. Polyxena's corpse lay where it had fallen, her white mantle fluttering round her in the wind that would carry us away from Troy. Bracing myself, I rolled her over onto her back. The deep gash in her throat made her look as if she had two mouths, both silent.

Silence becomes a woman . . .

Slowly, because the knot at the back of her head was snarled in her hair, I worked the gag loose and took it out of her mouth. Her eyes gazed up at me, unseeing. By the time I'd finished, my teeth were chattering and I had to turn away.

I looked down and saw, far beneath me, men like columns of black ants carrying loads up the gangways onto the ships. The huts would be empty now. I imagined the camp as it would be next winter, how the scouring winds would whistle through the deserted rooms. By next spring, or the spring after that, saplings would have taken root in the gutters, the advance guard of a forest that would one day reclaim its own. And on the beach itself, nothing left, nothing, only here and there a few broken spars bleached bone-white by the sun. And yet Troy's broken and blackened towers would still stand.

I looked at the burial mound and tried to say goodbye, to Patroclus, who'd always been kind, and to Achilles. I didn't grieve for Achilles then, and I don't now, but I do very often think of him. How could I not? He's the father of my first child. But saying goodbye to him that day was difficult. I remembered how he'd held my chin in his hand, turning my head this way and that, before walking into the centre of the arena, holding up his arms, and saying, "Cheers, lads. She'll do." And again, at the end, holding my chin, tilting my head: "He's a good man. He'll be kind to you. And he'll take care of the child." That voice, always so dominant, drowning out every other voice.

But it's the girls I remember most. Arianna, holding her hand out to me on the roof of the citadel before she turned and plunged to her death. Or Polyxena, only a few hours ago: "Better to die on Achilles's burial mound than live and be a slave." I stood there, in the cold wind, feeling coarse, lumpen and degraded in comparison with their fierce purity. But then I felt my baby kick. I pressed my hand hard against my belly and I was glad I'd chosen life.

Alcimus, beckoning urgently, was climbing the hill towards me. Obviously the ships were ready to sail. I turned for one last look at the mound. Somewhere underneath all the tons of earth the Myrmidons raised as a tribute to their lost leader, Achilles lies with Patroclus, their charred bones jumbled together in a golden urn. Even far out to sea, that mound was still visible, its red earth baking in the sun. And it must be there still, though the grass will be growing green above it.

Alcimus had nearly reached the top of the hill and I still hadn't managed to find a way to say goodbye. I thought: *Suppose, suppose just once, once, in all these centuries, the slippery gods keep their word and Achilles is granted eternal glory in return for his early death under the walls of Troy . . . ?* What will they make of us, the people of those unimaginably distant times? One thing I do know: they won't want the brutal reality of conquest and slavery. They won't want to be told about the massacres of men and boys, the enslavement of women and girls. They won't want to know we were living in a rape camp. No, they'll go for something altogether softer. A love story, perhaps? I just hope they manage to work out who the lovers were.

His story. *His*, not mine. It ends at his grave.

Alcimus is here now, I have to go. Alcimus, my husband. A bit of a fool, perhaps, but as Achilles said: a good man. And, anyway, there are worse things than marrying a fool. So I turn my back on the burial mound and let him lead me down to the ships. Once, not so long ago, I tried to walk out of Achilles's story—and failed. Now, my own story can begin.

AUTHOR'S NOTE

I'd like to thank Clare Alexander for many years of encouragement and sound advice, first as my editor at Viking Penguin and more recently as my agent at Aitken Alexander Associates. Simon Prosser of Hamish Hamilton has been throughout a most enthusiastic and supportive editor and publisher. No author could have a better team, and I know how lucky I am.

A special thank-you also to my copy editor, Sarah Coward, who always manages to be both meticulous and tactful.

Lastly, I would like to thank my daughter, Anna Barker, for being a scarily objective first reader.

Pat Barker is the author of *Union Street, Blow Your House Down, The Century's Daughter, The Man Who Wasn't There*, the Regeneration trilogy (*Regeneration, The Eye in the Door*, and *The Ghost Road*), *Another World, Border Crossing, Double Vision*, and the Life Class trilogy (*Life Class, Toby's Room*, and *Noonday*). She lives in Durham, England.